AMIRA

Book Two of The Sword and the Sunflower
a novel by Mark Bradford

Alchemy

Printed in the United States of America

First Printing, 2020

ISBN: 978-1-7336622-4-6

markbradford.org

DEDICATION

To those who came back because they knew the journey wasn't over.

ACKNOWLEDGMENTS

To the few.

AMIRA

Book Two of The Sword and the Sunflower

INTRODUCTION AND PRONUNCIATION GUIDE

Though you should already know how to pronounce these words from reading The Sword and the Sunflower, *I'm including them here along with the original introductory pronunciation guide.*

I find that when reading words one is not familiar with, it is commonplace for the mind to fill in the pronunciation. I also find it equally common that the pronunciation the mind comes up with is often times different than the author intended—some would say better.

Lest you experience this shock when finally hearing these words I present to you a pronunciation guide.

The caveat is that I default to you in the event that you like *your* pronunciation better than the one I provide here. Though I am the author and you are the reader, I find that you have the final say as far as pronunciations are involved.

Unless we meet in person. Then we can argue.

I am including this guide from The Sword and The Sunflower in case you are reading this without reading it first.

As per the Guide to simple American pronunciation markup[1].

---

[1] https://en.wikipedia.org/wiki/Wikipedia:Pronunciation_(simple_guide_to_markup,_American)

Stojan: Stoh JHAHN.

Anastazja: Ah nah STAH zhuh. Also, AH nah

Lucjan: LOO shehn

Budziszyn: BOO Dih Shehn.

Dagmar: Dag MAHR

Poliska: Poh LEE skah, also POH lah

Amira: Uh MEE ruh, also Uh MEER Uh

Mark Bradford

Amira

AFTERMATH

The great land of Amira—many many times the size of Poliska, home to the Saints and countless wonders—experienced something wondrous this day. For over one thousand years the dwellers of this land felt the touch of the ever-present saints. The people there grew up, grew old and died in a land that seemed to always have known the power of the Saints and those that became their arbiters. They were immutable, they were a constant and they were indeed powerful.

The Saints were considered invincible, and immortal.

But they were not. After a millennia of ubiquity, the constant of the Saints was broken; they were shown to be mortal and their true motivations would be exposed—in the moment it took to swing a sword.

The man that swung the unusually long sword stood before an ever-increasing audience of bewildered, excited and hopeful people.

Anastazja and Stojan embraced for some time. Opening her eyes she looked upon the decapitated statue on the raised dais. The body was in many pieces and the head lay upon its side—eyes wide with surprise. The mouth was contorted as if to express the beginnings of a question.

Stojan had clearly taken it by stealth.

She wanted to chop it up into smaller and smaller pieces, but did not want to dull her blade. She pulled back a bit from Stojan and asked him the immediate question.

"It is dead?"

He smiled and looked over to it. Picking up the sword he had dropped for a proper embrace, Stojan poked at some of the pieces.

"I am not sure if it was ever alive."

To him it looked like a normal statue—save for the fact that it had been sculpted with a most unusual expression, and was presently in many pieces.

"That was a Saint…?"

"It was what we now call saints, yes. Waste no reverence on them Ana, for they are interlopers."

She looked around at the interior of the church—admiring the windows, the solemnness and the woodwork. Her eyes finally fell upon the body of The Shaman.

"We have some business to attend to."

"Yes," she said, as she remembered not only the body before her, but the one of Fox in the antechamber nearby.

That was when they heard the voices.

A small group of people slowly filed into the chamber through the main doors from the front. One after another they came in. None had weapons drawn and all looked timid. Anastazja thought she recognized the couple that ran from her only an hour before.

The people looked around the great hall and made their way to the dais where Stojan and Anastazja stood. One after another the visitors' eyes widened as they saw the statue on the floor—along side The Shaman.

They did not attack; nor did they talk. Instead they filed on to the long chairs near the front. Those that had helmets or hats took them off.

Not knowing what to expect, the pair simply watched. Stojan was ready for some sort of attack but realized the demeanor of this group was quite different than the last.

Finally a woman in the front spoke. Her voice was timid and had both hope and sadness in it.

"Will we... will we still be able to gather here?"

Ana and Stojan traded confused glances. They looked at the statue and then the crowd.

Stojan eventually answered.

"Gather?"

The woman shook her head slowly as many traded glances of agreement.

"Yes, gather here. Are you now the bishop here?"

Confusion failed to leave Stojan's face.

"I am no bishop."

He pointed his sword at the man on the floor.

"Nor was he. I know not of your ways here, but an interloper has been dispatched."

The crowd's confused voices erupted in soft murmurs.

Ana wanted to leave the stage and run to Fox—to give him a proper burial. She felt exposed even though the crowd obviously meant no harm and was clearly without direction.

Stojan sheathed his sword—clandestinely running his thumb along the blade to see if he'd dulled it on the statue. He had not. Looking up to notice Ana's tiny smile of approval, he panned over the crowd.

"What is it you want of us?"

With that the crowd became silent and once again the woman spoke and looked around to gather consensus for her words.

"We... we want nothing. Except to gather."

She nodded and others joined in.

"We have no business in preventing you from doing so. You are free to gather here."

His last words seemed to impart happiness upon the crowd, as if he'd just made a great proclamation.

He had.

Awkwardly, he continued.

"There are many dead and..."

"We know. Others are attending to them and..."

Anastazja ran off of the dais to the room where Fox lay. Heads turned as she passed by.

In seconds she burst through the door to find two men gently moving him on a length of sturdy cloth with two long poles flanking it. They easily lifted it and were about to exit through the doors when they were startled by her entrance.

"I..."

One of the men started to talk as she interrupted.

"Where are you taking him?"

"I... we believe in proper burial. We are gathering the bodies outside."

She reached out to Fox's sleeve and touched him. Looking up through her hair at the men she spoke.

"Please be gentle with him. He... was a good man."

The men stared at Anastazja—now recognizing that she was part of the pair that had wrought so much destruction.

With much comfort the other, older man spoke.

"You can come with us? Please, accompany us."

Ana looked down and then back up at him briefly. She softened.

"Yes, of course."

Stojan continued to look over the crowd as even more entered. The feeling of being cornered had not left him, but he was most certain that these people posed no threat. Anastazja's flight from the room was quick and sudden and left him alone upon the stage with the body of the elder along with the rubble that once represented a saint.

They continued to file in.

The woman who had spoken glanced back at those entering the long chairs. She seemed pleased with the group as if it was larger than normal. Clearly she was in favor of such a gathering. What was to happen next had Stojan perplexed.

When all had filed in and every pair of eyes was upon him he stood in silence. He felt oddly exposed and decided to speak again.

"I know not why you gather. What has happened cannot be undone."

Instead of questions from the crowd he was met with faces filled with anticipation and interested silence. He had a captive audience of almost one hundred that day. And they wanted more.

He tried again to speak with finality, as this would allow him to leave. Perhaps if he just stated the obvious they could continue with whatever ceremony they wished and he could rejoin Ana outside the church. Though they did not block the exit, he felt compelled to stay. He spoke loudly and his voice echoed perfectly in the chamber.

"You are free of the saint that once dwelled here. It will not return and is dead."

Gasps from the audience, then murmurs. When he tried to continue he heard clapping—slowly at first and then louder and faster as more joined in. The sound erupted loudly and echoed though the chamber. It was a great and satisfying sound and Stojan had never heard such a thing—at least not as loud and dense as the applause produced by the large crowd. It was as if one great creature with many mouths spoke the same praise to him.

He stared and forgot about the pain in his side. After what seemed like an eternity, Stojan watched as the door at the back of the church opened slowly. A blonde girl peered in experimentally. The eruption of applause was heard even outside and Ana could not help but rush back in to see what could possibly be causing it. She knew not for what the crowd applauded.

They stared at each other from a distance, and both smiled.

Noticing Stojan's gaze, those gathered started to turn to see what he'd fixated on. The appearance of Anastazja once again caused many to turn and focus their applause on her as well. She quickly walked to where Stojan stood, and try as she may she could not become invisible during the journey.

She rejoined Stojan who reached out and grasped her hand in his.

Together they faced the crowd and for a few seconds more the clapping continued.

Reflecting on the moment later, they would both find it to be a surreal experience in which a crowd of strangers praised them for destroying something unexplainable while they stood before them, next to a man who'd just been murdered by a statue.

Fox was in good hands and Ana found the curiosity of the sound and the distance from Stojan was what drew her away from Fox, leaving him in the capable hands of the apparently gentle group outside.

She did not have the stomach to bury another man she cared very much for, but instead chose to go to the one that remained very much alive.

The odd satisfaction of standing before the crowd's applause was quickly replaced with an awkward silence. Before they could speak, the door at the back of the church once again opened and the men returned. Slowly they walked to the front and explained that they were there to retrieve the body of the elder.

Ana and Stojan found the people to be surprisingly kind and warm. They only wished to gather and be together as a community it seemed. Stojan (and Ana) had become the default leaders by their acts. The crowd harbored no ill will; they made no gestures to detain them or even disagree. It seemed they had been trapped and hexed for some time and their release caused much relief and gratitude.

In a short time the gathering turned into a funeral rite for both Fox and the elder. Though Ana disliked them being held in the same regard, her distaste was minimal and she was comforted by not only Stojan but the entire congregation. The well-wishing and kindness of such a crowd was very impactful and she had never felt such a thing.

She started to understand the power of such a gathering—for whatever reasons, for good or bad.

She was asked to say a few words at the funeral and did indeed have not only praise, but told a short story of her first meeting with Fox.

It seemed that the death of Fox when shared with the group provided much closure—closure she had never experienced at the passing of her own father.

She thought of him now and felt she borrowed a bit of comfort from those around her and imagined a similar funeral for her father.

Finally thoughts turned to Stojan and their next steps.

This group was more than happy to accommodate them but after some discussion they decided to make their way to the coast. Many repeated the stories of a beautiful ocean, and having no other objective this seemed the best direction.

A quest to see an ocean sounded better than just meandering in the opposite direction, after all.

THE QUEST FOR THE COAST

Stojan and Ana stayed for a few days with the citizens of the small town and much discussion was had about the Saints and the land of Poliska. The people were fascinated with having travelers from such a distance and a distant land. For all they knew, Poliska was part of a pristine land on the other side of the world.

In Ana's mind that was exactly what it was.

To Stojan it represented a beginning and an end. His recent realization that he'd somehow traveled seven years into the past was in and of itself a most difficult thing to accept. Having just passed the date of his daughter's death and the choice he'd made not to intervene multiplied the weight of the matter many fold.

Right now he was absorbing and living in the moments of what reality presented him with. Perhaps he would be able to properly embrace, process and deal with what he'd just been through.

Perhaps he already had, and that was the most disorienting thing of all.

His opinion of the denizens of Amira was slowly adjusting to what these new people represented. Instead of the minor interactions with those on the road he was exposed more deeply to people not much unlike those of Poliska; they just wanted to live their lives unmolested.

This small town was built recently, so was not apparently from the old world like some of the other towns. Because of this, it did not display any unusual tec or features. It did, however, benefit from the protective sphere of influence the Saint provided. That meant that items simply did not age nor deteriorate. Unfortunately for the citizens this preservation did not apply to anything living, which made for an unusual dichotomy of decay. This discussion caused Ana to wonder about dear Fox and what would have happened once he was buried. Were there these 'cemeteries' all over Amira with dead bodies in them that had not decayed in a thousand years? Or was dead actually dead? It seemed these burial areas were usually located next to a cathedral. She put the thought out of her mind and was happy the Saint had been dispatched and thus so had the effect on the surrounding area.

At least that's what she preferred to believe.

"Where will you go?"

The simple question came from an older woman they were dining with. She had the look of someone who spent a lot of time outside, but favored wearing very long dresses.

Ana cocked her head and continued to chew on the bread, attempting to relegate the question to Stojan. He looked back on her in silence, and clearly would not accept the responsibility of an answer.

"What will happen if we go back the way we came?"

"To the west, or the southwest?"

Confused, Ana responded with "To the west."

The woman smiled and replied, "You will reach The Coast. It is the great westerly edge of Amira. That is where you will find beaches, and the ocean, and…"

She trailed off quietly and looked regretful.

Ana's eyes lit up.

"And?"

Stojan watched the exchange like a bird in his loft.

"Well, I hesitate to tell you."

She touched Ana's arm.

"Let me ask you what your intentions are? Do you intend to explore Amira? Are you seeking other Saints?"

"Other Saints?!"

Ana was beside herself.

"Oh, I'm terribly sorry! It is none of my business of course! I just didn't know if... if you meant to explore. Or..."

The woman struggled to choose her words carefully and ended up essentially choosing the same she'd already used.

Stojan looked slightly amused.

Ana placed her hand on the woman's.

"It is fine. But are there other Saints so close by? How many are there?"

The woman looked slightly relieved. She didn't know if the foreigners were on just one one leg of a very long tour or if this had been a miracle of circumstance. She was unaware of the prophecy that The People spoke of, and the elder certainly hadn't shared before his untimely death.

Looking less than comfortable, the woman withdrew her hand and looked down.

"I'm sorry, I should not have mentioned it. I merely wanted to know where you would travel to."

Ana exchanged glances with Stojan. Neither, it seemed, felt any offense.

She smiled and waited for the woman to look up.

"I think we would like to rest—to find a place to settle for a bit. Is your winter coming soon?"

"Yes, but winter is most mild here, and to the southwest it is nonexistent. If you go to The Coast you will find so much coastline that some experience winter and some of it does not."

Ana's eyes widened and although she had become familiar with just how large Amira was, she still could not help but be amazed.

"How large is Amira? A coastline that knows winter and yet some that does not?"

The woman looked pleased and happy to have not offended her benefactors.

———

Though the large group that inhabited the small town here were friendly, they were not a replacement for The People that Stojan and Anastazja had spent so much time with. Doubtful they would ever feel they were among family here, like they did among the Navajo.

Instead, here it felt like a stop along a journey—though what that journey had become was unknown. In fact, to both Stojan and Anastazja it felt as though the journey had just ended. With that end had come triumph, and then disorientation.

Conversations were had about staying, seeking out the people and even settling down in Amira in a town far far away from the influence of a saint. After a few days of the topic popping up now and again, it was finally determined that they were in agreement: none of the ideas sounded ideal.

It was then that one of the people of the town came up with a suggestion that appealed to them both.

"Why don't you go on vacation?"

"On vacation?"

Stojan pronounced the phrase as a very foreign one indeed, as it did not quite make sense.

"Yes. Vacation. A traditional Amiran vacation."

Though the woman was enthusiastic, even some of the others of the group seemed confused. She continued.

"A traditional Amiran vacation means that you would travel away from your home and see new sights, eat new food and then return relaxed and rested."

Stojan summarized his understanding in one word.

"Exploring."

She nodded and looked over to Ana, then back to the tall man.

"That is what we have been doing for three years."

Anastazja giggled and added her own thoughts.

"Yes, as we said we have travelled from the far east to the Red Lands, and we have lived with The People—The Navajo—for some time."

She looked up at Stojan who seemed to want to continue them.

"We have eaten many unusual foods, and seen many unusual sights. We are, after all, not even from Amira. But..."

Both Ana and the woman hung on the last words.

"...I did not find any of this relaxing."

The woman froze—not sure of Stojan's tone.

Ana laughed an absurd laugh which caused the tiniest of smiles to cross his face.

Darting her eyes back and forth between the two foreigners, the woman eventually smiled with a look of relief.

Though there was much kindness and warmth among the people here, they still regarded Stojan and Ana as traveling foreign warriors with very strange ways. They had about them—most felt—a certain mysterious air. Cordial conversations were always punctuated with a certain apprehension—because of this no one was truly comfortable. They found Stojan's stoicism somewhat like having an unreadable wild animal in close quarters, and they found his companion to be a beautiful and disarming child that had been trained in the deadly arts—arts she was not at all afraid to use—this frightening talent was only enhanced by the curious ability of her hair to change color with her mood.

"Well, I thank you for the suggestion."

It was all Stojan could say to close the conversation. He much preferred the Navajo, as they spoke directly and without fear. Native Amirans were less direct and cared more about presentation rather than the substance of their words. He found it all taxing.

Perhaps a vacation *from* Amirans would be the best idea.

When it was clear that the gathering in the cathedral would be conducted every week, Stojan felt much motivation to move on before that. Fortunately Anastazja felt the same level of discomfort.

"Let us go to this coast then."

"For our 'on vacation?'"

"Yes Stojan, for our on vacation!"

The prospect of seeing an entirely different shore line at the end of the country of Amira did have a certain attractiveness to Stojan. He'd heard enough stories from the citizens of the small town to believe one out of ten. With fall approaching, staying in the warmer climate was the best course for comfort and survival. With The Coast being as long as was described, it would give them opportunity to find a city that was comfortable regardless of when they arrived. They could just move up or down until the weather suited them—and in some way perhaps this could be their 'on vacation.' All things considered Stojan had enough of running, of Saints and recent history. He had much to absorb and consider and no interest in doing either. He just wanted to exist. In that way he was the very essence of one on vacation—he just didn't know it.

With some additional supplies they said their goodbyes to the people of the little village that were now free of the influence of a Saint.

The Saints would no longer preserve them, thanks to Stojan and Anastazja.

Mark Bradford

Amira

DEPARTING FOR THE COAST

The relief that set in shortly after leaving the town was so strong that it caused Stojan to eventually comment.

"It is good to travel again, Ana."

As if in a daze Anastazja was slow to respond—realizing that he could not hear her smile she responded in kind.

"Me too."

For the next hour they fell back into silence—both appreciated the lack of thoughts.

Stojan mused about how easily Ana had picked up some of the mannerisms and the colloquial language of the people of Amira. She was well-learned for the average denizen of Poliska, but her time with the Navajo had provided her with as much teaching as she as would absorb; which was to say anything and everything.

Now she was picking up some of the language of the people of Amira, and they were much less formal. He marveled at how adaptable she was.

Was this simply part of someone her age, or did she had a unique ability to learn? Perhaps she simply had the willingness, and that's all one needed. It was an interesting consideration.

He was entertained by the fact that his thoughts could wander to such esoteric and ethereal musings. It meant they were not in danger, and had no real plan for now. For the first time in his life this actually cheered him.

Unfortunately, this feeling would pass.

"Stojan... will there be many cities on the way?"

Happy to once again speak, he replied.

"From what the people in the city spoke of, there should be many cities between here and The Coast. In fact there are a number along it."

"Yes, I would think we would encounter a number of larger cities, and The Coast should be densely populated."

He almost laughed. She had developed her own version of his habit of asking a question he knew the answer to. She would learn more subtlety eventually. She clearly had been listening to her teachers among the Navajo.

"Would you like to visit a large city?"

She thought for a few moments and began to nod.

"Yes, yes I would. I think I would like to see truly how the native Amirans live. Oh! But do you think there will be a Saint present?"

"I think they are always present. They are not all-knowing, and I do not know if there will be spies about."

"Spies?"

"Those who follow the saints, yes. Amira is immense so I would assume we can move about freely."

"There were seven."

"Ana?"

Stojan glanced over to her—startled by the dream-like quality of her voice.

"Stojan, there were seven of them. The elder—Clever Owl—he told me there were seven."

"When did he tell you this?"

"In passing, before we left the village. He was distracted and it seemed to slip out as part of our talk. He seemed to hurry our conversation along. I thought he had just picked the number but now I feel he knew for certain."

Stojan stroked his tiny beard, thinking of the many things the elder had withheld from them and his people. What else had he known or learned from his employ of the saint? What was he privy to? It was at that moment that Stojan thought he understood the action of the saint. The sudden impalement of the elder was not angry, erratic behavior; it was a calculated action to prevent him from revealing something he knew— something that would prevent Stojan from agreeing to go back.

"Well then there are now six."

Ana nodded.

"Then it is indeed doubtful that we will run into them in the great vastness of Amira."

"Yes, The People believed that they only controlled small areas."

Ana watched the sword strike in her mind again—she'd replayed it countless times. It happened mostly in her peripheral vision as she was looking into the sad eyes of Stojan at the time—she would never forget the look in his eyes that day. It looked like the last day of his life, but it had truly been the first day of it with her.

Confident that avoiding any future interaction with the saints would be an easily-accomplishable task, they continued towards The Coast.

Though they had a very rudimentary map, they also had the luxury of simply traveling west until they could go no further, because a great ocean would be in the way.

And they had all the time in the world.

Amira

A CHANGE

"What is wrong?"

The reserved man shifted his weight as he waited for an answer. Madison was unusually pensive this day and her concern was his. In all the years he'd served her he knew what was wrong before asking—this time, however, was different. It unnerved him, for she was his strength. After all, she was the bishop to a great Saint—there was no one in the land of higher office.

Eventually she turned to him from the floor—her curls making the rotation a half-second later.

"Him."

His eyes widened and he repeated the word back to her, for confirmation as well as clarification.

"Yes. Something is not right with the lord. He is concerned, and speaks of something that disturbs him."

"Disturbs him?"

It was all the taller man could do to respond. He just repeated her words back to her.

"Yes."

She stared at him intently and then spoke blasphemy.

"I think there are others."

"Others?"

Had the situation not been so grave she would have smiled at the continuous parroting of her words.

"Yes. Others."

She did not elaborate but instead continued staring—waiting for the enormity of her words to sink in. She waited more and finally saw the results of her words.

"What?"

His voice was loud—and incredulous. Coming from a traveler, it was blasphemy—or myth. Coming from her it was... disturbing.

"Who tells you this, who says...?"

"Carlin this is..."

She stopped, for what she was to say was to contradict everything she knew, and everything they'd known for generations.

He swallowed and continued to listen.

"Things have changed. Something is different, *very* different. I have seen a change in behavior. There is something different about everything. He acts as if... as if he has been hurt."

Her words were strung together as she attempted to make sense of things and distill them.

"My Lady Bishop if you say..."

"I do say Carlin. I do say."

She punctuated her words with a finger pointed gently at him, and allowed it to rise and fall with her discussion.

"Listen to me."

She looked over her shoulder instinctively.

"Something is awry and something has changed. I tell this to you only as you are my most trusted advisor. I expect instructions from our lord soon to confirm this."

Her way of speaking made him think there was more.

"And if it doesn't?"

He couldn't help but ask, and he didn't want to know the answer.

"Then Carlin, our way of life is about to change."

Her proclamation had come out of nowhere. Her assumptions were out of character and unbecoming of someone of such stature. What she spoke of was simply impossible. She was the most powerful person in all of the greater area. Her words carried the authority of the very Saint that resided there. Their cathedral was blessed with his presence. Though there had always been talks of other cathedrals and other saints, none had ever come forth to challenge them and the blessings of the Saint could be seen in tangible ways. In addition, were there not unexplainable things—miracles, amazing coincidences and the workings that were clearly because of his presence? And no one could dispute his longevity. For as long as anyone could remember, the Saint had been there—guiding, advising and showing his power over his surroundings. Things simply did not age—the building, the implements. It promised an everlasting life of anything that surrounded him. The congregation was immense.

———

That Sunday the congregation assembled as it had always done. Visitors and members gathered and filled the long seats. As always, they marveled at the building, the windows, the sheer and beautiful size of things inside. It stood as a beacon to others to come and marvel and be changed. An open heart would bestow anything and everything one desired. People reported ailments being healed, miracles occurring in the privacy of their own homes, and attitudes changing of those who would do them harm.

And for an even more tangible show of the power of the saint, selected members were able to store items in a special room. These items would never decay or break down. They were—like the Saint—ageless.

People came from miles and miles to see it and to be a part of it. The cathedral was not only the grandest in the land—according to the bishop and her flock—but yet paled in grandeur to the special monument erected to represent the very saint that lived there.

It was The Great Arch and it towered over everything. It leapt from one side of the cathedral to the other. It watched over the cathedral from afar and the grasses and paths were sculpted to encompass the most wondrous structure in the world. The arch was made of Amiran metals and stone and under the influence of the Saint, it had stood there for hundreds of years. It was a grand structure and yet a simple loop.

As grand as the great cathedral was, it was as if in miniature when compared to the arch. Madison knew this as fact—because she was one of the few who were allowed to enter it. Indeed she had made the great trek to the top from within and looked upon the cathedral from hundreds of feet above it. There she was able to take in the entire building and appreciate the height and construction of the arch. All bishops before her had been granted access; and so had a chosen few of the congregation.

In spite of these glorious sights and proof of her lord, she now felt unrest. Nothing could shake her faith except for the one thing: the very Saint himself.

Her talk with him was one of apprehension. She detected things in the conversation she had never heard before—things that she would expect from those who were not great and powerful. Searching her memories she could not recall a time when this was so.

Finally after much thought she decided to open the subject with him—in spite of the dangers involved. She needn't have worried; since the Saint was all-knowing it had anticipated this and summoned her. The resulting conversation had both put her at ease and charged her with a great quest.

It was with much pride that she once again spoke to Carlin and entrusted him with the results. He too was not only pleased but seemed to be exceptionally excited at the prospect. He felt singularly special for the opportunity—once it was truly made clear to him what was to happen. There was a plan. There was always a plan.

Mark Bradford

Amira

TOO SHORT SWORD

"You pulled back."

Anastazja looked at Stojan, and shook her sword at him slightly, accusatorially.

She looked unhappy—to say the least.

"I did."

"Why? You've never pulled back before."

Stojan considered this. Throughout her training he had always adjusted his intensity to allow her to learn. He considered her at this point almost an equal.

Seeing the thoughts cross his eyes she continued.

"You have been the finest teacher I could ask for…"

Uncharacteristically, he cut her off. Perhaps it was the rush of compliments that were about to come forth.

"How long is your sword?"

She stopped and blinked.

She looked at it again as if he'd somehow snuck in a replacement.

"My sword? How long is it? Why Stojan, it is as long as it has always been."

"And you?"

"Me? How long am I…?"

She responded with confusion and a bit of incredulity. She stared at him as she considered his strange words until…

She narrowed her eyes at his smile, and took one more step backwards and responded in an almost defeated tone.

"I am longer than I used to be."

"Yes. And your skills have grown and adjusted to your frame, Ana. However, your sword has not."

It was always a very intense thing to discuss the one connection she still had to her father. She had indeed learned the sword—thanks to Stojan—and excelled. She knew her father would be proud of his gift to her. And perhaps she had ignored the changes of late. She was a bit taller and as part of this her reach had changed. She now had an adult frame.

It was then that she realized her denial was in full display. It made her sad.

Stojan put up his hand, and then sheathed his sword—his way of communicating that he was truly done with practice and there were no tricks in store.

She did not sheath her sword and instead held it as if it was a new thing. In fact it was just the opposite. The thought of her outgrowing her little sword was unpleasant.

She continued to look upon it and asked her mentor a question.

"Could I not adjust my combat for a smaller sword?"

She knew the answer to her half-hearted question but waited for the answer regardless of the possibility.

"Anastazja, your style is unique—as are you. We have worked hard to develop it, and the sword and you are one. You have been intimately aware of the weight, the length, the feel. Your natural skill and your early blacksmith training has also played a part in it. Your hair has acted as a guide for us to hone your skill and your emotions to work as one."

She listened intently to Stojan's exceptionally complete answer. He had clearly been aware of this situation for some time.

"However; because we began training when you were younger, the changes in your body have made training a very fluid thing, and all aspects of your training have been equally as fluid—save for one."

She sighed.

"My sword."

"Yes. Your father was a very smart man to create two for you, because he knew you would eventually grow out of that one."

She looked upon it once again. It did indeed look small—too small for the kind of fighting she favored. Could she change her style to accommodate a smaller sword? She knew she'd been taught enough to know how to adjust for various shapes and sizes, and indeed Stojan had exposed her to other swords—even his unusually long sword. But capability and her prime style were two very different things. Knowing her weapon intimately is what allowed her to excel. Doubt in her weapon changed everything.

But so did denial. Imagining her weapon was longer than it actually was would have dire results, and explained why Stojan pulled back.

She had left an opening that up until now had been invisible.

She looked at him imploringly.

"What do I do now…?"

The prospect of seeking out a new sword should certainly be an exciting thing for her. But it was not. She could never have the proper sword, despite the foresight of her father. She would have to settle for second best. These thoughts filled her mind for some time, and her disappointment and realization proved why she had denied the fact for so long. Denial was easier.

And now suddenly she doubted her effectiveness.

Ana sheathed her sword, slowly.

Stojan approached her and put his hands on her shoulders.

"We will find a solution for you. And in the meantime you will have to be accustomed to being only half as great as I am."

She tilted her head in disbelief. She knew him to never be a boastful man.

"Stojan!"

He winked.

The absurdity of his statement broke her sullenness. She shook it off and wanted to engage him. That was of course exactly what he wanted.

He backed up, unsheathing his sword.

"Now, let us see just how horrible you have become."

With that, the two engaged in what was a most enjoyable session. Stojan, as always was a perceptive teacher and the last thing he would allow for her in this situation was to feel sorry for herself. They had been through exceptional times together, and a weapon that was shorter than necessary was not enough to dampen the mood.

He knew she would adjust until they found a more appropriate weapon.

Mark Bradford

Amira

A CITY OF MANY STATUES

Of all of their travels, Stojan and Anastazja had never come across a city larger than a small town. They knew there were larger cities in Amira just as there were in Poliska, but they had yet to encounter one.

The vast majority of their time in this country was spent among The People and in that they were thoroughly immersed in a civilization that was quite adept at hiding their numbers. Even the largest of Navajo encampments seemed like small, personable towns. It made Stojan reflect upon the anthills he'd been shown.

At last they were upon a sizable town and Anastazja was excited. Stojan was most glad to see this. Ana thought she detected a similar joy—albeit a stoic form of it.

The traffic in and out of the city had increased dramatically as they approached. Single horses, duets and large groups all traveled in and out. Wagons and even double-wagons were seen coming and going on the apparent main road they'd found.

It was always a good sign to see the trappings of civilization when one traveled to an unknown land—unless of course one was running from the law, being pursued by otherworldly creatures or those in league with them.

Stojan believed the likelihood that they were followed or pursued was slightly less than the likelihood that they weren't, so his demeanor and actions reflected this. Which is to say that he remained quiet.

As a single rider approached and overtook them, he performed the standard form of greeting by pinching an invisible hat brim, while Ana had the luxury of doing the same to her actual hat she favored on trips. The hat also served to minimize the viewing of accidental color changes that the local populace would not understand.

"Ho! A good day for travel, no?"

The man seemed friendly and had ridden up to ride in parallel with them.

"It is."

Stojan's response was emotionless but not unfriendly.

"Have you come far?"

Again the man seemed friendly, and although an excellent question, it was not out of place. It seemed to be one of only a few questions one was asked when traveling to and from cities in Amira.

"We are exploring, and look forward to a rest in a big city."

"Not a trader, or…?"

"Or what?"

He smiled, seeming to run out of words and options. He then motioned to Ana, who had remained silent so far.

"Education?"

She smiled and answered directly.

"Yes!"

He spoke to her now, finding a much more enthusiastic conversationalist.

"That is excellent. You have a good teacher to travel and learn. There is nothing better than to learn by treading the roads between cities in this great land. The more one sees, the more one can learn about… everything!"

His last response brought thoughts of Dagmar to her. She recalled the rather lengthy responses she received to her questions. Perhaps this man was similar.

Stojan watched the two converse and found his out to any further responses.

"How long will you stay?"

"It depends what we find, I think? Do you have knowledge of this city? Are you a native?"

"I come to the big city now and again, for festivities and to gain supplies I cannot get in my village."

"Which is it this day?"

"Well, both."

The concept of festivities had all but dissipated in Stojan's vocabulary. The thought of he and Ana remaining simply for entertainment had not crossed his mind.

Ana brightened considerably. When the stranger looked at Stojan to see his reaction, she caught his eye and while nodding enthusiastically, silently mouthed, *"On vacation."*

Her eyes were filled with excitement and mischief at this.

He blinked a slow blink and met the eyes of the stranger, whose own enthusiasm was wearing on the tall man.

"By all means tell us more of this entertainment."

The insincerity of Stojan's words were almost comical, yet the stranger did not seem to notice this, and saw it as a signal to enthusiastically continue.

"Well sir…"

He leaned forward a bit to catch up to Stojan and decrease his proximity. It almost seemed as if the tall man was making it a challenge to catch up and speak easily.

———

Fortunately for Stojan the traveler had a good deal of pressing business in the city. Because of this, he parted ways shortly after entering the city with them.

While Anastazja was engaged and presumably absorbing information, Stojan took in the sights of the city, the layout and its fine people. The latter was mostly to observe behavior of the prying variety. At this time he felt that they would be safe—at least from those pursuing them directly. There were also very few stares as the people tended to keep to themselves.

It was decided that they would seek out an inn and stay the night. Though Ana was most excited to explore such a large city, Stojan maintained that their location should not be embedded so deeply within —at least until more exploring was done.

"Jason said that it is not uncommon for travelers to stay in the homes of citizens here. In fact, that is a common practice for this area of the country."

Stojan had watched as they exchanged names, and was happy that Anastazja had told him her name was simply 'Ana' as that name seemed to not raise the same eyebrows as her full proper name did.

Staying out of the conversation, Stojan was deftly able to avoid revealing his own name. Ana thought him overcautious, but had no desire to be proven wrong so was more than happy to comply. They were moving to the west and thus The Coast, so she was thrilled to accept whatever precautions he thought prudent. The farther west they travelled the less likely they were to come upon anyone who would recognize them. Rumors and stories of epic battles traveled fast but could only travel as fast as the people who brought them with them. And these stories were more likely to have changed into something that fit the perceptions of those who repeated them and personalized them as their own. To that end, it could very well be rumored that the saint had met his demise at the hands of an entire group, or because of another saint.

When this point was made to Stojan, he remarked simply that The People also had a verbal history and method of transmitting information yet their stories remained pristine and identical.

It was a moot point to both and the theoretical discussion was dropped for more pressing matters—such as what to eat next.

The city was well-established and was as large or larger than any city Ana had ever seen. The same was true for Stojan and he remarked that it might just be larger than any he was aware of in Poliska. This fact made for exciting discussion and an ever-smiling Ana as they made their way through the various districts. The city boasted not only one statue to greet them, but Ana counted over ten on the first day they were there. Each and every time they passed one the pair couldn't help but to stare and wait.

None of the statues sprung to life and challenged them; none of the sculptures moved.

Not one blinked.

After a while they stopped noticing and it seemed even Stojan was at ease.

The buildings were impressive and none were of the Old World design. So to them these were what they considered to be modern construction and they looked quite similar to what they would find in Poliska. In this city, however, they encountered even taller buildings and some were of a grand design. It was most impressive. The city was well-established and her buildings were possibly hundreds of years old.

Districts were recognizably separate with homes being found in a hilly area, a section for travelers near the entrance and somewhat of a business district deeper into the city.

As with Stojan's urgings they did not venture in too deeply at first—a plan that made more sense as the city became a bit overwhelming and all-encompassing. In fact, Ana had never traveled so far into a city and not yet reached the center.

The people seemed generally happy—no more and no less than they'd encountered elsewhere.

Anastazja tried to imagine the people of this city conflicting with others on the roads as she'd seen years ago. Perhaps the more established a city was the less likely they were to conflict with others? The teachings of The People did not extend to well-established, very large cities.

She expected these Amirans to be more civilized.

"Stojan, what will we find at the center?"

He raised his eyebrow and motioned to a street to the right. They both turned as they talked.

"I have been thinking about that as well, Ana. I expect to find a cathedral at the center of each. However, what we have learned recently tells me that may not be the case."

"What do you mean?"

"Do you remember Saint John?"

"Of course."

"The Amirans had built a very recent town around the cathedral. It seems logical for the people to come upon these pristine buildings and then build near them."

"Why?"

"Because I would think they believe it is a source of safety and comfort."

This thought gave Ana pause.

"But the saints do not provide food, or water, or supplies."

Her perspective came not only from the teachings of The People, but also from her semi-nomadic life.

"No, they do not seem to. They do not seem to provide much of anything—save for their ability to preserve that which is inanimate. It would benefit me not to live near such a force. To me it would be not more than a novelty, unless of course it had the ability to keep a sword sharpened indefinitely."

"And if so?"

"Then it would rob me of my one simple pleasure."

Ana smiled slightly—the humor being diminished by her continued curiosity.

"But why then? Why do they attract followers? Why does something that is so immobile cause those to gather around it?"

"Perhaps it is a need for some.   I do not think they create this need, but simply appear to fulfill it. And their magic does help."

Ana was unconvinced.   To her it made little sense.   The elder had forsaken his people in exchange for being the servant of the saint.

"The weapon?"

Stojan looked at her, waiting for more.

"Stojan, the weapon the elder used on poor Fox that day."

"Yes?"

Her conversation would have to wait as they reached their destination—a large inn that was off the path a bit.

"I would try more Amiran food, and then perhaps we can visit a blacksmith."

All thoughts of saints and plots came to a halt in her mind.

The inn was just as Stojan had hoped; far from the main path but large enough to provide the workers with a lack of intimacy.   Meaning, they wouldn't gossip too much about travelers that looked out of place. And, they could get lost in the crowd.   Their meal was unremarkable and the discussions were short and cordial.   It seemed that no-one wanted to befriend them today.   They were left to their discussions and refilling their stomachs.

It was decided that they would stay at this inn and store their horses at the attached stables.   Their supplies were brought with them to their room—leaving empty saddle bags for anyone who wished to plunder them.

They found the city center to literally be a massive circle.   The roads all came to a circular hub with a park in the center.

"There is... no saint? No church? No cathedral?"

Ana looked confused and shocked.   Stojan rode with her around the circle and instead of exiting to one of the paths he led her to continue all the way back to the start.   Ana thought he seemed amused.   Onlookers thought the pair seemed confused.   It took many minutes to casually walk the circle on horseback.   No one gathered in the center on the tall grass.

"It would seem not, Ana.   I think there was something here but it has since left, or been removed."

They marveled at the large, perfectly-circular park. The center seemed to contain a small square patch of barren earth.   Exchanging glances, the two thought it best not to examine the patch, as there was no more of an exposed or obvious place to stand out.   Their curiosity would go unfulfilled, but it was the source of much musings by them.

Each day would be taken experimentally to see if they were noticed, or tracked.   Each day would be measured and the overall comfort would be noted. To Ana it would be an exhausting thing; to Stojan it was simply how he had lived for so many years.   To that end he kept his surveillance mostly to himself.

This continued for a week or more.   Their monies were holding up, but Stojan knew that at this rate they could only stay so long at a place designed for short stays.   Soon they would move on.

The day they were to depart, it seemed a direction unfolded before them.

Amira

THE SEER OF SIGHTS

"You must go to the desert—the great desert in the mountains to the west."

On their last day they stopped for a final bite of hot Amiran food. This was similar to what they experienced while staying with The People in that it was served on some sort of flat bread. Instead of being thick and hard it was very soft and rolled around the food within. Stojan found it quite enjoyable and remarked on his like of the spiciness.

This establishment had most of its seating outdoors—something the two had never really seen in Poliska. Warm weather continued year long and the people here made much use of it. Ana did not understand why someone would spend all day in the sun only to avoid the cool shade a building would provide.

Their discussion about the next destination had sparked a conversation with a man passing through. He wore finely-tailored clothing and had rings upon his hands. Clearly a business owner of much renown and wealth, they were surprised that he would spend much of his day in the sun eating. That was until they had sampled the drink.

Try as they might to avoid it the man pried into their business. Not wanting to make a scene Ana eventually said they were to travel to the coast to rest. In response to this the man felt the need to point out various landmarks, with the saints being featured prominently among the sights to see. It was perhaps that their saintless city caused the prevailing attitude that the saints were a far-away thing. His offers to provide guidance for a hefty fee were quickly squelched by Stojan.

"But surely everyone wants to see the sites of the west, and travel and see the marvels of the saints? You and your daughter have much to learn from such a trip. Why make a straight line to the coast when you can make the very trip itself a learning experience!"

His words were well composed and had been repeated many times. The man was selling travel with a guide, and his product was purchased by those with disposable wealth. Stojan had neither the interest nor the wealth to purchase his exorbitantly-priced service.

"I know many many things about this land, and have even inside knowledge of magics of Amira."

He winked at the travelers, one slowly closed eyelid at a time. His prospects were great with these two. He was more than convinced that they could afford him.

Finally out of frustration and inebriation, the man decided to forcibly offer his services—or at least his information.

He continued to talk with slightly-slurred speech.

His finger pointed off to the side—presumably in the correct direction and held his arm out as he continued. Squinting in the sun, he made his case.

"There lies a great pyramid. It is a pyramid that has stood since ancient times and therein also lies a great Saint."

Stojan was unfazed by the proclamation and waited for the arm to be returned to a more comfortable position. Unlike Ana, he did not look in the direction it pointed but instead looked into the man's eyes.

He moved his eyes to Ana and then back to Stojan.

"It is a great thing. If you seek the saints then this is where you must go."

At last he dropped his arm—looking slightly defeated. He spoke incredulously.

"Surely you seek the saints? On a long trip such as this? They are the wonders of…"

"We do not seek the saints."

"What?! You clearly have…"

Stojan's demeanor was severe as his eyes were unmoving. It was a disconcerting habit and it made those who spoke to him wish to look away when he did this.

"They seek us."

He stopped, as if he had been slapped. For many moments he stared as if his brain was resetting. His eyes went wide with shock and he all but moved his chair away—pressing his back into it. His eyes darted between the two travelers rapidly in a look of madness. Ana was taken off-guard by Stojan's honesty. Perhaps it had been employed to shut the man up.

"Then that means… You…"

He continued darting as his voice grew louder. He looked them up and down—seeing them for the first time that moment and taking stock in their appearance.

"…the two of you. You are those who defeated—nay dispatched—Saint John."

Anastazja smiled a humble smile—as if she'd been just told her recipe for coffee cake was delightful. It was the acknowledgment of someone whose capabilities were certain, and the action was so true that one simply agreed with a cordial smile. There was no hubris, and this humility made it seem even more like a precious treasure had just been uncovered in plain sight. Or perhaps a deadly, deadly weapon.

The silence was deafening and hung heavily between them. The man took a nervous drink.

He swallowed—not knowing how to continue, or what to ask. His attempt to impress travelers had been flipped upside down.

"Tell us all you know about this saint in the pyramid."

49

It was Anastazja that saved him from any more discomfort. Appreciating that the two would continue to speak to him—and meant him no harm— he spoke. He enthusiastically told them everything he knew, suspected and pondered. He left no bit of information out, for he imagined that he was helping two who had been prophesied to change Amira for the better forever. And perhaps they would share enough information to provide him with an even greater product, for surely he could tell of his meeting the two great warriors. In fact, perhaps would even refer to them as his friends. In the man's mind, a decimal point moved to the right.

To Stojan it seemed like the man was doing a very believable impersonation of the departed Dagmar.

Mark Bradford

Amira

.

A CARROT FOR A DONKEY

"This vacation seems to bear quite the resemblance to one of your quests."

It was the first thing Stojan had said in a while after leaving the city proper. When a reply was not forthcoming, he continued.

"In fact I cannot seem to tell the difference. Perhaps you can help me?"

Ana could no longer contain her breath and laughed out loud. She had intended to answer seriously and do her best to mislead Stojan with her answer, but his own sarcasm had preemptively won.

"Oh Stojan! Yes! A quest to find the great pyramid!"

"We have already found a pyramid. And it was indeed great Ana."

Anastazja thought of her ever-present book—the one she had read countless times since she had received it from the Navajo library. She wondered if they would encounter another library in Amira, or once again find the Great Library of the People. When their quest for The Coast was over and they'd visited the great black pyramid they could then revisit the Great Library. It seemed that their future was filled with excitement now.

The only thing that dampened her mood was her missing sword. Stojan had helped her come to terms with the denial, but the fact remained that very soon it would have to rest and be replaced. She smiled broadly nonetheless.

"On to the next city?"

"Not directly."

She waited for more and was rewarded for her patience this time.

"With the maps and directions we've seen I think it best we camp outside of cities for a bit. I think I've had enough of city life for a while."

"Really?"

Again her mood brightened. She would once again practice… and walk. Why Stojan had not brought this up sooner she did not know, but it made her happy.

For some time they traveled along the road and then when it seemed appropriate, they detoured into the forest. The trees here were larger and fought the sometimes-sparse brush for nutrients. To Ana it looked like a forest recovering from a great drought—one that had won the battle and was just now becoming more dense; however, the fight was daily as both the trees and other plants fought to bring green to a very hot climate.

Regardless it provided the cover they needed. As was their desire, they followed a river and camped near it. It was far away from the road as to make discovery anything but intentional, and close enough to the river to fish and gain clean water. Camp was set up quickly.

"What do you think of the tale of the pyramid?"

Stojan unsheathed his sword while sitting, and sharpened.

"I think it is a carrot."

"A carrot?"

"Yes, like the kind tied to the end of a rope and held in front of the…"

"*Donkeys?*"

She finished his sentence, seeing him struggle to remember the name of the animal.

"Yes."

"So you believe it is just a story to allow him to be hired."

"If there are no sights to see then one does not hire a sightseer."

She sat down under their common tree.

"So does this mean we no longer quest for it? You think it doesn't exist?"

Her disappointment was surprisingly minimal and was tempered by patience.

"Oh it probably does exist. But much about it seems exaggerated. And yes I am willing to visit this pyramid on the way to The Coast. Or perhaps Ana?"

He asked of her with tenderness, attempting to manage her minimal disappointment.

"Perhaps we would visit this on the way back."

Back. Back to where? The single word gave her pause and made her think of a time and space she had not yet considered. She'd only thought of the ocean and them spending an infinite amount of time at The Coast —traveling up and down until they found the perfect climate. It was the closest she had ever come to thoughts of settling down.

Resisting the urge to call her name to conjure her from her thoughts, Stojan went back to sharpening. The sound of the wet stone brought her out of her instant journey to The Coast and the future.

As if he could hear her concentration return to the here and now, he spoke without looking up.

"Will you be gone long?"

She smiled.

"No."

Still smiling she turned and sought out her own space among the trees.

———

The next morning saw the pair much rested—so rested that Anastazja was beginning to think that city life may not be the best fit for them. This thought was put on hold until they were able to test it again.

Consulting the simple map they'd purchased, they continued on their journey to The Coast—by way of the dot on the map that supposedly marked the great pyramid. It would take some time to reach the pyramid, let alone The Coast, and this gave Stojan ample time to convince Ana that it would best be visited going, rather than coming. And perhaps by then a new quest would have presented itself to her.

He found her interest in these quests far more entertaining than he would ever let on. They were both mindful of the dangers of keeping their distance from the saints and Stojan simply did not want to deliver them into the arms of one of them.

As before, they followed both the closest road and the most obvious river that would take them to their general destination. The fact that their destination was literally spread across as much as 1,000 kilometers made their direction quite lax. Ideally they would let the weather dictate their direction; if it became too hot they would veer to the north, and they would do the opposite if it became too cold. Amiran weather—they were told many times—offered any and every extreme possible. The pair had only seen some of this as their travels had taken them to the south west. The horrible winters of the north had not been experienced and serious planning would have to be made if they were ever to venture there.

Poliska had its share of all four seasons and both had experienced cold and snowy winters. Here they had the luxury of simply adjusting the weather to their liking by traveling. And this they did, day by day.

Days and weeks passed as they travelled in the lands that sometimes reminded them of The Red Lands of the past, and sometimes seemed as if the trees of the north were encroaching. Some forests were quite thick but they made sure not to travel too deeply into them. The value of both roads and rivers were not ignored. Each day brought them closer to this coast they were promised. The weather stayed hot to mild as they made their way and the teachings of The People had more than prepared them for the environment.

As pleasant and distracting as the journey was, Stojan could not deny the feeling that slowly grew stronger each day. He would not share it with Ana but kept it to himself as he pondered it—this was easy enough as there were ample quiet periods and was never considered strange for one such as him.

But the feeling remained. It greeted him in the morning each day and wished him well at night, and it could be summed up in just four words.

He was avoiding something.

Though he thought that their journey was in their hands—and that they both deserved this rest—he could not stop thinking that there was something he was to do. To him it felt as though they had not just figuratively—but literally—gone off their path.

Perhaps it was years on the run; perhaps it was their interaction with a saint, or perhaps it was simply a desire to settle down? Did he tire of travel? Did he long for Poliska? In his mind Poliska was his homeland, but no longer his home. The complications and recent resulting clarity had made it clear that Amira would be their home for some time; if not permanently.

Ana was as comfortable as he was traveling together. She was living day to day and enjoying their time as a duo. Each day was an opportunity to learn, to grow. Her optimism was fitting for one her age, and it served to fuel Stojan in ways he could not explain. In turn his strength and wisdom kept her grounded.

He was smart enough not to seek adventure, as it had always come to him.

But had it? Was it not his choice to agree to the bishop's job? He had gone on his own quest—he realized—and that fact made him almost laugh out loud.

Anxiousness was not his forté and was actually quite foreign to him. He had been above all a patient man and it had served him well.

But patience did not seem to be the answer in this case. He could not act if he did not know what he was to do. Or perhaps it was that he did know?

Perhaps this is what provided the conflict.

Mentally he felt he'd made progress.

Now all he had to do was figure out what this thing was. His concentration was broken by the cawing of a distant bird. It stood out among the sounds of the forest and the other animals.

It brought him back into the here and now and he looked around at the surroundings, his horse and Ana.

"Stojan do you see it?"

He blinked and attempted to look in the direction she looked, then pointed.

It was a plateau. And perched high atop this was something of an off color. Amid the reds and oranges and browns was something of a color they had not seen in some time—it was a tiny dot of blue.

Ana had clearly been scanning the horizon as Stojan was deeply lost in thoughts.

He squinted to see the pale blue structure. There were no edges to be seen, but instead it looked like something round, as if a great boulder had been painted blue.

"A marker?"

"Yes, perhaps it is a marker of sorts for travelers. A place to allow those to locate themselves on a map."

The roads they traveled on were sparse and not well worn. Before Ana could speak, Stojan seemed to have read her mind.

"It is quite far—up and away."

Ana listened as Stojan clearly had a point to make and there was no use in objecting… yet.

"We have not seen other travelers for some time, Ana. If this is a building of some sort, or even a village atop a hill, then we would have encountered some traffic by now."

She frowned.

"I cannot see any buildings."

"Nor can I."

Ana looked over at Stojan. Her question did not need to be vocalized as it was quite obvious what words would be next.

"*Yes.*"

When she smiled a confused smile, he continued.

"Yes, we can go to the strange object atop the hill, but we must seek shelter first. According to what the sightseer told us, there is a city nearby. Or at least there should be."

His phrasing made it seem like an absurd decision, but it did not dissuade her from her enthusiasm. She nodded quickly.

"Although I do not think it is the great pyramid we were told of. I do not believe they are so round."

"This is also not a desert."

Ana spoke the obvious, not knowing if Stojan was chiding her, or providing his input. She realized it was the former.

"It is a steep peak, but there is a road that does lead to it, and it seems to meander gently."

She nodded.

"We have much daylight left."

Stojan thought of how much of their travel was in valleys and the tactical disadvantage that provided. To see the land ahead from a peak was definitely welcome—but the steep cliffs at night would be deadly.

They made their way up the road that went to and fro instead of in a mostly straight line.

"Stojan, I notice that some of the roads are intentionally longer than they need be."

"Yes, I noticed that as well. Much work has been put into building roads that have gradual inclines—but at the expense of time and distance. One must travel much, much longer on these meandering roads."

"You think these are built?"

"It is possible—it seems unnatural to have such sections of the rock to be such a uniform width for so long."

"Amiran tec?"

"Yes."

"You think they were able to carve out the very rock—for many kilometers?"

"Yes."

Ana fell silent for a time and then posed a question to her tall companion.

"Stojan do you now believe in the power of the saints and the Old World?"

"What do you mean?"

"If you believe they could accomplish such a grand task, do you now believe that it was a wondrous civilization?"

She waited and hoped for an interesting answer.

"Anastazja, I do not think civilizations are great. I believe that one can be great, but the more people involved, the less chance of greatness."

It seemed she was indeed the recipient of interesting answers. He continued.

"In all the statues we have seen, have you ever seen one erected of a group?"

Her face showed her child-like confusion.

"Um, no?"

"Perhaps even the Amirans of the Old World knew that as well. They knew a group was not great, but instead it was the individual that accomplished things."

Her question about roads had not been answered, but now she pondered not only the great machines that could possibly create hundreds of kilometers of roads, but also what consisted of a group—or a civilization.

Her silence told Stojan that he had given her something to think deeply on, and this gave him much satisfaction. It made him feel that he was sowing the seeds of wisdom with someone who truly embraced them.

He himself thought of the shaping, the carving and the planning involved in such a monumental endeavor. Though the roads were more of outcroppings and jagged paths, it seemed they could very well have been flat and easy to travel so very long ago. At least that was what both Dagmar and the The People had taught them.

It took some time to approach the structure, as the road indeed had swayed back and forth. It took much more time than expected as the eye drew a straight line while the road and the horse did not.

Unfortunately they could only go so far.

Amira

A JOURNEY DENIED

"Well, that is that."

Anastazja stared downward and slowly dismounted. Stojan did the same and backed his horses up a few steps.

To him the scene was all-too-familiar. The trail had come to an abrupt end in the form of a cliff. Many meters away the road continued, but before them was a chasm.

Ana moved towards the edge slowly, and Stojan found this action quite disconcerting.

"Ana, be careful."

He touched her shoulder as he spoke, and the graveness of his voice made her stop. She too was reminded of their encounter with the rope bridge many years ago. Her anger and frustration had caused her to go out in the middle of a storm, and the result was lethal. Or should have been.

Ana touched her hair.

"You can hold on to me."

Stojan kept the multitude of comments to himself and approached with her, hand in hand.

"It is steep!"

"Hundreds of meters."

The two stood as closely as they thought prudent and looked down into the gorge. It looked like a section of the great ridge they were on had been carved out—for what purpose they did not know. The edges were mostly flat on either side. Suddenly the massive rock they traveled upon seemed less solid.

Ana blinked and Stojan pulled her back a bit.

"Stojan I am OK."

It was then that she looked into his eyes and saw something new. He looked uncertain, pensive. There was a certain anxiety.

"Stojan... are you afraid? Of the height? Of falling in?"

Composing himself he responded.

"My dear Anastazja it is not the great fall that concerns me; it is the sudden stop at the very end."

She smiled and squeezed his hand tightly as if her hand laughed along with her voice.

With that the two backed up further and taking a deep breath they both surveyed their surroundings. The lands were of rich oranges and reds; rocks and outcroppings continued to challenge the sky and some of the ridges they traveled on were visible from here. It was a barren land that did not welcome green.

Their attention was once again turned to the very inconvenient chasm before them.

"There is no rope bridge this time."

"You assume I would allow you to cross it?"

She made a mock frown.

"Oh I would force you to come with me this time!"

They took the opportunity to rest the horses a bit before making their way back down the road. Though she was disappointed in being prevented from seeing something new, she knew it wasn't the Great Pyramid she'd been promised. One positive of reaching the end of that road was the vantage point, and they had not only taken in all they could, but in surveying the surroundings, a small city had revealed itself.

As with their travels in the south the sky always looked larger and the land was always in stark contrast to it. It was a sweeping vista of colors, and the small city also stood for exactly that reason.

Amira

A VIBRANT CITY

With only a few hours of daylight left the pair arrived at the city proper.

Notably the buildings were of a design they had not seen before. Instead of wood, it looked like the buildings had been shaped out of some sort of stone and painted. Each building was a bright color with oranges, yellows and reds being the most prominent—in that way they mirrored the environment. Some of the windows were rounded and no glass was employed. Flowers were seen hanging in the sill of most windows—adding even more colors to the presentation.

Most roofs were also unusual and made of curved reddish tiles. It made for a colorful welcome to the recently-thwarted travelers.

All buildings were just one story, and taken in with the setting sun it made for a vivid experience.

"It is beautiful."

Stojan looked to Ana in response to her words and saw the delight in her eyes; when she viewed beauty her face reflected that.

"We have encountered a unique people it would seem."

Taking their eyes from the building, they looked to the streets for the denizens of such a colorful city. Those milling around reminded them of the Navajo they'd spent so much time with. These people were of a darker complexion and almost without fail grew their black hair long. Their clothing matched what Ana favored with thin leathers, tassels and furs worn here and there. Indeed one would think the pair resided here— the match was so accurate in Ana.

The road leading in was thin and looked to be seldom used. To Stojan this was no surprise as the only place it led was to the building on the perch. Following that trail further took a week or more to reach the next city.

They were at the back door, mused Stojan.

The denizens seemed unfazed by their entrance and neither greeted nor ignored them. The looks they did receive seemed friendly enough.

"Will there be an inn? All the buildings look like homes."

Stojan considered Ana's question as they rode past building after building. They did indeed all look like homes—warm, inviting little colorful buildings. In some cases, an older citizen sat on a bench outside looking quite content to look around. They sat and lackadaisically looked here and there—no one stared at them, but instead looked just long enough to give them a good, polite look.

When it was obvious that they all seemed to be homes and no inns were forthcoming, they turned to the nearest building with a pair sitting outside.

"Hello."

"Hello."

The man shielded his eyes in response to Stojan's greeting—the setting sun making him a bit of a silhouette upon his horse.

Ana smiled and raised her palm in greeting as well.

Again, the facial features and mannerisms transmitted very little about the mood of the man. His similarity to The People struck Ana as well.

Stojan dismounted—feeling it unfriendly to yell down to the older man from horseback. Ana stayed mounted for the moment as she was unsure of what was to happen next.

The man stood up in response to Stojan's dismounting and it seemed that both men were polite.

"You are welcome to stay here with us."

Stojan glanced at Ana and it took much effort not to respond with *Just like that?*

Ana saw this as an opportunity to dismount as well, did so and absentmindedly pet her horse.

As the man's wife nodded slightly in agreement, Stojan chose to answer.

"We are grateful. We are just stopping to stay a night or two on our journey."

"To The Coast."

Anastazja's eyebrows came together as she chose to enter the conversation.

"You know of The Coast? Or do you know of…?"

Though she did not finish, the man waited before responding. It appeared he had as much patience for her unfinished thoughts as did Stojan.

"Those that pass this way typically are on their way to The Coast. Or at least they have been told to seek it."

"We have been told to seek it, and the great ocean that exists."

After an uncomfortable pause the man motioned with his arm to guide them.

"Your horses—you may bring them to the back."

The older woman stayed seated and had both a permanent smile and squint upon her face.

Stojan and Anastazja complied quietly and walked their horses to the back of the colorful building. Unlike in the other towns, the buildings here were spaced apart a bit with each having a plot of land behind them. The plot was so well manicured that at first Ana thought it a natural occurrence. Upon closer inspection it was an arrangement of rocks, and cacti and all manner of environmental items that appeared natural and inviting. The immediate landscape was a reflection of the owner of the house and they found this to be true for each and every building.

The owner of the house provided his name as well as the name of his wife and it was at that time their suspicions were proven correct. For indeed, each person in town they encountered was named with the same convention as their dear Navajo brothers and sisters. Their hosts— Proud Jonathan and Janet Armadillo Skin—welcomed them into their home.

It was with trepidation that Stojan and Anastazja provided their names. So uncertain did they seem that the inquisitive looks continued for some time.

"Brother, you need not hide from us."

They exchanged glances not knowing what to say.

"But you may hide *with* us, if you so choose."

It would seem that day their confusion was unending.   Stojan's forwardness proved to be the proper course of action in the present environment.

"We hide nothing; we are familiar with your people, we think."

"Tell us then, Stojan."

"You are part of The People?"

"All people are part of…"

Stopped by the touch of his wife on his shoulder, the man winked at her sheepishly and restarted. His humor and disdain for an immediate direct answer was well known to her.

"Yes, we are a part of The People.   Many years ago a part of us settled here.   Or rather, we resettled.   Our people lived with the Amirans for some time.   Some were in cities, some as a part of the forests.   There came a time when many of us chose the relative safety of hiding in plain

sight. That was when a part of us became The People of the Ants."
They nodded, but neither decided to speak further, or interrupt the old man. He looked like he had much to say.

"I am not permitted to speak your true name until you speak it first, Stojan. You need not share it with us, but know that we will always keep it safe."

As Ana started to speak Stojan cut in with his response.

"Perhaps tomorrow. But we are the visitors and wish to learn about you, and your surroundings."

With that the two made a comfortable rest at the home of Proud Jonathan and Janet Armadillo Skin.

Soon afterwards, they headed to bed and Ana found their room to be the closest thing to her actual bedroom she'd stayed in since meeting Stojan. It gave her pleasant thoughts of her years with her father in their house. The interior walls were painted a neutral brown, or perhaps this was the natural unpainted color?   Regardless, she was grateful as the bright colors were enjoyable to see from the outside, but looking at them inside was overwhelming.   A soft bed was always welcome, whether it was under the stars or in a room with much hospitality.

They found sleep quickly and felt a trust in their environment—made easier by the fact that they kept all of their belongings with them in their room.

The next morning the four enjoyed a breakfast together as the sun greeted them. The dining area was clearly positioned to watch such an event unveil, and the sun painted the surroundings with rich oranges, reds and even yellows.   It shone over the hills, rocks and distant mesas —including the one in question with the mysterious blue structure upon it.   Stojan found the couple did not make small talk but instead spent their first moments smiling, sipping tea and staring.   Stojan and Ana enjoyed their hot beverages and breakfast items that were very similar to what they'd enjoyed with their stay with The People. They just traded glances and enjoyed the show. After watching for some time she no longer felt the couple rude for not speaking.

"He seeks The Saint on High."

For the first time his wife spoke, and her voice was surprisingly soft.

All heads turned to her as she continued.

"You both do, do you not? You've come to see the saint, and you seek guidance on how to reach him."

Stojan furrowed his brow a bit and blinked away the bright colors, but allowed Ana to speak.

"No, we did not come here to seek out a saint. We attempted to visit a building but the passage had collapsed. Assuming it is a building?"

"Yes."

"Instead we seek The Coast. We are on a long journey to see it."

Her excited eyes darted from Stojan to the couple.

"We are told it is immense and all manner of climate may be sought there."

The couple exchanged glances and looked back at their guest—their faces now more serious than before.

"Then you do seek the saint."

"No no. As we said we have no interest in saints. We have seen no cathedrals."

She nodded towards Stojan—looking for confirmation. He did indeed nod, but was watching his host carefully. Something had raised his suspicions again.

After a pause that was entirely too long, the man finally smiled.

"We have no cathedral here—you need not worry."

The subject was changed to them being poor hosts and not speaking to them during the sunrise. As people who were related to the Navajo, they had many things in common—their hospitality, their outlook on family and accepting those worthy to join their community and even their altruism. It was the latter that stopped Stojan from pushing any payment on them or wondering about any ulterior motives.

They agreed to stay the night and enjoyed the company of their hosts. It was decided that they would explore the city by themselves. Their guides decided it was best for them to see things through their own eyes instead of the eyes of those that had 'looked upon the city too many times.'

As they first thought the city was essentially residential. When they pursued an explanation they found that each family participated in the trade of goods, the creation of goods, and the care and feeding of animals. It was a self-sufficient society and much like The People they did not use currency. Instead, altruistic participation in the health of the community was the prime concern of all who lived here. They simply wanted to live, and be content and support each other.

It was because of this attitude that Stojan found the ominous words of his host so out of place and disconcerting.

"Do you think they have much to do with The People, Stojan?"

Ana asked him simply while she munched on a treat they'd been offered in passing by a home. Though there was nothing approaching an eatery or inn, those who dealt heavily in goods often times offered treats to passers-by. This was one such occurrence.

"They seem the type not to be fully cut off. I would think there may be some sort of commerce or exchange."

"Exchange?"

Ana continued to munch on the lightly sweet, rolled bread. She moved her sword slightly on her hip as he spoke. Though they'd been cordially asked to keep their weapons at the home of their guests, Ana would have none of it. Stojan's opinion did not differ.

"Goods, services, information."

"Information. You think they are in communication with The People?"

"Indeed. I think they know far more than they are telling us—which is their prerogative of course."

"You think they lie?"

"No. Not directly. If you meet for battle with an unknown opponent do you immediately announce what weapon you will use, what training you've had?"

"No."

"Have you then lied?"

She thought, then smiled.

"No."

For a man that presented himself in such stark, black and white mannerisms she found Stojan to continue to surprise her with his understanding of nuance.

They continued their tour of the city. It was a vibrant painting come to life. The exploration was refreshing and interesting to them both. The citizens seemed to be content in what they did, how they lived, and their beautiful city. It was a contentment that came after many years of hard work as part of a thriving society, and Stojan mused that this was a sort of resting place for those elders that wanted to settle in an environment with others who were in the same stage of life. Neither knew if this was something that had been planned, or if it had just come about after many years. Regardless they found their tour enjoyable, and were met with quiet regard especially for such people who were obviously out of place. Little conversation was made, as if these people were used to confused travelers passing through. Ana felt much conversation was had after they had passed by, but had no real basis for it.

"You think they gossip?"

Stojan asked but it was clear he agreed.

"Yes."

"Well, perhaps we've found what they replaced their currency with."

Ana just smiled and imagined someone offering a good story about travelers in exchange for a crate of grain or even a horse. The images stayed with her and enhanced her smile for the walk back to their lodging.

One difference these people had with the Navajo was that they sometimes ate in their homes. While The People preferred to regard meals as not just a time to consume but a time to come together and learn, these were people who happily sat in the privacy of their colorful homes and ate with each other. It was at one such meal with their guests —two days later—that Stojan decided to reveal his true name.

"Jonathan, before we leave I would like you to know my true name."

At this he brightened. Nothing had been said about it during their stay so he was quite pleased that Stojan had broached the subject.

His wife, however, did not look as pleased, but rather looked apprehensive.

Their stay had been uneventful and quite pleasant. Fully rested and recharged, they found their hosts and the entire city to be much like the Navajo with one minor exception—there seemed to be very few young people. Most all of the residents were what they would consider old or elderly. That was not to say that they did not work hard and were not part of an active community. The fact was that there were no children— or even people of Stojan's age.

It seemed to Ana that despite his words about them holding back, Stojan had found trust in these people. She watched the unveiling of his true name, and especially the face of the one known as Armadillo Skin.

The woman watched intently as her lips parted. It looked to Ana as if she was going to reveal the name simultaneously. As it turned out she was not wrong.

"Watchful Raven."

Indeed the woman had formed the words at the same time Stojan had, but silently.

Their response was not to react unusually—or to laugh, or to smile. In fact they had absolutely no reaction to Stojan. That reaction, it seemed, was reserved for Anastazja. Upon pronouncing his name, both heads turned to Ana. They looked and waited. The tension of their expectations weighed heavily on her—so much so that it showed in more than her face.

As her hat hung on a rung near the door, so did her protection from prying eyes.

Her hair was now the color of a sunset, with tendrils of reds and oranges mixed in.

The woman's gaze was that of one in shock. Her mouth fell open and stayed that way until she mouthed a single word.

"Sunflower."

As time had passed Anastazja's color changes had become such a part of who she was that Stojan paid it little mind. To him it was as normal as a facial expression. Her anger in battle had been managed and utilized so effectively that it had hardly come up of late. Their travels had revealed little conflict save for the training, so this color change came as a bit of a surprise to him as well. It seemed that their hosts—in particular the woman—was quite aware of who they were. She appeared to be in tune with what they sought, and had suggested they actually seek the saint in the cathedral. In this at least she was wrong. Stojan felt a bit exposed, but had offered his name for just such an occurrence. He decided to show some of his hand so that they would reveal theirs. In this he was successful, albeit slightly embarrassed—not at all comparable to the level his companion was currently experiencing.

"So you are they."

"We are just travelers."

"You are the only two who have challenged a saint and won."

"We were lucky."

"You have come here at this time to once again challenge a saint."

"No. You said you have no cathedral here."

Ana nodded as her hair slowly turned to blonde.

"But you mentioned The Coast."

"Yes, we travel to the coast of your great country…"

"We are on vacation!"

Anastazja smiled a triumphant smile as if the statement would explain their intentions.

For the first time the pair looked confused.

"Well, you will not be able to visit The Coast."

"Well, why not?"

"Because…"

She paused and placed her hand upon Ana's.

Ana looked into her eyes as she felt the warmth of her wrinkled hand.

"Because Watchful Raven and Sunflower, The Saint on High means to destroy it."

Amira

IN THE SHADOW OF THE CATHEDRAL

Stojan sat up in his chair to a very stiff posture—which was to say he barely moved.

"Destroy The Coast of Amira? Why would he do that?"

Her hand still on Ana's, the woman continued.

"Because he no longer wishes to be here. His plan is to destroy the coast and the rest of Amira to destroy all saints."

"How do you know this?"

Ana pulled her hand away and moved it to her side; the movement was instinctual as that was where her sword would be—had it not been hung up out of courtesy.

It was the husband's turn to speak.

"Because…"

"You said you have no cathedral."

Ana had rudely interrupted but her frustration was obvious.

"We do not. But there is one nearby."

"The peak?"

"Yes."

"We intended to visit it."

"It *is* a cathedral. We live in its shadow."

Ana looked at Stojan—amazed that their tiny blue dot was indeed a cathedral that housed a saint. So quickly had they yet again found one.

"There were others who made the journey to it. The ones that did return spoke of a great weapon in his possession—a weapon of mass destruction for all living creatures."

When the two gazed back with an incredulous look, he insisted.

"It is true. Do not underestimate their power. Perhaps they mean to kill many; perhaps they mean to devastate the land. Perhaps it is both. It is an odd thing—this power they wield. Sometimes I think they themselves do not understand it."

"Interlopers."

The old man smiled and looked at Stojan with some pride.

"You are indeed wise, Watchful Raven."

Stojan took a deep breath and folded his arms.

"What do you suggest we do then? It seems this saint interferes with our on vacation."

Ana did not know what to say and instead just watched the conversation unfold.

The old couple exchanged glances. It seemed that Stojan was very willing to take the next step. His willingness confused Ana considering that she believed he wanted to avoid the saints and not move towards them.

"You need no convincing?"

Stojan turned to Ana to address her shock, but before he could answer the old man spoke.

"We will take you to the other elders of our village to give you what wisdom we have."

With a confused Ana, a seemingly calm Stojan and two excited hosts, their dinner was hereby disregarded in favor of an immediate meeting.

———

The meeting with the elders was surprisingly short. Unlike The People, the denizens of this village were less formal when it came to leadership. To Stojan it appeared simply that these leaders told them to seek out the saint, discover his true plan and most importantly, to 'be careful.'

Ana had mixed feelings. For all her talk of quests, she now found herself on one with not only the sanction of the elders of The People, but with their full support. It made her wonder if a quest was really what she wanted, or if perhaps one was enough. Stojan was of no help as his mood seemed not only supportive but nonplussed. She wondered if he was placating her, knew something she didn't, or was just genuinely happy to travel with her—regardless of whether they were in danger or not.

In her heart of hearts she knew it to be all three.

The room of elders was the neutral brown Ana had come to understand as the standard wall color of the village. Their meeting place was one of the few exceptions here in that it was a much larger building with an equally large room inside. Though it seemed to be built as a hall, they were told that it too was someone's home. These people did not believe in creating a structure for a purpose; but instead adding a purpose to a denizen's home. This was no different and was complete with a bedroom and plot of well-tended land behind it.

The walls were populated with figurines as brightly colored as the building exteriors. They stood upon small shelves, or stood guard in a corner—making themselves known as a bright spot in an otherwise soothing interior. Intermixed with them were tiny intricate sculptures of glass and metal. These were in contrast to the organic look of the dolls —but somehow fit in. Ana wondered which one of the homes housed a glassblower, and thoughts of that led to a furnace, which then led to…

She blinked and exited her thoughts as they continued the conversation.

"We do not send you to spread his power, but to end it."

"What power does he currently have?"

The elders exchanged glances and waited briefly for the one with the best answer to speak first. This time it was a taller woman adorned with many tiny beads.

"We believe with the weapon he possesses he will be able to destroy the coast at a distance. A great distance."

"Then we have two problems."

"Oh?"

"We have no way to reach him, and we have no way to destroy him. Surely someone would have already done this."

Before they could answer, it was Anastazja that spoke.

"Why have you not sent warriors to do this?"

She panned her eyes around the large table.

"We lived with The People for some time and learned of many warriors. Do you not have warriors to send to dispatch him?"

Stojan nodded his agreement. He too wondered this but had his own thoughts on the matter. The woman spoke again—feeling that she had the floor.

"We are not warriors, but a people who wish to simply exist."

"In the shadow of a great destructive force."

They all turned to Stojan and some faces showed that they did not appreciate his assessment. He continued—much to the dismay of some.

"What occurred with Saint John was our doing and our choice. We were not employed as mercenaries to do the bidding of any people. We did so of our own free will. We wish to explore Amira. And like you we wish to simply exist."

"But if you travel to The Coast and the saint gets his wish you will NOT exist."

The man pounded the table. He was angry and did not appreciate the sudden turn of events. Judging by the eyes of even those who remained calm, neither did the others.

Ana watched and thought she saw panic in the eyes of one elder.

"Perhaps we will simply seek elsewhere to go then."

The anger and tension of the room continued to climb as Stojan spoke matter-of-factly. When everyone remained silent, Stojan did something that Ana now half-expected. He folded his arms and sat back in his chair and smiled. She was the only one who was not confused—though this was marginal.

They all stared at Stojan—angrily, incredulously. Mouths half-formed words, glances were exchanged. When it looked like they could take no more silence he at last spoke.

"Then perhaps you can tell us what is really going on."

Anger and tension quickly turned to submission. Ana thought she might have seen a small amount of relief too. The elders all looked closely at Stojan's face. They saw no stress, no anger and no friction. Instead they saw a slight smile. He knew something.

"We are an honest people. We did not mean to mislead or be dishonest with you. You are honored guests and what you have already done is much loved by us. We will tell you everything we know."

"At last."

Anastazja listened intently as the elders told the story of how they came to know of the saint, their initial pilgrimage to the cathedral and the results. It sounded to her that the last interaction was many, many years ago, and their story was less of a story and more of a rumor. She wondered if it had been pieced together from many travelers or just one.

"He only accepts those that can help him."

Stojan raised an eyebrow.

"And, it is not a chasm."

"It most certainly…!"

The elder continued and cut off Ana, or perhaps it was Ana who had interjected.

"It is a bridge, made of Amiran tec."

"We saw no bridge."

"It is hidden."

"And?"

"And he controls it."

Ana was oddly elated.   A saint that controlled an entry and only let certain travelers in. It was a fascinating quest. Stojan, however, rolled his eyes.

He spoke while Ana pondered.

"You believe this saint will allow us passageway?   Then why did he not accept us the first time?"

They froze.   None even looked around. It was as if Stojan had told them all to pause.   Finally one pushed his chair away and walked to a wall. He returned with something small and shiny.

"Because you did not have this."

He gingerly placed it on the table and it made a distinctive metallic thud. It was a bit heavier than it looked. At least one of the elders looked like she was going to snatch it back and withdraw it from the discussion. Ana looked it over and as her eyes handled the object she simply asked what it was.

"A key. It is a key to the bridge. It is said that the saint can sense it."

"So you think it unlocks it? This is Amiran tec?"

Ana glanced around the room—searching for more like objects.

"It is a key of sorts.   We think he extends the bridge instinctively when he senses it. Or it is the Amiran tec."

Stojan shook his head slightly.   He realized they were just as confused.

Indeed the line between Amran tec and the power of the saints was blurry. He did not know where one ended and one began. And sometimes they overlapped.

"If you carry this with you, the bridge will greet you."

Stojan and Anastazja accepted the small object and Stojan's last words made Ana slowly turn to him. He did not meet her eyes.

"Do you have a shovel?"

————

The conversation that occurred after the meeting was devoid of any talk of quests, saints or cathedrals. Instead, the group of four had a meal together and chatted cordially about the village, the bright colors and the gardens of each.

The elderly woman was quite proud of her yard and would talk endlessly of it. This was welcomed by all three as they all were lost in thought— her talk of cacti and flowers and arrangements made for a constant background noise, as if they all sat by a babbling brook.

The next morning they were up with the sun, enjoyed a small meal with their hosts and were on their way.

Amira

THE SAINT ON HIGH

As the two made their way up the long winding road, Ana thought about the small metal and glass sculpture in her saddle bag. She wanted to handle it, to toy with it and stop to see what it did—if anything. However, they both knew better.

As they once again approached the chasm they halted their horses and dismounted.

Ana smiled and brought forth the object from her saddle bag.   The sun was reflected in both the metal and the glass. She found the weight of it impressive and insisted she hold it as they approached the chasm.

They edged forward—one slow step at a time. When they were as close as Stojan would permit they simply waited.   With the tiniest of sounds something did indeed happen.

Out of the very cliff face itself came a great section of road.   Unlike the unkept path they travelled, this massive rectangle rose into view as a black square adorned with only an orange line down the center.   It was not a constant line, but was a repeating pattern of line segments.

They backed away slightly as it continued to rise and finally stopped— sealing the path perfectly. What was now before them was an unbroken path forward. The bridge looked out of place and was unlike Stojan had pictured it.   There were no hand railings nor visible supports, instead along either side were metallic curved barriers.

Ana gripped the device tightly and thought it felt warm—though she could not tell if the warmth came from within or as a result of the bright sun.

"We should take the horses."

Stojan—with horses in to—walked slowly across the newly-formed path with Ana alongside him. The path was as solid as if there were hundreds of meters of rock below them. Ana did not know if she should sprint or proceed with gingerly steps. She felt she was fighting to somehow do both. Eventually they did cross the length of road and once across they stopped.

Guiding Ana to walk further, he watched the bridge as they proceeded. When they were about fifty meters away, the bridge started to disappear from view. It was at that point Stojan stopped them and went to his saddle bag.

Off to the side he searched within the dense but low brush. With a smile he began to dig. When he was satisfied, he returned to the bags and brought forth a brightly-patterned cloth. He walked over to Ana and outstretched his hand.

She handed the object to him and simply asked, "Why?"

Without a word he took it and carefully buried it, covered it in a brightly-colored cloth and refilled the hole. Dusting off his hands he returned the shovel to his bag. At last he answered.

"So that he may not take our means of escape from us."

In their travels they had seen many cathedrals. Each one was slightly different but in many ways they were similar. They all possessed certain designs that made them very easy to spot.

But this one did indeed look different. The building was at the very top of the hill in a flat clearing and stood proudly overseeing everything below. It had intentionally been built at the highest spot, it seemed.

Stojan just nodded as the two made their way up the trail—now mounted — that was quickly becoming a solid road. The effect was familiar to them albeit backwards; overgrowth gave way to a black road that looked pristine.   Cracks gave way to seamless pavement.   It mirrored the experience they had when they first arrived in Amira—just in reverse. If the effect was constant it meant a saint did indeed reside here.

Ana looked up from the road—realization showing on her face.

"Stojan this means that…"

He politely let her finish though she gave him an opportunity not to.

"…there was a saint nearby when we first arrived in Amira."

"Indeed Ana.   I believe the conveyance would have not survived all of those years if one had not been present. And the building."

"And the roads."

She finished the thought—bringing her full-circle to her realization. Stojan smiled as Ana stopped in her tracks.

"What is it?" Stojan raised an eyebrow and stopped as well. A pleasant breeze silently blew her hair out of place as she sat.

"How should we proceed? How…"

The tall man was silent, but rather than ignoring her, he was contemplating how to respond properly.   Ana looked at him with concern, but not fear.

"We will proceed with caution. If my understanding is accurate then we have more to fear from his minions than the saint himself."

Ana thought back to the Saint animating the statue—the dais it stood upon, even the sword that seemed to be forever bonded to its hand. If Stojan was right then indeed the Saint could do little other than animate a statue and threaten them.   What exactly would have happened if they had not approached the saint in the cathedral of Saint John? Would it forever mock them from the place it was affixed?   And for that matter, what hold did it have on those like the elder?

Up until now Ana had just assumed that there was much, much more to the saints and those that followed them.

"Ana?"

Stojan had watched in silence as Anastazja had collected her thoughts. Though he was entertained by her silent musings, he was not particularly comfortable with standing out in the open.

"We provide a very stationary target here. Shall we continue?"

She blinked.   Slightly embarrassed, she continued and her horse enthusiastically matched the pace of the tall man's in an effort to make up for the pause.

"Stojan?"

She brushed the hair from her eyes and looked over at him.   He continued and did not return her gaze.

"There is so much I do not understand about the saints. There is so much that does not make sense."

"I agree Ana.   We are strangers in a strange land, and we have only recently arrived.   Our understanding cannot be anything but disappointingly incomplete."

There was no response as she continued to process her thoughts and Stojan's words. He chose to continue, however.

"And fret not; we do have an advantage for any questions you may have."

"Oh Stojan, what is that?"

They rounded the hill and both Ana and Stojan stopped—dismounted their horses.   He turned to face his blonde companion—the building immediately behind him.

"We can simply ask him."

Anastazja looked at the domed building. She had initially thought that the dome was a small part of a larger building; it seemed quite the opposite was true.   The dome was very large and had only a small rectangular building attached to it.   To Ana it looked as if a giant sphere had been pressed into the earth, with a large belt placed around the perimeter.

As expected it was beautiful and in pristine condition. Unlike the other cathedral she'd seen, this one had no stained-glass windows. In fact, it had no windows at all. The door was smooth and like other Old World Amiran buildings it had no knob. They pushed it open and it offered no resistance. Carefully they entered the building and chose the short stairs going up. It emptied into a large room. As the door closed, almost all of the light left the room. Their eyes slowly adjusted.

"I know why you're here."

It was a voice that whispered in their ears and it caused them both to look around—to recoil from an invisible stranger standing right next to them.

There was no one next to them, however.

"Tell us then, so that we may save much time."

Stojan spoke with certainty and capitalized on the willingness of the interloper to speak. He was mindful of their position in relationship to the door, and when first entering had not seen any statues. Instead he had seen a mostly empty room.

Ana looked up and around. The voice in her ear made her uncomfortable and she continually shifted as if she'd bump into it at any second. She grabbed her sword but did not unsheathe it—taking a cue from Stojan.

He, however, did not shift but remained still and looked forward. Since he had nothing to look, at he did just that.

"Dude, relax."

This time the voice was different, as if there was something other than single-minded malevolence present. Stojan raised an eyebrow as Ana's face approached something comical.

"You don't have to be all uptight."

"Show yourself."

The being did not heed Stojan's reply, and the two started to search the interior. The lengths of light started to brighten, revealing a most interesting room.

The light provided came from thin strips hanging from a section of the room and it shone a subdued lighting far dimmer than the sunlight they were just recently bathed in.

There was very little in the domed room. The walls sloped upward to form the interior of the dome and the room was quite spacious. Absolutely no decorations were found and Stojan noted that the walls were not smooth, but instead had a sort of scaffolding lining them— almost mechanical in nature.

A desk of some kind with a few chairs was off to a side, and prominently in the very center of the room was a massive contraption that was the most elaborate otherworldly machine he'd ever seen.

The device was affixed to the floor and was a sort of cylindrical base with a very large cylinder mounted atop that. It had to be a good fifteen meters high or more. Protruding from it were all manner of dials and controls. In that way it reminded him of the conveyance they'd used to travel to Amira, though instead of the dull metal, this had been painted a uniform, drab white.

Ana thought it frightening to behold and most confusing of all was the great cylinder that was pointed upward toward the inside of the dome. Thoughts of the thing that was used to end the life of poor Fox crossed her mind. This was much, much larger and the magnified size only served to increase her fear of it.

It was a great weapon indeed.

She imagined it being fired and destroying a good portion of the dome in the process. It was a cathedral with a great weapon mounted inside of it, atop a hill. This saint had at his disposal the means to destroy much— from afar—it seemed.

"I can't."

The tone of the Saint was most curious to both and it emboldened Ana to join the conversation.

"Why not," she shouted upwards towards the dome.

"That's not how it works for us, you know?"

"That is not what we have seen."

"Yeah, I know. Statues, and all that stuff."

"Stuff?"

"Hey so have a seat or something, and let's chat."

The two exchanged glances, but did not sit.

"It's OK, I'm not going to hurt you. Man, it's nice to talk to someone. This has been... well this is all... it's been a really long time."

"So tell us why we are here then."

Stojan was not amused.

"Man, you *are* impatient. You just got here. OK fine. You're here because you think I'm going to wipe out the coast and go all epic on you. That's not gonna happen. That's not what I'm all about. Hey, seriously, have a seat."

Ana shrugged and looked over at the two chairs. They looked comfortable and made of wood covered in leather. The being speaking was decidedly different than the previous saint they'd met—not only in demeanor, but also in language. This one was harder to understand and spoke in a casual manner.

"Suit yourself."

The warning seemed slightly ominous, but the speaker continued.

"I'm here like the others, except I think my situation is different."

"What about the weapon?"

Stojan motioned with his chin, though he was unsure if the being could actually see him.

"What? *Dude.* That's not a weapon."

At this pronouncement the device seemed to come alive—slowly moving and rotating. Impressive mechanical sounds could be heard from it. Ana drew her blade and Stojan did not stop her.

"What is it then?"

Ana yelled as she pointed her blade at the thing, knowing it would be of no use. It would be almost like fighting a building. Perhaps if they sat, it meant to crush them with it.

"It's a way of trying to find home."

For the first time Ana heard sadness.

"I've looked for a thousand years and it's not out there. That's not where we came from."

We.

Stojan reflected on both the emotion and the use of 'we.' This being clearly knew there were more. He'd come to understand that they were far from all-knowing, but this one did seem to be aware of the others—as well as his limitations. He was a stark contrast to the other saint.

"A thousand years…"

Ana spoke almost reverently as she whispered the words.

"Yeah. That's a really, really long time to be in one place. Disconnected, but connected. Mobile, but immobile. I've had nothing to do but search."

"You were searching for home?"

Ana almost felt the saint smile at her question.

"Yeah. Home. The door's closed but I thought maybe there was another way. We don't really see stuff like you do. Time, space—all that nonsense is like sorta the same thing. But I'm still trapped here."

Before they could respond, it shouted.

"Hey! But you can help. We can open the door again!"

"The…"

"Yeah, the door. It's not that far from here. We could open the door again and then we could all just return."

"You want to go back?"
Stojan added, "You have no interest in conquest—submission of these

94

people? Surely this is a trick."

"No no, man. I think we all want to go back. The door was closed and we were trapped here. See, others would have come through, but the door was closed. If we just open it again then we can all go back. Then we're done."

They stared at the inside of the dome. It was odd that there were no statues at all. Perhaps they had been destroyed, or perhaps this place was not even a place of worship. It made no sense.

"How did you become trapped here?"

"Ooh, that's a good question. It wasn't my first choice, I guess. When I came through I sort of bounced around in the valley for a while but I didn't take hold. It's pretty confusing—like totally confusing. But then this place just had enough... I dunno, like *softness* to accommodate me. I think I get it now, because after all that looking, I think I felt what some of the guys here felt. And that's probably why I was able to survive."

It seemed like the machine moved to and fro as it spoke—dials rotating here and there, almost punctuating some of his words. It was similar to how one waves a cane, or removes a pipe from one's mouth while speaking.

Ana imagined that the saint was actually inside the machine.

Stojan for the first time felt some curiosity regarding the saints. He'd previously defined them as evil non-corporeal beings. But now, there was much more. This one in particular seemed almost friendly, with little or no interest in their affairs.

But he did not trust him.

Him?

It did sound like a decidedly male voice, but Stojan was not quite sure if he heard it with his ears or with his mind. He would not be taken off-guard by a being such as this just because it seemed cordial. It was still evil and an interloper.

"Where are you?"

Stojan's sudden question stopped the saint's conversation. It was silent as Ana traded glances with him.

"What? Where am I? Dude I'm right here."

Again the device moved slightly.

"So you are trapped within the contraption before us."

"Well no. I'm here. *Here* is different for us. I mean, man, you're a hard one. I know people are like skeptical, but…"

Again Ana looked at Stojan. She seemed to be enjoying the exchange more than he was. To her it was a surprisingly light-hearted conversation.

"Then show yourself."

"I told you, I'm here. This is all I got for ya."

"Then how is it that you propose to open this door?"

"Well, *I'm* not going to do it. Well maybe I can. If you can find something that I can inhabit, then I can come with you."

"Come with us?"

Ana's surprise was genuine.

"Yes! I can send you to where the door is and give you the proper instructions on how to start it. I mean, how to open the door again, then you can just do it. I mean it's not rocket science… well, wait maybe… yeah I suppose that's exactly what it is."

Ana thought she heard it laugh.

"Enough of this nonsense."

Stojan had listened long enough to the saint.

"We have come here in error."

Ana touched his sleeve—sensing that he was about to end their conversation. She shook her head as he continued.
"We were told that you possessed a means to destroy a great many

people. But instead you say you wish to end the reign of all saints?"

"Saints. Yeah, that's what I'm trying to tell you man. Can't you talk some sense into him?"

Ana looked embarrassed at this.

"Like tell him that I'm trying to help you get rid of us. You don't have to go around and just stab stab stab to get it done."

At this Stojan thought he heard a different tone—one of anger and perhaps desperation.

"And you think the others will be in agreement to this plan? How will they get to this door?"

"Oh they don't need to be in agreement."

Stojan raised an eyebrow as it continued.

"When the door is open they will just go through it. And they don't really need to be close to it. Near, far, close—none of that has any meaning to us."

"Just like that?"

"Yeah, just like that Stojan. But in reverse."

"You know my name?"

"Of course. I know tons of stuff about you and Anastazja. We are all aware of things. Sort of felt it when you... well, you know."

Stojan glanced at Ana—she looked hopeful at the prospect.

"Why haven't any of the others proposed this? Why haven't any of them attempted to leave? They enslaved the hearts of the people of Amira and yet you seem to be so happy to leave. Why have you not attempted to do this if you have truly been here for a thousand years?"

Stojan looked at Ana while he spoke, in an effort to drive the point home. As much as he enjoyed the look of hope in her eyes, he did not want her to be persuaded and misled by this evil being.

"OK. All good questions, but really, why? I'm telling you now that we can do this. We open a door, we all leave, and that's it. OK maybe there's a bit of societal issues that would need to be cleaned up, a vacuum created here or there, etc."

"Answer the questions."

After a long pause it answered in what sounded like a defeated voice.

"Because I just figured it out. And I figured how to ignore the other voices."

Stojan realized he did indeed want to sit down.

"Other voices?"

It growled and then screamed. Ana almost covered her ears. The massive contraption moved quickly back and forth, which was to say it lumbered slowly. Still, there was a sense of urgency to it, and the sound was otherworldly.

"We are running out of time."

"Tell us what we ask then."

Stojan was firm. The saint did not possess a means to threaten or even affect them; it had no minions and seemed powerless. This saint was trapped in a dead end atop a mesa with no way to affect the people of Amira. And if it could be believed, it had cut itself off from the other interlopers. This meant that his and Ana's location would not be reported.

The device stopped moving and there was silence in the great room for many moments.

"I can only stop listening to the other voices for so long. Then I hear them again. Then they know everything *I* know."

Ana's eyes widened at the prospect.

"Yeah, I know. It's enough to make you go insane. I started to get used to the quiet. There's a lot going on out there, and a lot that has gone on for hundreds of years. Things changed recently. So look. Let's just do this. Like right now."

Before she could speak it continued.

"Yeah yeah, 'or what.' I know, you give me an ultimatum, or just refuse, or just walk out. Or you say 'why us.' You're already here, and you're not freaking out talking to a telescope."

It seemed that just when they were understanding the saint, it used words to perplex them. Most of what it said could be deciphered, but not all. It used terms and language that was confusing—and perhaps intentionally misleading. Stojan still had many questions.

"What do you want us to do?"

Ana had interjected before Stojan could speak. This prompted an enthusiastic response from the saint, and a look of apprehension from Stojan.

"Finally! OK. here's what I need you to do..."

A PLAN UNFOLDS

"Do you completely understand what it is we are to do?"

Ana looked over to the tall man as they rode. The saint had explained—impatiently, erratically, irrationally—what they were to accomplish.

Stojan summed it up in one word.

"No."

Ana could not help but laugh.

"Stojan! Then what are we doing?"

"I do not completely understand, or agree with it. But I understand enough for us to accomplish it. Assuming this is not at all an elaborate ruse."

"You think it is a trick, don't you?"

"Yes, of course. It uses us to accomplish something it cannot. You and I have learned enough about these interlopers to know there is no kindness in their hearts."

He scoffed at his own choice of words. A thing that did not have a body, did not have a heart.

"Stojan, if you think it a trick then why did we agree to do it?"

"Because it may allow us to do something that we could otherwise not do."

"And what is that?"

"To get rid of the ones we call saints—all of them."

"Yes. It said they would leave."

"Of that I have much doubt."

"You sense deception?"

"I feel that they will not be in agreement so easily. One thing I have learned is that they are ultimately selfish. His motives are no different."

"But you think we have enough information to complete his goal?"

"What I hope, dear Ana, is that we have enough information to complete *ours*."

As they understood it, they were to try to find a vessel for the saint to travel in from the cathedral to the great doorway. He would assist them and open the door. Once open, it would draw all the other saints through it. It explained that opening the door in the first place had drawn them in, and a saint on this side of the door had closed it. In a way they had all been trapped here. Since the door had been closed on this side they were powerless to reopen it. With the resulting chaos and catastrophe, so many were lost—including the special Amiran tec—that they were unable to open it again.

When asked who closed the door, the saint had said that it was one of them, but quickly changed the subject. That fact was of particular interest to Stojan.

They were assured that opening the door was of no danger to anyone, and that it would automatically close once they were all through it. This too Stojan took exception with. Since they were all intimately selfish, he doubted all could be convinced to go through.

In addition, the saint had no minions; no congregation. Almost a century ago the last of his congregation had left or died, he said. This too did not ring true and sounded particularly ominous—regardless of the nonchalance that was used to relay it. It had been alone for all of those years, and the pilgrimage of the Navajo turned out to be the final congregation member making it to their city with his trinkets. The last person had left hundreds of years ago—perhaps longer than that.

As it turned out, the saint did not open or close the bridge. Instead he merely allowed it to work. Something about the trinket was causing him to focus attention and when he did so the bridge just worked. It was not actually a key at all but rather, a carrot.

"Stojan…"

Ana broke him out of his musings. Her voice was gentle and perhaps afraid. He turned to her immediately and searched her face. She seemed to be taking an inordinate amount of time to find her words.

"What if we turn the world upside down again?"

She was genuinely frightened. This quest was far beyond anything they had yet done. The dire consequences could be global.

Stojan looked at the girl he called his daughter, and with much kindness and comfort he replied.

"Well then, Ana, it will once again be right-side-up."

CONSIDERATIONS

The map had pointed them to the southwest. They had a great many miles to go, so stops in towns and cities were a must. Unfortunately they were now traveling *away* from The Coast. They would have to put their plans on hold and as Stojan had remarked, they were now 'off vacation.'

Cities in this local were spaced so that travel could be had within the day. In spite of this, Stojan preferred to make a camp between cities when they saw fit. His reasoning was that they would maintain control and be able to assess things from afar.   He did not share that this also gave Ana the ability to practice and go for walks, though this was mostly why he did this.

"Have you seen any unusual animals of late?"

Ana turned and answered Stojan's parting question. It seemed to her that he'd found a new way to say 'please be careful and return to me in one piece.'

She smiled, almost giddy at the prospect of another walk.

"No, nothing really.   I do like the forests here; they remind me of the forests we moved within when we were with our friends."

Stojan simply smiled, as nothing else was needed. It was clear she knew exactly how he felt about her walks.

As they had moved slowly to the southeast, the forests did indeed become more dense and—despite the surrounding areas— more lush with green. They were very similar to the forests to the north. It reminded him of Poliska—just much, much warmer.

With that, she quickly disappeared behind a tree and was not seen for some time. He thought this a good time to sharpen his blade.

Stojan sat and sharpened and considered. It had only been recently that he'd destroyed one of the saints; now he had agreed to assist one. His opinion of the saints—all of them—had come from the single encounter he'd had. This one was markedly different—almost friendly and probably insane. While the previous saint had been absolute and clearly wanted to rule, this one just wanted to escape. And in escaping he would bring the rest of them with him.

The impression that the other saints would not agree with this was strong, as well as his opinion on the truthfulness of the saint in the great dome.

There was more to this quest than just opening a door, and Stojan had no intention of allowing him to escape. Perhaps there was no door and obtaining a vessel other than the great tube was what he really wanted? Any story would suffice to convince wayward travelers to allow him to escape.

A story about opening a door to rid the world of saints seemed perfectly tailored to two such as Ana and Stojan. What were the last travelers promised?

And it seemed this saint was disconnected from the others. But—Stojan considered very seriously—since when? He knew of his name, and Ana's, but did he not know of the loss of his brethren? If a saint is dispatched, surely they would be alerted to the loss, yet he did not speak of it. Or did he? Was the death of the saint the very thing that allowed him to detach? The saint's mannerisms and language were quite foreign. Being trapped in a machine for one thousand years could very well have made him insane. And perhaps that was the fate that befell them all. At one time were they benevolent?

Stojan dismissed any thoughts about kind beings that were intrinsically good. They were not. They wielded great power and saw mankind as playthings, regardless of whatever promises they made.

And this included his current quest.

He would have to be very careful for Anastazja; she was understandably impressionable and thus much more susceptible to this kind of ruse.

Stojan thought long and hard about this and what was to unfold before them. In fact, so deep was he in thought that he did not notice Ana's return.

"Hello Stojan."

Amira

A CROSSROADS

Stojan immediately looked up.   Though the voice was that of a woman it was not Anastazja.

It had been the first time he'd been surprised in a very long time. He sat in mid stroke of his sharpening and froze.

There were others; he knew it and could feel it. But she stood before him alone.   His thoughts went from berating himself to retracing what had happened to understanding how much time had actually passed to how many were truly in her group, and then… Ana's safety.

He smiled.

"Stojan? You're most friendly. I trust you'll remain that way, especially since your sword is already drawn."

The woman was adorned in light robes and rested her hand on a long staff almost as tall as she.   Around her neck was a necklace made of wood and metal with two cross pieces—large but simple. Her face was the mid-tone dark Stojan had come to recognize as the standard skin tone of Amirans. It was not as dark as the Navajo but not as light as he and Ana. Her hair was black and curly and almost floated upon her head. It made him think of a mushroom. She was about the same age as Stojan and he thought her to be not unattractive.

While she spoke he continued to think. His musings were accelerated and he attempted to make amends for finding himself in such an unaware position.

His body was immobile but his mind was not.

The smile on her own face dipped slightly as the timing of the conversation seemed to be off. He did not immediately reply, nor did he respond with a well-prepared quip. He just sat—prone. Her entourage had him surrounded. He should have leapt up and immediately formed a stance of challenge—sword out in front of him with his back to the tree.

They'd advised her that this would most likely be the case, with the worst-case scenario being that he would just charge and run her through. The decision to confront him alone at first had not sat well will everyone. Yet there he sat, not responding and behaving like she was to say more.

And it was uncomfortable.

A sizable group might be out searching for his partner and he had no way of knowing just how outnumbered he was.

"Are you dumbfounded? Why do you not speak?"

She spoke loudly, with tones of authority in an attempt to rouse him to respond properly.

He looked around and then back to her.

"The forest is not the echo chamber you are used to. Perhaps it has less power than you think."

"What!?"

It was maddening. He was not rational. She watched as he put away his sharpening stone. His extra-long sword did indeed look sharp—he had done an excellent job. Before she could recover from her angry interjection he spoke again.

"This is the part in which you tell me our destination."

She blinked.

"You don't want to know who I am? You have no interest in why I have sought you out?"

"I am sure you will tell me without any prompting."

He stood, and kept his sword out. It did not appear that he would attack. This did not provide any comfort as his long legs could bring him to her faster than she could react. And the sword would certainly find her. The staff she relied on was not a weapon and would be of no use. She felt oddly exposed now, as if she'd stepped into a cage with an animal.

That was when a number of her men both came to her rescue and somehow prevented any further conversation.

Stojan looked to both the left and the right. In they came—armed with short swords and wearing light leather armor. They were clearly a group of men under the hire of the woman before him, and it was easy to see that they had not seen any real battle in some time. None of them looked fresh; as if they had traveled for some time to be there. It made him wonder just from where they'd come to ambush him.

"Where is she Stojan?"

He kept his sword out and his eyes on the men. Though they flanked him he did his best to be aware of each and every one of them.

"You don't know? Surely you've surrounded us, yes?"

She couldn't tell if he was being arrogant or was just a simple man. At least he was straightforward. She would not tell him of her instructions, but instead motioned to the men to remove him along with everything at the campsite. He came along quietly. In fact his compliance would have been suspicious had it not been foretold by her lord.

To his slight surprise they did not take his sword but instead just had him sheath it. He wasn't sure if it was inexperience or poor planning, or something else. Judging by the hubris of their leader, he thought that her experience was with speaking to congregations, and the men in her employ were city guards at best. She was out of her element and operated as if given limited instructions. He was not wrong.

ALONE

This walk was more welcome than most as she now had a lot on her mind. In fact it seemed her life was now filled with plans on top of plans. This walk would also not see her draw her sword. She was, however, mindful of what it meant to lose herself in thought too deeply. To ignore her senses meant to allow something to sneak up on her, and that was a task she herself thoroughly enjoyed. No animal would steal that from her today.

Her movements were lithe; her actions were as one with the breeze. In moving about the brush and the trees, she once again found the flow of nature and became part of it. It readily accepted her as a ghost—able to travel within and through it. Her walk had reawakened her awareness of this and reminded her that swordplay was not her only skill. She gave in wholeheartedly and embraced her walk—the sights, sounds, scents and even the feel of the forest floor through her short boots. Her clothing did not exist, instead she felt naked on her walk.

For some time she was lost in the embrace of nature. Her awareness of what was around her expanded—this included both flora and fauna. She breathed it all in deeply; its air filled her lungs and the rest filled her soul. She let herself go for what felt like hours. Indeed it had been a long time that she let herself wander, explore and embrace.

Then something changed.

She stopped and became still to consider what was different. Was it a sound? A scent? An animal call? Perhaps it was a lack thereof.

Being mindful to not let this out-of-place thing cause her to be unaware, she proceeded slowly and cautiously. She would make her way to this disturbance. It was obvious after a short while that it was indeed a lack of sound. The animals had become quiet, and the closer she moved to the quiet, the more she realized which direction she was going.

It was whence she came.

She continued—focusing on the sound and her surroundings. Though she was intent on finding her way back, she was also aware of what was behind her. Nothing would take her off guard today.

She eventually made it back to the camp and although her instincts had already told her what her eyes would see, it still came to her as a surprise. He was gone. And not only was Stojan nowhere to be seen, but both horses as well. She tip-toed around the camp. Her nose sniffed the air as her eyes searched the ground. There had been many here, and as far as she could tell there had been no struggle. He went willingly, or at least did not protest physically.

Ana looked down at the spot she last saw him sharpening and could still see his movements upon the sword.

For many moments she stared while her mind raced. For the first time in a very long time—nay for the very first time ever—she was alone.

Her first reaction was to run in the direction they'd gone. With some tracking perhaps she could possibly determine the direction, eventually. But what then? They were about a day's ride from civilization in either direction. Her horse had been taken and with it all of her supplies. Everything she owned now was worn upon her. At least she had her sword.

There was no panic, however. Her face showed very little emotion as she turned. Instead of running as fast as she could to the nearest road, she did something unexpected. Maintaining both a dream-like state and an odd heightened awareness of the surroundings, she moved slowly.

Anastazja went back into the forest and once again sought the embrace of the trees.

Her mind had been given a problem. With it came the realization that she'd never truly been alone. Even when her father left her, Stojan was already there to be with her. This understanding occupied her mind for some time as she continued inward.

Then she sat under a large tree. Her knees were bent and her hands were on her sword. She'd plunged it into the ground in front of her and between her knees. Both hands rested on the hilt as she stared ahead and looked at nothing and everything. There she sat—alone and exposed—in the middle of a forest with no name, in a country that was foreign to her. Though her home had been taken from her, her new home was with Stojan—wherever that was. But now he too had been taken from her.

She did not become angry, or scared, or desperate. What came over her was a state of mind that she would never be able to describe properly when asked. She just *was*. And there she sat, staring, existing. But it was not long that she was alone.

From her left lumbered a great animal. She'd heard and smelled it when she entered the area. She knew what its fur felt like because much to Stojan's shock she'd crept up and pet more than one of them. The animal's fur was a black that looked like it had been lightened by the sun slightly - a sort of faded black that was almost a brown. It made a path straight to the girl under the tree and sniffed the air as it approached. It weighed at least three times as much as she did and its claws could shred the bark from a tree.

When it reached her, it gently touched its nose to her hair and sniffed.

Then the black bear sat down next to her.

She continued to stare ahead. She saw trees, grass, forest and animals. She barely blinked and continued to watch nothing, and everything.

She did not look or turn her head as the animal eventually got up and lumbered away. The relative silence was only broken by the strange croaking calls from the tree nearby.

Amira

A PARTING OF WAYS

It seemed the less Stojan spoke the more his captors did. They were searching for answers and although they had apparently been given instructions that foretold his actions this day, they were still confused. It was all too easy to retrieve him. This made him consider his own actions. His reasoning for allowing them to take him was so that their interest in Ana would be diminished. In fact, as far as he could determine, this was exactly the case; they had been told to extract *him*, not *them*. Perhaps if Ana had been there they would have captured her, or they would have fought together. At the moment it seemed the logical thing to allow them to take him, and spare her. Her tracking and survival skills were excellent and had been taught by a man who was forced to be on the run for years. But she had no supplies, and his attempts to get them to ignore the second horse were not heeded.

He would understand what this was all about, and then come find her.

It would be a small thing to allow them to put some assistance between them and her. Then he would make his escape and bring her horse back with him. If he had remained they would have spent the majority of their time sweeping the area for her. And, the ensuing combat might have left him injured or allowed some of them to seek help. There was no way to tell if they were part of a larger group.

Yes, he would allow enough distance and time to pass before making any kind of escape. Then he would retrace their steps and be reunited.

Nothing would prevent that—no man, woman or saint.

This plan was excellent and would have worked perfectly had it not been for the second ambush that occurred only minutes later.

Stojan was the first to notice them. His hands had been shackled to his horse in an odd configuration—made stranger by the fact that he was still armed. It seemed that the foretelling of their saint had not included the basics on how to capture a prisoner and subdue them properly. Or they had been given conflicting information.

Or…

The group that approached them had been well-hidden and had been hiding for some time. They knew the path. They knew they'd be there.

As the prisoner kept in the center the few blows that were exchanged did not reach him. Their conflict was short lived and his captors seemed to give up far easier than expected. This gave him much pause, as he had also given up with very little resistance. Was there some sort of hex upon them? Did free will not exist? Suddenly he felt less control. Surely his reasoning for giving in was sound, and had given him a level of control—not a loss of it.

These people just appeared as if they had no experience in this sort of conflict. Their force of twenty or so had been easily outnumbered by at least a factor of two. It seemed that none of them had a stomach for battle and of all their talk of faith, the only person that was willing to die for their cause was the man in the very center of the conflict.

The oversized entourage made their way to a nearby city—and this was clearly where the newcomers resided.

The good news for Stojan was that the city was not far from where Ana was left, and this meant if she tracked them in the proper direction it would be simple to find her once he escaped. But now there was something else—curiosity. Those who ambushed had themselves been ambushed. And the newcomers had knowledge of their whereabouts. A mole? A spy? A traitor? Or something ever-present? To him it smelled of a saint. In fact the saint in the great machine could very well have orchestrated the entire event. The more he thought on this, the more it made sense. The Saint on High had set them both up, and then notified the others. This was their chance to do in the only people in one thousand years who had destroyed one of them. Perhaps some had threatened them, but his was the blow that made seven into six. It also explained their lack of interest in Ana. They were not a pair, but instead they were simply interested in the tall man with the sword—a sword he was still allowed to wear.

His certainty turned back to confusion.

He listened in on the conversation of the lady bishop—her proximity to him making this an easy task. She herself had some uncertainty, as if she kept a secret that was eating at her—a secret she hoped was not true but was slowly revealing itself to be just that. Stojan imagined that this woman probably hadn't stepped out of her cathedral in years. She was given a task with little information and now others had come to usurp her.

His musings kept him from worrying too much about Anastazja, but his stamina in the matter was wearing thin. This was the first time they'd been apart since he met her. In fact, their companionship had been without a break since then. Perhaps she needed a break from him. His attempts at humor did not alleviate his concern, and his ploy to put distance between them and her now had him in doubt.

What had he done?

THE BISHOP LADY MADISON

"It is a cruel, sadistic, detached creature that is completely powerless to do anything positive."

She froze.

The aftermath of the capture had been that the two had been placed in a makeshift cell. In fact, it looked like a formal building of some sort that had been repurposed. Stojan thought it an inn of some kind. They were quickly rushed into the room by the others and he thought he detected some sort of additional skirmish. He now had doubts that this was the origin of those who ambushed his captors. His annoyance at the situation was only tempered by his belief that he was only slightly less confused than those who detained him.

He guessed the instructions to the newcomers were on par with the vagueness of his current cell mate. He continued yelling at her—in response to her constant praise of her saint.

"It wants nothing other than worship, and I've come to understand that it does not even want that."

Finally she spoke one word with bitterness.

"Oh?"

"Yes. And this it only wants because it thinks it keeps it safe here, in its cocoon."

"You seem to know much about the motivations of a great being."

"It is not a great being. It is different, but its wants are petty."

She folded her arms.

"And? And what about its needs?"

He scoffed at this.

"I know nothing of his needs."

She looked him up and down, and thought he knew much more than he was revealing. She thought him strange and too cold. He was hiding something and spoke without elaboration. She would attempt to retrieve more information.

"Tell me Stojan, what exactly do you know of the Saint that you are not revealing? Surely you would not want any harm to come to Anastazja…"

When he tried to speak, she continued.

"…especially when that would be due to you holding back."

He narrowed his already-narrow eyes.

"Lady, you know more than I do. I am not in their employ; I do not worship them. Surely a traveler such as myself knows less than the committed servant? Why do you threaten me so?"

"Oh I do not threaten you; I merely explain that it is in your best interest to be cooperative. You want your daughter back and I want escape. We work towards a mutual goal."

"For now."

"Oh? You think things will change when we escape?"

Rather than answer immediately, he considered for a moment before continuing.

"Why does your saint not free you?"

He stared.

She returned his gaze. Unfortunately for her, blinking was not an activity he regularly participated in.

Slowly her face contorted into anger and she erupted.

"You are a fool—a smug fool who will be responsible for the death of his daughter!"

Somewhere deep inside him a voice agreed, *I already am.*

When there was no response, she decided to try a different path.

"This is the way it has always been Stojan."

"No, it is not."

"I have the ancient text—the book of the Old World. It is quite impressive and can show you the way."

"Your book is from before they came."

"Not them, *him.* For it is the second coming, as foretold."

"No. Whatever your book tells of, it is not this. These are interlopers released upon this world by accident and have taken control by deception and stealth. They are weak, formless creatures."

Her eyes widened.

"No Stojan! *He* is a Heavenly being. We can only aspire to such greatness; to such purity as he shows us."

"There is nothing pure about the twisted pleasure of the suffering and misleading of others."

He pursed his lips slightly. She marveled at how still he stood. She had heard of his speed; his reach and his agility with his blade—yet he stood so still. One would think he was casually conversing but she knew better. Whatever stance he had chosen was to maximize his reach and potential damage to those that would attack him. She could not suppress her feelings of amazement at this.

"I have seen more than one of these saints. They have nothing in common save for their selfish desire to survive."

She shook her head.

"If they arrived with any sanity, there is none left after one thousand years."

"The Book."

"I have seen books—more books than you will see in your lifetime. Each one was from the Old World and kept safely away from the prying eyes of your saints. They are not all-seeing."

"All wisdom is contained in The Book, and it matches what they share with us."

She pointed at him.

"We are lucky they share this with us! We have but to accept it."

They. She'd said it.

His lack of expression and reaction was annoying to her. He was clearly unmoved. His conviction was absolute. Had he seen as much as he said?

"Books do not contain wisdom. Nor do interlopers. Only we contain wisdom for one can only gain this through experience."

He finally tilted his head down—ever so slightly.

"And suffering."

For the first time she saw some sort of emotion.

"The Book was written so that we would not have to suffer. The Saints are here to end the suffering."

He lifted his head up ever so slightly and raised an eyebrow.

"Oh? You and your congregation no longer suffer?"

Unconvincingly she responded.

"Yes."

He seemed amused at this.

"Just like that?"

When she did not immediately elaborate he continued.

"No suffering, no pain? What do you all feel then—just pleasure? No strife or conflict—everyone living in perfect harmony?"

His tone was unpleasant and she realized she was conversing with a man who had spent his life suffering.

"Perhaps Stojan it is finally time to end your suffering."

To her surprise he smiled.

"You mean to kill me?"

She blinked in confusion, then tried to continue in a softer tone.

"No no... I meant that..."

It then became clear that he would not receive her word that day, regardless of how important or true it was. He was very stubborn and solid in his beliefs. In fact, he seemed to have more faith than she possessed. In this she was very confused. He was unwavering. Perhaps he was fanatical, but fanatical to what? His belief seemed to be rooted in opposing the saints.

He waited for a response. None was forthcoming. He did not speak again for some time.

———

Her recent attempts to goad him into some reaction had not worked. How this man could possibly have the reputation he had baffled her. There was no way he possessed that level of control. She was grateful, however, that he was not what he was rumored to be because in her attempt to produce a reaction she had pushed too far.   If he was who they said he was, she wouldn't be considering new ways to get him to cooperate to escape.

Instead she would be dead.

It was then that there was a knock at the door.

"Move away from the door or be run through."

The voice was gruff and shouted. There was no fear in the voice as it commanded and seemed to do this merely for convenience.

They had been hastily shoved—quite literally—into the room together. There had been much heated conversation outside of the door after that, then some sort of scuffle, then silence. But soon after came the voice.

They both complied and moved away from the door. His sword still lay upon the bed with her scarves wrapped around it.

The large man that opened the door had hands like a bear. His eyes were all over Stojan and looked immediately to his belt.

"Drop it."

Stojan pointed to his chest, in a mock effort to determine who he was looking at.

Stojan carefully pulled the small sword from his sheath and dropped it upon the wooden floor.

The man looked relieved at the compliance and laughed.

"Kick it towards me, man."

Stojan once again complied and gently kicked it towards the massive man. It slid easily and stopped at his foot. It looked more like a dagger in his hand and he looked it over.

"Ha. You're not who they say you are. Or you are probably a lair. A shame you didn't kill her."

Without looking at the woman, he backed out of the room and left.

She looked at him with some appreciation. It had worked. The guard was focused on what Stojan wore at his waist, or what he would have in his hand. If Stojan possessed a weapon, it would not be hidden or ignored. And upon finding a weapon on his person, it had fulfilled the need of the guard. He didn't even consider the minion of the saint, for all of her perceived power was removed when she was separated from her cathedral. Stojan wasn't even sure if he noticed the sword masquerading as a staff. He was caged, but whole—and they were now unaware of this. Even better—they were convinced of the opposite. His trading her sword for his and then hiding his as inconsequential had gotten them through this moment.

A shame you didn't kill her.

She thought about the parting words of the big man. Their expectation had been that they would go at it and Stojan would—in anger—run her through.

He hadn't.

"Why are we here?"

She blinked away her musings. He was staring at her again and she looked him up and down. She gave away her only weapon and he was once again armed.

A shame you didn't kill her.

Now she was afraid. It was this fear that allowed her to tell the truth. She couldn't help but look at him and hear those words again.

"I was told to capture you, and was given your location. My lord told me that you traveled on that road."

"Capture me, but not kill me?"

"That is correct Stojan. That is all I was told, other than that you were a very dangerous man. Unstable and mad."

He raised an eyebrow, as if he had received a compliment. This was not to her liking. Perhaps he was mad and unpredictable.

"And who told you this, who sent you again?"

"My lord."

"A saint?"

"THE saint."

He narrowed his eyes at her and took in her demeanor.

"It is clear to me you do not believe that, do you?"

Her fear was mixed with sadness now.

"No."

"And who told you that?"

"He… well, no one has told me that."

"Why hide anything from me? We are alone and captured."

She exhaled.

"I detected a change in him. The way he spoke seemed different. He did not tell me directly."

She sat down and looked troubled. Looking at the floor she continued.

"His words were… different. His mannerisms. Everything. Something had happened. There was uncertainty and his choice of words were confusing."

For the first time Stojan saw her without her facade. She looked at last vulnerable and confused. And she continued.

"I voiced my concerns to my lord. His responses at first continued to confuse me, but then he changed, and assured me. He is so powerful, and knows so much, Stojan."

She looked up at him—searching his eyes for compassion. She was met with indifference.

"We have a beautiful cathedral. And a wondrous sculpture that is actually a great structure. I have been inside it—The Arch. So huge is it that it dwarfs our great cathedral."

Her eyes were wide as she spoke of the wonders of her congregation and her saint.

"But every so often there was talk of other saints. This talk was not allowed and those were shunned or expelled. Our city is my congregation. It is large indeed."

The more she spoke of wonders, the less he seemed impressed.

"But what changed then? What was diff..."

"You did."

He tilted his head at her interruption.

"What?"

"You did. There was much talk of one who destroyed a saint."

She looked up at him as he approached the bed. Her face tilted down as her eyes reached up to him. Her voice was soft and there was a quiet defeat to it. At last she spoke her truth out loud.

"You cannot destroy another saint if there is only one."

He righted his head again, but did not speak.

"That was when I knew. I think that he sent me to retrieve you but instead of delivering you into his hands, they have arranged for us to be delivered into the hands of others."

"Troublemakers."

"Sadly, yes. All of my years of service and my one transgression has made me disposable. I believe that the disposable non-believers were set against each other—each believing they were doing the right thing in service. And Stojan, you were the bait."

He folded his arms.

"But I think you and your people have stumbled through the trap."

"What do you mean?"

"If what you say is true, then we were all meant to kill each other. That would be a very tidy affair, would it not?"

"Yes."

Her eyes were distant as she considered his assessment.

"We would retrieve you and fight to the death to bring you back."

"Then why didn't you?"

"I…I have no desire to die."

"Even for him."

"*Them.*"

She surprised Stojan by correcting him.

"If there are more, and he has lied to me, then my death would be meaningless. And…"

"You were confused."

"Yes. I was no longer certain. My faith had been shaken and so had my trust in him."

"And thus you were no longer of use."

She narrowed her eyes. His words were all too truthful and painful.

"But what of the others? The others who captured us?"

She considered his question.

"I think they were also sent from a saint to capture us."

"Yes, I believe you are correct. That I think is certain. I meant to ask why they too did not outright attack."

"I…"

She did not finish. This was new territory for her and it was all very overwhelming. Instead Stojan offered his own answer.

"Their timidness may have worked against the master plan. It seems that the saints have sent their chaff to be disposed of, but their chaff have yet failed at another task."

She frowned.

"Indeed they had no stomach for a fight. Perhaps it is much easier to pledge one's life in the comfort of a great cathedral than demonstrate it in battle. And yet another advantage to our surrender—they had no motivation to fight and we gave them no reason."

She drew her eyebrows together, and he in turn studied her. She had been removed from her element and thrust into a betrayal—a betrayal she had unfalteringly believed in. And now she was a prisoner with him only because of the ineptitude, lack of experience and lack of faith of those who were also betrayed. Their free will had worked against the saints and in their favor. But the limbo they now enjoyed would not last long.

She looked at the floor for some time. Eventually she looked up at him as a different woman. She had now truly absorbed what had happened. Her value had changed in an instant—the instant she questioned her lord. And now she was someone else—empty and devoid of any power, any control and any value. Her eyes were wide open and filled with tears, and to Stojan it appeared as if she had aged more than ten years. Her voice was solemn and quiet yet still retained some strength and dignity when she finally spoke.

"What do we do now, Stojan?"

He thought before responding, and his stare encouraged her; at least he had not turned away or laughed. Though he was her enemy, he was the only person currently in her life that could actually validate her existence. She was sure that if she had perished, the story to the congregation would be that she died in fighting for the cause. Her replacement would...

Carlin.

That was her mistake.

Stojan watched as the preoccupation was shown upon her face. He would not respond while she was so engaged. Lucky was she to be trapped with someone so very patient.

Defeated, she exhaled a tremendous sigh and she thought she emptied the entirety of her lungs. It was the signal that she was ready for his response.

Unfortunately for her, his response came in the form of a question.

"What do you know of The Great Black Pyramid?"

Mark Bradford

Amira

THE GREAT BLACK PYRAMID OF EGYPT

"What? What does this have to do with our escape?"

"It has nothing to do with it save for what my destination will be afterwards."

"So nonchalant about all this Stojan."

She shook her head in disbelief, and continued.

"We are in dire straits and you wave your hand over the actual escape to what you do next. Is it not of importance? We could and probably will be killed!"

She didn't hide her dismay.

"We will either escape, or we will not. If we do, then my destination is of tantamount importance. If we do not, then there is no reason to plan for it."

"Plan for what?"

"Our demise."

He was a consummate professional. Any doubts that he did not match his reputation were long gone by now. She was still alive and had the fortune to have not have been his latest victim. The self-control he exercised in not ending her life when she prodded him about his daughter was very appreciated now. Instead, his skills would be used to help her escape. And these skills were not just swordplay. She had greatly underestimated him in what he was capable of. From what she was told he was a rogue and just a violent, unpredictable element that had to be extinguished before he caused any more harm. But he was much more than that. He clearly was versed in something more than armed combat —his skills transcended that. He was a tactician first and saw things on a much grander scale than she would have considered possible. Her mistake was assuming he was just simply someone skilled at the sword. He was thinking a few moves ahead.

But once they were free would he then kill her? She wanted to ask but was afraid of the answer. She would focus on escaping and whatever his plan was. Then she would make a break for it. If she could reach her men then she would be safe again.

"I have heard of it."

Her answer was so delayed and timid that he paused while considering what she was responding to.

His eyebrow raised as he crouched down and sat—he did this slowly and looked into her eyes the entire time. It was if a wolf had just asked her, 'So, what exactly do you taste like?'

"Tell me all you know."

Compelled, frightened and strangely curious she went on to tell him everything she had heard. 'Til now everything she was told was filed away as myth or lies. But she treated it all as fact as she did her best to fit it all together and distill it into a cohesive story. She was quite amazed at just how much knowledge she'd accumulated on it. The vast majority of this knowledge was never shared with her saint as it was all considered blasphemy and designed to weaken the will of her congregation, but it did not stop her from listening, or retaining it. And now she was composing a succinct report—not for her saint, but for the one man he was afraid of.

He listened and took it all in. The information improved his mood for the more he had to work with, the more control he had over what was to come.

Or so he believed.

As it turned out she needn't have spent so much time on it.

———

Before the end of the day they heard a knock at the door again. This time it was not the massive thuds as the last time but instead a knock that was almost polite. Stojan stood.

They exchanged glances—having not been given instructions. Madison spoke questioningly.

"Come in?"

At that they heard arguing as the door opened. What Stojan saw was a man clothed in such a way as to put any bishop to shame. Upon his feet he wore sandals and leather shin guards dyed black were strapped to his shins. Around his waist was something like a skirt with a long rectangle of black hanging from his belt. It looked like a decorative armor skirt a woman might favor. His chest was protected by a great plate that wrapped around but left his midsection unprotected. Armbands wrapped around his biceps. Everything was colored black and adorned with strange symbols that looked both artistic and descriptive. He knew not if it was an actual language or some sort of ceremonial markings. Instead of a helmet, he wore a headdress that looked like it had been carved from the skull of a strange animal and then brought back to life. In this way it reminded him a bit of The People and some of their ceremonial dress. However the man looked almost like an artist—as if he had just performed in a play—for all of the attention to detail he did not look menacing in any way. And the armor looked like it would not survive even one battle.

The man behind him had clearly been doing his best to convince him not to enter. Stojan did not draw his sword so as not to play his hand. Perhaps this man would pay little attention to it—after all he had entered without considering where they were in the room.

He stood proudly, carrying a staff that was adorned in black and gold.

He smiled at the two of them.

The other man made his way in and it looked like the man with the staff was about to swat him. He turned to him and said "Enough" in irritated tones. Turning back to them, his irritation turned once again to the triumphant smile—so quickly as to appear completely insincere.

"I am Darius—Pharaoh to The Great Luxor."

Clearly this was to make an impact on the two.   He smiled widely awaiting the awe and wonder that was to come.

When no response was forthcoming, he looked them up and down and then glanced at his assistant momentarily.   The other man shrugged slightly and looked ever-fearful.

Seeing no other option, he looked them over once again and continued.

"You are my prisoners and will accompany us.   You have been summoned. My lord has foretold of all events and sent me to retrieve you."

Stojan made a frown of consideration. This to him was a good thing.

Madison stood and folded her arms—not in defiance, but simply because she was cold.

When there was no objection, Darius turned again to his partner and chastised him.

"See? It is just as Luxor has foretold. There will be no conflict this day. We are in no danger and they are forced to comply under his great power."

Stojan thought about unsheathing his sword and striking the man down. Surely he could if he wanted to?   There was no hex upon him.   He entertained the idea of striking down the assistant as a test, but then thought better of it.

"You will come with us and face him—it is a great honor!"

Stojan thought Madison was rather reasonable compared to the fanaticism of the oddly-dressed man before him. It took some effort not to smile too broadly. But, as usual he kept his feelings to himself.

"But of course."

Four eyes went wide at this—the four that did not belong to Stojan or Darius. It seemed they were both in agreement.

With that, Madison stood up and eyed up both men. The assistant did the same.

Smiling greatly, the self-proclaimed pharaoh turned and left with a few words to his assistant.

Still wide-eyed the man motioned meekly with his hand to both Stojan and Madison.   Stojan did the same with Madison.   One by one they left the room with the assistant bringing up the rear.

Amira

CAPTIVE

The destination was just a few weeks away. Madison and her men had traveled much farther to reach Stojan and Anastazja. In fact, they had come almost halfway across the great country. It explained the demeanor of the men, and the rag-tag appearance they had when he first saw them. Madison had been warned to keep a low profile, but had been provided with less supplies than warranted for such a journey. It was indeed clear to her that this had been intentional; the plan was to have her exhausted men meet their demise at the hands of Stojan. Though he was outnumbered almost twenty to one, she was sure that his cunning and freshness would have won that day. Not for the first time she shuddered at the prospect of dying at his hands. She felt a certain comfort that she was doing the right thing by following his lead. If she was ever lost in the forest this was the man she would want at her side.

The two were kept together in a carriage of odd design. The conveyance was made of a material that was neither metal nor wood. It was colored in some of the gold and black Stojan had come to recognize as the decorations of this saint. Instead of large wheels of metal and wood, this had smaller wheels of a black flexible substance. It was much lighter than it looked and had been tacked to two gaudily decorated horses that easily pulled it.

There was no enclosure save for a room and supporting bars that held it up. Otherwise it was completely open to the elements. They could easily just leave. Not only was Stojan allowed to keep his sword, but neither of them were bound in any way. Stojan seemed very pleased with himself and almost smug—a fact that annoyed his companion to no end and caused more than one exasperated conversation.

"It was foolish of him to confront you directly."

"And yet this was exactly what you did."

Madison thought for a moment and frowned.

"Yes… But it was what was decreed."

"Yes."

"Yes?"

"I don't understand."

"He was merely following the promise of his saint, as were you."

"But you could have killed either one of us."

"Most certainly."

His tone when saying this was not to her liking as he could not hide his enjoyment. It was not a laughing matter and the fact that he was so certain about the ease of taking her life made her uncomfortable. She fought the fear and frustration and focused on finding an answer. Though she seemed to be in a good position—both figuratively and physically—she desperately needed to understand what was happening.

Timidly she asked the question she didn't want to know the answer to.

"Stojan… why did you not kill me that day? Is it the same reason you did not strike this man down?"

She looked around as if someone might be within hearing distance. She looked at him as he sat next to her in relative comfort. She would not look away or interrupt him as she learned to wait for his entire answer.

For the first time his face turned serious.

"No, they were very different reasons. But both are related. If your enemy has a belief, then it is their weakness. He believes I am compelled to be compliant so in being so it increases his belief. But instead of his saint being in control of me, I am. Therefore I am able to do what I wish, when I wish. And I am currently armed. If they believe a magic spell has been cast upon me then I will allow it to be true."

"I see. And I had a similar belief?"

"What were you told?"

She exhaled and thought. It made her feel guilty.

"You would be captured easily and my lord would prevail. His word on the matter would be absolute and true."

"And what do you think would have happened if I had resisted?"

"Stojan, I have not yet seen you fight but I am thoroughly convinced I would not be here speaking with you."

"You are correct."

Again she felt the shiver of fear—like having a bottle of poison sitting next to your drink. You were in no real danger if you were careful not to drink from the wrong cup, but it was a very uncomfortable arrangement.

"But why did you not kill me? There was no reason not to fight."

He turned to look into her eyes for the first time—adding to her discomfort. His demeanor became even more serious.

"Because I cannot predict the exact outcome of a battle. I am no good to Anastazja dead or injured. And if you left with me, presumably you would leave her be."

She tried to look away but was lost in his eyes. She'd never seen a more determined gaze. Indeed their instructions dictated that they ambush Stojan and there was little mention of his companion.

"I have learned to be patient."

"So in allowing us to take you it caused us to ignore her?"

"Yes. It was a number of things."

"I believe you. You are a tactician at heart. But what about this man?"

She glanced to the rider of one of the horses pulling their cart of Amiran tec—his gold and black coverings glistened in the sun.

"My plan was not to abandon Anastazja for very long. Once you and your people had taken me far enough away, I would have just made my way back."

She was most appreciative of his phrasing. She knew what *made my way back* entailed. It was not a pretty thought.

"When these people ambushed us it changed things. But now they are taking us to the one place I knew Ana would go."

Realization crossed her face.

He nodded and looked forward once again.

It was quite an adjustment to be caught up in what was now happening. In a very short while she had gone from the second most powerful being in all of Amira to someone who was swept away in a current of events that she had no control over. She was a spectator but was fortunate enough to be sitting next to someone who was apparently thinking a few moves ahead at all times. His ability to plan and understand situations was an amazing contrast to her saint.

But it spoke to her intelligence that she was still alive. In her hubris she could have had her men fight to the death when ambushing Stojan. Likewise, she could have battled those that captured them. Madison had thought on her feet and although her lord had told her what was to occur she herself had to adjust. She was then just as responsible for both of them still being alive. This thought comforted her for the first time and served to lift her from the depths of despair she found herself within. Finally she felt the tiniest bit of control and had found herself again. She knew herself to be a leader and not just a blind follower. Taking her saint and her power from her had left a vacuum in its place, and in the following days she'd been lost without purpose or pride. But she was starting to fill it again—ever so slowly.

And the last person in all of Amira she would have ever considered was the one helping her fill it.

"Then why do we not simply escape?"

"I have told you."

"Tell me again please Stojan."

"There is no way for me to search all of Amira. And it is doubtful that Anastazja stayed at our location for long. We have been forced to move past the window of opportunity I had to escape and search for her."

Madison continued to listen as Stojan matter-of-factly shared his plan.

"I have no magical means to locate her; therefore, I must travel to the one place that I know she was interested in visiting."

"The pyramid."

"Indeed. And our captors are taking us there. I need not search for it, or wait outside of it for her to appear."

Madison thought about someone infiltrating her own cathedral—it was not merely a building, but far more than that.

"It is probably much more than a pyramid; just like my own cathedral was just the center of the city."

"I would agree."

"Are you not concerned with how she will get there? We took everything with us including her horse."

"Yes you did."

He smiled slightly but she did not pursue it. She looked down at the odd construction of the carriage; meeting his eyes at that point was to be avoided.

"I must trust that she is capable. I cannot search such a grand area for her, and though it looks like escape would be an easy affair, we are still surrounded by many armed men. I have no doubt their leader is as fanatical as you and would exhaust all of his men to kill me should I try to escape."

She panned the surroundings with her eyes and looked over the men and the horses. Indeed there were many.

"But now he brings two great prizes to his lord, does he not? In pristine condition."

She thought for many moments and had one final question.

"How can you remain so calm?"

He turned his head to her and met her eyes once again.

"With everything I have just explained to you, Lady Madison, how can I not?"

Mark Bradford

Amira

A COMMON DESTINATION

"I am looking for the great black pyramid."

Anastazja's demeanor was direct, and a bit intense. The man on the horse was taken aback at the young woman walking along the road. She wore decorative clothing, appeared to be armed but had no supplies save for a tiny backpack. He would have been surprised that it contained no food or drink, but instead an empty wineskin and an item that might be considered rather valuable in some cities: a book.

"Howdy."

She continued to walk alongside him. Though she was alone, she did not seem afraid and looked to be properly nourished. He did not think she had recently escaped some sort of imprisonment, though that was the most likely.

She stared and waited for her answer.

"Oh."

His charming smile was replaced with seriousness.

"I don't know about pyramids. Black pyramid you say? Where's it supposed to be, young lady?"

"The west."

"Well we're in the west. Say, you need some water? Where is your horse? Are you…"

"Where is the nearest city?"

She cut him off in her pursuit of an answer.

"The town is just up ahead. You want to ride with me?"

"Yes."

Before he could go on to dismount, then gingerly help her onto the horse, she had stepped onto his boot at stirrup and leaped onto the horse behind him. She rode behind his saddle and appreciated riding bareback. He didn't feel her land and the horse did not seem startled.

"Y… OK then."

He grabbed his hat and pulled it down slightly, smiled and pushed his horse forward.

They rode in some silence as he recalibrated his perception to what had just happened.

"Uh, what do I call you?"

He tilted his head back slightly as if this would signify that he was speaking to her rather than the horse.

"Anastazja."

He considered engaging her in some sort of conversation on the way, but thought better of it. It could be a trap of course; a young woman needs a ride, distracts the rider and then they are both set upon by bandits. Then she conveniently escapes. She might even have a dagger at his back right now.

"A hot one today."

This was the best he could do to fill the silence.

"Yes. But I have gotten used to it."

His eyes moved back and forth as he tried to make sense of her, and the conversation.

"Is there someone in this town that would help me seek the pyramid? A sightseer?"

"A seer? I don't think they have any seers in the town. We are not much for that sort of thing."

"No, not a seer."

He dug at his belt and passed her his water skin.

She grabbed it and then shortly afterward returned it to him. He smiled —happy that he'd at least made some progress with his passenger.

"You can ask around. I have to meet a man, but…"

"Thank you."

"If it is further out west, maybe it's on The Coast?"

"I do not know, I was told by the sightseer that it is to the west, in a desert."

"Well, a lot of these parts are desert—desert and red rock."

"There are also forests."

"Well yes. Is that all he told you—that it's in a desert? That doesn't help much."

"He said it was the largest building in all of Amira, and it had a light atop it that reached the sky."

His eyes widened at the prospect.

"Oh, my."

After what was once again a very long bout of silence, they finally reached the town.

"Thank you."

He abruptly turned so see she had already leaped off the horse. She had not disturbed it with her exit.   He wondered if she was a performer or even a horse trainer. He watched her walk away and decided to impart some wisdom.

"Hey!"

She stopped and turned.

"You OK?"

He thought he saw the first sign of emotion in her.

"No. Not yet."

She turned and ran down the street before he could say any more.

Amira

THE WANDERING TIME

As best she could determine, the pyramid was in the west. It seemed that everything was in 'The West' and she made no attempt to hide her frustration when making this point.

Most had not heard of the pyramid but those that did always focused on the light that sprang forth from it. Her best information came from a man that said the light had gone out years ago and some had said it was a sign of sorts. No one seemed to know exactly what it signaled, but it was a sign to be sure.

The more days passed, the more she suspected she may never see Stojan again. Her anger and frustration was hard to hide and more than once she had to run from a group of onlookers as her hair represented her feelings on the matter of this lack of information.

Did Stojan keep her calm? Surely her self-control was not any more present with him at her side. No, this was a supreme frustration of being separated. This ambush was intentional and perpetrated with a calculated malice to separate them. But why? Did they mean to torture her? Perhaps they thought by removing him, she would flounder and be lost. Or perhaps they simply wanted only him and she was lucky enough to be wandering nearby. The last thought only compounded her loneliness. She felt insignificant. Was this the end of her journey? Was it enough that Stojan had appeared at just the right time to walk her through growing up? Was this to be the next step—alone and settling down in a way that she had hoped for?

In a short time she had proved herself to be an excellent blacksmith apprentice. Her skills returned to her quickly and she found it all easily as not only had she grown in stature but was even stronger from training and practicing with the sword.

More than once she had considered crafting her own. Perhaps this was truly the next step. If she was to do this, it would take some time to not only mentally prepare but to sharpen her skills to do so. Though she was excellent as an apprentice, she had much to learn as a blacksmith and her sword-smithing skills were almost nonexistent.

Thoughts of training created frustration and just served to make her feel even more alone in the world. There was only one man that she would have wanted to train her to be a blacksmith. He had produced a sword with no equal. And there was only one man that served to train her to use it properly.

She called them both father, and they were now both gone.

And every day that passed lessened the chance of Stojan joining her again.

She touched her hair and pulled it into view.

A walk. That was what she needed and what she had robbed herself of ever since she had settled in the city to recuperate and generate a small amount of monies. She'd insisted that she be paid at the end of every day, and leveraged that by working the first day for free. The man was nice enough and she'd gained his trust this way. He looked and behaved nothing like her father and this made her work a bit easier. She felt disconnected, but performed well. He was impressed with her skill and asked more than once how she had come to know so much about the trade. Ana saw no reason to lie and told the simple truth that her father was a blacksmith, and that he had passed away years ago. That seemed to suffice as a story—once she added that she was from the far north. That too was not really a lie as the conveyance that brought them was docked there.

Soon she would have to pick a direction. Her blacksmith skills gave her the luxury of being valuable in any city she settled in, it seemed.

According to the Amirans, the west was the largest part of Amira. At one point she could have just followed the light to the pyramid, but it had now supposedly gone out. And even the great light of the pyramid had its limits—it could not be seen from anywhere. She would have to be close enough—perhaps one hundred kilometers or so.

Or so the Amirans had told her. The story changed each time with some saying it was still lit; others saying it went out; still others saying that it had only recently returned. Clearly it was a rumor that no one who spoke of had ever seen directly.

Ana had traveled north a bit in search of a larger city. Her thought was that she could find more information about the pyramid and even find a seer similar to the one they'd met.

Each day that passed, it seemed that Stojan was farther and farther away. In her mind it was an ever expanding circle that would be impossible to search. He could have sought out the pyramid; he could have continued on the path to the great doorway. He could even be searching for her right now where they last parted. He was an excellent tracker and had taught her much about living on the run. But her skills in the forest were like no other; even The People were impressed with what she could do there. If Stojan pushed himself to find her in the infinite wilderness of Amira, he too would be lost forever while she toiled away in a random city.

The thought infuriated her and made her sad at the same time. She was powerless and her only refuge was patience.

And the man that taught her this lesson was gone—or worse.

She put much effort into avoiding the thought that he was already gone. Those that took him could have had him killed, or made an example of him. It was Stojan that—after one thousand years—had destroyed a saint. After all of that time he had proven that they too were mortal. All of their promises were nothing if they could be struck down.

Her knowledge of them was great as she'd not only been one of the few to truly have direct contact, but she had been privy to the teachings of the Navajo. And they had told her everything they knew because they saw her as part of a prophecy. But hadn't Stojan been the one to make this change? Wasn't he the one they now feared? Perhaps this was why they came for him and not her. If there were truly seven, he had reduced them by one and now there were six. For all of their grandstanding it seemed that they too knew fear.

Her mind was thus occupied as she worked as the apprentice to a blacksmith in a city whose name she'd forgotten, so that she could earn enough money to travel in a random direction to find a man who was in all probability already dead.

She let the hammer drop without the bounce of a repeated action. It stayed where it was—only producing a few sparks in protest.

She stared at it and the embers.

"You're tired. Go home."

She turned to see the blacksmith looking at her from the doorway.

"I'm fine. I will leave when this is done."

"What bothers you?"

It was the first time he'd asked anything personal since their initial meeting. She didn't see it as an intrusion so she opted to answer. She continued hammering, but this time slower so he could hear her words.

"I'm searching for someone. Amira is so vast and I know not where he has gone, but only a hint of where he might."

The man seldom showed much emotion, but now was uncharacteristically curious. He wiped his hands on his apron as he spoke.

"A boyfriend? A family member? Where did they go—or where might they have gone?"

She stopped once again and without looking spoke more to the hammer and less to the man.

"I do not know. I truly do not know."

"Well surely you have some..."

"I said I do not know!"

She gripped the hammer tightly as she pulled it back to strike the metal again. The man watched as the light of the forge showed the definition in her arm, down to the tiny hairs that sprouted on it and could only be seen in the right light.

He was again impressed at how strong she was. He glanced at her hair, but did not show any emotion. She turned just as he was moving his eyes back to the hammer, and then her own eyes. She knew he saw it.

"When did you know?"

"I am not dumb."

He guffawed.

"I knew the second day you worked for me."

"My hair did not…"

"Not the hair. Your way with the tools, your ease with the heavy equipment. There are no traveling blacksmith apprentices that are young ladies, you know. There is no such thing. And your strength."

She put the hammer down.

"I knew I would see the magic eventually."

"And now that you have?"

"I worry only for your wellbeing."

"What do you mean?"

"It does not matter to me what color your hair is. You are a good worker. But if I have figured this out, others will as well."

"Others? What others?"

"The Saints."

He lifted his blackened hands to shoulder height.

"They are all around us. And if you do not believe that, then know that their minions are all around us. *That* you can believe."

"And?"

"And they will come for you."

She exhaled—becoming thoughtful.

"You think him dead?"

He shook his head and considered his response.

"What happened?"

"He was taken from me. Captured. I am certain of it."

"Then it seems likely that he would be brought before one of the saints. And it seems impossible that he would still be alive."

Her eyes went wide with anger as he continued speaking.

"And it also seems impossible that one can destroy a Saint."

"You joke?!"

He shook his head and looked at the floor. He was clearly embarrassed at his attempt to lighten the mood and be in good spirits.

"No. I... mean to tell you that it *is* possible—that he *is* still alive."

"I grow anxious. I should leave."

She dusted off her hands from the work, then wiped them on her own apron.

"I can not stay and work while he is still out there. You have been very kind and I thank you for that."

The man still looked down at the floor. He knew the inevitable. She was a fine worker, but he also knew she was transient.

"I will pay you today's wage of course."

She walked over and shook his hand then restored her tools to where they belonged and removed her apron.

He had indeed paid her, and she decided to stay the night and leave at first light. Where she would go she was uncertain. Her sleep was uneventful and lacking any useful portents. There were no ambushes, no battles and no surprises. Her only recourse was to seek out the one place she was fairly sure he would go to find her—The Great Black Pyramid. More than once she had been told to seek out a man before she sought out the pyramid. He would know. He would know what to do, they said. Seek out this sage, they said. There was even talk of portals. All of this piqued her interest, but she had endured and considered it heresy 'til now.

Her restlessness had won and she gave in. In frustration she joined a group traveling to the city favored by him.

At least that's what they told her.

Amira

THE SAGE OF SEDONA

As she plunged back into the middle of the Red Lands, she was once again astounded at the colors. The landscape both amazed her and reminded her of her Navajo brothers and sisters. Where were they? Could she somehow contact them? In all of their time together they had never discussed how to find them or seek them out. At the time it seemed a given that she and Stojan would be with them for the foreseeable future. Their abrupt leaving saw only poor Fox following them and his subsequent demise. So as far as she knew, word had never reached them of what had happened, their whereabouts or their direction.

She was alone and without a way to contact Stojan or her extended family. Perhaps the man they called The Sage of Sedona could help. She was told that he was not only very wise, but knew of the workings of the saints. In fact, she'd been told a tale of him actually being summoned to The Great Pyramid. If anyone could help her find it, he could. And perhaps he even knew of The Saint on High.

If Stojan still lived, then he was involved in the quest for The Coast, completing the task of the Saint on High, or was seeking out The Great Pyramid. The latter made the most sense; it was the one place that he knew she wanted to go. If she traveled there and he had accepted whatever fate befell him, then that would be where they would meet.

She almost smiled at the prospect of having three separate quests. The Saint on High was most certainly mad; The Coast was probably just a shoreline of some kind and The Great Pyramid was probably an ancient, decrepit structure that wasn't even as impressive as the pyramid library of the Navajo.   It was all so very silly. Stojan was so very accommodating of her flights of fancy and her companionship seemed to be his only pursuit and reward.

Yes, the black pyramid would be her final destination, by way of this great sage.

———

Like their trip to the mad saint, the paths their group chose was filled with great ridges that jutted out from the rock. Sometimes they trailed them; sometimes they made their way in the valleys. It was all very beautiful and each night she thought of Stojan as the sun set.

As they made their way into Sedona she noticed that the rocks looked like great sculptures. The colors were still of oranges but the reds were more prevalent. This Sedona had even more red than the Red Lands themselves. Or perhaps it was at the center of it.

She was told of magical portals that existed in these lands and it made her wonder if these were the doorways the saints had come through, and the destination of her original quest. He had not spoken of many doors but just one—surely the sage would not only help her find the pyramid and Stojan, but the very door itself. And if that was the case they could then summon the saint and open it—pulling through all saints and ridding the lands forever of them.

Suddenly her path had crystalized. All paths intersected at the Sage of Sedona and the Great Black Pyramid.

The ride into town was like a deep descent into a cavern. Through the week or so of travel she had felt that the air was different. As it turned out, this part of the country was closer to the sky and because of that the air was clearer, she was told.   It meant that newcomers fell asleep faster and would tire easily.   The Navajo had taught her that though the land was indeed closer to the sky, it was because there was simply less air to breathe. This fact had scared her upon learning, but she was consoled that there was still more than enough air for everyone.

Indeed she felt this was a fleeting feeling now and then, but never more than that. To her, the most impactful was the bright colors and the air of mystery the surrounding land had. With the Navajo, she felt reverent about the land and the wildlife. Here there was something else; as if a portal would threaten to manifest next to her at any second.

The small group she traveled with did their best to convince her of the magic that was in the air here and that strange things were afoot.

———

Descending into the land of Sedona the Red Lands became redder; the rocks became even more impressive and the air even more mysterious. This did indeed seem to be the heart of the Red Lands. It was the perfect location for a sage. The outcroppings seemed like they had been carved by powerful winds that had cut rock. The tales of her companions told a different story, however—along with portals and magic they relayed that this land had been mostly underwater and great rivers flowed for thousands and thousands of years. The cataclysm of the saints had caused the lands to dry up and bake in the sun, and this was what was left.

Sedona was once underwater and that was the door that the saints had come through.

To her, the information was uncertain and each tale contradicted the last. It made her think of the teachings of the Navajo; though each story seemed mysterious, there was a certain logic to it all. These people seemed to try to outdo each other with each subsequent story—and the more fantastic the better.

Her brief encounter with the Saint on High included a description of where the doorway was located. He had said it was actually at the bottom of Amira and not in the west and he had not described it as a desert. Wax-A-Hatchy was what he called it in passing. When pressed, he had simply said it was the center bottom of Amira. She found his directions immensely vague for such an enormous land. His guidance did not include roads, landmarks or cities. Instead, it was as if his information had been told to him second-hand. It was this that gave her much thought and made her mind wander as to just how the saints interacted with their followers. Was that how they learned? Neither saint demonstrated that they were all-knowing or all-seeing, so just what *did* they see?

How did they come to know what they knew? The Saint on High was trapped, with no way to leave. He seemed powerless in actuality. There was nothing menacing about him and he was not in a position to destroy anything. What knowledge he did have seemed like gibberish. Even upon taking a human form as a statue they could not forge a sword, train a horse or prepare food. They were alien indeed. Her quest was to find the great doorway and somehow find a vessel for him to inhabit. He would then do something that both terrified and amazed her—he would jump from one location to another. If he could do this, then it meant the saints could conquer the entire world. So much of what the saint said made little sense. Stojan had said that he was most probably mad anyway.

But if they allowed the saint to leap from his cage to the doorway were they not releasing him upon the world? Would he truly open this door? Or was this simply his way of escaping his prison?

It made her feel sick to think they would help the saints in any way—especially if they were expanding their reach. Stojan had comforted her in that his own plan would prevent that.

She had much to do, it seemed.

And now she was going to meet someone that could help her reach this great pyramid. Perhaps he could even be enlisted to help; at least he would provide the proper information to find it.

Unfortunately for her there would be no audience that day.

———

"What do you mean he's not here?"

She had decided to pay for some lodging as it would be only a night or so, and staying among the rocks and trees seemed less desirable alone. She could not hide her disappointment and anger.

"He is not. He has business out and about—he is a powerful man and…"

"Well when will he return?"

The man's politeness was impressive, but it would not last forever.

"I do not know. He was summoned and made haste just last week."

She had slept through the night and appeared at what was apparently a magistrate office of some kind. Like the other buildings in Sedona, this one was very similar to the buildings of the colorful city. It was made of a bright mud or plaster of some kind and had curved tiles that served as a roof. The office was one of the few two-story buildings in the town. So interested was she in seeing him that she had gone directly here at sunset. Had she been with Stojan, she most certainly would have taken a scenic route to the destination. It allowed her to marvel and take in all that it had to offer while Stojan planned routes most tactically.

But now she had come a long way to reach this sage, and she was not even sure if it was on the way to the pyramid, or worse had increased her time to reach it.

Her already-apparent frustration and impatience was growing.

Ana's attempt to pause and stare an answer out of the official worked.

"Are you passing through or staying? I can leave word and summon you as soon as he returns."

She said nothing.

"I can also send word to you if I receive information on his estimated time of arrival."

She smoldered. It had been some time since she'd been angry, but now she felt powerless and the vague information of the sage's servant seemed like a ruse.

Though the man was in his 30s or 40s, he found it difficult not to be intimidated. Her stare was intense, her dress was unique and her hair…

"Oh."

He blinked and somehow looked impressed, terrified and amazed. He smiled and repeated the word.

"OH!"

She drew her brows together. Her sword remained sheathed.

"What?"

She shouted the word in an irritated voice.

"Please come with me!"

———

"Juan!"

That was the only word Ana heard clearly. After that there was much yelling and arguing. The official had taken her back through a number of chambers and hallways. The interior was similar to the colorful village in that the interior walls were the same neutral color. Like their meeting room, she'd seen that this was also decorated with shelves and small dolls and various artwork. As they traveled to the inner chamber the number of items increased. What started out as a very light sprinkling of accoutrements turned into a densely-packed arrangement of items—with some of them being very odd-looking. She detected smells of incense and perfumes—similar to what she had experienced with the Navajos years ago.

Resisting the urge to run up, grab and examine an item she stood ready for whatever was to pop out of the inner chamber.

It was the official again. He trotted as if to get out of the way of the next person who was to emerge.

She stared at him and waited.

"Ana?"

The man that appeared looked bothered and skeptical.

She looked him up and down and he was slightly shorter than her and dressed unusually. He was wrapped in something like a robe but with large pockets on the outside. Underneath he wore a silken shirt of a brilliant pattern that was quite lovely. His feet were clad with strange shoes that looked rather flimsy and not appropriate for any kind of climbing, but had made his emergence almost soundless. They had one thing in common it seemed; they both wore essentially the same kind of hat. He too wore a wide-brimmed hat with tiny tassels that ended in little balls. Perhaps he too had met...

"Dagmar?"

The man smiled incredulously.

"Anastazja?!"

The assistant looked on in amazement.

"You're so…tall!"

So swiftly did she move that the assistant stumbled back in fear and before he knew it, she had swept his master up in a tight embrace.

"Good lord you are…"

He grunted in delighted discomfort as the air left his lungs.

"…strong."

She pulled him away and looked into his face.

"Dagmar you live! We… I thought I'd never see you again!"

He smiled and looked her up and down—searching her face, her hair, her clothing. He was impressed by the presentation. She was clearly a warrior now and had been for some time.

"And I, you Ana."

There was an odd pause as both of their brains moved to the same realization. She allowed Dagmar to be the one to speak it aloud.

"And… Stojan?"

He tilted his head and body to look around her—thinking he was just behind Ana. Tilting back he looked into her eyes. Gently he had asked her the question she had no answer for.

"Where is he…?"

She saw the apprehension and fear in his face, and although she knew not for certain, did her best to assuage it.

"I believe he was taken, Dagmar…"

Dagmar blinked and cut her off.

"Where are my manners? We stand here like strangers. Please, let us go downstairs and sit and talk please."

She nodded—slightly in a daze.
Quickly they were at a gorgeous wooden table inlaid with rich colors of

all types of woods. It was covered in something that looked like glass but had formed to the slightly irregular shape of the table top. She touched it with her hand and it was not as cold as expected. It was no surprise that Dagmar had surrounded himself with all manner of Amiran tec.

The assistant quickly brought refreshments in the form of a sweet tea served in the most pristine, clear and perfectly-formed cups she had ever seen. Along with this were some sort of jagged, triangle-shaped breads that were crispy and salty.

The assistant bowed out and closed the only door to the room.

She ate and drank after removing her backpack and sword. She realized it was the first time she'd removed it in a long time. The thought made her sigh as she continued the conversation.

"Oh Dagmar. He was taken from me…"

Seeing he face, she continued hurriedly.

"No no! I believe he still lives. We were settled in between cities. I returned from my walk…"

The man smiled as he fondly remembered his time with the pair.

"There was no sign of a struggle, but everything—including Stojan—was gone."

"What did you do?"

"I was distraught. I did not act right away. They were clever in taking him while I was gone. I think they were following us for some time. I blame myself for not noticing them."

Dagmar shook his head.

"Nonsense."

"'Tis true. I have noticed in the past. But nothing was left, not even the shovel."

"Shovel?"
She smiled at his confusion.

"Yes, Stojan insisted on it when we met the Navajo again."

"Navajo… again? You've met the Navajo?"

"Oh yes, we lived among The People for some time!"

His eyes went wide and he seemed truly impressed and delighted.

"Ana this is amazing. You have done so much since we parted ways."

"Yes! And we met with the Navajos again. And you? How did you escape? I thought you were imprisoned?"

Her questions were rapid-fire and interspersed with her tale. She fought to both fill him in on years of experiences while she grilled him questions. It was the intense conversation of two people who had not only missed each other, but had lived though amazing times in their respective absences.

It would take some time explaining her time among the people. Moving on to what had happened with Saint John and Stojan's choice, she then attempted to relate to their experience traveling to The Coast to being on vacation.

Just as she was exhausted from her stories, it was Dagmar's turn to tell of his release from the port, his travel and search for Sedona and ultimately his establishment as The Sage of Sedona. He had apparently sought out Sedona for the same reason she'd been sent by The Saint on High—to find the doorway.

"Yes, it was why I sought out Sedona—I was told that there were many portals here and it seemed to be the proper place for the doorway that released the interlopers upon us."

"And?"

"And I was very much mistaken. The doorway—I think—is not a magical thing, but once again Amiran tec from the old world."

"Oh. Do you think you found it? What will you do? Do you have a plan?"

He laughed.

"Oh Anastazja, I have very much missed you!"

She laughed as well.

"Stojan has reminded me of asking less than ten questions at a time. I've slipped into my old ways without him."

He leaned over and touched her arm.

"I am sure he still lives."

"Of that I have no doubt."

Her resolve was impressive, and he did not disagree—Stojan was a survivor and had much to live for.

"How exactly did you escape?"

He considered her question.

"It was not exactly an escape. I had been enlisted as the preeminent expert on Amira. It was my ego that truly trapped me—not them. I felt terrible as time went on. My biggest accomplishment was translating an ancient book. I am familiar with some of the languages of the past and struggled through it, but was only able to translate some of it. I do not know why it was needed, but I ultimately failed. With the merchant gone there was very little to do. I believe my work was for someone not actually in Amira."

Her eyebrows went up.

"Not in Amira? Where then? Poliska?"

He smiled.

"I know not. There are many other lands besides just Poliska and Amira."

After a long pause she refilled her glass and decided to make a proclamation.

"I am on a quest!"
"You are?"

"Well, we were. It was why we travelled. Our original destination was…"

"Preempted?"

"What?"

"Please go on."

"We found The Saint on High."

"You found another saint?"

"Yes. He was like no other; he spoke like no other."

Dagmar could have said many things to prompt her to go on but all he could do was stare.

"He occupied a cathedral that was truly strange. It was a metal dome and instead of a statue, he inhabited a great weapon."

Again, Dagmar kept quiet lest he interrupt her train of thought again.

"We thought it was a weapon. It was said that he was poised to destroy the entire coast—The Coast of all of Amira. But he denied it. He said it was not a weapon and instead he was just trying to open the door again."

"Fascinating."

Dagmar, the Sage of Sedona, the great knower of Amiran tec and history, was now in the remarkable position to be told things he had not yet known. He absorbed her words with relish and delight.

"Stojan did not trust him. His plan was to send us to the great doorway and then he would appear there."

"Appear?"

She nodded.

"Uh huh. He would appear in a vessel that would contain him. He called it a 'soft space' and that all saints require them to exist."
"Ana this is amazing. It confirms what I have believed for very long."

His eyes seemed to dart around the room—as if he was looking for something to show her.

"OK."

He smiled at her response.

"You have truly been among Amirans for some time."

She tilted her head in confusion.

"Oh, please. Please go on. I did it again."

"He said the doorway would pull the saints back through it—even if they did not want to go."

"That was where you were headed?"

"Yes, we were headed to the doorway. It is located at the bottom of Amira. In the center."

He remained silent.

"Dagmar do you think this is possible? It would rid us of the saints forever."

"I do not know. Ana, you have told me so many amazing things I can barely keep up. It is one thing for me to endlessly research the Old World and the saints."

He shook his head.

"It is entirely another thing to have experienced it in the way that you and your father have."

She smiled weakly as her emotions conflicted a bit. She was thrilled to share with Dagmar, and was happy to discover him alive, but she missed Stojan and reliving her travels was emotionally exhausting.

"For the first time in over one thousand years a saint has been destroyed. And it was you and Stojan that have done this. I am overwhelmed that I have come to know you and he."
She was truly taken aback by his words. They were obviously spoken with sincerity and pride. He looked astounded and humbled.

"Well, thank you."

She giggled uncomfortably.

"Thank you, Oh Great Sage of Sedona."

He laughed and the two shared their respective embarrassment. She took a deep breath as her face became serious.

"Oh Dagmar. What will we do about Stojan?"

He smiled the tiniest of sly smiles. His look gave her hope that he had some sort of Amiran magic at his disposal.

"Ana, Amira so very large—to search for him would be very difficult."

"No!"

"What..?"

"No Dagmar. I think I know where he has gone."

"You know who captured him then?"

"Oh... I had not considered that."

"Wouldn't he just go to the great doorway because that is your quest?"

"That wasn't our first quest."

"Ana I am confused."

She sighed.

"We were told of a great black pyramid to the west. It sounded so amazing and Stojan knew of my excitement to find it on the way to The Coast. I think he would go there."

Dagmar rubbed his naked chin.

"You think if he escapes he will go there looking for you?"
She suddenly looked sad and downtrodden. The conversation had made her consider things she had not yet thought of. In seeking the Sage of Sedona she had not weighed what Stojan's captors had wanted. What if

they were taking him far, far to the north? It would be a monumental thing to brave the extreme cold and snow of the north to find him there. And even if he escaped to make his way all the way back to the west on a hunch—the same hunch she had sustained herself with—it was almost impossible that he would be there at the same time.

She now felt without purpose or direction. It had been a fallacy to think this. He was lost to the great expanse of Amira. She was lucky that he was replaced with Dagmar, but that was all she could now hope for.

Dagmar watched as she stared—lost in thoughts. He looked upon her features and compared them to when he had first met her. She'd grown so much and was a woman by all measures, but he still saw the little girl in her now, and she looked lonely.

And lost.

He touched her hand again as a tear emerged from the corner of her eye.

"Ana. We will sort this all out. We will find him—wherever he has gone."

Her watery eyes looked back into his.

"Stojan is like no other. He is strong and is a survivor. He will indeed escape capture and we will find him—soon. This I promise to you with all of my heart. I am so very glad that you have returned."

He brightened considerably upon saying this to her, as if he had one more secret.

"And! See?! What are the odds that you would find me?!"

She smiled and inhaled the tears that had found their way into her nostrils.

"And you were not even looking for me!"

She laughed and he found this to be the most delightful sound he had heard in years.

The two continued to talk for some time as they enjoyed another meal— so much time had passed. They watched the sun set over the gorgeous land known as Sedona as they walked through the streets that night.

Her lodgings were quite comfortable. As the Sage, he was not only the resident knower of all things Amira, he was essentially the ruling body of the town. He was both a Sage and a Mayor—the latter he accepted with some hesitation as politics and the rule of others were not his desire. He sought knowledge and the pursuit of all things Amira—and that included the saints. He'd been given a gift with Anastazja's appearance. Dagmar was as eager to learn as she was to relate her adventures.   Oddly, someone he knew turned out to be someone who provided so much new knowledge. Of all the sources, he thought she was the most reliable, that alone made him ecstatic, and finding someone he had a hand in saving was in found in good health made him all the more cheerful. It was truly a good day. His concern now was absorbing this knowledge properly and deciding on a way to help her find Stojan.

Like Ana, he now had a quest of sorts. But unlike Ana, he was at a great advantage in finding the pyramid.

He'd already been there.

"You what?!"

The next day during their breakfast he broke the news to her.

"I have been to this pyramid you describe—clearly it's the same one, there are not many great black pyramids in the west of Amira."

"Dagmar, it seems like in Amira everything is 'in the West.'"

He laughed.

"No doubt you know just how large it is, but there is much to the east and to the north."

She nodded.

"But you do not want to go to the north."

"No?"

"Well, at least not during the winter. It is even colder than Poliska and in some areas the snow falls for days on end."

She looked at the vivid colors and breathed in the dry air.

"I am no stranger to winter, but I will take your word for it Dagmar. I think Stojan and I have avoided more than one winter here in the west. And that was our plan for The Coast—to travel up and down until we found the perfect climate."

He considered what she said for a moment.

"That is actually a very good plan."

She smiled again and waited. She was starting to remember how easily his conversation could go astray. She would make a mental note not to tempt him again.

"The pyramid? You have been there."

"Oh yes."

He puffed up a bit as he spoke.

"I was summoned there once…"

"For what?"

"The Light of Luxor had dimmed and was in danger of going out."

"The Light of Luxor?"

"Yes. It is magnificent. The great black pyramid has atop it a great light —the most powerful in all of Amira. It shoots up into the night sky and can be seen for many miles."

"And it dimmed?"

"Yes. The Amiran tec needed some…adjustment."

"Dagmar, I must tell you something."

"What is it Anastazja?"

Sheepishly she continued.
"I do know that you have knowledge of Amira and the Old World. But I believed most of what you said was…"

"Embellished?"

She looked confused at his choice of word.

"Made up."

He smiled.

"But now I see that you are deserving of your title and I am sorry that I ever doubted you."

He stopped walking and focused on her eyes.

"Ana, that is the nicest thing I have ever heard anyone speak to me. Thank you."

They were both energized by her renewed faith in his abilities. What was an insurmountable obstacle now seemed possible with him as her guide. Truly The Sage of Sedona was what she had hoped—and more.

A week passed as they discussed their options and plans. Though she was growing restless, she knew it was best to be prepared than go blindly forth to find it by herself.

In addition, Dagmar had something he needed to do. It was an appointment he had with the people of the town, and it was something he did almost every week. She was intrigued by this public side of Dagmar and wanted to learn more.

Near his building a stage of sorts had been set up. Many of the townspeople had gathered and a respectable amount of them were children. She was able to get a seat near the front and she found this was where the little ones sat as well. They were all rather excited about the show that was to take place. Some of them spoke with her and were rather taken with her attire, her weapon and even her hair. At the moment it was the blonde it had always been.

Apparently these kids looked forward to these short performances, and more than one had volunteered to join him. It was a magic trick and he always told them afterwards that there was always an explanation for magic of this kind.
What she saw that day was truly a different side of Dagmar. Though he was still a bit awkward in public, his delight at amazing them and then explaining things was clear. This was his calling.

As with his other performances, he would make something disappear, or appear, or cause one thing to change into another. Then when it was all done, he would demonstrate just how he did it, with a special door here, a thing hidden there.

The equipment he used was amazing to her and she suspected it all was Amiran tec. How he came to possess this tec was a question for another day—or perhaps not. It was his Amiran tec that saved her life a few years ago, and she was in no position to be unappreciative. Instead she would simply enjoy the show.

Seeing Dagmar demonstrating things to children made her smile inside and out. And soon they would rescue Stojan—she told herself.

———

She remained quiet for the rest of the day, but just before bed she asked Dagmar what they were to do now. She had only a vague idea, and after some time had passed he had told her of what he knew of the pyramid currently. Something was going on, and Stojan had not been reported at the pyramid. Dagmar told Ana they would wait and see, and that he had those who could inquire. They had recently returned.

"Dagmar, do we simply wait for Stojan to arrive? I'm confused. Can we not rescue him *before* he gets there?"

He thought for a bit.

"Right now Ana it is the best plan I have. Without knowing exactly where he is, that is all we can do."

Before she could insist, he seemed to predict her question and had an answer ready.

"I have pried to the best of my ability. Even those left in charge do not know where they are except that they are on their way back. In fact, it is all very vague—too vague."
She listened to the possible intrigue.

"I feel there is a plan on top of a plan."

She pulled her head back while shaking it.

"Oh, that is too much for me Dagmar. I do not want to know about plans on top of plans. I just want to save him."

He exhaled.

"I know this Ana, but I am trying to help him as well. And I too am frustrated. Nothing these saints do is straightforward. They are like many minds acting as one sometimes, and other times they are like children—or both."

She could see he was indeed very frustrated with what he was dealing with—far more so than she had considered. His face showed desperation, but also kindness and patience. Since she had arrived she'd done nothing but demand that they rescue him, and Dagmar had complied. He had dropped everything he had been doing to focus on her and Stojan. She realized just how much her single-mindedness had pushed him and how much he was doing for them.

It was then that she softened and attempted to find balance between the panic of finding Stojan and pushing this man too far who had done nothing but help. She would have to learn patience. She and Dagmar were on the same path now.

"Dagmar, I am sorry."

She genuinely took him by surprise and he blinked away his confusion as she continued.

"I know you are doing everything you can. I hope that I have been helpful?"

"Well of cour…"

"There must be something I can do to help you."

He was touched by the change in demeanor and all frustration was now lost. He smiled at her.

"Thank you Ana—I will try to think if there is anything I have not asked of you, or told you."

He laughed.

"And I will keep my own answers to under an hour!"

Dagmar requested that a good meal be prepared for them, as his tastes were much more in line with home cooked food and less in line with the kind of rations one uses when traveling. His job as the Sage of Sedona definitely had some advantages—and he was all too willing to enjoy them. They ate a cold soup along with a number of items similar to what the Navajo served on flatbreads. It was all served to them in an inner chamber that was beautiful and most remarkable.

The room looked like a room for banquets, but Dagmar explained it was normally used for meetings. It reminded her very much of the room in which she met the Navajo recently—including the trinkets that adorned the shelves. This was different in that most of the shelves were empty, however. Their dinner was mostly quiet and filled with the sounds of two people who were delighted to eat. Ana's eyes were on her food and the most barren shelves.

When they were finished, Dagmar had a new line of questions, and the excitement with which he asked almost startled her.

"Ana tell me more about what the Saint on High told you—specifically how he would help you once you reach the door."

She related to him everything she knew even though most of it confused her and sounded like magic. It seemed that Dagmar was very interested in the vessel the saint talked about and she did her best to describe his requirements. Dagmar did a considerable amount of nodding and digesting.

"I am worried that he will use his weapons of destruction of the masses —that he will trick me."

"I do not think so."

"Dagmar, how are you so certain?"

"Because I think I have seen them and they are not under his control."

"You have seen these weapons?"

Ana was incredulous. Dagmar was witness to unfathomable destructive forces.

"I think I have."

He looked uncomfortable now, and there was a certain gravity to his words.

"My employment by the saint was not originally to fix the light. In fact, he was not really aware of the brightness of the huge light it seemed. Instead he wanted to become a master of such weapons of destruction. He is very paranoid. In fact he may be the most paranoid of them all."

Ana scoffed. They all seemed equally insane and paranoid to her.

"No, it is true. He is a master of a great fortress and the largest repository of Amiran tec."

"Then what does he…Dagmar! You did not help him did you?!"

She was incensed and frightened. He took a deep breath and tried to compose his words. To her, he looked ashamed and calm at the same time.

"Ana, I failed. So much of Amiran tec has decayed or been destroyed. Some of it still remains pristine due to the saints—which they have no control over."

"I know this, Dagmar."

"The weapon is like a great arrow. There were once many spread throughout all of Amira. This one is near the pyramid and still works, I think."

"So you succeeded in arming him in such a way as to…"

"No. I failed."

She was skeptical. Dagmar had used his skill to increase the power of a saint many-fold.

"You see, I believe I understand the device, but its purpose is not for what he intended. The device is actually meant to destroy things in the clouds. It relies on things that used to circle the very world, but they have all fallen out of the sky. For the weapon to work otherwise something would have to be very…"

She shook her head and believed he was trying to confuse her.

"None of this makes sense to me Dagmar."

He put his hand on her arm. He had told her too much. So many ideas and thoughts plagued him. He knew he needed to make things clear for her and he had just lost ground.

His face changed. He was now more than excited and anxious.

"I have something to show you again."

"Is this about the vessel?"

Without answering, he walked her to a set of doors that were flat and ornate with metal knobs. Around the knobs was wound a length of strong thin twine. He put his ear to the doors slightly and then unwound the length of string. He then opened the doors quickly—almost apprehensively. It looked like a closet of sorts, or a pantry. There were some small shelves on the sides and one large one in front. Stacked along the pantry shelves and strewn on the floor were what apparently populated the shelves of the room at one time. In fact, it looked like these had been hastily placed in the little room. As Dagmar would explain, she was right.

Staring right at them was a statue that was about a meter tall. Like some of the other items in the closet it looked like an ornate doll. What she found odd was that it looked like it had been designed just for the dark area on the shelf. It sat with its little legs hanging down from it. Whoever made it did so with the shelf measurements in mind. Why someone would do that and then keep it in the dark made no sense.

She looked at the opened doors in case it was some sort of glass and had missed it, but found it was wood. One of the now-opened doors had some sort of scratching on it as if someone had taken a dull stone and tried to draw on the wood. She walked closer as Dagmar glanced at her.

The large doll was rotund with equally fat legs and arms, and appeared to be male. Highly colorful, it wore a frilly shirt, ballooning pants and had bracelets around both wrists. The fingers looked like thick sausages and some of the color of the tips of the fingers had been rubbed off.

She stopped.

"Dagmar what is it? What did you do here? Did you make this?"

He looked closely at the big doll and was peering into the painted-on eyes.

She found it unsettling. In fact, she had the urge to take a few steps back.

"Dagmar..."

She leaned forward to look at the face of the doll, then looked at the hands.

Then she looked at the inside of the door with the scratches. She took two steps back.

"Dagmar! Close those..."

He smiled. And just as he was about to assure her, she yelled at him.

"Now they know I am here!"

He looked genuinely confused, and half smiling still, he slammed the doors closed and did his best to wind the twine around the handles.

"No no..."

She backed up a few more steps as he assured her.

"Ana, it is not alive. It is just a small statue."

"Then what made the scratches?!"

"Well I believe it did."

She grabbed her sword hilt.

"No Ana, I do not believe it is alive *now*. I think it was at..."

"Was it alive when you trapped it?!"
He walked away from the doors to join her and reconsidered his method of explaining lest she cut him off again.

"Let me explain in full please. One day I walked into the room and I saw it move. When it detected me, it started to run and then immediately froze and fell over. It was a terrifying experience that was only softened by how comical it looked when it fell."

She nodded and did not interrupt.

"I watched it for some time and called my assistant. I did not tell him what had happened but asked that he remain in the room. For some time I watched it and eventually just told him we would be storing all of the dolls in the storage area."

"So you were able to bend it and make it sit on the shelf?"

"No, he did. He sat himself on the shelf."

"And the scratches?"

"I think he was trying to test his environment."

Ana drew her sword.

"We must destroy it Dagmar—this is our chance to destroy a saint easily! If Stojan was able to do this…"

She did not finish and noticed that Dagmar looked entirely too relaxed. He looked at her sword and for the first time realized it now looked too small for her.

"Ana this one is different. It seems that it becomes inhabited with a saint from time to time, but only for a few seconds or perhaps a minute at a time. Then it is gone for days."

"Well, where does it go?"

She looked around the room—the walls and the ceiling. Swinging her sword to accentuate where she looked, she continued.

"Is it in the walls, in this structure? Is this a cathedral of sorts?"

"No. That's a good question actually! I came across this doll months ago and periodically I would find it in a different position. I had scolded my assistant more than once about allowing someone to fool with me."

She smiled at his compliment and slowly returned her sword to its home as she listened.

"Ana, I think something odd is afoot with one of the saints. And more importantly…"

He looked into her eyes with promise.

"I think we found your vessel."

Her eyes widened as her mind raced.

"You think it is the Saint on High? You think he tries to reach out? Oh! Do we just wait for him to inhabit it and speak to him!?"

"I had not considered that until now—until you told me about his plan. Perhaps he is trying to find you, or perhaps this doll is a soft spot that is near the great doorway?"

Dagmar now looked less certain. Somehow, he or Ana had confused his original train of thought. Ana looked excited, however.

"What do we do then?"

She grabbed Dagmar by the shoulders—an action that never ceased to surprise him.

"You have a plan?"

He smiled sheepishly.

"Yes, I do."

She released him and he stumbled back slightly—still smiling.

"Ana, I will go to the pyramid."

"No."

His smiling and proud face at once fell in confusion.

"No?"

"No."

She was very serious and her one-word answer confused him all the more.

"No Dagmar, *we* will go to the pyramid."

"Oh... Oh! Oh no Ana. You are safe here. I have been there before. It is much too dangerous."

"Why?"

"Why wh…"

"Why is it much too dangerous Dagmar? I have been trained—by Stojan. I am far better in a battle than you are. And I have…"

He swallowed and decided not to let her finish listing her grim accomplishments.

"I understand, Ana. I do."

He nodded and smiled most convincingly.

He started to reach out with his arm to console her. She did nothing but stare back at him with her blue eyes—a few strands of red blocking the view of one of them.

He withdrew his arm.

"Oh dear. I see there is no negotiation here."

She did not speak and he found the whole affair most uncomfortable.

Mark Bradford

Amira

THE ROAD TO LUXOR

It would take about a week to reach the pyramid at their best speed. Initially they thought of bringing a horse for Stojan, but then decided to do something much easier—they'd just steal one. Even better than that, they would be lucky enough to recover both of their horses.

Dagmar's description of the pyramid was nothing short of magical. He'd explained that it wasn't a cathedral; instead it was a castle. In fact, it was one of many castles from the Old World. Each castle was a small city unto itself with commerce and visitors, and lodging and food. Even exotic entertainment was to be had. Each castle was run by a lord and they all participated in a sort of competition. And in the land they were traveling, the castles were all huddled together. One could walk from one to another to another all in the same day.

It was hard to imagine a building so large as to be a castle and yet be so closely located next to their enemies.

"They were not enemies but instead in league. Well, some of them."

This only served to make Anastazja less able to grasp as to what they traveled. She decided that it was simply a giant pyramid and would sort out the rest.

Much to Dagmar's dismay, Ana continued to insist on her daily walks. Though his protests were for her safety, it was clear to both of them they were actually for his. In spite of hinting at carrying a few Amiran surprises, he was no warrior and thought her to be infinitely more capable than he was. After hearing her stories, he was horrified and convinced. He had never taken a life; she had taken many, and was prepared to add to that number to save Stojan.

Fortunately for him the excursions did not result in an ambush, or an animal attack. Regarding the latter, Dagmar was in awe over her handling of the rabid wolf. He found her story amazing and had to work hard to force her to tell it. Her relaying of the story was short due to her humility on the matter and Dagmar knew not to push too hard.

Then they saw it.

As the sun went down on the third day, they saw it reach into the sky. It was a thin beam of white light that stretched itself into the cloudless night.

"Well, I have no doubt where the pyramid is now."

They exchanged glances and marveled at the most powerful beam of light in all of Amira. They were still at least two days' ride from the castle-pyramid and yet the light was visible. Dagmar enjoyed the look of amazement on Ana's face and was happy that in all of her travels he could still introduce her to something that would invoke such a response.

He didn't tell her that according to what he had read, the beam could be seen as far as Sedona. He'd never seen it and wondered if even the saints had their limits as to what they could preserve.

"How does it work, Dagmar? Does the saint in the castle make it light up?"

"No. He simply allows it not to break down."

"Then what makes it light up? Is it like the mushrooms in the pyramid of the Navajo?"

"No, I do not think so. The Light of Luxor requires much energy. The pyramid itself generates it somehow."

That answer seemed to more than satisfy her curiosity. In that he envied her; she could ask just enough questions to understand something but then no more. For him it was like a curse in that he couldn't stop until he knew as much as there was to know.

And he had a bad habit of filling in the blank spots with his own guesses.

It was Anastazja, however, that had filled in the intentional blank spots in his plan to rescue Stojan. He did not dare tell her the entire plan as he knew she would not approve. She cared for him as much as he did her it seemed. Dagmar felt disingenuous for doing, this but believed it was the only way. And if he was wrong, then she need not ever know anyway.

Her walk on the night before their final ride found her not just walking, but practicing. It was unfamiliar and she was once again reminded of her undersized weapon—but she attempted to persevere.

She could rescue Stojan, or find that he'd already been killed. Or he simply might not be there. If he was not, then her next destination would be their original quest—to find the great doorway. There really was no other option than to find him; however, it all sounded so impossible.

At least he had an idea for how to enter the pyramid.

After what seemed like hours, they prepared to turn in for the night. They made preparation and although the day had been hot, the night was rather cool. It was a comfortable rest for them both, but each wondered if the other would actually sleep that night—for so much was happening around them and Stojan it seemed was at the very center. In a way it gave Ana some relief that she could operate without their interest in her. But how long would that last?

Dagmar had many grim thoughts as he started to doze off. His plans would have to be put into action but at what cost? Finally his mind came upon a solution that gave him peace. Just before dozing off he spoke some quiet words to Ana.

"Tomorrow I think I have something to show you."

ARRIVING AT THE PYRAMID

The size of the pyramid played tricks on Ana's sense of size and distance more than once. She was convinced they were closer than they were—twice. So large was the structure that it affected many in that way. As they arrived in the middle of the day, she discovered another secret of the pyramid: it wasn't black at all. Instead, it was a great four-sided mirror. Almost the entire surface was covered in these great square mirrors—all working together to create what looked like an almost seamless surface from far away. As they approached, the pyramid was actually sky-blue as it reflected the great sheet of almost pristine sky above them. Dagmar explained that it was black at night as it had little or nothing to reflect. Immediately, Ana wanted to see the pyramid up close and admire the great beam on the top. It appeared that though this light was powerful, it could not be seen during the day. Dagmar explained that the beam only turned on at dusk and turned off at dawn.

"Automatically. And it had done that for hundreds of years—perhaps more."

"A great light that produces no heat like all Amiran lights."

She was in awe again. He laughed, however.

"Oh, these lights definitely produce heat."

"There are more than one? *Lights*?"

"Oh, yes. The great light atop actually comes from an entire room of lights. And to be inside this room is to be cooked alive, even now when only a few lights remain. They are very, very hot."

He rolled up his sleeve to reveal an oval scar on his left forearm.

"I knew the room was hot but didn't realize that each of the bulbs was also very, very hot. I thought perhaps what gave it power was what made the room so hot. I was mistaken."

"Oh that looks like that must have hurt terribly!"

"It did, but there are salves and ointments in Sedona that soothe and heal and they are made from nearby plants."

"Yes, the Navajo taught us of the green plants that can cure and heal many things."

She looked at the pyramid as she spoke.

To Ana, it was clearly a structure of pure Amiran Tec—an entire magical building that reminded her of the great library of the Navajo.

As Dagmar had said, there was very little outside of the structure, and that in and of itself was the entire city.

How the denizens of the pyramid found food, raised animals and other necessities were a mystery to her.

Dagmar was able to demonstrate this by the land surrounding the pyramid. In the middle of the desert was a lush area with trees that she did not recognize. Instead of pine cones or great branches, these trees seemed almost naked with just some great broad leaves at the top. As they approached she saw that these leaves were actually taller than she was. Once again size had played tricks with her eyes in this magical land of the great pyramid. She'd never felt more immersed into a different world than right now.

Many people came and went around the pyramid and the surrounding green. It was a beautiful scene with grasses, arching trees and mountains in the distance. Farms were sprinkled here and there and everything was split in two by a river. The builders of the pyramid had chosen a lush area to be sure and the river provided ample water—perhaps more.

Dagmar had much to say on the subject but his self-control was greater than his need to teach that day. Ana thought he looked unusually nervous, but also said nothing of it.

They kept their distance and made a great arch around the building. His plan was not to remain hidden but to move about calmly as if they were part of the city folk.

They made their way through a bit of farmland and rested. The people here looked like others she had seen save for the abundance of black and gold in their outfits. Never had she seen so much importance placed upon the fashion of a people. Though she would be considered stylish and perhaps a bit flamboyant in her dress, everything she wore was for function over form. If it looked good too, then so be it. However, though the folk were at least friendly, they were quite downtrodden. She felt that each and every one had a burden upon them. Ana could not quite understand why or how. She knew they lived among the pyramid, but seemed free to go at any time.

Dagmar was not shy in speaking to some of the villagers and introduced himself vaguely as a traveler passing through to The Coast. It made Ana wonder just how close The Coast was and where exactly Stojan was. She tried not to think too much about it but did pester Dagmar about his plan, how they would get into the great structure, and where he thought Stojan was. At last, the conversation revealed that the farmers who lived in the surrounding area were actually those that supported the great structure. They were counted upon to produce all of the goods and services for it, and if their contributions were not to the liking of the saint, then they were replaced. As familiar as Ana was with the cruelty of the saints, this fact made it even more apparent as to their true nature. She was sickened but tried hard not to show it.

It was decided that they would move away from the pyramid to find a place to settle for the night.

The next day Dagmar would enter the pyramid alone. From what Ana had told him, it would not do well to have her be discovered as well. The saints would know that they were a pair, but they would not associate Dagmar with them. And—he reminded her—he'd been here before. His vagueness and her anxiousness worked hand in hand to make her a most stressful companion since they arrived.

A MOST CURIOUS SCULPTURE

Their morning was quiet and uneventful. As the sun rose, they ate a small breakfast while feeling insignificant amongst the pyramid and the mountains. It made for a stunning backdrop to what was to come. Each was lost in thoughts. Though Dagmar could not predict exactly when Stojan was to arrive, Ana felt it would be imminent and her intuition told her it would be that very day. She was hesitant to ask Dagmar what he was to show her and kept her thoughts to herself.

She stole a glance at him or two that morning and the seriousness in his eyes was something she'd never seen before. The only thing that had come close was her memory of him looking down upon her after her fall and miraculous healing by the bridge. He was unusually silent and had Stojan not been relatively so, she would have felt uncomfortable. Traveling with her stoic companion had made her appreciate silence and words when necessary—they meant more that way.

But that was not normally so for Dagmar—in fact it was quite the opposite. So curious and interested to share and make his knowledge known that he was always a whirlwind of chatter. But not today.

Eventually he took a deep breath and motioned to her to mount her horse. It was decided that each day they would pack their camp until Stojan arrived so that they would always be ready. Today was no different.

The ride was taking them away from the pyramid to a path in the lush surroundings. She noticed that the lush area was a localized phenomenon in that in every direction the environment turned back to dry desert. Dagmar disputed that this was the doing of the saint and that instead it had been caused by one of the many disasters that befell the

Old World. Waters had been diverted through purpose or accident and had created this special green place in the desert.

As they travelled, the green was about to turn to brown and it seemed they had come up to their destination. Among the trees was a large hill that Ana was not so convinced was natural. She was right.

Dagmar took her hand and gently walked her around to the other side of the green protrusion. He had never touched her before save for her hugs and this seemed almost fatherly. She noticed his hand was smaller and smoother than Stojan's.

He pulled some of the vines away from a section and it appeared to be a door. He smiled at her most gleefully and commented simply as he let them in.

"I am afraid to do this at night."

Curious, she followed him into the dark area. It was not a cave, but a large building. It reminded her of the darkened building they'd seen many years ago in a port in Poliska. Like it, this was dark without windows and had a metallic echo to it. This enclosure was even larger than the last though they were told that no water was present.

Ana detected odd smells similar to what she'd experienced previously; smells that reminded her of earth. It was both pleasant and unpleasant to her. She knew it wasn't a scent she would normally detect and instead had come from deep within the ground.

Finally, Dagmar reached the portion of the wall he'd intended to and although he said it quietly she distinctly heard him say "Ahh, here it is."

The click resulted in the building coming to life with lights emanating from strips hanging from the ceiling. As she had barely detected it was indeed a sort of rounded building—though not as perfectly round as the habitat of The Saint on High. Were all buildings from the Old World rounded like this? Were they all made of metal? She barely had time for any other thoughts as her eyes adapted quickly to the light. It wasn't the lighting that held her attention but the thing in the very center of the huge one-room building. It was a metal sculpture. Never had she seen something so beautiful, so serene and delicate and yet apparently made of metal.

They had entered something like a shrine or museum. The sculpture was sleek and looked like it had purpose along with form—she even thought there was a direction of sorts to it. Absolutely devoid of any hard corners, it looked like it had been sanded smooth. The hands that made this were indeed skilled and if any machines were involved they were so advanced as to be almost unimaginable. It was beautiful, of a silver material and had simple decorations upon it—a symbol here and there. The item looked so delicate and solid at the same time and it was perched upon a delicate base that ended in small, round black circles. She thought perhaps the base was equipped with wheels so that it could easily be moved from one location to another lest they damage it.

It was almost human looking in that it was symmetrical and had a body.

Dagmar smiled proudly as if he had constructed it himself, or perhaps summoned it.

She walked around it in a circle. It was huge—and occupied the space that perhaps five or six horses would, standing next to each other. Then there was the portion that simply jutted out from either side. She knew that the metal should have bowed and dipped from the weight of itself, but it did not. And then there were the strange mounds that erupted from the slats on either side—adding even more weight. But rather than bow down, the slats seemed to be bowing upward with a tiny curvature.

Unlike the rest of the sculpture, these mounds had an opening to them with tiny teeth—almost like someone was trying to represent the rays of the sun on a cloudy day. In the middle of the rays was a small cone with a curly design on it. She wanted to reach in, but something about it was menacing.

She had a feeling that there was a proper front to it and was certain she was standing at one end of it. Walking up, she gingerly placed her hand on the material and ran it along the length. There were many sharp angles on one end and on the other, everything was smooth. Finally she noticed the very front of it. It was the only area that did not seem to be made of metal, but rather was constructed of glass. Like other Amiran creations it was the clearest most delicate glass she had ever seen. And there were more than one panel of glass. It was a sculpture with windows.

Dagmar continued to stand back and allow Ana to walk around the sculpture. He was clearly delighted by her reaction to it. Again and again she circled it—so determined to figure it all out.

She looked at him, then the sculpture. Back and forth were her glances as she smiled as if she'd been given a great gift and could not unwrap it, but was just to feel her way to the answer. Many minutes were spent in touching it, walking around it and exploring it. Marveling at the way it just stood there perched and challenging to defy gravity, she was lost. She ran her hand along the smooth, wide surfaces, and her fingers around the two large circles and just watched as the light played off of the thing made by those that lived one thousand years ago.

Finally, her enthusiasm crashed as she remembered their impending meeting with Stojan and those that absconded him. The sculpture was ethereal and amazing, but it had no purpose. It served as a distraction—nothing more. Soon they would leave the building and cover it back up.

Seeing her dismay, Dagmar ran to her. Seeing the concern on his face she turned apologetic.

"Oh Dagmar, it is majestic and gorgeous! I appreciate that you..."

She did not finish her sentence. Her silence was caused by his action on one side of the thing. She turned and followed him.

It was a door. She saw the seams and the tiny indentation that acted as a handle. He pulled on it lightly and stepped back as the door swung open. At the same time, a portion from within also unfolded to reveal something in miniature that almost made her laugh: stairs.

He smiled at her and beckoned her to enter with him—which she gleefully did.

The interior was lit not only from the strips above but from tiny unseen lights within. The experience was familiar. While the conveyance they'd traveled within for a week was of metal and little comforts, this device seemed to be created with comfort in mind. There were a total of four seats and each was huge and covered in the most supple of leathers she had ever felt. Beige and tans were used throughout with appointments of small strips of shiny, finished woods. It was the carriage of a king or queen, and it was in the shape of a soaring bird.

Clearly this was the royal carriage of those that once ruled in the great pyramid.

It was extravagant, luxurious, delicate and entirely impractical. It also seemed too delicate to travel along the roads.

Dagmar motioned for her to remove her sword and enjoy the seat and she gladly obliged.

She ran her hands against the armrests and looked about the small enclosure.

Dagmar was now smiling ear to ear as if he yet still had a secret. He did.

Gingerly he made his way down the steps and to one of the walls of the rounded building. Ana peeked out to watch him and that was when she realized it was not entirely round but had two flat walls and a rounded roof. Dagmar was at the wall that the thing faced and after feeling for something and producing a satisfying click, he pulled hard to reveal a giant door. Pushing and pulling quickly, he separated them as light flooded the large one-room building.

The opening was so huge that the conveyance could be rolled through it.

He returned slightly out of breath and closed the door behind him. The stairs folded back in as the area was sealed.

He reached over her shoulder and pulled at a strip of material. It was like a thin scarf with a bulky head made of metal—like a snake with its tongue out. He pulled it across her chest and then inserted it into an item next to her opposite leg. This was all done rather awkwardly and his proximity to her made her slightly uncomfortable. She moved her arm to motion her thoughts and found she was now bound by not only a strap across her shoulder, but one across her lap. Quickly her face turned serious and she was about to voice her concern. Had he trapped her?

He pointed with his finger rapidly as a small amount of panic crossed his face.

"No no! No no! Here press that!"

She looked at him oddly and did as he said. The red rectangle clicked and the device unraveled back into the wall.

Relieved, he looked at her smiling and pointed to the empty seat in front of her.

"Come up front."

"Then why did you...?"

Dagmar motioned for her to move one seat forward and once again she was reminded of the conveyance of the past. In front of her were many intricate designs and above it was a sloping window that followed the delicate curve of the room.

On either side were also windows. The glass looked too delicate to last if there were any bumps in the road. Surely they would shatter if they encountered a ledge or rock.

He sat next to her and although their areas were identical his had the addition of a protrusion placed most inconveniently directly near his chest.

Reaching around it, he pressed various things with his hand and she thought she heard gentle chimes.

Like the conveyance, this seemed to have tiny lights that danced, and living paintings that moved. The chair was exceedingly comfortable and made for a perfect viewing area of the area just outside of the carriage, though the design was such that the protrusion in front blocked the view for many meters. A chiming once again occurred, but this time it was persistent and rather annoying.

Dagmar fastened his own strap and then motioned to Ana to do the same. Suddenly there was a light lurch as the carriage rolled outward. Dagmar fastened his own strap and the chiming stopped.

She gripped his forearm tightly.

"Dagmar! Are we to go for a ride? Does it move under its own power? What makes it go?"

He smiled as the device rolled into the sunlight. In front of them was just some scrub, sand and a rather flat road. Dagmar focused ahead and using the protrusion was able to steer the carriage onto the road. Again he looked rather nervous. Their rate of movement was barely that of a walk and no match for even a slow trot.

"OH!"

He undid his belt strap and let himself out of the conveyance. She turned but was quickly restrained by the straps.

"Dagmar?! Where do you go now? What are you...?"

She thought about undoing her own strap and pursuing him. In moments he returned again. Sitting back down and once again restraining himself, he spoke without looking at her.

"I forgot to close the doors."

She just nodded.

"Please do not be afraid."

"Well why would I be..."

That was when she heard the sound. It was a whirring, then a whooshing, then she thought she heard something like a scream. It was constant and the sound built up, and it sounded like it came from the front—perhaps even from the large protrusions on either side.

She looked over at Dagmar who was intensely looking down at the lights and things in front of him. He seemed to mentally be going over a checklist of sorts—so lost in thought was he.

Finally he glanced at her and back at the window.

Pushing something forward the carriage moved, but this time much more rapidly than before. She looked out the perfectly-clear glass and watched the trees and sand as they rolled forward. She found the whole affair rather bouncy. Though the seat did a fine job of cushioning her travel, she was not sure if this was going to be tolerable for much time. The Amirans of old must have enjoyed that sort of ride or been so averse to shocks as to cushion things with the tec to the point that it was intolerable for those of modern day Amira—or Poliska.

That was when she noticed just how fast they were going.

Even the fastest horse had never traveled as fast as they were moving now. Dagmar continued to focus ahead with a glance now and then to the side. He was particularly interested in something in front of him that resembled the compass he'd shown her years ago. So quickly did they increase their speed that she imagined she was being pushed into her seat. She was.

She felt the pressure on her back, but when she felt it in her seat, her eyes went wide and she gripped both arm rests.

Dagmar continued looking forward as the carriage tipped upward.

"Dagmar! Be care…"

She did not finish her sentence.

At first she thought they hit a rather large bump in the road, but it was clear they were not coming back down.

She looked at the ground, and the sand and the mountains in the distance. Then she heard a strange sound below them.

Since Dagmar did not look alarmed she just braced herself for what was to come.   They continued to move upward.   The sleek carriage that looked too delicate to travel—even if made of the amazing Amiran metals—was not designed to roll along the ground. The metal sculpture that reminded her of a bird was designed to fly. She closed her eyes in disbelief and took in the sounds and the movements.

"Ana, it is best to open your eyes."

Finally, she complied with Dagmar's gentle request and realized that not only was her belief true but that she herself was experiencing it directly.

The carriage was no longer climbing up into the sky but instead seemed to be rolling along in the air.

She took a deep breath and realized that she had been gripping her arm rests so tightly as to almost damage them. She released them as her eyes filled with tears.

Dagmar took his eyes off of the amazing view to look over at her. Before he could speak to comfort her, she spoke softly as tears ran down her cheeks.

"Oh Dagmar. We are inside one of the great machines that painted the sky with lines."

He smiled back as his concern turned to happiness. It seemed that he too was tearful at this moment.

He did not correct her as he was not certain if this particular conveyance was able to paint the lines seen in the skies of old. But he had given her something amazing that day.

The two spent the next hour or so flying over an unpopulated area west of the pyramid. In fact, Dagmar was able to point to the short wall in front of them and demonstrate their direction.

Before she could ask, he made it clear that he was to show her The Coast that afternoon. Anastazja had many questions for Dagmar and not once did she look at him when she spoke. There was far too much to see, absorb and embrace and she meant to take all of it in. From time to time she'd imagined what it would be like to travel in one of the machines and look down. She always thought she would be able to look directly down for some reason, instead of looking out through a window. Perhaps there were conveyances like this once that had a glass belly that one could lay upon and watch the world pass by underneath. But right now, she was enjoying being able to see below her at an angle.

Dagmar spoke of the cities and the rivers. He spun many tales of the Old World and how and where people lived. He told of a great coastal forest of trees that were many times taller than any she'd seen; trees that were red instead of brown and were the width of a small house. He pointed out lakes and told her of a great hole in the earth—so large it was as if a whole section had been scooped out. She asked if this was what the moon had been formed from and he told her he did not think so, but was unsure.

Like the other conveyance she had been in, this one had the ability to make the inner chamber hot or cold at will and he demonstrated that to her.

"You must make it colder as things get hotter?"

"No, actually it tends to get much colder the higher you go, Ana."

She moved on to other questions and took it all in. He continued his stories and tales and facts and no matter how sensational, how embellished they seemed, how wondrous they all sounded, she believed every single word because she was now in a flying machine that was over one thousand years old. Constructed by a people she thought were only myths and kept in pristine condition by creatures that were inexplicable.

And somehow Dagmar had learned to operate it.

"Dagmar, how is it that this…"

"Airplane."

"…this air plane is still functional at such a distance from the saint?"

"Ana!"

Dagmar smiled a proud smile like a teacher that has made an impact on a pupil.

"That is an excellent question!"

She beamed as he explained.

"Yes, the effect and influence of the saints is felt for only a short distance. They do not seem to have any control over it. And it is usually little more than a kilometer at best."

"So then how is it this works at all and is in such perfect condition?"

"Because I think his influence has decreased."

"You mean it shrinks?"

"Yes that's exactly what I mean. I think his influence spanned many kilometers at one time, but for some reason it has withdrawn into the pyramid. And I think it is exactly why the great weapon was still preserved."

For the first time she looked sad. She did not like to talk about such unimaginable weapons. To know that Dagmar had seen one and even attempted to fix it while in the service of such an evil being made her question things. Seeing such a change come over her, he attempted to both cheer her up and explain things once more.

"Ana, please do not judge my actions. I truly would never have made it work for him. In fact, I barely left with my life. And I am ashamed I tried to use it."

She looked out the window and admired the puffs of clouds—it was a surreal experience and the talk of destruction seemed out of place. She looked back at Dagmar.

"You tried to use it?"

He swallowed and she saw something desperate in his eyes.

"I was so angry at what I had seen in the pyramid. So much of Amiran tec being wasted; so many people working so hard to have everything taken from them because of the ignorance of the saint. He has the means to help people but in his stupidity squanders everything! When he found that I failed—and even working on the light did not please him —I almost lost my life. So I decided to use it when I escaped."

"Dagmar. What do you mean?"

"I tried to use it on him—on the pyramid."

She was oddly fascinated by this but said nothing.

"I felt horrible when I tried because I did not know if any innocent people would lose their lives. But ultimately it did not work."

She spoke quietly as the conveyance hummed around her. It was truly a private conversation in the sky.

"Why not?"

"Because it is like an arrow that will only go toward a flame—even if you point it at the thing you wish to destroy. I should go back. I have left many notes on its operation though I think they are mostly useless."

For many minutes she looked past him out his own window. With the good came the bad. The Navajo had taught her that everything had two sides and these amazing things were no different. They too told her that sometimes good and bad were simply how something was used. Dagmar had attempted to use a horrible thing to benefit Amira. Instead of being shocked and disappointed, she should instead be embracing all the good he was trying to do. She brightened and smiled while she stared. And her eyes returned to him. Dagmar was taken aback as if she had seen something outside of the window and he too smiled.

"Tell me more about how the air…?"

Taking her lead, he happily turned back into a teacher.

"This runs under its own power. And as long as it is kept in the sun, it

209

has the power for a journey. In a way, it must rest for some time between travels."

"How long... how far can we go?"

"Oh my. This conveyance can go for over one thousand kilometers, perhaps more."

He pointed to a circle in front of them.

"This tells us just how many more miles we can go."

Ana had heard the Amirans speak of miles many times and assumed that it was just another word for 'kilometer.'

"Let us make sure we return before we run out of whatever powers it, or it becomes too tired."

He nodded, becoming serious. She noticed something else.

"Dagmar! Did that already happen to you?"

He laughed sheepishly and told her of how he thought he was stranded when he took the conveyance for a ride for the second time. That was when he learned of its ability to renew itself in the sun.

So many things raced through her head. This was a tool and a weapon against the saints. It would allow her to travel almost anywhere in Amira and reach things in hours instead of months. Dagmar possessed a miracle machine that was even faster than the conveyance she'd spent a week within. She voiced many questions to him, and Dagmar did his best to answer and sum them all up in one response. He smiled and took a deep breath.

"Oh, I have been to many places. Yes, I may go almost anywhere, but one of the limitations is that we need a long path of land that is extremely smooth and without trees or buildings. Even a few larger holes can damage it. No, I do not know how to fix it if it breaks, but it should not need any kind of repair for some time, hopefully. We cannot use it to look for Stojan because we must fly very high for it to work properly I think, and those on the ground will see us. Most of the controls are automatic and I dare not try to steer such a thing in the sky. It takes off and goes up and mostly goes in the direction I initially choose. I believe there is a way to guide it in the same way one rides a horse and directs it.

But I am afraid to do that yet."

He took another breath, and it was his turn to ask a question.

"Ana, you told me of the doorway. I came to Sedona looking for the doorway, but you say that you know where it is."

She looked afraid at this train of thought, but answered in kind.

"Yes. We drew a crude map and the Saint on High mentioned the name of the city."

"Waxa…"

"Yes, something like that."

Dagmar manipulated one of the moving paintings and made it large and small before her. It was of a shape that was green and brown, surrounded by a light blue. It had many lines on it and in a way they looked like black lightning strikes.

"Ana, I believe I can find the doorway."

He pointed to the painting that she now realized was a map—a rather large map.

"Dagmar, what is this…?"

She watched as once again he made it grow big and small, and she saw words appear as if from nothing.

"It is an unusual name, to be sure. I did not know how to spell it, but it is so unique that I did not have to."

Waxahachie.

There it was in front of her.

"If the doorway is indeed there, at least we know where it is, and how to get there."

She instinctively looked out the window—as if she could see it from high in the sky. She could not, or perhaps she was looking right at it. There was no way to tell.

She grasped his arm once again and searched his eyes.

"Dagmar, what are you thinking?"

"I am thinking that this has been our destination the whole time."

He winked at her shocked face.

"No, no Dagmar. I am not ready to do this… and Stojan. He needs us. He needs me. We should all do this together!"

She was upset, but respectful.

His tone was comforting and he realized just how out of her element she was. Though she had done things and seen things he had only imagined, his possession of the Amiran tec was nothing short of a miracle—a miracle he was already used to.

"I meant only to find the city and then return us, but I think it is at the limit of how far we can travel in one trip."

"Oh, we do not have enough energy to reach it?"

"I think we do, but then we would have to let it rest in the sun for some time—possibly days or a week."

Relieved, she released her grip from his arm. He was sure that he would have more than one bruise from the trip and made a mental note not to be so sensational in his presentation of things to her.

He explained to her that he had taught it the destination and that they were now returning to the area near the great pyramid. She watched as he demonstrated.

On their return trip she asked about their visibility, and why he was not worried about being discovered.

"The storage area is far enough away from the Pyramid and the farms are all on the other side of it. And if we left at night I could not show you anything."
"And you could not see."

He nodded, but not convincingly. Before landing he was able to point out the location of the weapon. It was just a square with a thin road leading away from it for just a few meters. It surprised her just how close it was to the camp. She did her best to entertain his interest in showing her, but found it all so horrible. Surely thoughts like this would have entered the minds of the Amirans that built it?

Bringing the conveyance back down to earth was as exhilarating as it was reaching for the sky. The bounces at the end did scare her, but she was too thrilled to notice. She marveled at the patterns of the farms and remarked that they seemed like patches on a quilt. Dagmar was truly a master of the machine, in spite of how terrified he looked when they landed.

Once the machine was properly, stored Dagmar explained that he would have to bring it back out into the sunlight to allow it to rejuvenate for a few days before it could be used to full capacity again.

She hugged him and thanked him for the amazing journey. Ana considered it a once-in-a-lifetime experience, but he told her that he had many trips planned for her and Stojan.

Unfortunately she was overwhelmed by it all. Stojan's rescue was more than enough, but now she was intimidated by the great pyramid, and then had just been shown a device that she had only dreamt of being close to. She had flown above the highest bird and literally among the clouds. Then there was the weapon.

It was too much to take in and Dagmar had the opposite effect on her. While Stojan could sum things up and reply with just a few kind words, Dagmar would expand on anything she would say and exhaust her further.

It was all too much and she found she just wanted to sleep.

As the night fell, Dagmar made his way to the pyramid as Anastazja waited in their camp.

Dagmar had made sure that Ana understood what they were to do and what his plan was. She was grateful for his interactions and uncharacteristic lack of embellishments, and he was equally as grateful for her lack of questions. Together they made a most silent pair as neither wanted to breach this current delicate balance.

She would not walk this night but instead just wait, and think, and stare at the great beam that now emanated from the point. As Dagmar had said, the pyramid did indeed now look black.

Ana continued to stare as she thought about Stojan. Would Dagmar simply emerge with him a few hours later? Were they too late and something terrible had happened, or was he even here?

The building was so large, so impressive and so imposing. And it had a saint inside.

If Stojan was captured and inside then what did they want with him? As far as she knew he was alive. If they had come to kill him then something changed because there was no indication of any bloodshed that day. What exactly could Dagmar do by himself? Surely her skill would have helped.

Clearly she had not listened to Dagmar's parting words instead spent the entire time worrying.

———

When morning came, there was no Dagmar. She checked the camp and surrounding area more than once and wasted much time since she had been periodically up almost every hour waiting and listening anyway. The closer they had moved towards the pyramid the more vague his information had been—or at least that was the way it felt.

She ate and pondered. How long should she wait before she should become concerned? Dagmar had almost lectured her about not coming with him and it took much convincing just to let her come with him so far. She had no intention of staying in Sedona while someone else just disappeared. But now he had disappeared. She contemplated a walk but did not want to abandon the camp and her thought was that he would return the second she would wander off. And this had been exactly how she had lost Stojan.

No, she would stay and wait—no matter how long it took.

Minutes became hours and hours became an afternoon. Surely the horses would need to roam, thought Anastazja. A light ride for each one to keep them from harm's way was the prudent thing to do. And with that she did indeed take each or for a ride before the sun went down. She was able to see the farmlands and houses up close now and was surprised at how many dwellings she saw.   This castle-pyramid was essentially surrounded by another city.   If there were hundreds or even thousands living in the pyramid then this was indeed a large city.   On her second ride she encountered more than farms.   This time she came across merchants selling some dry goods and even those offering a bit of food. In fact, she saw every kind of business save for one: an inn.

She imagined a decree preventing such a place from being established, but then thought it silly.

Her rides had essentially allowed her to circle the great pyramid and as the sun would only have an hour left, she turned to once again wait at the camp.

Upon approaching the outskirts of the pyramid, Ana again was taken aback by the enormousness of the structure.   It was so perfect and shiny and menacing.   It brought fear to her heart and she had thought many times upon the structure and the saint within.   From conversations with Dagmar, she'd learned that it was not like any of the other cathedrals she had seen before.   It was decorated lavishly and the inside was impossibly large.   Her mind chose not to fill in any other information—a fact she was most grateful for.

Anastazja was finally able to see first hand just what it would be like to enter the great pyramid.   Her first quest was being fulfilled.   Months ago she had hoped Stojan would indulge her and allow them to visit.   Now she was seeing the outside up close. She would have never imagined that this would be how her visit to the supposed pyramid would have occurred.   To her it was just a comment from an inebriated man trying to convince two travelers to hire him.   But it was all too real, and it was massive.

And the closer she moved to it, the more ominous it felt to her.
Once again the size played tricks with her eyes, and what she thought might be a doorway for a person to pass through, was actually a set of double openings that would allow an entire group of horses and carriages to ride through side-by-side. It made her wonder if the creature that lived here was also massive, but then remembered that if the saint were to take the form of a statue it would probably not be much larger than her.

The opening was so close and many other horses were tied as well.   It seemed to her that very little harm would come if she just waited in the same area for his return.   The ride had revealed that there was just one main entrance, and the existence of the horses there only solidified this point in her mind. If Dagmar did not make his way out shortly, she'd have but a quick ride in the darkness back to the camp. The moonlight and stars had help from the beam, so the ride would not be in total darkness.

She tied her horse—which happened to be Dagmar's—to the nearest post and stood beside it. The area had an entrance sloping down with paths leading in. That is to say, there was a path leading in and one out. What made them so distinct was that these paths actually moved. The ground itself was slowly sliding—one in one direction and one in the opposite. People stood upon it and allowed it to propel them. Some walked even though the ground moved and to her it was as if they ran. Sometimes someone would stumble as the moving ground met the ground that did not.

It was the most luxurious thing she had ever seen—a walk that did the walking for you.

Ana edged closer and closer to it as she tried to figure out the workings. Every so often she smiled at a passer-by and attempted not to look too amazed, lest they think she was a traveler from far. There seemed to be two groups of people who came and went—people who looked exhausted and downtrodden, and those dressed well who looked to be guards or mercenaries. The former tended to carry things in crates; the latter was more apt to make eye contact with her. She imagined that hundreds, if not thousands, lived in the magical castle. The amount of food needed would have to be immense and being hand-delivered like this would simply not make sense, yet she did not see any carriages of food. She assumed some was raised indoors somehow.

Before she could turn away, she was politely bumped by a number of people using the path that went inward and as she tried not to make too much of a fuss, she found herself now among them. And effort to walk back away through them was met with resistance and stern glares. She was now riding the moving ground with them. Taking a deep breath she looked ahead and watched as they all sloped inward. Instinctively she placed her hand on the black railing only to find that it moved as well. The Amirans had thought of everything.

She looked up and saw hundreds of rectangles that softly glowed. She wondered if these were the kind that were cold or the kind that had burned Dagmar. In her mind, she reserved these dangerous lights as only being the ones atop the pyramid.

Proud that she stumbled very little, she exited the moving walk and continued to be part of a dense group moving inward. The path opened to a wide hallway and there were people crouched down. She was certain they were panhandlers wanting a coin here and there to improve their fortune.

It was all very big.

Unfortunately, as she passed through the large doors she happened upon more than one statue that was indeed great in size—probably almost three meters high. Two flanked those who entered and they looked inhuman. Unlike other statues she had seen before, these were painted black and looked very much like strong men wearing skirts made of leather or metal slats. They held spears that were resting upon the floor. The most remarkable thing about them was not their size, accoutrements or skin color. Instead—thought Ana—it was their inhuman heads. It was not as if they were wearing helmets; these men had the heads of an unknown animal in place of their human heads. The snout was elongated —far past that of any wolf or dog she had seen before. The ears were also long, thin and pointed upward. The facial features were perfect and as disturbing as it was for her, there was a certain harmony as if it made sense. If one of these came to life before her she would have been terribly afraid. In fact, she stared at them as they passed through to the point of almost bumping into others passing them by.

She wondered if these were depictions of the true nature of the saints.

She walked up a ramp and then moved to some stairs. She would turn back shortly—as soon as she could breathe a bit and step aside from the influx of people entering. The interior was lit by many tiny points of light in both the ceiling as well as posts along the way. Some posts produced light while others did not. She did not know if this was intentional or if some of the Amiran tec had failed after so many millennia.

What clearly hadn't failed was some sort of system of moving air. Barely inside the pyramid, she was rewarded with strong, constant gusts of cooler air. In fact it was so cool as to be slightly uncomfortable on her skin.

Ahead were small structures within that almost looked like a village and just as they were rounding a corner she was finally able to see some of the actual interior. It stretched for hundreds of meters all around, and thousands of colored lights flickered and flashed and twinkled. The lights she thought were fireflies on the water conveyance that brought them to Amira so many years ago were put to shame as these were many times brighter, many times more active and many, many times as abundant. They had a way of demanding one's attention as if each and every light twinkled to beckon her to look closer.

People milled about below and walked through the aisles upon aisles of tables and boxes from which the lights emanated. The people seemed to walk slowly, look upon the lights, then continue walking. It reminded her of the candle-lighting ceremonies she had been told about that occurred within the cathedrals. In fact she participated in one at the small cathedral of Saint John on behalf of Fox and the other departed. But here no one was lighting candles. They were simply looking at the lights.

Again, she almost bumped into another visitor as the scenes were so transfixing. She was deep inside the pyramid-castle and the foreboding continued. She looked to the stairs heading down and from that vantage point she took in the entire opening of the pyramid. It was filled with the boxes and people and everyone was bathed in the ever-changing lights.

Or so she thought. She panned her eyes around and realized that she was just looking at a small portion of the actual building and that this was a section of the lower floor as seen from above. She was two stories up and now at the top of stairs that resembled the moving walkway. She grabbed onto the nearby railing as the opening gave her a little vertigo. She stood and watched as people moved onto the stairs and then stood still. Though they did not move their legs, they all moved down in a very orderly and consistent fashion. Looking closer she saw that—just like the walkway—the stairs moved of their own accord and were protected by a glass barrier on either side. Ana felt exposed as she just stared and marveled. Each step was just emerging from the balcony at the top of the stairs. One after another they emerged in perfect precision. Each star had teeth like a gear and meshed with the one in front of it, and the one behind it.

She had to try it.

Watching one or two people step onto it at a time, she was able to see just how easy it was. After a minute of this she knew what to do.

Then she was on it—and smiling broadly. It was so gentle and solid. She expected it to bounce for some reason, but it most certainly did not. Her sheath rubbed against the glass as she rode it down. So much of the expansive area could be seen now and little of it made sense. She affirmed that cathedrals were the most confusing of any building she could ever enter. Amazing and frightening at the same time. From the thin tables along the wall to the sculptures and sitting areas, to the boxes with lights and...

That was when she saw the pointing.

At the bottom of the stairs were three men. They were trying to hide their interest in her but they stood out because one of them pointed directly at her. She reflexively looked behind her and back again. The stairs were so long that she was able to tell that indeed it was she that they pointed at, not the group of four men at the top of the stairs.

She looked back again. Scanning the expanse she looked down—it was probably too far to jump, and she would land on unsuspecting people. People were packed in behind her and there were some in front as well.

"Ana!"

It was Dagmar. He was among those at the bottom and he looked very uncomfortable. His stance was that of someone who had something sharp pressing against their lower back. The man holding him from behind reinforced that perception. He mouthed a word to her over and over but she could not hear it.

"Run."

She wanted to run towards them—to skewer the men near him and then take him away.

Instead she stood still and waited as the stairs brought her to them. Those in front of her cleared out and left an open path for the last few meters as they scattered. The crowd was starting to notice the commotion.

It was unfortunate for the men who did not realize just how fast Ana could draw her sword—which just happened to be all of them. Before they could react, she had leapt from the moving stairs and impaled the largest of the three. The metal went into his chest followed immediately by her boots. The other man turned as the one holding Dagmar did nothing. Barely landing, she pulled the sword from the now horizontal man and swept it up and fit it between the man and Dagmar. It bit into his arm and took it off at the elbow as the other dropped the dagger it was pressing into his back.

He looked at her, not in horror but in complete surprise—as one looks at a seemingly gentle animal that has demonstrated not only unexpected quickness, but a level of lethality that should be impossible for such a creature.

Dagmar's surprise was not unlike the man that was just restraining him, but as he slowly turned he was just starting to realize how close the sword swipe had come to the back of his head. Reflexively, he touched his hair as he backed up.

The man remaining in service started to run and Ana glanced at the two fallen men to try to assess what was to be done next. A woman screamed as she saw the carnage and the crowd erupted in an ever-expanding circle around her as their awareness of the situation grew.

"No no! You shouldn't have come."

Though his words were fast, he did not reprimand. He looked grateful but also sad and scared.

"Dagmar, what has taken you so long?"

He stared at her hair—a mixture of blonde and red now—and tried to compose both his response and his perception. They glanced around as they hurriedly spoke.

"Ana I know I told you not to come. And I know that I am delayed, and…"

The men at the top of the stairs were talking with others now but did not move to come down them. Dagmar rolled his eyes as his brain struggled with conflicting thoughts.

"You are right to come of course. They were right that you would."

"Would? Would what?"

Dagmar was being unusually still and Ana was perched to grab him by the shoulder to pull him along.

"Ana."

She stopped and looked at him. To onlookers it was as if she was about to strike him down; to her it was just her stance.

"There is no escape. They have Stojan."

Her sword felt heavy just then and she drew her brows together.

"Where Dagmar? Why are you here then? Were you trying to escape?"

She glanced again up the empty stairs—the men remained in place, but no one was allowed to use the moving machine it seemed.

"Ana, I am sorry."

"What? What Dagmar?"

His stance was wrong. He was not trying to run. She was conflicted and knew what not to do. The man without an arm started to moan on the floor now.

Dagmar looked at the man and then the floor in front of him. They were now surrounded by at least twenty men and closing in quickly. Dagmar was not moving and had accepted his fate it seemed. Anastazja was not so accepting and would have willingly cut each and every one of them down. But alas Stojan was here, and Dagmar was no longer willing to fight. Something was not right.

In short order they had totally surrounded them and moved them down the large aisle.

She knew not what to do and the experience was as if she hovered above herself. Only the ringing and the tweets of the machines around her could be heard and the lights could be seen as she walked with the men in a dream-like state. She wanted only to see Stojan and they were obviously taking her there.

Eventually they entered into the largest area she had yet seen. She looked up and around and it was then that she knew she was directly under the very tip of the pyramid. Ana scanned along the walls and realized that the great castle had perhaps as many as thirty floors with walkways along each floor. A tremendous amount of space was simply open. The construction boggled her mind as she continued onward in her ethereal state. Her last look was at the very ceiling where it looked like it was a special balcony of sorts.

They stopped.   Shaking off the dream-state, she realized she had sheathed her sword and did not remember what had happened to the moaning man on the floor.   Things were eerily quiet now and she could not even hear the faint noises of the machines.   It was just the two of them surrounded by a very large group of men.   They seemed to be escorting them as much as they were being protective of something, or someone.

At any moment she expected Stojan to appear with a man holding a sword to his back—or worse.   They gathered at the base of a feature of the large room.   A large doorway exited and three separate rooms were off to one side.   The scale of everything was an order of magnitude larger as the hallway could be used to drive entire carriages through it.   The rooms to the side were the size of great dining halls and she was sure that there was even more that she could not see.   Everything was so large and oversized.   So much space was wasted.

Even the feature that sat on a great chair was massive.   It looked like the dog-faced guards that flanked her when she first entered.   It seemed that the entire interior was designed around the gaudy thing and it filled at least two stories just sitting in its ornate black and gold chair.   They gathered in a seating area near the oversized feet.

Finally coming out of her daze, she noticed the man standing near them.   He was dressed to match everything else, but his ornate and flamboyant outfit was in stark contrast to his demeanor.   Looking tired and injured, he stood not so upright but was doing his best to present an authoritative visage.   She thought he was perhaps injured as he was using his ornate staff for more support than he was trying to let on.   He'd clearly been through something serious.

That was when she realized just where he might have sustained his injuries.

Stojan.

She shook her head and brightened.   Ana looked around excitedly— assuming that he would be there somewhere.   Unfortunately in the huge mis-shaped room, he was not to be found.   The apparent leader was now gesturing to some of the men.

"Everyone is out—all of them!"

He flailed one of his arms angrily and about half of the men broke up and left. She craned her head back and forth, and stole glances at Dagmar. He looked so sad and resolute now. What had happened? Reacting to the situation was difficult as she was torn between protecting Dagmar, being worried for Stojan and absorbing all the absurd sights and sounds. She just wanted to run and to take them with her. She'd just killed a man and hadn't even thought much of it. But now she was frozen with indecision. She couldn't act in either direction because of her conflicting emotions. And Dagmar was no help.

As the men spread out, they started yelling in all directions. They needed no other directive and apparently had done this before.

She stood and stared at the man in front of her. He was clearly the leader and dressed in an animal helmet that resembled the large feature just behind him. He looked like a miniature of it.

Unceremoniously, the man walked backwards and sat down on a raised square. Ana realized that it was a sitting area that was much more comfortable than it looked. He held onto the staff and just looked down.

"Dagmar, what is happening here?"

He turned to her slowly and with some uncertainty replied.

"An audience."

"A what? An audience?"

He looked around at the men that continued to surround them, to the leader who sat and to the great feature they gathered around.

Ana thought about her chances of attacking the men around her and running. It seemed Dagmar would not come with her if she tried. And where was Stojan?

After an eternity, the man stood up again and told all but three of them to leave. She watched as they left and positioned themselves far away—on balconies, at the tops of the great stairs and in the center of the room with all of the blinking lights. Something was going to happen.

The remaining men eyed Ana but did not draw weapons. They looked frightened, but not of her.

"On your knees."

A man shoved Dagmar down to his knees and he easily complied, as if this was a ritual he'd been privy to.

Ana, however, did not comply. She was more confused than defiant. And her constant looking to Dagmar for cues was exhausting and frustrating.

A man reached for her shoulder but she violently shrugged him off.

Dagmar looked over to her and once again said a word without speaking it.

"*Run.*"

She shook her head and whispered a reply.

"No. No, I want to see Stojan."

That was when she heard the laughing. It was not in the great hall, nor from one of the nearby men who now all knelt suddenly. It was not from the leader dressed so oddly. It was from all around her and it was deep and bellowing—yet somehow hollow.

She looked up eventually to the giant statue that sat in a black ornate chair. And it was looking at her.

Without moving anything other than its head, it spoke. She grabbed her sword hilt and was the only one standing. It was frightening.

"Welcome."
She looked at the leader, then Dagmar. They all were transfixed by it. She drew her blade and no one stopped her. Ana was apparently the only one who had not witnessed it coming to life.

It smiled.

"You surely do not need that. Put it away before you injure another of my followers."

Dagmar glanced at her through the corner of his eye, but kept his main focus upon the great statue. His reverence for it disturbed her. The leader knelt with much difficulty.

"If you do not show reverence then you will not see Stojan."

Still looking at Dagmar she took a knee and allowed the sheath to drag upon the floor in the process. The floor was soft and had perfectly drawn patterns upon it. There were no seams that she could see, but it was clearly a cushioned material. There was no sound in the great hall or even from anything in the entire building that she could see. She was unable to understand how they had cleared out so many people so quickly.

"Where is he? I kneel now. Bring him!"

Her defiance surprised even Dagmar. She was nonplussed by what was occurring. He looked at her and her red hair.

"Fetch me the blasphemers."

The leader waved his staff immediately upon hearing this from the saint and the men reacted quickly. She stayed kneeling as eventually a group was brought in. They looked upon it with horror as it turned their head to them. A woman screamed a meek scream as she saw it move. Apparently the people being brought in had never seen such a sight. Ana had never considered how much or how little the saints inhabited statues to incite awe and fear. This one kept quite hidden, she mused. Why such a grand presentation was hidden made no sense. The people being brought in would probably be converted on the spot—yet he hid.

Once they were assembled around them she looked at some of the faces and most of them looked at her with recognition. A redheaded girl with a sword was a sight they had all been told about. It was her time now to do what she needed to do.
She stood and yelled as she ran toward the thing. She didn't notice the man standing with the help of his staff as he shook his head to unseen men behind her.

Within seconds she was at the base of the thing and swung her sword against its ankle. Amazed gasps escaped many in the crowd as she did this which obscured the defeated warning from Dagmar.

"Nooo."

Her first instinct was to provide a slice and then a return strike, and this saved her considerable pain and damage to her arm as she quickly found that this was made of something other than stone. It was not solid, yet was like hitting another sword and it rang like a bell. She barely held on to her sword as it vibrated and shook on the upswing out and away. The pain was visible on her otherwise focused face.

The leader looked shocked at the occurrence but ultimately took no action. Nor did anyone save one—the great statue.

It laughed.

"I cannot be destroyed, little one."

She backed up and pointed her still shaking arm at him.

"You have been destroyed before! And you will be!"

"I have not been destroyed. You are mistaken. I am clearly here and always will be."

He panned his head around those assembled below him and then looked back down to her. She looked around at this and all were on their knees save for her.

"Would you like to try again?"

The saint was beyond arrogant to the point of serenity. He had accomplished something that required her help and planned it most excellently.

A statue of this size should not be able to be destroyed by a sword and she knew that, but it seemed like the right thing to do. She had to do something and was the only one willing to, so she believed. But now, all she had done was scratch some black paint from the monstrosity that was apparently made of metal.

Dagmar continued to look at the floor. The leader still looked injured but relieved while his men looked impressed. The many villagers that had been forced to assemble did not look at the saint—they looked at her. Each one had the look of disappointment and defeat. Each one looked as if their only hope had been dissolved in one moment. And it had. He had done it and done it well.

"Did you want to see Stojan? If so I would do as you are told, as you have demonstrated how powerless you are. Otherwise, I will just have him executed."

She swallowed hard and looked at Dagmar. He did not meet her eyes.

As her hand released her sword she re-gripped instinctively and sheathed it. It seemed her will for the moment had given up but her reflexes did not.

The great dog-like head addressed the crowd and the men shepherding them.

"They may leave now. Go and spread the word and talk no more of any nonsense."

The villagers left and Ana could not help but meet the eyes of more than one of them as they did. A young disheveled girl looked at her in a way she'd never been looked at before—with need and sadness. It made her doubt herself and—not for the first time—reality.

Once the people were disbursed, most of the men returned. Ana just stood awkwardly as she waited. She flexed her hand as she was in considerable pain from the strike.

"Bring the cage."

This time it was the leader that spoke for the first time. His voice was weak and not at all what she expected.

Men wheeled in a large cage that could contain a horse—although it was perhaps not tall enough. However, it certainly could hold a large animal, or a number of people. Dagmar looked up with added interest upon seeing this. For the first time she thought she saw something positive cross his face. On top of the cage were linens that were brightly colored.

She shook her head as she looked from Dagmar to the leader to the great statue.

"I'm not going in there."

"Yes of course Ana."

It was Dagmar that spoke and interrupted her. He was standing now and the look in his eyes told her to comply.

"He learned early. We *can* trust the Sage of Sedona."

The great statue was smiling a toothy smile and seemed quite pleased with himself now. If it had any doubts about Dagmar, they were dissolving as they spoke; however, he was still cautious.

"I think it is best if you accompany her."

Instead of objecting, Dagmar walked to her side as they opened the giant cage.

They placed them in, but first removed her sword from her. Dagmar did his best to comfort her while at the same time backing her into the cage with him—thus doing the job of the men for them.

"Dagmar! What has gotten into you!?" She shook his hand off of her arm with some anger. He just continued to push her into the cage and she almost stumbled.

The men slammed the door behind them and then went to work with a rather thick looking lock and chain. He just continued to motion to her to calm down and keep quiet.

"They took my sword. What am I supposed to do now?!"

"Of course they took your sword."

He spoke out of the corner of his mouth while smiling at the men. He was managing her and displaying a compliant persona—ever the showman.

After giving the chain and lock a good tug the man backed away. Dagmar whispered to Ana while still smiling.

"You still have your backpack."

"Yes what of it…"

"They would have taken it too but didn't notice because it is so small and.."

"We are still in a cage Dagmar!"

Though she was outraged she managed to keep her voice down as well. It was then that she almost lost her footing—because the cage moved.

He grabbed her arm gently and spoke.

"Ana, just do as I say here and listen, please."

She relaxed and tried to push all of the thoughts into a small corner of her mind so she could focus on the multitude of problems at hand. She had never felt so out of control. First the capture, now this. And now she didn't have her sword. And where was Stojan?

She grabbed a bar and held on as she listened. The cage was moving and turning slightly. A little of the linens was hanging down in the back now.

"Dagmar are we moving?"

He spoke quickly and clandestinely to her.

"Yes. Yes, please listen. They are raising the cage. I have seen them do this before, but I was never in it. You must not reveal anything you know. He only knows what he is told. Remember that, and what he knows all of the saints will know."

She nodded and watched as the surroundings changed to reflect the height. She could see more of the surroundings and the inside of the pyramid. It was truly empty of people now and only a handful of the men along with the leader remained.

"I think the quieter you remain, the more he will reveal to us."

"Well, what difference does that make now?"

Dagmar looked at her and for the first time his eyes showed hope. "I think soon I will have something to show you."

With that they were now at eye level with the great head. It spoke again in its hollow bellows.

"Ahh. There you are."

Ana glared but did not speak.

"Thank you for your demonstration, little one. It was exactly what I needed to quell the uprising."

"What do you mean?"

Her tone did not challenge but was just curious.

"There are many followers that believe in nonsense—nonsense such as the existence of other powerful beings such as myself. Imagine."

Ana noted that he could easily reach over and presumably crush the cage along with them in it. It frightened her, so she concentrated on the dead eyes and then his head moved. Ana did not see it as a thing, but rather a puppet moved by a being she could not imagine. She replied.

"But there are."

She was ready to flinch, or even hold on to the thick bars, lest he backhand the cage and instantly kill them. Instead he just maintained his demeanor.

"Of course."

"What?"

"Of course there are. How could Stojan have killed one of us if there was only me."

She was confused. He had maintained a very stern rule over his followers and it was clear that the "blasphemy" was that they believed there were other saints.

"Then why…"

"We are now alone. I'm fully aware of the others. And what Stojan has done."

"Where is he! You said I could see him!"

"Yes I did."

It was so calm and even-tempered. There was no grandstanding or threatening. He was confident in his supremacy over them. She once had thoughts of traveling the country and smashing any and all statues she saw. Things were a bit more complicated than that.

"And?"

"I lied."

She looked at Dagmar then back to the face as it swayed too and fro—or rather, she did.

"Stojan is not here.   No, something unfortunate happened.   The men I sent to capture were themselves taken over by others. An ambush upon ambush upon ambush."

Though he related bad news, he still maintained his even demeanor.

"This sort of thing is expected now that we all can communicate so efficiently.   When we all seek the same goal it is not surprising that we eventually intersect. But I now use this to my advantage."

"What do you mean?"

"Well, now no one has Stojan—I am told—and none of us has learned anything new—until now."

He smiled and she was sure that if he breathed he would have exhaled upon her.

"That you are important—important to him that is. So though no one has Stojan I have the next best thing: you."

She folded her arms and was sure the movement was going to make her sick. Dagmar continued to be silent.

"So, though none of us knows where Stojan is, once he learns that you are here he will come for you and I will have both you and Stojan.   And I possess the greatest fortress of them all. Do you see these walls?"

Again she expected it to lift its hand and point, but it did not.

"Along them are hundreds and hundreds of sleeping quarters.   I have been amassing an army and this army resides within my pyramid, while the villagers toil and provide food and services at some distance.   And yes I know that the others know this as well.   It is an odd game we play now as nothing is hidden—thanks to Stojan."

"Dagmar, did you know this?"

She turned to him and asked him incredulously, as if she was watching a great performance rather than conversing with someone. In a way, she was doing both. Before he could answer the saint continued.

"Because of his dispatching of St. John, things changed greatly."

Dagmar moved his hand in a circular motion, as if to prod Anastazja to keep him talking. She picked up on the suggestion.

"What changed? What could have changed by one death?"

She looked over at Dagmar who seemed very pleased with her question.

"Oh, much has changed. We hear each other so clearly now. We are almost as one again, save for the one who flickers…"

He was obviously leaving something out, and that was clear even to Ana. She moved her hand in the same circular motion as Dagmar had, and then realized he would not understand it. Dagmar grunted at this.

"And…?"

"And the one who trapped us here."

For the first time he did not seem amused.

"I will keep you alive—for if I do not they will know, and they will let Stojan know."

"Why do you tell me all of this?"

"Why would I not tell you? The more you understand, the less likely you are to do something stupid. And if you do something stupid I will have to kill you. I've killed so many of you. But it is you who we are talking about. Yes. You behave and then Stojan will eventually come here. Then I will have you both. Then I will increase my followers many, many fold—and with it an army. Eventually I will have all of Amira."

She sat down on the floor of the cage and it absorbed her quietly. The saint was considering his words and thinking out loud. She was no longer part of the conversation but just an ornament he looked at as he spoke. She shifted her weight as the floor had a protrusion or two and it had poked into her buttock.

Anastazja had had enough, however. Stojan was not here and the saint used the lie to trap her. Dagmar's behavior did not help. She was inside a cage now—suspended from a deadly height—inside an unimaginably large and fortified structure. Dagmar was complacent and Stojan was gone. And this saint was indestructible. It all made her doubt anything and everything she knew.

And now she had to relieve herself.

"Dagmar…"

She stood up and shifted her weight back and forth.

"I have to…"

He drew his brows together and then understood.

"Oh! That's perfect."

"What? Dagmar you do not understand."

"Oh but I do. Yes! Tell the saint that you have to and then pull those linens down."

"Dagmar I don't want to do that in front of you while we are…"

"Trust me, Ana."

She yelled to the saint that she had to relieve herself and in no uncertain terms told him she didn't want him watching her. He seemed nonplussed.

She carefully pulled the linens down. They were made of an amazing fabric that was thin but let very little light through. When done, she turned away from Dagmar and started to undo her belt.

"Oh no. No no Ana."

She turned, annoyed. He waved her over to the back where he had sat for most of the time. Dagmar ran his hands up the bars to where they met the top of the cage. She was sure she heard a click and became frightened as the back side of the gate started to fall inward. Surely the cage would topple and they would fall to their deaths.

"Dagmar!"

He smiled and held it in place. It wasn't the outside of the cage, but an inner wall that had been painted to look like a set of bars. He then pointed at the floor at a small half square.

"It is a door, Ana."

"I do not wish to fall! I cannot climb down."

"No, it is a door to a small area underneath. Once you enter the bottom of the cage I will fold this wall over it and to all observers it will look like you have disappeared."

"And... And then what?"

"I will get them to lower the cage. They would have to let me out anyway as I will offer my services to fix the light."

"I thought you fixed it?"

Looking slightly sheepish, he responded.

"Well, my fix quickly failed. I realized what I did wrong the last time. I was so angry at burning myself I just left it and they all believed it was brighter—through sheer faith."

"What of the saint? Surely he himself checked on it."

Dagmar looked introspective just then—as if he had a secret but by mentioning it, the reality of it would be dispelled.

"Ana I have a theory."

She looked behind her and turned to him with a frightened look on her face.

"Dagmar, hurry, at any second he will reach over and remove the drapery!"

"That is my theory Ana."

She turned her hand upwards in a plea to get him to continue.

"I do not think he can move."

She dropped her hands as Dagmar nodded as he spoke.

"I think he can only move his head. I think that is why they always take great pains to remove all from the building when he speaks. And why he used this cage to bring us to eye level."

Her mouth was open. It made her angry and happy at the same time.

"Now, please go into the area below. You will know when to come out. And when you do, please be careful."

Though her bladder provided urgency, she did indeed open the small door and enter the chamber below. There was ample room to lay and a few tiny holes let a little light in. She was prone and felt defenseless. If the cage came crashing down she would be killed instantly. Suddenly, she felt as if the ceiling of the small face was closing in on her. The air was hard to inhale and had an odd smell. In seconds she would suffocate! It was a horrible decision to enter the tiny area and she would perish in...

"To all observers."

She realized where she heard Dagmar say the exact phrase—when giving performances to the children. Her eyes were tightly closed and her concentration was split between fearing the fall, dealing with the enclosed space and thinking she would just relieve herself where she lay.

"What is this?"

It was the saint, and he sounded confused. For all of his power, he saw the world through two oversized eyes many meters in the air. And it seemed that for all of their otherworldly intelligence they had little common sense.

Dagmar's voice was more muffled now due to the fact that he used only sound, while the saints could be heard in a room—and in one's head.

After a short wait, there were some bounces and mechanical vibrations. The cage was indeed being lowered and finally it hit the floor with a thud. Then she heard yelling and the sounds of the large chain being removed unceremoniously from the door along with the large lock.

"I do not know! She made her way down somehow. She leapt to the saint's lap and then made her way down!"

It was Dagmar and he was an excellent liar. The footsteps above her were hard and heavy and it sounded like he was being forcibly removed. She continued to hear much talking and less arguing.

After a short while she was reminded that she had an urgency to take care of. It would not do for her to have an accident in her clothing, especially in the cramped space.

She hoped the door above her would open. She pushed and it did not. She pushed again and realized that the special wall was now on top of the small door. Her panic would have gotten the best of her had she not found a similar thin door at the back of the compartment. It was now visible in the enhanced lighting. Her heart was beating fast and she squeezed a latch experimentally. The door was about to fall open but she held it awkwardly with her arm. She sighed a deep breath and listened intently in the odd position she was forced to exist in.

Dagmar had said that she would know. But when? She waited as her bladder and arm complained to her. It seemed like forever and soon she would just simply have no more control over either. She would have to give in to both momentarily. It was just when she was ready to give up that it seemed to get darker within her prison. She instinctively allowed the door to drop a little and it was almost as dark outside of the cage. Experimentally, she allowed the door to open more and finally allowed it to open completely.

It was painful to shimmy out of the door and she did her best not to shout loudly in pain. No one was there to stop her. In the distance she heard yelling, and her eyes took in the relatively brighter surroundings. None of the points of light that normally illuminated the interior were lit. The only lighting was provided by numerous points of light nearby that were red. She looked around quickly to take it all in and heard yelling all around her. The saint made no sound as of yet and she thought this odd. His minion was gone along with everyone else. She decided she would trace her steps and in doing so remembered the place at which she'd struck the saint's ankle. That was when she saw something she thought she'd never see again: her sword. It had been propped up right next to the area she had barely scratched. Once again something made her happy and sad at the same time. They obviously decided it would be placed on display to show that he could simply not be harmed. They were probably planning many things like this to cause awe and coercion throughout the ranks of believers and non-believers alike. She ran to it and was stopped by her intense desire.

Terrified and angry she did something that could cost her everything.

She squatted and relieved herself upon the foot of the great saint. It was satisfying in so many ways and even if he struck her down then, she would have still enjoyed it. No retribution came as the distant yelling continued. Finally when done she grabbed her sword and sheathed it. She was renewed and would find Dagmar. She knew that his desire was probably for her to escape under the cover of the eerie darkness but she had to find him. Unfortunately, she did not have to wait long as she was witness to something that broke her heart.

Much yelling occurred and at first she could not determine from whence it came. Finally she looked straight up at the tiny balcony that Dagmar had described as a room of lights. Someone was struggling with a group and much yelling was heard.

"NO!"

It was a voice she did not recognize as a figure plummeted from the area. It descended quickly, only to land atop the cage and then bounce onto the floor.

Broken and contorted, and covered in seared skin, it was Dagmar and he was not long for this world.

She stood only a meter from him and she crouched down to caress his bloody face.

He took a deep noisy breath.

"No, do not speak Dag,…"

"It is done. It is done Ana. The light is as bright as ever."

She whispered her response as she continued stroking the hair from his face. Thin wisps of smoke arose from his clothing.

"But you said you would extinguish it?"

"It is as bright and hot as it ever has been Ana."

He smiled despite his massive injuries.

"Oh no. No Dagmar. Please do not leave me."

She cried and held his hand. She no longer cared about time, or being recaptured.   She no longer cared about any who dwelt within the pyramid. She no longer feared the saints. Her eyes were wide open as she cried and she felt the warm tears roll down her cheeks. Her boots and the floor were covered with a spattering of his blood. Ana brushed his face one last time.

She stood. She was no longer in a daze. Whether something was surreal or not, it became clear what was happening and what she must do.

She ran for the exit. She would not draw her sword, nor would she pay any attention to yelling. The moving stairs had stopped and she ran up them without regard for whether they would spin her in place or suddenly move downward. Three, four, sometimes five stairs were taken at a time as she ran up them. In moments she was at the top and had to slow lest she keep leaping upward with no more stairs.   Continuing to retrace and make her way through the red lighting, she passed more than one of the large guards she'd seen before. She paid none of them any mind. None would be as fast, none would have reacted in time and none would remain without a hole in their chest if they stopped her. All of her energy was put forth into this rapid travel to find the exit and finally she found it.

Running to either side of the now frozen walkways, she made her way to a set of double doors.   They were closed and a man stood in front of them.   He looked confused, but not menacing.   She stopped a few safe meters from him. It was just the two of them in the huge hallway. She stopped and caught her breath as she watched what he would do next. The two stood and watched each other. The man's focus went from this new person that had appeared to the lights and then the doors. From what she could see he was not armed. It was then that the lighting changed— gone was the eerie red and now present was the familiar torches of varying sizes. They both blinked as a click was heard behind him. The doors were opening.

She smiled.

As he was about to stand in the ever-widening opening to block her, she put her hand on her hilt and shook her head. He watched as the crimson hair shook back and forth with it. Her eyes remained on him as he froze.

Unfortunately, he did indeed attempt to block her exit and as she entered the outer areas he grasped his throat in an attempt to stop the bleeding. He had not seen her draw her sword as she passed. When he pulled his hand away there was the tiniest of blotches on his palm.   And that was the last day he spent in service to the pyramid and the saint that dwelt within.

To her surprise the horse was still tethered. It was unhitched and she was mounted before she knew it. She rode swiftly to her camp.

Though she did hear an unintelligible shout, she paid it no mind. In a very short time she reached the outer farming areas and the location of her camp. The cool wind was refreshing to her as she stopped her horse —not at the camp, but at the group of people in the road.

They turned to her and looked upon her with shock. They blocked the way and she just wanted to leave. There was nothing here for her now and Stojan was still out there somewhere. The people did not look menacing but instead looked exhausted and poor. They were both adults and children. She had no anger towards them, but did indeed want to pass. One of the children pointed and this caused a number of gasps to erupt from the crowd.

"It is her."

She recognized them now. They were a good portion of the group that had been forcibly assembled in the pyramid and this was the worst thing that could have happened to the saint—she was seen to be alive and well.

"You live?"

She brushed the hair from her head and took a breath. Her horse was most grateful for the break. The group started to move towards her—to surround her from all sides. This made her uncomfortable as she searched their faces. She would have cut them down to escape but it looked as if they meant no harm. Even if they did they were apparently unarmed and looked as if they had no hope or energy left. Until now.

Lacking any other options or even a route to leave, she decided to speak to them.

"Yes, I live, but my dear friend is dead. His last act was to return The Light of Luxor to its full glory…"

She thought quickly.

"…as a signal to all that it is we who hold the power. It is not the saints."

In concert, they all turned to the pyramid in the distance, and the extra-bright beam that emanated from it. She believed her own words as they were essentially true.

"Does his power not grow stronger?"

She answered the woman in the crowd.

"No. He is weak and cannot even move. What he has done will be his undoing. I will find my father and destroy this saint."

Yet more gasps—this time she knew not why.

"You are indeed The Sunflower. Look at her hair."

She shook her head slightly to bring some into view, and noticed that her discussion had apparently calmed her down enough to allow it to revert to her natural blonde, before their eyes. Even in the low lighting it was apparent.

"Sunflower."

She would normally have been embarrassed at the attention, but so filled with purpose was she that it came easily now.

"I am. And I will destroy this saint. Each and every one of them will die. We will be free to live our lives as we are meant to be."

More than one was touching and petting her horse. She was hungry and thirsty, and did not know how long the horse would stay at ease before it was spooked. She needed to end the conversation and be on her way.

"Tell them… tell everyone what has happened. Tell them that The Sage of Sedona has brightened the light as a signal to all. Tell them that I have escaped…"

She thought for a moment. This was her chance to send a message to Stojan.

"Tell them that The Sunflower lives and now searches for Stojan."

With that, she pulled her horse gently from side to side—as if to signal that she was leaving. It worked as they pulled away.

She added a parting instruction.

"And stay as far away from the pyramid lest you lose your lives."

The rag tag group watched her depart. There was much talk of what happened and the news would spread quickly. These people had been the most vocal about the rumors of the one named 'Sunflower' and her quest to destroy the saints. The word of Stojan destroying Saint John had spread quickly—just as the news of their fighting prowess had. But as rumors do, the news changed and flowed to fit the narrative of those who spread it. Some said that there was a great man touring Amira in a quest to destroy the saints; others said a young girl with magical powers was the one who was destined to do the same. And it was said that she had a companion that was just as powerful. Some said it was her own father. Regardless of the form the rumor took, it spread like wildfire and one thing always remained constant: someone was bringing destruction to the saints.

The gathering in the pyramid was the saint's attempt to quash any remaining hope surrounding his fortress. All others had been forced into submission and this last group would turn the tide for him. They would spread the word of his new capture, and the promise of him containing the now-roaming Stojan. He would have them both, and had displayed as much to them. His generosity in letting them live was his way of demonstrating his power and influence. He needed them to tell those in the surrounding area of what he had accomplished.

His own bishop had failed miserably when their ambush had been taken over by a surprisingly large force from the north. Many men had been sacrificed to allow him to escape and bring word to his saint. All that remained were a handful of men and his minion. The game had changed and this new open communication made it quite difficult to encroach upon the spheres of influence of the other saints. Until now, his relative isolation and great structure had allowed him to enforce the fact that he was the only saint. Some saints did the same while others were happy to allow it to be known. There was so much distance between them that this mattered very little. And for the most part they only had glimpses of what each other was doing. Things had changed considerably with the destruction of one of them. Now the awareness was constant and almost maddening. It was a bit like the old times before they had come through the door. But they still could not communicate, only listen in.

The most important change was the hardest to adjust to.

There were no more secrets.

———

Ana rode into the night—not to the camp but to the area described by Dagmar. Tears again filled her eyes as she thought about what she'd just witnessed. She rode hard and without regard for her or the horse's safety and in a matter of minutes reached a low outcropping in the sand and rock. In the moon and starlight she could see the grayish platform. Immediately she felt disappointment—as if the building was missing. As she became confused, she noticed a bit of the drab paint was missing from a circular area. It was a door. It reminded her of the unusual doors on the water conveyance she had rode within many years ago. Experimentally, she tried the wheel that was inset and hidden partially by the semi-darkness. It turned. When it would turn no more she pulled and was rewarded by a circular hatch. It was a dark tunnel. Had she not been so absolutely angry she would have been terrified to descend it. One step after another were placed onto a ladder along the side of the tunnel and she did not care if the door closed behind her and sealed her in the metal tomb. She felt as if she would rip the door off of its hinges in anger if it did.

At the bottom of the ladder she came upon a similar door and found a square next to it that had sustained some sort of damage. She tried the inset wheel again and was rewarded with a door that opened slowly and heavily. She entered a small room and was again reminded of the water conveyance. Though not as crammed, the furnishings were similar, spartan and mostly grey. In this case, they were a reddish grey as round lights along the walls were lit. She was reminded of the machines in the pyramid that tweeted at her as she approached flat structures that beckoned her with lights and sounds.

As she approached the row of squares and lights something moved. She inhaled as it gently fell to the floor. It was a tiny, brightly-colored sheet of paper. She picked it up and it was no larger than her hand. Turning it back and forth she saw that one side had a shiny strip on top and the other side hand handwriting. She recognized it as Dagmar's.

Placing the paper on the desk area, she moved to a closer view. It seemed that he left exact instructions on how to operate things. Having dropped the paper she read it now and became impatient at all the notes. In fact, there were twenty or more of these kinds of square notes all over the desk area. They stuck to the things that looked like windows and hung on by some unknown means.

She was in a hurry. She felt a pressure to act, to react and make them pay. She could not decipher note upon note, and now she had dropped one.

Her hands into fists, she was about to slam them down when she noticed the arrows. There were three notes. They were written in jet black, thick ink. They read respectively, "This," "Then this," and "Final."

She didn't see the delicate keys that were in the locking mechanisms, nor the elaborate rigged levers he had in place. She did not read the notes upon notes that were crossed off as Dagmar had struggled to learn more about the weapon. She only saw the note that said "Final." It was next to a large red disk and it glowed of its own accord. It would glow, then stop, then glow again.

She slammed her hand down upon it in anger.

That was when she heard the voice. It was a woman. She had the most distinct and clear voice Ana had ever heard. At first Ana thought she'd just awoken a saint, but instead realized it was coming from the large desk area. It had recited something that did not make sense but was now gently counting in a distinct accent.

And it was counting backwards.

She stared at nothing as she listened. Finally when it said "one" it said something that was not a number. It said "launch" and after a short pause the room vibrated.

Terrified, she ran from the dimmed room—out the door and up the stairs. Ana bumped hard into the metal door as she exited—so panicked was she. What had she done? What had Dagmar done? In her anger she had just struck out at the thing that mocked her. She was out of her element and immersed in magical workings that were not meant for those of present day Poliska or Amira to dabble in. And now the building shook because of it. The rumbling was unlike anything she'd ever heard. A storm was brewing and was emptying an entire night's worth of thunder upon her all at once.

She climbed the stairs and thought daylight had already come. In a way it had.

Exiting the tunnel she looked to the land nearby and saw a great fire. Something like a sun come to earth was glowing in the distance. It was close enough that she could feel the heat of it, but far enough as to allow her to see all of it at once. At first she thought a great thing had come out of the sky to land upon the desert. Instead, it was moving the opposite direction and there was more to it than the ball of fire. It was just as Dagmar had said, but it was impossibly large, and white, and it did have fletchings.

An arrow.

It leapt into the sky and left a trail like the air planes of old. But it was painting lines here and now and it started on the ground.

As it continued into the air, it reached for the heavens.

Again she wondered what she had done. Her heart sunk as it spread far, far up only to arch back downward and move towards the only thing remotely as bright as it.

The pyramid.

The beam shone into the sky with absurd brightness. Surely this was the true glory of the light Dagmar described. Followers from all over now would be able to see it and be awed, inspired and terrified. It would draw those seeing it for hundreds of kilometers to it. He had indeed returned it to what it was as part of the Old World, and he had given his life to do so. It was now white and bright. And hot.

And it was the last time anyone would ever see the Light of Luxor, for it was about to be extinguished.

The great white arrow reached the bottom of its arc and disappeared into the pyramid. The light went out and in mere seconds the black triangle became white and orange. It was as if a great mushroom grew from it—made entirely of clouds and smoke and light.

She stared.

Her fear had turned to awe. And this then returned to something that surprised her. It was anger. She had no way of knowing if the poor farmers and folk who surrounded the pyramid were safe, but from the distance it looked like a highly localized event. Because of this she had no remorse for what she had apparently done. She wanted the saint to die—to be extinguished forever like the great light atop his cathedral. And she wanted the same for each and every saint that remained.

And she was going to do it herself.

They had taken her father and her home. They had taken Dagmar and Stojan. And they had taken Amira from its people. They would do this no more.

She continued to stand and watch. Stojan had destroyed St. John. Ana had destroyed the saint that dwelt within pyramid Luxor. If the deceitful elder was to be believed, that meant there were five left. She would search for Stojan by way of these saints. If there was one landmark that would draw them together it was the location of the saints and she already knew where one dwelt. He too would pay.

She folded her arms as the cooler breeze dissipated the great mushroom and cooled her skin. Her red hair blew in the breeze as well. She was angry—far more so than she had ever been; however this was anger with a purpose, and it was sustainable. Perhaps her hair would never go back to its original color.

———

Ana rode into the night to her camp. To her relief it was still there. Very little had been left there save for a makeshift seating area and a place where a fire had been made. There had been no need for coverage as Dagmar explained there was very little rain—even in such a lush area. Apparently what moisture remained was burned off in the intense sun upon morning. Even her horse was still there.

Would she sleep, or would she make haste to leave? She dismounted, and collapsed against a tree. Breathing deeply, she had no thoughts. Only images entered her mind and she felt as if she was only an observer; watching the saint, viewing the massive impossible interior of the fortress. Then she saw Dagmar fall. She thought about how kind he had been to her since she arrived. Instead of finding a figure who was ruling over his city with guile and deceit, she'd found a man doing quite the opposite. Dagmar had gone from someone trying so desperately to prove that he had knowledge of Amira and the secrets of the Old World, to someone who just wanted to explain things. And he had dropped everything to help her. She owed him her life from years past, and he'd given her a fighting chance yet again. She owed him much. He needed to be remembered for what he had done. Dagmar had put so much effort into teaching her, and showing her things and…

The arrow plane.

What would she do about it?   Who did it belong to now?   Had he told anyone else about it?   She was almost certain she was now the only person that knew about it.   It was a burden she did not want to dwell upon.   Images of their flight made her feel peaceful, but perhaps it was best left alone now.   It would have to remain in its house for some time. She had too much to sort out and the most pressing of matters was whether to remain in the camp and be found, or ride into the night. Neither was desirable.   Her body was tired, but her soul more so.

She stared for many minutes as Dagmar's horse hung its head down.   He was ready for bed too, unburdened by the choices she would have to make.

She heard them coming and was happy that being so lost in thought had not made her defenseless.   Standing up and unsheathing her sword she was ready for them.   Her horse did not seem startled by the newcomers which gave her pause.   She recognized them right away and was relieved.   Some of the group that stopped her on the road had made their way to her.   How long had she been lost in thought?   The four smiled and gingerly approached her.   They stared at her sword with fear.

They looked like a family to her and she had clearly frightened them. She sheathed her sword with the assumption that it was not an elaborate trap.

"We… we are sorry to have bothered you."

It was the adult woman who spoke.   The man took his turn now as he glanced from his wife to Ana.

"We wanted to offer our home to you.   It is not safe out here.   Our farm is nearby.."

"And we thought you should stay with us."

Ana wondered if they would be taking turns the entire conversation.

"That is very kind but…"

"We would be most careful.   It is dark and no one will know it."

The woman cut her off just as her husband had then cut her off.

"And it is not far.   They will come for you."

"We owe you."

Ana was confused. She did indeed destroy the pyramid and presumably the saint, but she had not yet done anything directly for them. And the latest comment by the mother made them all glance at the children.

"He is gone now."

It was then that Ana recognized the little girl; it was she that had looked so disappointed at Ana. Now she did not. Rather, though she still appeared to be tired and dirty, she now looked most excited. The father continued the mother's words.

"We had been rounded up. We do not think we would have been allowed to leave. Their plan was to convert us or we would..."

The mother pulled her daughter's shoulders towards her and ended the man's sentence.

"Because you were unable to harm him and we were witness to this they decided to allow us to leave—for surely we would tell others of your failure."

Ana nodded.
"But that is not what we will tell of now."

They glanced behind them at where the pyramid once stood; where the beam once pierced the sky.

"Please come with us."

It was the little girl. Until now both children had remained silent.

The situation had been reversed; no longer was the little girl looking at her with disappointment. Instead she was staring at Ana as if Ana was a saint herself.

She sheathed her sword and walked toward the children. Kneeling to them, she spoke softly as the little girl and boy stared into her eyes and hair respectively.

"I will come with you on one condition—that you do not look upon me as if I am a saint. I am not. I am just like you."

The little boy swallowed and continued to look up on her hair with wonder. It seemed her hair would not remain the color indefinitely and was changing before his eyes. He was the only person other than Stojan to witness the change so closely. And despite her words, he found her absolutely magical. He would speak about this for some time.

Ana nodded slowly as the little girl and boy did the same.

She walked her horse as they walked Dagmar's, as she felt uncomfortable riding with a family in tow. It was not too far that they had to travel to find the farmhouse. It was a building that had been repurposed and was made from the Old World. Again, Ana thought about the great influence of this particular saint; he had kept much in perfect condition but as Dagmar had said, he must have grown weak or changed recently.

She would sleep very little as she considered herself a liability to the family. Rather than occupied with thoughts of her own home in Poliska, she thought of what was to be done now, and the safety of the people who had opened their home to her. Most of her time was spent cleaning up and attempting to keep her distance from them.

It was not a social visit and she started to feel a certain kinship with Stojan now. Had he not stayed the night in a house with an innocent young girl and worried about her safety? He had gone so far as to stay in the barn.

Innocent girl.

She smiled.

The thought of staying in the barn with the horses greatly appealed to her now. Wishing them all goodnight she made a place for herself there with the horses.

The night was uneventful. Her worry of retribution need not have happened. Any of the men that had been loyal to the saint had now dispersed. Even the most power-hungry of them found it difficult to make any headway with the most powerful of all castles now laying in ruins.

None would search for her.

Ana was very grateful for the food, water and supplies provided by the family. They were thankful beyond words for what she had done and offered any and all monies that she would accept. Her compromise was that she would sell them Dagmar's horse. The way they looked at her continued to make her uncomfortable however, and she was grateful for her night alone in the barn.

That morning, she had one task to complete—she would do her best to seal the entrance to the great weapon. Dagmar had said that this was the only great arrow that lay dormant in the structure, but she did not want to take any other chances.

She had been marginally successful at sealing both doors, however, her sword made short work of all of the equipment and sliced, shattered and destroyed the delicate workings she found there. The notes were scooped up and would make tinder for her next fire. None of the lights had been on and everything had seemed dead to her anyway.

She found as she rode away that she was unusually satisfied at destroying the Amiran tec.

Her first stop would be Sedona to tell the people of Dagmar's demise. She wanted to ensure that his death was properly represented and understood. He had been a great man and his efforts were just as responsible for the demise of the saint as hers was. There she would leave word that her mission was to visit the saints one by one. This would also be the needed bread crumbs for Stojan to catch up with her.

She paid no mind to the fact that said bread crumbs were not selective; others who did not wish her well would also use them.

Upon leaving the area surrounding the pyramid, she happened upon some of the farm folk as well as the local merchants. Each and every one of them stopped and stared. Each and everyone of them did not turn away without a wave and a smile—news had spread very quickly indeed.

She was pleased to see that where the pyramid stood was now a collapsed crater of rubble, and the destruction looked highly selective. The nearest building or farm was a safe distance away and had not been harmed in the process.

Though she rode past it at a gallop it felt like slow motion. The scene was surreal and gave her a new appreciation for the size of the previous structure.

She stared as she rode and watched carefully to see that no saint climbed forth from it—whether as a whole body or just a giant head.

She needn't have worried as such devastation was beyond the capacity of the interloper to adapt to. His present container had been shattered as thoroughly as his castle. Indeed there was one less saint. Ana made haste for the magical land of Sedona.

————

The ride to Sedona was relatively uneventful. As much as it would have troubled Stojan, she did make sure to take a walk each and every night on the way. The edge of her dear sword had been seriously dulled by the strike at the saint statue's ankle. Doubtful it would ever be the same. This feeling just compounded the sense she had that it was time to retire it in favor of a better fit. The trip alone was creating a building anxiety within her. Had it not been for the walks she surely would have gone mad—she mused. But each day that passed made her appreciate just how fast the air conveyance had been. It would have made the same trip in an hour or so. She marveled at this and thought perhaps that she should have put it into service. A shorter trip to Sedona might have been a good way to test it. Thinking that a week-long trip was now considered short made her realize just how many amazing things she had seen. It seemed that nothing was out of the realm of possibility.

To her pleasure she understood the downside of traveling by such an amazing conveyance: there would be no time to think or walk or practice. In that way the travel seemed too fast. What did the Amirans do to think and consider things? If the travel was so fast that would mean very little time for such things. She shook her head in disagreement. This would not do—to go from one town to another within hours. The times between the cities were what allowed her to regenerate, refresh and renew. It wasn't just her body—but her spirit. Dealing with the people and the restrictions took a toll on her and the time in nature undid this toll. She found the times in which she was restricted from practicing and walking to be those in which she was the most at unease. It made her crabby.

Immediately she felt better about not pursuing the plane of the air. Though it might have made her quests easier, it would have robbed her of countless days of practice, healing and meditation. Her hand and wrist were finally healing from the unfortunate strike at the metal statue. She was saved from breaking her bones only because she chose a slice rather than a strike. And her muscles built up from training and as an apprentice had presented a hardy foundation. A lesser combatant would have broken their wrist. If she simply took the air conveyance she would be entering into a new situation tired, unhealed and downtrodden.

It was these thoughts that cheered her on the lonely journey she was now on—back to Sedona.

Retracing her steps with Dagmar was relatively easy as she had not only been paying attention, but had been taught to navigate by Stojan.

The weather along her journey did not make things difficult though she would have not minded the rain. She embraced the sun and absorbed it as she walked. As she let go, she was reminded of the imagery of the last few days and this imagery made her think of what to say to the people of Sedona.

She had come a long way and speaking to the people invoked a small amount of panic. What would she say? The last time there was a funeral she was unable to speak any words officially, save for the few she and Stojan had said after burying her father.

Eventually, she let go of any prepared statement, and all images of her standing on a great balcony to address the entire city were dropped in place of a more realistic chat with his assistant. She then moved on to other thoughts and the center of these was Stojan. Was he still being retained? Was the bishop of the great statue saint injured directly due to Stojan? Was this due to a skirmish that allowed him to escape or was it simply a matter of a forced prisoner exchange? In her heart she knew that Stojan was alive and well and out there somewhere. She just needed to find him. Strangely, she had been comforted by the confusing vague words of the saint and his minions. In all probability he had escaped.

It was the day before reaching Sedona that she felt at ease about him. Because of this, she turned her attention to something other than finding him—she would locate the very door that had brought the saints to this world in the first place.

And she would reopen it again.

RETURNING TO SEDONA

The morning brought a beautiful sunrise and lit up the structures surrounding Sedona. The sun brought to her attention the reds, oranges and yellows. Even the browns vied for her attention in a concerted effort to implore her to perceive the beauty of it all. She needed no coercing as she drank it all in, and was no stranger to appreciating every color—the blues of the skies and the lakes; the greens of the trees and the grass; the browns of the trees and the animals; and the yellows of the fields of sunflowers.

Now she added many shades of orange to her palette of appreciation.

As she rode into town, no one made much fuss over her and she preferred it. Her pace had been very quick and it was doubtful word had reached them yet. She would be the first to arrive from the city of Luxor.

Ana made her way directly to the building in the center of town in search of the assistant. It took some time to find him as he was apparently fulfilling some of the duties that Dagmar would have handled.

"My lady?"

Ana quickly glanced behind her in confusion and then back at the man who had spoken those words. She pointed to her chest.

"Me?"

"Yes. Yes, of course. Anastazja."

It was Dagmar's assistant and he had returned to the building of government. She had been waiting patiently in the room in which she'd first met the man.

"I…"

"Please come with me to the chambers."

He backed her along gently and respectively. He seemed to be a slightly different man and in place of his trepidation and fear was a more calm and professional leader.

They sat and as was tradition he offered her more of the cold tea. She gladly accepted. Ana unsheathed her sword and leaned it up again her chair. It was a habit she had when sitting sometimes because she did not want to remove her belt. It unnerved some and in this case served to be a demonstration of what had happened. He looked at it with surprise. The well-lit room showed the damage that had been done. To him it looked like the sword had been mistreated and was used to chop firewood and then had been banged hard against a large rock. Indeed Ana had not even attempted to sharpen it during her journey.

"Oh my."

She looked at him and took a breath. He was not asking where Dagmar was. He was smart and cordial enough to wait for her to explain why she had come alone, and for that she was very thankful. She sipped and gathered her thoughts and continued to appreciate his patience.

"Dagmar was captured."

He listened and did not interrupt as she exhaled between sentences.

"He told me to stay back. Stojan was not… Dagmar did not return. He was supposed to, well I expected that he would be in a matter of hours. It was so huge—that pyramid!"

Juan nodded as she continued to attempt to sort her thoughts in real time.

"I could not wait for him. I went out to stretch the horses. I suppose I was stretching too. I usually walk. At night that is."

Juan just looked on and his face looked sad.

"I went in. It is filled with wonders. Never have I seen something so huge, and filled with…"

She looked down, then up. Her voice was cracked and quiet. It was filled with grave sadness and said very slowly. She choked out the words as her rambling came to a halt suddenly.

"Oh… He fell."

She was silent as her eyes filled with tears. The man's face mirrored hers in sadness as she revealed the part he knew already to be true.

"He… we were trapped. He's so clever. He's such a good man. He was…"

She sniffed the tears from her sinuses.

"Take your time, Ana."

"Oh… he is gone."

She cried. And as she wept, the man named Juan sat and swallowed. He tried to remain calm and supportive, but seeing the girl cry as she delivered the news was too much for him. He too cried and for moments they sat in silence—absorbing what had occurred from both that of the messenger and that of the listener.

"I did not know what he had planned. He sacrificed his life for me. For us. For us all."

He blinked and listened to her hoarse voice.

"The saint was immense."

She inhaled sharply just then as Juan spoke for the first time.

"The saint? You saw him? In person?"

She swallowed as her face changed.

"Yes. I did. I struck him. I tried to dispatch him in the same way that Stojan had… St. John…"

At was then that he noticed her face change and it would not be the only thing to alter itself in the conversation.

"I failed. I failed at first."

"We saw it. The beam. The great Light of Luxor. We saw it nights ago as had been foretold. We feared the worst because Dagmar had always said that as long as he was alive he would never ignite it to its full brilliance… because that would signal that the saint had won."

She tilted her head and was happy that he was speaking instead of her.

"He thought he knew how to ignite it properly but would do so incrementally sometimes, he said. But when we saw the beam all the way back here in Sedona we thought all hope was lost—that they had absorbed you both into their castle."

"Have you seen it before?"

"No, I have never seen it, and that was the first time I have seen the beam."

"It was the last."

"What? What do you mean?"

His face was filled with confusion and hope.

"It is gone. Along with the saint."

Her words sounded so fantastical to her own ears, yet she said them proudly. Her tears were no more and she spoke as one who had fought a battle.

"When Dagmar was no more and I had escaped, I used the weapon of the Old World. I destroyed the saint and his castle. I have seen it up close. It is no more. It is rubble. It is a hole."

Again the man looked upon her as he had when they first met—with awe and trepidation. She was sitting up now with her shoulders back. She was proud of what had occurred and what she had called into action. The man said but two words.

"It worked."

She nodded. He had a distant look now, as if remembering all the notes, all the conversations and rants of his employer. He looked again at Ana and smiled.

"He has not died in vain, Anastazja. He has allowed us to triumph. What you have done is not a small thing. I think even the action of your father does not compare to this."

He dabbed his eyes.

"You should be proud of what you have done."

She swallowed, but said nothing more. Her hair was a mixture of blonde and red now—reflecting the tumultuous feelings she currently had.

"But they will come for you. Were you able to steal away in the night? You left in stealth under the confusion?"

"Oh no, I did not. I have to find Stojan. He still lives. I am sure of it! And he cannot find me if he does not know where…"

She looked at his eyes.

"What? What is wrong?"

"You left word of where you would travel next?"

"Yes of course, how else will Stojan find me? I told them I would travel here first. I had to tell you and your city of Dagmar's demise—of his bravery!"

"Yes I…"

"Why do you look concerned?"

"Because Ana, they will come for you. I fear you may have brought much conflict to Sedona."

"No. There was no other way. I think you are wrong for a simple reason."

He was surprised. Her words were bold.

"There is no one left to come for me."

"No one left? What about the people?"

"Those who farmed the lands outside the castle were not loyal to the saint."

"But surely…"

"And those who were, were present in…"

"In the castle?"

"Yes."

"All of them?"

"I can only hope."

He thought much on what she had said. Surely there were others still loyal, but this was almost unprecedented—save for what Stojan had done. Without a saint, there would be doubts in their minds, and still those that were loyal. There were those that would still believe. But Ana had removed all doubt and not only destroyed the saint, but his great dwelling as well. It was the grandest destruction that had ever been wrought in modern times. And it had trumped what had been done before; not only had a saint been dispatched, but also the very castle itself. And—if Ana was right—every man and woman that was part of his militia.

The weight of this was felt by the man and Ana could see it in his eyes. She was the most wanted Amiran in the country now, or she would be when everyone had learned of what she had done.

"I will not be staying long, so you need not worry about me Juan."

"No?"

"No. I will be on my way tomorrow—if you will allow me to stay the night here."

"Of course."

"And take two things with me."

Her eyes looked left and right and he thought he saw her smile.

"If I may keep Dagmar's compass?"

"Oh!"

He started to look around the room as if it was laying around.

"I already have it. It was part of his things left at the camp with me."

Her face was a mixture of appreciation and sadness.

"Yes of course you may keep the compass. You may have any of his personal belongings that you desire. You were family to him and he spoke very warmly of you. He was quite fond of you—and your father, actually."

She smiled and he returned it.

"But what is the other thing?"

Her eyes betrayed her and she glared at the double doors at the end of the room.

His eyebrows went up.

"The doll."

"No Ana, I do not think…"

"Yes. I must have it as it is part of my next quest."

Deep down, under all the sadness and exhaustion, the words filled her with glee. She stood up from the table, and he did the same. He had no intention of trying to stop her but knew enough of the object to fear it. It was a saint in miniature if Dagmar was to be believed. And he had no reason not to.

She motioned to the doors.

"I want to take it with me. It will show me how to open the door, once I unite it with the Saint on High."

"Oh dear."

"Please."

With that and much trepidation Ana was allowed to take the doll with her. Juan, as it turned out, was not able to come up with a reason for it to remain that was acceptable to her.

She slept in the same quarters she had when she first visited Dagmar and again found them to be very comfortable. Sedona was a very nice place to stay. It was warm all year round and welcoming enough, and not too large as to be overwhelming. However it did make her miss the green of the woods. Granted, woods of this type could be found nearby, but not near enough for her liking. There was something about the enveloping hands of nature when walking through a dense forest that made her feel safer than just four walls. She was free *and* secure at the same time.

Before bed, she laid out all of her things—including her belt and her sword. Taking it out one last time for the day she looked at it again. It was indeed damaged. Her father would probably see it as a challenge and spend a fortune in time and effort making it right. She smiled when she realized she was not quite correct. Nay, he would spent a fortune in time and effort coaxing and mentoring her to fix it herself. Because of that attitude she was still an excellent blacksmith apprentice. She missed him too.

Anastazja fell asleep smiling.

———

She woke as the sun was greeting the entire city of Sedona at once. Ana closed her eyes and drank it all in with her skin. The rest was deep and rejuvenating.   As far as she knew, no great hoard of followers from Luxor had arrived to wreak havoc during the night. She would find Juan and make sure everything was all right. The doll still lay dormant behind the double doors—as far as she knew. Knowing what Dagmar had told her and what the saint had admitted, anything the doll saw and heard would be relayed to ALL saints. Just like her last interaction and demise was relayed to them all.

That last thought gave her pause. What did it feel like? What had the other saints experienced? It was such a bizarre thing to consider—this communication they now possessed. They were aware of everything they all experienced, but they were now also aware of the destruction. She did not know if saints experienced fear, but thought it would be a very good thing for them to learn now.

She was coming for them all.

Just then her stomach reminded her that there were more pressing matters.

She dressed and gathered her things. It was a habit that she could not break. Having lost her sword, her horse and most of her belongings, she had no intention of losing any more. Exiting her room, she almost immediately encountered Dagmar's assistant. He was very happy to see her that morning. He asked to have breakfast together and she happily agreed. It was most delicious and during the meal Juan insisted on making sure she had enough supplies going forward. He added both rations and monies. She refused the latter but he said that Dagmar would have wanted her to have some. It was the first time she had seen the man push something hard and because of this she eventually agreed. It was not a small amount.

It was then time for her to be on her way, and with trepidation the doll was revealed. It sat on the shelf contentedly but did not move.

She glanced at Juan and asked if it was alive again. He shrugged and looked fearful. He did not want to be viewed by all of the saints at once.

"I…I do not know…"

She grabbed the leather wrappings she had requested. The original linens were refused by her as not being secure enough. Fortunately the doll was frozen in a relatively compact shape and she began to wrap it immediately. It looked like it was made of ceramic and might be quite fragile. As she finished the tight cocoon she wrapped the head and then the eyes last. Could it hear her? Did it even matter that the eyes were covered?

"What will you do now?"

Ana considered the question as she was not as sure as she had been the previous night. She sat back down and Juan followed suit.

"I assumed I would have to bring this to The Saint on High and…"

Juan did not finish her sentence for her, as she hoped, so she continued.

"Join? Allow him to leap to it somehow…?"

"Hasn't he inhabited it before?"

"I thought you and Dagmar knew this? Dagmar mentioned that it had come alive more than once."

"Yes it has, but…"

"But what?"

"This is new to me, Ana, and all very fantastical. Dagmar was a great teacher and spent much time explaining this. He was able to show me that much of what I see is not unknown or magical. But…"

He looked at the cocoon on the floor.

"The saints are a different story. They truly are magical and unknown."

She sighed.

"What troubles you Ana?"

"It is some distance to The Saint on High. It is even a greater distance in the opposite direction to the great doorway."

"Oh?"

"Yes. I have seen both. I do not know how to proceed. Do I travel to the saint or just to the doorway?"

She had been so certain, so he was honored that she was discussing her plan with him. But much to his dismay he did not have an informed answer."

"I do not know how or… Perhaps we can summon him? Or perhaps if we wait long enough he will appear and we can simply ask him? I am not sure if this is a good idea."

She considered this. The thought of saving a month of travel was worth the wait. Her biggest fear was that Stojan would be lured to the pyramid because of her and then captured. She no longer feared that. With the breadcrumbs she was leaving, he would follow her to Sedona and her next destination. And now she had to decide what that would be.

"I think that is a good plan. How long until he appears? Have you ever caused him to appear? And how long…"

She smiled at the bewildered man. She was asking too many questions at once. He too smiled, and then laughed nervously.

"I have never seen him appear, but from what Dagmar told me it lasts only minutes and without warning. The doll has not attempted to do anything nefarious other than try to escape when he was placed behind the doors. You wish to summon him right here and now?"

She nodded. The idea of communing with the saint and going directly to the door was very appealing now.

"Tell me Ana, how did you reach The Saint on High? Dagmar once tried to reach it but found that there was an impasse."

Again she smiled. Carefully removing her tiny backpack, she wordlessly opened it and removed one of the only four items she kept within.

It looked fragile and was made of metal and glass and clearly of the Old World. Juan gasped with amazement.

"Where did you get that?!"

"Stojan and I were given this as a means to reach the saint."

He looked closer at it and resisted the urge to reach out and play with it —he had learned his lesson the hard way with Dagmar. Amiran tec was almost never what it seemed.

"Did you... dig it up?"

She smiled again.

"Yes this, time I had to. When they took Stojan, they took everything including the shovel. But fortunately he buried it again. I thought perhaps that was his way of saying he was OK."

"OK? Shovel?"

"Yes, I dug it up with a stick. The shovel... Well, Stojan thought it was a good idea."

He stared on in complete bewilderment, as her eyes widened.

"Do you think?!"

Once again she assumed he knew more than he did.

"That you... Ah...?"

"That I may also use this to recall the saint here?   He opened the drawbridge for us."

She became very excited and placed the object on the table. It hit hard and dried earth flaked off of it onto the table top. This would have annoyed Dagmar had he still been with them, thought Juan.

"Help me unwrap it. Just the head!"

Quickly the wrappings were removed and the doll was placed on its side. The remaining cocoon made it impossible for it to remain upright.

She grabbed the device and then touched it to the doll—first to the head, then the body, then the head again. Nothing seemed to happen. She placed it next to the head and backed up and waited. For many minutes she waited and stared. Just when she was ready to give up, she thought she saw it move.

"Ana. I do not think this is a good idea! Perhaps we should take it outside of the city, or somewhere else?"

He looked around the room and then circled the table.   What could the saint see? Would it know where they were? Suddenly the thought of summoning a saint here and now was not to his liking.

"Ana!"

It was one thing to have it become animated randomly in an almost comical fashion. It was another thing to intentionally bring this evil into their inner sanctum.

"What?!"

"I do not think..."

"Did it just...?"

She glanced at Juan and back again. It was still and immobile, and lifeless. She sighed as her thoughts turned to the long journey.

"Dude."

She focused her eyes on the present. Juan all but leaped up. He clearly had never seen this kind of possession before. She had actually seen it so often it was almost common to her.

They both tilted their heads to match the doll's head on the table as it lay upon its side. It was a comical sight as the pair stared.

"That's him."

Juan was ever so confused and Ana spoke and not in fearful, or reverent tones—but instead with anger.

"Why did you lie to me!"

"Hey! C'mon. I didn't lie to you. Hey this worked—whoa. I'm not here anymore, I'm *here* now? Wow."

Juan whispered out of the side of his mouth as his eyes remained transfixed.

"He speaks gibberish?"

"Answer me!"

"OK! Hey I have a head or something but the rest is... Hey, it sort of moves. Where am I? It's pretty bright in here. Who's this guy?"

Ana moved the small Amiran device away from the doll—thinking it would somehow dispel him. She was angry and had felt betrayed. It had no apparent effect, however.

It looked as if Ana would take her sword out and smash the seemingly confused doll, but just then it did answer.

"I didn't lie to you. I kept everything a secret, but then I couldn't hold on any longer. And then the voices came back and they knew what I knew. And I knew what *they* knew. Man... It's even worse now. It's a lot clearer."

Ana relaxed slightly.

"Where is Stojan?"

There was a short pause and Ana was ready to scream at it again. Juan was shaking his head and had backed away a few steps. He looked around the room for a weapon of his own.

"I don't really know. Remember, I only know what everyone else knows, and they only know what somebody shows them, or some dude tells them. And maybe I sort of know what they might be planning, maybe? Kind of?"

His voice almost squeaked at the end. Juan was clearly unnerved by the exchange. The voice was in the room and also in his head.

"You know nothing of Stojan right now? I find that…"

"Well, here's the deal—one dude sends his guys to get him, then the other sends his guys to get *them*. But because everything is clearer now, a third guy sends his guys too. What happened? Yeah, I don't know—I only know what they see, not what their dudes see. Since everyone knows what everyone knows now it makes it really hard to surprise anyone anymore. And…"

He trailed off as Juan listened intently. Anastazja found the conversation not to her liking.

"And?"

"And, well, they're all getting a little anxious. They're kind of selfish, you know? That first guy just wanted to get rid of some of his men. And for the first time they are afraid of something."

Juan was sure the doll was going to say 'Ana.' She asked the question herself.

"And what is that?"

"Well, they totally don't want to die!"

Juan was in amazement; he was in the presence of a saint that was directly communicating with them. In addition, it was revealing to him the inner workings of the saints. It was a unique and once in a lifetime event, and Ana seemed to regard it as if it was an every day occurrence. Suddenly, hundreds of questions entered his mind. This would be an opportunity to record and learn. Dagmar would have been ecstatic. But Juan wanted no part of it.

"Why do you not ask where Stojan is? Do you know his whereabouts?"

"Oh, sort of. I didn't think he was with you. Man, now you're the uptight one. I got a glimpse or two from the flickering one."

"The flickering one?"

Juan again whispered.

"What do you mean?"

"It's hard to explain. We're not all here, you know? Well, one of us isn't. I didn't figure it out until like just now. Hey! So let's go now!"

And stood back and folded her arms.

"Where? Where is he?"

"I told you I sort of know what they planned, but not where he is."

"Where do you think he is then!"

"Oh my god. I told you I don't know. It hurts enough to think about what they planned and are thinking. They wanted to capture him. They all had the idea one after another and were all like one-upping each other. And I don't think that worked out great. That's all I know."

Juan had heard enough. It had no real information and the longer it was here the more it would learn about Sedona. He was about to ask Ana to terminate it when she abruptly changed the subject.

"I will help you open the door."

The painted-on eyebrows moved upward.

"OK! Where are you? You near it now?"

"What do you think?"

Juan looked at her.

"About..?"

"Do you think it will be safe to transport this to the doorway?"

She nodded before he answered—which was easy as he was frozen in indecision.

"OK, I will do this, Saint on High. But know this: if you lie to me or try to cause harm I will smash you instantly. And the moment you learn of Stojan's whereabout you will tell me."

After a long pause, it smiled and spoke.

"So, how far away is it from where you guys are?"

Amira

THE JOURNEY TO THE DOOR

Equipped with Dagmar's compass, supplies from Juan and the now-rewrapped doll, Ana said her farewell to Juan.

"Ana, I wish you only the best on your journey. May your quest be successful."

Juan's choice of words were not accidental, as he knew she would much enjoy a mention of her quest. She smiled, hugged him and mounted her horse.

"If I may offer a bit of advice?"

"Juan? Yes, of course."

"It is about the word you leave regarding your whereabouts."

"Yes? So Stojan may find me. You do not think I should leave word?"

"Well…"

"How else is he to find me, I have to leave word."

"Well, yes, it is not whether you should leave word or not, but rather how selective you are with whom you leave it."

She looked at him and waited.

"I would say leave word with a select person—someone you trust."

"So I should not tell those in Sedona where I am going…"

"Yes, in this case you can trust me."

"Hmmm."

This was all she said as she rode off. He shook his head as he watched her go.

———

As she left the town, she waved at a few people, and was even the recipient of shouts of "Good luck." She only smiled or grabbed the brim of her hat as she had learned to do in these situations.

According to what she and Juan were able to figure out, the journey would take her a month or so to complete. Juan had access to very detailed maps that Dagmar possessed and had collected over the years. These maps were mostly printed somehow on very large and thin sheets of paper—like the books of the Old World. In fact, Dagmar possessed books that were just maps. Juan had suggested that they go through his things and she choose what she wanted. With the immediacy of finding Stojan, and opening this door, she felt it best to leave it for another time. Privately, she did not want to sort through the personal belongings of another person that was dear to her. It felt much better to be angry than sad. And this anger would hopefully give her the energy to reach this doorway. The land of Waxahachie was some distance to the east, but was essentially as far south as Sedona. For this she was grateful—there would be no worries of bad weather as far as she knew.

Every so often the doll would make muffled sounds. Surprisingly if its mouth was kept bound it could not speak—even though some of the sound was not made outside of her ears. She found this curious, but was very glad. Otherwise it would have driven her to much annoyance to hear it speak almost constantly like a chatty companion. That was a stark contrast to Stojan who enjoyed their silence when appropriate. .

The combination of map, compass and compact saint made for a very efficient route—at least that was what she believed.

With these things in place, Anastazja set forth on a month-long journey to find the great door that had opened one thousand years ago. Through it had come seven beings and this brought forth catastrophe upon catastrophe in which the world was turned upside-down. Great quakes occurred and countless people lost their lives so that humanity was reduced to only a fraction of what it once was. The great civilizations that thrived at the time lost not only their people and their special magic tec, but the knowledge to maintain and recreate it.

Somehow this door was sealed—by one of the beings themselves. It was too late, as the destruction had been wrought.

And now a young woman was on her way to reopen this doorway. With the help of one of the saints they would pursue a common goal—to finally rid the world of the interlopers.

Her personal desire of seeing the great pyramid had turned into a grand quest to save not only her people of Poliska, but Amira and the entire world.

And yet this did not weigh heavily upon her for one simple reason—she was much too angry.

The doll once again was making muffled noises. It was an odd thing as she still heard some of it in her head. After riding for some time, she finally stopped, dismounted and removed it from the saddle bag. Ana slowly undid the wraps around its head.

"Where are we goin'?"

"What do you mean? We travel to the door."

"Yeah, but like right now?"

The head turned slightly as the eyes darted around. Ana had propped it up in her saddle bag so that only the head was visible—she had no desire to have it escape. It looked around at the trees, the scrub and then the sky.

"Like we should be on a road."

"I prefer not to travel on the road unless I have to. And you said the roads were indirect. We can make better time this way."

"OK."

She once again started to wrap his head but he protested.

"Do we have to do that?"

"Yes."

"Why though?"

She exhaled and looked around.

"Why does it matter to you?"

"Well, I think it would be nice to chat."

Her blanched look was unconvincing, but eventually she released the wraps she was holding, but made sure the rest of him was tight.

"Fine."

She hopped back onto her horse and continued—now with the brightly-painted head of a large doll peeking from one of the bags. She soon regretted this action as the doll was rather chatty. Her awareness of the fact that all saints were aware of what it saw and heard made her very hesitant to respond. She was hopeful that its view of the countryside would not truly reveal her position. Random trees and shrubs should not be of much use to those who would want to find her. And at the urging of Juan, he was the only one that knew she was on her way. Of course now that The Saint on High knew, the other saints did as well. But they would have to communicate that to their followers. It all hurt her head. She already regretted unwrapping it.

"So this should take a month, huh?"

There was no response.

"You know, I didn't really think the vessel thing would actually work. I tried many times and then one time I felt a push. That's crazy huh? And here I am."

The saint had already adjusted to the fact that Ana chose not to respond to most of his questions. Every so often he would ask a question, or make a comment that she would acknowledge. He was surprised at her level of resilience, and how little information she divulged. Finally she yelled back at him in frustration as she pulled her horse to a stop.

"Why do you persist in these questions! You know I will tell you and your brothers very little."

"I'm just makin' convo, ya know? It's not like I had a lot of people to talk…"

She had once again bound his mouth, but this time she bound his entire head and then shoved him unceremoniously back into the saddle bag.

She made a loud guttural sound not unlike an animal while urging her horse forward. Her plan was to use as direct of a route as possible and camp between cities using them only for supplies when needed. She did not take her walk for three days, and when she finally did it was with some trepidation. Thoughts of the doll untying itself, or somehow alerting others that she was on her way ran crossed her mind. Fortunately she encountered nothing like this and the saint was thoroughly subdued within the bindings. That was when she decided she would check in at night with it.

"Do you know where Stojan is yet?"

She had moved the doll and propped it up against a tree as she sat by the small fire.

It blinked and then smiled.

"Campfire? Nice. You know, I thought it was lonely up in the observatory, but this is in a way like a lot more…"

"Where?"

"What? Oh, Stojan. You… you… you're not a good listener you know?"

She waited and poked at the fire. He took in as much as he could and answered.

"All I know is that the three groups met up, or at least should have by now."

"That's it?"

"Yes. Why would I… oh yeah."

She just stared into the fire and shook her head at the oddest companion she could have possibly chosen. It made her upset to think of it as helpless or even playful.

"Do not think that just because you are trapped in the form of this doll I believe you are not an evil and powerful saint."

"That's hurtful. Dude. I'm right here."

She realized she was upset at herself as well, for now she did feel it was a companion—a talking plaything of some sort. But if she was successful it would be gone along with the rest.

"Then provide something useful to me, or I will bind you again and store you."

"Uh, what do you want to know…"

Seeing her eyes light up with obvious anger, he quickly continued.

"…besides where Stojan is. Sorry. Like I said, I know what they see and are told so that means none of the guys made it back to…"

"Where, where are they from then?"

"The saints? Oh, they're both from the north. Yuck. It's getting pretty cold there now. Do you know I had no concept of 'cold' until I came here? I mean I had no concept of a lot of things, actually."

"They are both in the north? How far? Where?"

"Well, they're at the top of the country, but still many miles apart."

"How many are there?"

"Excuse me?"

It seemed her question had taken him off-guard.

"How many saints are there?"

"Oh. Here? Well, not *here* with us, ha!"

Ana's face was without friendliness as she stared into the fire instead of the animated face of the doll. She poked at the fire again with her stick, and watched as the embers rose into the air. Building a fire was not something she normally did, but this night seemed particularly cold.

"Seven."

"Finally."

"Well, there were seven. But now there are less."

Soon there will be none, thought Ana. Her anger mixed with a mild irritation—the thought that speaking with this saint made her less desirous of destroying it. But then, if her quest was successful, she would not be destroying him or the others. She would merely be sending them back from whence they came—forever. She mused over this while she listened to the roundabout way the saint used to communicate. Combined with his gibberish, it made obtaining answers taxing. Thus she only half-listened.

"So there's really five—including me. I've been here for a while this time!"

"What?"

She looked up.

"This time I've been here for a while, you know…?"

"You've been here before?"

"Well, oh! Ha! I'm totally confusing you. I mean with you here. I'm bouncing back and forth, but I can't figure out how I'm doing it."

"You go back to your cathedral?"

"My cathedra… oh, yeah. I do. I didn't think this would work, but then it did and then I went back and then came back. Totally weird."

Ana got up for her seat and without a word started wrapping the head of the doll.

"Wait… c'mon…"

It could say no more as she finished the bindings. She then placed it back in the saddle bag again, as she had done every night. And every night the saint protested. Her routine had been to only unwrap it at night just before bed, ask it the same question about Stojan's whereabouts, then wrap it and keep it in the saddle bag.

Sometimes it was able to extend the conversation by volunteering information, sometimes it was not. She wondered if Stojan would use the time to ask strategic questions, but over and over again she reminded herself that every question and answer was made available to the other saints. Just asking a question could tip them off to her intentions, and they already knew she was on her way to the door.

And they would know exactly when she would get there.

For a few more nights the saint was unwrapped, asked where Stojan was, and then rewrapped under protest. This night was different. Ana had a new question.

"Tell me, why is it the other saints do not want to go back?"

This question gave the saint pause and he considered his words for some time.

"Who said they didn't?"

"You said that they would be pulled through the doorway. Why would they have to be pulled? Why would they not work with someone from Amira in all of these years to just reopen it? Why am I the first?"

"OK, ok, good questions… OK, you're right. Some of them don't want to go. In fact, I think it's only me, and one other that wants to go back."

"Why?"

"Why don't they want to go back? Well, unlike me they have it pretty good here I think. You people like this sort of thing. You want something to tell you want to do and be all…"

It looked like the doll was struggling to use hand movements to help his description, but to no avail.

"…awesome and stuff."

"Awesome and stuff?"

"Yeah. Awesome, amazing. Something to look up to and make them feel that... Wow, look at me. I'm getting all philosophical on you. Look, I dunno. They like the power. For as weird as it is to be here, I think they kind of believe what they are telling everyone."

"And what made you different?"

It laughed. As always, it was a hollow sound.

"Well, I don't believe I'm a telescope."

Ana waited for more information, but when none was forthcoming she just sighed. This lead the doll's face to change for the first time.

"There's a lot of harsh in the system right now. They don't like the kind of stuff we talk about. Kinda set in their ways, y'know?"

"No."

He rolled his inanimate eyes.

"I mean they are totally against us talking. They don't want us to open the door."

"Yes, I knew that."

"We should be careful."

"I know that."

Ana was again exhausted by the cryptic conversation. Finally it asked one last question before she attempted to wrap it.

"Can you do me a solid...?"

———

The travel had been remarkably uneventful, and although she was very grateful for it, she couldn't help shake the feeling of being watched. Her walks usually put her in tune with the natural world around her, so she was more likely to watch an animal than it her. However, this was something else; it was like being in the middle of a city but the people were invisible. She chalked it up to talking to a doll on a daily basis and the effect it was having on her perceptions in general, or this would be a month-long journey and her companion of all people was a saint.

Despite this, the trip alone had worn thin on her. More than once after her walk she would return to her camp to collapse under a tree, rest her face in her hands and cry quietly. She was drained beyond the point she thought she could go. Hope was in short supply and she had mostly run out. It was becoming doubtful that she would ever see Stojan again. Even her traveling companion did not know where he was with any certainty. She had willingly plunged herself into the bottom of Amira and was possibly thousands of kilometers from Stojan. There was no real way to connect with her friends, the Navajo, and she carried the burden of opening this doorway upon her shoulders. It was really too much for her and she was uncertain how many more weeks of this she could tolerate before just giving up. She sighed a very deep sigh this morning to gather the strength to continue. Today she would go into town to maintain her bearings and purchase a few items at the local market. It was an experience to see what new things were on display there, and the local fruits and vegetables were a cheerful supplement to her diet.

This town looked much like the others she had seen along the route— each was small and compact and those that dwelt there were most concerned with just being left alone. People were friendly, but kept to themselves. They enjoyed life in the warmer climate and made the best of it by working hard. In a way, it reminded her of the remarkably colorful village of elders she and Stojan had visited in that there were a number of people that came 'out west' to settle here.

This was true for the man across the aisle she was now looking upon.

Her gaze was light, then became a stare as she looked at his face and his mannerisms. He met her gaze and for many moments they looked at each other. The recognition that now showed in her face was mirrored by him as his mouth opened slowly.

He ran from the marketplace and she immediately gave chase. The man was no match for her speed and she caught up as he reached his horse. He stood upright with a very straight posture and put his hands up as if she was going to rob him. He was catching his breath now and looking at her face, her attire and just stared—at her hair.

She said one very accusatory word at him.

"You."

Mark Bradford

Amira

WHAT IS OLD IS NEW AGAIN

Her eyes were narrowed and she looked at him with suspicion. Ana recognized the man and had been up close with him some time ago. Though his skin was darker and his clothing was a bit different, he was still the same man. He was not Amiran, but like her was from Poliska. It was one of the men that were tasked with holding onto her and Stojan back at the port of the conveyance—one of the few she did not try to kill.

Without much prompting, he just started talking as he stood in front of his horse as if to guard it.

"There was much turmoil the day you were there. The merchant disappeared at the same time you did. There were rumors as to where you went. Some said he took you to a Saint; others said that you had captured him. I was not…"

The man looked down at the ground—seemingly embarrassed—as he continued.

"I was not privy to most. I was new and their ways were distasteful."

Ana thought of the man, his demeanor. He seemed to be perpetually surprised that day and more than anything he seemed out of place.

"The work was short-term."

He seemed to be confiding rather than explaining.

She continued to listen and it appeared that day Anastazja had absorbed some of the stoicism of Stojan.

"I immediately left—I knew that was the right thing to do."

His eyes widened and looked into hers.

"You must believe me—I... was only there for the money."

Though accurate, his poor choice of words painted a picture contrary to what he was trying to convey.

Ana saw the confusion in his eyes, but he seemed to be sincere.

"You left?"

"Yes. I left, immediately. I returned to Budziszyn. I thought that they would find me—force me to return. But, they were disorganized and confused. Without the merchant they knew not what to do."

Ana's attention was wavering. The urgency of his conversation was misplaced. Though it was remarkable to have run into him, she simply didn't care. She had other matters to attend to.

"I was able to rejoin my wife."

Ana smiled cordially. He smiled as well and looked into her eyes.

"There I worked and I..."

She tilted her head at his hesitation.

"I sold your father's horse, and used the monies contained there to find passage here."

"The conveyance?"

"Yes. It had come back with some Amirans and they were returning to their country. This country. My wife objected but..."

She narrowed her eyes and judged his actions. Her tone was bitter and disapproving. Her face looked sour.

"Well you have done well then? You were able to make off with our horses and monies."

He looked at her with fear—a fear that reminded her of their first meeting in which she spared him.

"With the commotion, it was all I could do to leave them. But I have something to tell you."

She inhaled—growing tired of his dramatic ways. He was a stark contrast to the way Stojan communicated and the conversation made her miss him all the more.

She folded her arms.

"It was not long ago—in the city. That's when he came. I did not recognize him at first. But then I knew. It was him. And shortly thereafter is when it happened."

It looked like the man was about to cry.

"That's when it happened, Anastazja. I did not see it myself—only the aftermath."

"Speak! Tell me! What are you talking about? You waste my time."

Her hair began to show tendrils of red.

"All those people—men and women—laid bare, slaughtered. Tens of peoples. With such absolute anger."

His eyes were distant and showed terrible, terrible fear. She'd seen him fear for his life when he thought she was about to run him through. This made that look like he had been smiling—so terrified was his expression.

For the first time, his words held interest for her. The noises of the crowd and horses were now a distant, muffled sound. She listened intently.

"He killed them all—every one of them. It was like a man possessed…"

"Who?"

"None could stop him. All because his…"

"Who?! Why do you tell me thi…"

"He killed them all because of her."

This he said as if it explained everything. It did not. She looked into his eyes half-expecting to see the scenes protected upon them.

She was going to repeat herself as he continued. His eyes wet with tears looked deeply into hers and he spoke very slowly.

"His daughter."

Her eyebrows came together just as slowly. He continued.

"I thought it was you, but I see that you are alive and well, Anastazja."

"Stojan…"

His name escaped her lips. It was as a whisper. Almost a question.

He nodded.

"I am confused now seeing you. He killed them because she was allowed to die."

He swallowed hard as she looked at him—her own eyes showing the sadness he conveyed.

"What do you mean to tell me this day? That Stojan…"

Bits of conversations overheard, accusations thrown, and situations described all coalesced in her mind now—the slaughter, the deaths, Stojan's years of running.

"That he killed at least fifty people over the death of his… you… his only daughter."

The words fell upon her like a burden.

"But you are here."

She shook her head, not wanting it to be true, but knowing it had come to pass. A year ago when he made his choice to be with her it was to let his own daughter die. She had always imagined that he simply wouldn't be there to protect her. But instead it was as if everything was left to pass. Not only had he not intervened, it had been allowed to happen again— just as it had before.

The possibilities filled her mind. The moment she was at the church and saw the saint fall was the moment he would have been transported there. But to do what? To stop himself? To prevent what had caused her to die in the first place?

It made no sense. Would the saint have made good on the promise? Surely they were powerful, but the concept boggled her mind.

"Why do you share this with me? What good is it to know this?"

Her voice creaked as she spoke, and she shook her head—her black and blonde hair moving from side to side.

"This does me no good now, and only causes me pain."

She looked genuinely pained and affected. Missing Stojan, she was vulnerable and the news made it hurt all the more.

"Does this entertain you? You seem like a saint in this way."

His eyes showed the shock and horror of her words.

"OH! Oh no! No no, please please!"

He moved to comfort her but saw her arms were at her sides again and he would clearly and efficiently lose his life for attempting it. It only added to the look of horror and fear in his eyes.

"No no! Oh I am terribly… I am so sorry. Please, please for…"

"Then why did you tell me this?!"

"This is not what I meant to tell you. I am so sorry it was some…"

"Enough!"

She put her hand on her sword.

He looked down at it, but instead of fear she saw some joy in his face for the first time as he stared there.

"Because."

She looked down at her side, as if there was something out of place, and looked back at him.

"Because I kept it."

He smiled, weakly but proudly.

Opening his mouth to speak again, he thought better of it this time and ran to his horse.

It was then she realized what he meant.

He ran back to her carrying a black wrap that was all too familiar to her. About to unwrap it, he caught himself and instead presented it to her as one would present a babe wrapped in blankets—gingerly, respectfully and with great care.

She took it and immediately recognized the smell. The fine leather wrap still had the scent she remembered and the hint of oil from within.

For a second she thought it was a trick and darted her eyes back at him. He looked back expectantly as one does when presenting a gift and awaiting its unwrapping.

This she did carefully as she laid it down. Slowly unrolling it, she finally revealed the only other connection she had to her father.

Her sword. Not the sword she wore at her side that had become too small for her, but the sword he'd crafted for her in the hopes that one day she would grow into.

She looked upon it. The oils and tight wrapping had continued to preserve it. The look of the wrapping showed that the man had kept it very safely in his possession.

Without looking up to him, she spoke.

"How did you know?"

He thought about what she meant and responded.

"I did not. I did not know if I would ever see you again. I felt terrible about spending your monies and selling your horse. I could not sell your sword. I knew it was yours. I unwrapped it but once and saw the place for its sister to lay next to it. That confirmed that this was yours."

He spoke with compassion and honesty.

"You kept it all this time?"

"Yes. And when I heard about the…"

He stopped talking abruptly, not wanting to sour the moment for her.

"I am glad it has once again found you. Please take it."

For the first time in many days, Ana's heart was filled with joy. She smiled brightly and stared at it in the sunlight, and the image brought her back to the the time she'd unrolled it for Stojan—before she came to know him as her father. For some moments she felt fulfilled; she had a gift from her father and was whole again.

She looked back at the man, slowly wrapped the sword again and paused.

He smiled but looked apprehensive.

He flinched as she moved instantly in front of him and did something he thought she would never do.

She hugged him. He felt the softness of her embrace along with the strength of her arms. He smiled a relieved smile as he was grateful she did not kill him that day.

ANA AND HER NEW SWORD

In a few minutes, she had bid farewell to the man and acquired some additional goods at the market. The path outward was straightforward and in no time she was among the trees again.

After traveling a short while on her own, she took respite under a tree. Once she was confident she was alone and could proceed unmolested, she indulged once again in unwrapping the gift. This she did slowly and with reverence; watching it unfold gently and half-expecting that the sword would be gone and that she'd imagined the whole experience. It was not, and the large sword was indeed pristine.

Unsheathing her current blade, she held it to her chest, closed her eyes and thanked her father. Ana placed it carefully in the loop next to the larger sword and picked up the new blade at last.

Using the cloths provided, she wiped the blade slightly and moved it in the sunlight. She was taken off-guard by both the size and the perfection of it. She had started to grow accustomed to the undersized sword and as Stojan had suggested, it had affected her style and her efficiency.

This new blade was heavier, larger and longer—but it was not wider. Care had been taken to make the blade width identical to the smaller sword for a number of reasons. She once again marveled at her father's craftsmanship and appreciated the steps he'd taken to create it. To the observer, she was simply staring at and through the blade, but her mind traveled to the time in which she watched him create it. Closing her eyes, she smelled and felt the heat; heard the impacts from his hammer.

She watched his large hands shape and reshape with care and love—all because she requested it. His monumental efforts were engaged because she deserved it. A swordsmith of his caliber would not have wasted the time to create not one, but two perfect swords had he not believed she not only deserved it, but would commit herself to master it. To master them. For many moments she experienced this, and was lost in thought and memories and emotions.

Finally, she thought of how she would have made him proud and opened her tearful eyes.

The sun was bright on her sword and the scene had a surreal look due to the sunlight previously illuminating her closed eyelids. As the lighting returned to normal, she pulled the sword away from her face and simply said two words.

"I will."

It would not be obvious to any who watched as to whether she was promising her father that she would make him proud, or if she was committing to finding Stojan.

Mark Bradford

Amira

CHAOS AND A NEW PARTNER

Everything was confusing. She hurt and was sure something had struck her. Attempting to wipe the dirt from her eyes alerted her to another problem. She touched her forearm and felt the heat of pain as her hand inadvertently forced some gravel into the as yet unseen wound. She squinted hard. The yelling and noises were coming from all around her and mostly above her and that was then she knew she was laying in the gravel and stones. Every movement equaled a new pain as she tried to prop herself up, wipe her eyes and get a bearing.

The sounds of metal on metal contained now as some light finally reached her eyes. She attempted to focus them as the sunlight made her head hurt.

The odd wagon that she and Stojan had been in was on its side now. There was chaos as men and women clashed around her. Some had swords while others did not. Some were in metal armor while others wore leathers of various design. It was an intense and confusing battle as there seemed to be more than two sides. This was when she realized that some of the combatants were her own men and she watched from her place on the ground. Judging from the cart and her position she surmised she was thrown from it somehow.

A horse ran past her sans rider as she searched for faces she would recognize. There were many men now, and more were entering the field. They all came from the same direction and had attacked from that flank, and more were spilling around to this side. To her left, she saw the ostentatious bishop and he was clamoring to mount his horse. There was panic in his actions and he looked wounded. Dust and gravel continued to fly as the chaos continued and she tried to get to her feet.

Madison propped herself up on her elbows but then collapsed again from the pain and dizziness. No one was near her and she made less of a target here, she thought. Perhaps she would just sleep a little…

"Surely you can find a more suitable place to lie down."

The voice was nearby and was not like the others. It did not shout but was still loud, and she recognized it.

There was pressure on her arm now; she was being lifted into the air. The pressure hurt, and her arms stung as she tried to regain her footing. She just wanted to sleep, but the dust had entered her lungs and she was coughing weakly.

The hand held her as she finally stood and blinked, and continued to cough. She squinted at the sun, then at the man before her.

Stojan.

He was breathing deeply and rapidly like he had been in battle. In his other hand was his long sword and instead of shining in the sun, it had a dull reddish look to it. The particular color stood out to her and would haunt her for some time as she would never quite see that same color again.

She tried to speak, but only coughing escaped her lips and her chest hurt. He released her arm as she was now standing of her own accord. He turned quickly as he was approached by a man she did not recognize. The sword swing was easily parried and Stojan's return swing cut the man across the chest. He backed up a step or two as Stojan threatened him with a thrust. The man glanced at Madison and back to Stojan, and began yelling.

"They are here! I found them both!"

Stojan rolled his eyes, glanced at his companion and ran the man through.

"You did not need to do that."

He withdrew his sword as she watched in horror. The blade was now a shiny red, but would not be for long. He looked around rapidly and efficiently—surveying the situation. She could only follow suit slowly as she was still regaining her composure and the noisy, deadly scene was closing in on them. There were so many men and the entire area had become a battlefield. Now and again, she recognized one of her men only to see him die at the hands of another.

"If you want to live then follow me."

Her daze was almost lifted and was replaced by the harsh clarity of what was happening around her. These men were possessed and more and more were dying at each other's hands—and they were in the middle of it. Was he defending her? She shook her head to gain clarity and regretted it. Her brain was in no mood to move that fast. She struggled to keep up with Stojan as he moved about quickly with his long legs. He never quite ran, but shuffled around very quickly. His speed and accuracy made him a most deadly combatant on the battlefield and she swallowed hard seeing this demonstration of the man that had come willingly with them in sacrifice to his daughter's safety. She deeply regretted the prodding she'd done while they were both trapped in a room together.

Two men attacked Stojan from his flank and a supremely wide swing cut them both almost simultaneously. Her attention was divided by his prowess and watching her own back for attackers. Fortunately for her at the moment, only so many men could attack at once, and many were divided into their own separate battles.

More than once she saw two combatants joined by a third, and the resulting confusion as they decided who's side the newcomer was on. That was when she realized that there were indeed three forces at play here—her small group of men, the men of the pharaoh and a new large and heavily-armed group.

"What has happened here?!"

She screamed to Stojan over the battle as she checked her backside again and again.

When he was clear, he yelled back to her.

"I have never experienced an ambush. Now I have experienced three."

"Three..? Again? Who was it?"

He stopped and lowered his sword.

"Lady Madison, you all look the same to me."

She ran to his side again as he was the only element she could count on. There was too much chaos to determine who was friend and who was foe. And for the time being he was more friend than foe, and was doing an excellent job of maintaining an amply circle of safety for them both. It would be a surprisingly long time that they would remain in the chaos. Stojan later explained it as having to do with the participation of more than two forces. The third element just created a continuous chaos until all were exhausted.

Even Stojan was tired and though he had been eyeing up a horse, all had left the battle—leaving only those on foot to fight the final vestiges of the conflict.

Finally, the two faced each other as she approached him closely, but with apprehension. She spoke first.

"Are you all right?"

He squinted at her and surveyed the area. There were many dead bodies. Weapons were also strewn about as they'd left the hands of their owners when they died, or was the reason for them to do so.

"I am as well as can be expected for someone who has been fought over like some sort of treasure."

His expression was not gentle and he appeared to include her in those that would treat him this way. After all, she and her men were the first ambush.

She reeled slightly from his words and tone. She was still convinced he would kill her.

"May I sheath my sword, or will you again try to abduct me?"

Her eyebrows came together as her eyes widened.

"Stojan…I…"

"You *were* the cause of all this."

Fortunately for Lady Madison, Stojan was in agreement with them traveling together. She knew of a nearby city and it was agreed that they would make their way there to gain supplies, refresh themselves and find word on what was happening in the world. The city was to the north so although they were backtracking—in Stojan's opinion—they would seek it, as it was the nearest civilization.

Madison was appalled at the apparent indifference Stojan displayed at going through the pockets and purses of the dead. He explained that it was something he had always done and being on the run for some time had made him an opportunist. He reminded her of another reason why it made sense.

"They no longer need it."

She herself was able to find a short sword that was adequate, though was quite repelled by having to clean it first. She annoyed Stojan when she attempted to also apply her cleaning skills to him as he was covered in the results of the battle, but due to his skill almost none of it was his. Despite the protests, she was able to make him ready for the city and they made it by nightfall.

WAXAHACHIE DOOR

Upon reaching the town outskirts she consulted her map. Ana had referenced it so many times that she believed most of what she saw was already committed to memory. She was right.

They had arrived near the 'X' drawn on the map, but there was no more information. It was up to her companion now to guide her.

Today she kept him wrapped up and decided to venture into the city itself. The sign outside of the city proper was wooden and well-crafted. In rather bold letters it said "Welcome to Waxahachie." She saw this as a good sign—literally and figuratively. It would be prudent to check on the locals as well as her ability to stock up on supplies. Whether or not the door worked as promised, she would need to refresh herself and her horse, and perhaps staying in an inn would be a treat when it was all done. Then she would find Stojan.

Like some of the cities in Amira, this one greeted the traveler with a statue. He stood on a pedestal and looked to be in excellent condition. It was a depiction of a man standing against a slab of rock. He wore a long coat of sharp design and it unfurled slightly as if it was blowing in a breeze at the time of sculpting. In his hand he held some sort of papers and his other was open with palm forward. A tassel was tied around his neck. The sculpture was a slight greenish and she had come to know that this meant it was metal and not stone. Below it was an inscription too small to read, and laid about were many tools as if a nest had been prepared. She trotted in and eyed it all suspiciously.

The city was in good repair and she found the locals to be exceptionally friendly. The Amirans of the west were typically hard-working and open to conversation and these were no different.

She spent little time surveying everything and was efficient about obtaining a few supplies as well as information. Ana did not dare ask simply where The Great Door was, but instead inquired as to the statue that greeted her and the odd nest of tools.

"It's a tradition here, and I hear tell that other folks do it as well."

"Do what?"

She brushed her hair from her eyes and waved her now removed hat as a fan. Waxahachie was rather hot today.

"The tools. We put 'em around the statue."

"For what purpose?"

The older shopkeeper eyed her up and down. Her questions were very straightforward. She had the directness of a local, but dressed as a foreigner. And she had a particular accent that he could not place.

"Oh. They stay sharp and don't rust. And well, it's just lucky."

Her hand froze in mid fan.

"They stay sharp?"

"Well, from time to time. It don't always work. But, you know, it's a tradition and people like that sort of thing. Plus, it's supposed to be good luck. Say—you're not from around here, are ya?"

She placed her hat back on her head and smiled an unconvincing smile. Grabbing the brim of her hat she exited with a simple word.

"No."

Her eyes were wide as she sought out her horse and promptly left town. The innocuous, greenish statue of the handsome man who most certainly died over a millennium ago was now an eerie reminder of her task at hand. She rode past it and in slow motion she turned her head to it— hoping that it would not move when she did so. She needn't have worried as the statue remained as still and lifeless as it had when she first arrived.

It only blinked when she was no longer looking.

———

Outside of town she found a place with a bit of cover to stop and shade her horse.   It was far enough away from any passers-by or unwanted guests, so she unwrapped the head of her small companion.

"We are almost there."

She was quite pleased at the simple phrase and had mentally shrugged at having to deal with the usual exuberance.

"Yes. Which way now? We are just outside of the city."

It turned its head and then struggled a bit with his bindings.

"Let me see the map. Bring it here to me."

She unrolled the large scroll and brought it to him.   He examined it carefully in silence and then struggled a little again with his bindings.

"You will have to release me eventually."

"Yes, as we discussed. Which way?"

It narrowed its eyes and pointed with his head.

"That way. We should see a hidden structure low to the ground."

The saint looked particularly irritated at being wrapped, just when Ana assumed it had adjusted to her way of doing things.

"How far?"

"I would say just a few miles."

"You seem more certain now."

It smiled but said nothing more. She kept the wraps off of the head, mounted her horse and began the short trek.

After a mile or so, she looked down at it. He seemed to be struggling with the wraps, or was at least uncomfortable. Did a doll understand comfort? She looked down at it and yelled to the top of its head.

"You seem less talkative of late."

It stole a glance up at her and then continued watching ahead. She shook her head in annoyance. Just when she wanted more conversation it would no longer speak, or spoke less. It was less friendly and all business.

"Are you afraid? Is that it?"

Again it did not respond. Finally it yelled at her without looking.

"There, to the right—off the road."

Ana now saw a structure that had collapsed. It was clearly another Old World Amiran building with impossibly thin walls, probably made of metal and was none too attractive to look upon. It was in decay, but still managed to look menacing and bland at the same time. She was impressed that a building so abandoned would still be intact. An area that was presumably once windows was now just an opening. She thought surely she would find a nest of something residing in there. When she voiced her concern, the saint said with some certainty that it should be safe and that there was no real place to nest.

"Why is it still intact?"

"This is not the door. It is just the entrance."

A few clouds passed overhead—giving them a reprieve from the heat. She dismounted and looked upon the slate grey building. It was perfectly rectangle—or once had been. Now it looked as though all of the windows were missing and part of it had caved in. The earth appeared to flatten out as they approached the building. It was as if someone had made sure the surrounding land was quite flat, but the land had protested and shot up an edge, a crevice or a crag here and there.

"You can free me now."

She looked down to see a very flat, bright path leading to the caved-in area. It was made of sectioned stone in perfect square segments. The closer she was to the building the more pristine they were. She spun quickly to the saint in the saddle bag.

"Is there a saint here?!"

It shook its head and did not look at her.

"No, there is no saint here besides me."

She reached into the bag and pulled out the doll. Standing on its own it would be no taller than a meter or so, but was very squat. His girth was the product of artistic license by the sculptor and not due to his eating habits. She had fashioned the wraps so that the back was a sort of handle, and she made use of this to carry it into the building—much to the dislike of the saint.

"I said unwrap me. I can not help you to open the door if I am subdued."

Though it had annoyed and irritated her throughout the trip, she now realized that the flippant, scattered thoughts of the saint—along with his almost-gibberish way of speaking—provided a sort of comfort. She'd forgotten the magnitude of both the entity that was contained as well as the quest she was on. It was this thought that explained the apparent change in demeanor—and language. This, she realized, was welcome because she had almost formed an attachment to it.

"I will not unwrap you until we reach the door."

"Then enter here and go to the right..."

It guided her into the building and was quite aware of the layout. The section still standing was mostly devoid of items and had remarkably not been overcome by scrub, or even gravel. Why the area had not at least been taken over by the blowing dirt and dust, she did not understand. Surely though with such a great opening, the interior would look just like the surroundings. His comment about a saint not being here did not make sense. Something had maintained it over the years—somehow.

"We have to take the stairs."

After the confusing comment, he continued to direct her to a door with a metal bar set across it. It reminded her of the second Amiran building she'd entered upon coming here—the library. She pushed the bar and it gave way. The stairs were dimly lit with lights emanating from twin eyes affixed to a box near the ceiling. The light was ugly and harsh and there were boxes like this every few meters. They were quite similar to the boxes with the red lights that lit up when the pyramid had become dark.

After descending a number of stairs and landings, she wondered just how far they were to go. It was quite intimidating, and she had never been this far underground. In fact, she found that the air was stale. Ana stopped and plopped the doll down against the wall and exhaled.

"How far are we to go? I do not like this!"

"If you would untie me perhaps you would not be so tired."

She tilted her head in confusion. His comment came with some irritation.

"I am not tired. I am afraid of being this far underground. It is unnatural. It could collapse at any moment. We were not meant to…"

"Nonsense. The structure is large. It runs for many miles underground. And the controls are likewise underground. We are more than halfway there. You are afraid?"

It laughed a condescending laugh.

Frustrated and embarrassed, she grabbed the saint and continued through the stairs and landings at a more rapid pace. Her thoughts turned to just wanting to end this. Any affection she had for the saint had been dispelled with his laugh. They were evil creatures and he'd fooled her into thinking he was different and possessed some kind of humanity. He was just like the others and now he had reverted to his true personality as he guided her like a servant.

Finally, they reached a door and hallway at the bottom. There were items scattered on the floor—a shovel, some bags, bits of metal. The door was open and looked like it had been forcibly broken with a great gouge in one side. She could not tell if this forced entry had just happened or had been there for some time. The more she saw, the more she was convinced a saint had been here somewhere, but the saint contained in the doll had denied it.

She walked through the door and found a larger area that looked as if a battle had taken place within. Structures and boxes and cubes were there, along with a chair or two that was on its side. The chairs were similar to such chairs she had seen in other Amiran buildings. These actually had a branch-like design underneath, instead of flowers they sprouted wheels.

It looked like someone had angrily gone through the area in search of something. She recognized some of the larger cubes and desks and looked into the drawers that had been pulled open.

"Through there."

She blinked, looked down at her companion and then looked to where he was looking.

"You should untie me now."

"Are we at the door?"

"It's through there."

She did not untie him but walked him past the scavenged area and through the door made of glass. It did not open as other doors, but had been half slid into the door frame. She pushed it a bit more and squeezed through. There was another room and this one was lit with a softer white light. The sun, it seemed, was peeking through rectangles in the ceiling. She'd seen this sort of thing and now understood that this was not sunlight but artificial light created with Amiran tec, for surely they were many, many stories below the earth. Boxes upon poles protruded from the ceiling at regular intervals. A large barren wall had been painted a very bright white. Off to the side was a very large painting of intricate design. It looked as if someone had written a very large page in a book as the detail was perfection and the colors were vivid. The giant square looked to be by itself as the space next to it was just the pure white—as if someone had torn down those giant pages.

The saint squinted now and his attention moved from the giant square to a desk area set up in front of it some distance away. The desk looked wooden and although some chairs were on their sides, one of the wheeled conveniences was upright and in front of something that produced a bit of colored light. She recognized it as one of the living pictures that she had seen more than once now. In fact, she remembered the last time she saw something remarkable like this.

Wide-eyed, she dropped the saint onto the floor and he hit it with a hard plop and immediately fell on his side.

"What are you doing?!"

"This! This is all a great weapon! You mean to destroy things! I have seen such Amran tec before and have in fact used it. You have a weapon of mass destruction. You mean to use it."

"Shut…"

"You have lied! Again! You've shown your true colors."

"…up!"

"Do not talk to me that way!"

"This is *not* a weapon! This is what a control room looks like, you moron. Put me on the chair so I may see better. You still have me bound."

"I..!"

"Just do it. I can't cause any harm with my head. Ugh!"

Timidly, she did as asked and he mumbled while looking at the picture in front of him, and then glanced up to the wall with the large illustration on it.

"Unbind me. There is a problem."

Again he was all business. She was frustrated and hurt at what had transpired. He had never been so rude with her. And now he was simply looking over everything. They were strange partners in a business that benefited them both.

"You will promise this is not a weapon?"

"Yes."

She unbound him and halfway through, he wiggled out of it, stretched and jumped onto the chair. The board in front of him with letter keys was used by his fat fingers with some difficulty.

"There is a problem in the back."

"The back?"

"The door. The door itself."

"This is not the door?"

"You people are idiots."

"What did you say?"

The saint ignored her and continued to touch the letter squares. He did not clarify what he had said under his non-existent breath. To her amazement, the giant wall painting changed instantly to another illustration. It was a large circle, and it was colored orange with all manner of lines drawn upon it. The lines were extremely thin and there was writing too small to make out.

"We fixed this already."

He growled and hopped off of the chair and ran to a set of doors. She followed him—leaving the wraps in her wake. As she went through the double doors, she was taken aback by the echo. Stairs went down to the base, but these stairs rang like metal and were exposed—like a ladder that had been turned into a set of stairs. They were arched to a wall that then opened up into a cavern.

It was huge.

Slowly she went down the stairs, and being able to see through the sides of the steps gave her a bit of vertigo. At the bottom she stepped off and looked around. It was a shaped cavern, as if someone had used a great tool to dig a perfectly circular opening in the rock itself, as some of it was partially exposed. Into the tunnel was laid great lengths of metal and very thick ropes made of what looked like twined metal. The opening had to have been a circle measuring no smaller than 10 meters in height. The resulting tunnel went on for many hundreds meters and turned slightly in a consistent manner. If it had not turned she wondered if the tunnel would have just ended in a pinpoint—so huge was the monster of construction. Along the tunnel was a cylinder that flexed and had protrusions of many pipes upon it. So precise and particular were the fixings and attachments that it would take years and many hundreds of people to construct such a thing. It was lit every so many meters by the familiar strips of light. It smelled of earth and metal, and every footstep was absorbed in the vastness.

The little doll was waddling quickly and jumped into a small yellow cart that looked like it was designed for him. The thing had shiny metal bars protruding from the front and he used it to steer with. With a lurch, it took off and rode along a track that was on the left side of the thing—the inner curve of the great tunnel.

He talked to himself as he rode off quickly.

She just stood and looked around and took a few steps back. He had given no instructions and was thoroughly immersed in the thing. The saint was clearly very familiar with it and took to it as if he had had a hand in designing it.

She took the time to catch her breath and release some of her frustration. The tunnel and thing inside it was the most intimidating and awesome construction she had ever seen. Even the great pyramid of Luxor was not as frightening as this, for contrary to the saint's affirmations to the contrary, it did indeed appear as a great weapon. If the shaft pointed upward and did not curve she would have been convinced that it was the home of one of the sky arrows she had unleashed. Perhaps it really was a door.

Her eyes scanned around and she looked over some of the unfinished area of the carved rock. Along with the earth and metal smell was something new now—an odd, unpleasant scent. There were bits of metal and a few small pieces of something white. There were also tools strewn about—some looked like they would be used by a blacksmith while others were delicate contraptions.

A set of large double-doors was off to the side and they had an unusual seal upon them. Like most of the doors, there was some damage as if someone had hurriedly pried them open—or attempted to keep them closed. They looked very important and she wondered what was behind them. A well-worn track was in place there.

The small layer of dust on the floor was also not present near a normal-sized door. Glancing over her shoulder, she reached for the knob in silence. With some difficulty it opened. She was startled by the white thing that immediately peeked its head out and then fell. What she thought was a head, was in fact a hand and was attached somewhat to a body. An unpleasant smell slowly wafted out as the bulk of what was in the small closet pushed the door open.

It was filled with skeletons.

Some of them still wore clothing and the remains of the dead still clung to the arms and legs. She froze in shock and fascination as she attempted to make sense of it. Before she lost too much time and was discovered, she kicked the hand and other bones back into the closet and pushed the door closed. A click told her it would hold. The smell was not pleasant, but it was not as odorous as she expected.

Next to it were scratches in the rock. They were uniform and looked like someone was keeping a tally.

She once again heard the quiet whirring of the small, three-wheeled carriage. She had to shield her eyes as a bright lantern was affixed to the front of it and almost blinded her as it rounded the corner. Ana lifted her hand to shield her eyes and it rolled to a stop. The rotund doll leapt off of the ride.

"It is done."

He walked over to her with a look of satisfaction and excitement on his face.

"Upstairs. Come with me."

When she did not move and did not look excited, he stopped a few feet away.

"Where are we going? I thought this was the door. Is it up ahead in the tunnel?"

"The whole thing is part of the door. This structure. Come now. It is sensitive and only works for a short time. You don't want to be in the tunnel when this is on—especially with that metal at your side."

She shot him a curious glance, but it was clear he had no desire to explain further and started hobbling up the stairs. She followed behind him and tried not to look through the stairs again but focused on the back of his head. She thought that just before he entered the door at the top, he glanced down at the storage door.

Once back into the more comfortable space she asked more questions.

"Now what? Do we just wait? Will it pull you and the others through?"

He rolled his eyes and stopped in his tracks while mumbling a quick response.

"Why are you so stupid?"

"What?"

He turned his head and spoke loudly and with some anger.

"You ask questions whose answers you would not understand, so what's the point?"

"What's the point? Why are you so angry?"

He jumped upon the seat he had used before and immediately began squinting and hit a letter or two. The detailed drawing on the wall changed and no longer showed any orange, instead the circle was green now. Many numbers were there as well, and they changed before her eyes faster than she could blink.

When he started to smile broadly the drawing changed again. At the top of the circle was a bulge and it was orange now. His smile subsided.

"Well, you can do *something* now."

He jumped off of the chair and told her to follow him. She trailed behind him and almost had to run. Again he made his way down the stairs and almost fell—so hurried was he.

He went straight to the double doors and pulled them open.

"In here."

She followed and what she saw made the great weapon in the other room look tame.

It was a wall as high as the cavern and it too was circular. She expected it to be a window into the tunnel and in a way it was. It was a massive metal disk. Much shiny metal and pipes and lengths of metal rope reached out from an inner circle. She felt like she was staring at a great point of convergence—everything spoke of all paths ending here. If the mass of metal fell, it would easily crush a horse. In front of it was a sort of pedestal made of metal and stone. It too was circular and she felt the construction of it different from the massive thing that was not only on the wall, but was the wall itself. Scorch marks were on the floor as if someone had started a number of fires here and the room had a smell she could not identify; the scent was unlike anything she'd ever inhaled. All Ana was able to determine was that it somehow smelled unnatural. On the floor were bits of sharp objects. To Ana they looked like someone had shattered many ceramic pots. Some pieces were very vibrant while others were dull. Some of the pieces even looked like they had melted and not shattered.

The large doll turned to her and looked oddly proud.

"Here it is. This is the door—or at least the thing that you people would consider a door. And you're going to help me open it now."

He reached over to a crate on the floor and dragged it to a part of the wall. A large lever was pulled and she felt as if everything had gone silent. The smell had changed to the scents of a thunderstorm, but no rain fell and no thunder was heard. Her hair felt lighter and her skin felt as if something was crawling on it. Just then she remembered her sword.

"I thought you said I should not be wearing this!?"

"You're fine."

He smiled an unconvincing smile and hopped off of the box. He stretched his thick arms and walked up onto the dais. Looking down at the scorch mark, he looked up at her menacingly.

"Let's see if it works this time."

"This time? You have tried it before?"

"Oh yes."

"Why am I here?"

There was a humming now—it was not heard in her ears but within her bones. She was beginning to become scared. It felt like a room she should not be in.

"If this does not work, I need you to return that lever to the other position and turn this off."

Her face became incredulous and her lips were contorted.

"Why can you not do this?"

He shook his head in condescension.

"Because my vessel will be destroyed again."

That was when she felt the tingling. Instinctively, she reached for her sword—only to find that she could not move.

"Yes, there is paralysis and then some pain I'm told. Remember… if this doesn't work you have to pull that lever or we'll burn out another section and that will take years to fix with people like you. Plus it will kill you."

He smiled and truly looked like he was enjoying this. The humming was getting more apparent. Her speaking was labored.

"What do you…mean…again…destroyed?"

"You people are such idiots. How many generations does it take? I thought I would need you, but you were just my mule, kid. Once you reached the city I knew it was my turn."

"Turn…?"

"You got it, right? You knew I was different. I sent The Saint on High back to his observatory. I kept him in this shell so he could get you here. No, he couldn't do it on his own."

He poked a thick thumb into his chest and looked proud.

"I'm the only one that can do this. For many years I didn't take hold— just like the others. But when they did I continued. After hundreds of years I realized this was what my existence would be. Your people did a very thorough job of chasing me out of your country, however. So many statues and buildings destroyed, for what? To keep The Saints out, when you were really just keeping *me* out."

As he spoke, she tried to move various muscles and found that the harder she tried the more her effort was opposed. It was painful. Interestingly, she also found the reverse to be true—the slower she moved, the less resistance and pain she felt. It reminded her of when she would play her game of touching the animals and moved ever so slowly. She turned her head while he spoke. Behind her was a faint outline of a body, as if a fire had blasted it and left only a human-shaped, scorch mark as a reminder.

Her eyes widened in horror as he continued and turned her head back towards him. She started to slowly move her right hand.

"And for many generations I have tried to open the door. Only recently have I been privy to more than just a feeling or an intention, and I have gained more control over where I go. I've been able to keep so many things preserved because of it. This facility is just one. Your predecessors have done a lot of work for me, and you were just the messenger. I had bigger plans for you. You seemed so clever? But you're just as dumb as the rest."

"The Flickering Saint..."

"An apt name, yes? Like a flame that jumps from candle to candle. Unlike the others, I have so many congregations. Mind you, they are small and in some cases it is just a curiosity. Because of me, they believe there are thousands of us, or that we can be anywhere."

"What of the...Saint on..."

"Oh, I sent him back to his abode. I can change places with him at any time now. He is trying to possess this shell even now. He was very confused but taught me much about pushing the others out. He is clueless about what we are doing and trying not to listen."

Ana felt a slight relief that her relationship with the other saint had not been a ruse, and that he had not actually lied to her. He seemed quite harmless compared to the thing that possessed the doll now. The humming in her bones was almost intolerable now, and her right hand was in a different kind of pain from gripping metal.

"The room..."

Her voice now seemed sluggish as if she was drunk. She meant to ask about the room with the horrific contents.

"Oh, your predecessors. I've tried this for many of your generations. Most of the building, the reconstruction, the testing, the aligning... Some of this was destroyed at the time we came through. And then the door was closed. And then the earthquakes, and the shifts and..."

He frowned.

"Oh, you mean what happened?"

He smiled.

"They were my helpers—so eager to be the aid to a saint! I don't have bishops like the others; instead I enlist the help of those who are ever so devoted. You're the exception, but you had the means and the cleverness to make the trek with me in one piece. And your friend had the vessel. And the one you call The Saint on High was convinced that he could possess it—thanks to me. And thanks to him I learned how to block out the others when needed."

He tilted his head with a self-satisfied wink, and then turned behind him to look at the circular structure. Some of it was highlighted with tiny arcs as if there was a tremendous lightning storm going on behind it.

"You... don't really need... me..."

She surprised him. He did not turn, instead he continued to survey the thing in front of him as she looked at the back of his head. He wanted to make sure this time it worked before watching it pull him in and vaporize her.

"Well, you are actually clever! No. I don't need you. If this succeeds it will create a doorway that will destroy this room. If it fails it will create enough energy to kill everything inside it. Either way you will die like the others. I can't have you or them warning anyone, can I? Then I'll have no helpers, and I have exhausted most of the fetish dolls in this area. Finding a vessel has become laborious at best now. You're such a good listen..."

That was when she threw her sword. It wasn't much of a throw, but more of a release. True to what the saint had said it had been a dangerous idea to have that much metal on her person. He assumed it would just cause an additional arc of energy and he wanted to be sure she was dead.

As he went on and had his back to her, she'd unsheathed it with the intention to strike him down. It would be so easy to shatter the little thing with him in it, and the first strike of her new sword would be to kill a saint.

But the energies had acted to pull it in. The sword pointed to the center of the door. It competed with the pull of the earth itself and had won. The sword dangled from her hand as it pointed like a needle on a compass, and he was standing in the way. She could not raise her sword and exert enough force to strike him. And she was much too far away. There was only one thing she could do to make a difference.

A tear ran down her cheek as she decided she would give up the most cherished possession she now had. It was short lived and the action would most certainly kill her too. At least Stojan would know what happened to her—if there was anything left of her afterward.

She let go of the sword and it traveled rapidly to the very center of the door—where all the tiny pieces and parts converged.

Unfortunately, the saint turned too early as the sword was about to pierce his head. A slight movement allowed him to dodge it, so instead of his head it struck deeply into the very center of the device—where it was most sensitive. It landed with a terrible noise.

Infuriated, he turned fully to face her as a ring of white erupted from the machine. She could now move as his face contorted into fury. It seemed she had pierced the very heart of the device and it had become unstable. The center dimmed but the entire wall was now lit up with sparks, and arcs and light.

Their eyes locked as a tiny explosion ejected her sword and it landed between the two of them.

She looked back up as arcs of lightning leaped forth of their own accord and attached to anything within range, including the doll. It stumbled slightly now, and spoke.

"Whoa. I was… and now I'm…"

The doll quickly spun behind it to look at the device as if for the first time, then spun back to face Ana. His arms were out demonstrably and he shook them when he spoke. He had an uncertain smile.

"Dude I…"

Just then thick arcs reached the doll as it began to shatter in place. Sections of it separated into pieces that were flung to the floor. He looked into her eyes.

"Awww…"

It rolled its eyes in disappointment as it acquiesced to its destruction.

"Whatever."

She grabbed her sword and made for the stairs. Tendrils and arcs were reaching for anything and everything in the room. An arc leapt at the sword as if to threaten her. As she reached the top, she looked back to see the doll in pieces all over the floor and its shards mixed with the shattered remains of the other attempts. This time the destruction had taken with it not an empty shell, but another saint.

Ana reached the stairs and made her way out of the building as fast as possible. She had neither the time nor the interest in noticing the giant display that now flashed many warnings in red—and the alarm system that would have sounded had it been not disabled hundreds of years ago by an irritated interloper.

The humming continued and she thought she felt her skin once again feel as if something was lightly rubbing against it.

At last she made it out of the building and almost crashed through the door in the process. She did not slow her pace as she continued running. Thoughts of the great sky arrow were prominent in her mind and gave her feet even more urgency. She believed behind her would be a great explosion with the powers the saint brought to bear. He had boasted that he'd tried the door many times before, and yet she felt fear as she ran. It may have been the fact that she was probably the only one of his assistants that survived, or perhaps it was being up close with the impossibly complex and large machine. Or perhaps it was because she had been the only human in a millennia to sabotage the workings. Regardless, she kept running towards where her horse should be. How far was far enough? She only felt the wind on her skin now, and the sun on her face, but kept running.

Finally she stopped to catch her breath. Her hand hurt from gripping the sword so hard and she all but had to peel it from her palm.

She stared at it, and kept staring in amazement. It was unharmed and shined brightly in the sunlight. Whatever the very center of the door was made of, it had not been any stronger than the steel of her sword. She closed her eyes and remembered the scene. The sword had been enveloped in the lightning and energies and she was sure it had been melted. Yet here it was—intact.

With an enormous grin she jumped up into the air and yelled with the sword above her.

"YES!"

She ran her hand along the length of it—feeling for any pits or scratches. She found nothing and quickly sheathed it. The tiny hairs on her right arm were still standing on end and she wondered if it was from the energies she'd been exposed to or just because she was such a confusing mixture of fear, release and excitement.

She noticed the building—or rather—the lack thereof. In the place of the half-destroyed structure was a small blanket of dust that was settling. At this distance, the dust cloud was still at only a meter or so in height, yet nothing protruded from it. The building was now gone.

The ground rumbled and she crouched down to touch it and to catch her balance instinctively. The ground was now indeed rumbling and vibrating, but was already subsiding. There wasn't much she could discern at this distance other than dust clouds that were erupting everywhere and went off into the distance as far as she could see. Every so often she would see a tree topple or a group of trees fold inward. It was frightening, but would have been worse had it not been moving away instead of towards her. Something massive was moving away from the building and leaving a small cloud of dust in its wake. Something invisible, or…

She could see animals in the distance that were running from it—and birds that had taken flight. It moved away quickly and instead of traveling in a straight line, curved slightly. She lost it behind trees in the distance. As she watched it move farther and farther away it looked like it had subsided.

And thus it was that the doorway the interlopers had used to come into this world was not just closed, but now destroyed irrevocably. And although one saint had escaped, another saint had been dispatched forever. Anastazja had been responsible for the destruction of not one ,but two saints. She and Stojan had all but wiped out half of them. There were now four left—if those who spoke of it were to be believed.

She stood back up to her full height and scanned all around. There were a few clouds in the sky and like much of the land here, the ground had grass and trees mixing the browns of the gravel with the deep greens of the elms, oaks and ash.

There was one thing missing—her horse. If she could not find him then she once again would have lost not only her horse, but the rations she'd

319

just accumulated—and she was looking forward to some particular treats from the market.

At least her arm stopped tingling.

But what now? It appeared that once again she was alone, and this time she was in what once may have been a city but was no more. The saint that in actuality had led her here, betrayed her and had left—presumably for the nearest statue. The one that she had almost grown fond of was gone.

The Saint on High was no more.

She sighed and stood in place and laughed. It wasn't the laugh of joy, or of humor. It was the laugh one produces when one sees the most absurd of things, and each week produces something more absurd than the last. It was the laugh one laughs when one has almost all of one's possessions taken from them again and again. Now, not even her horse was present. She had water and the other silly things in her tiny backpack she refused to remove. This just drove the point home all the more that she should not let go of them. Ana sat upon the dusty earth and removed her pack. Her arms and exposed skin were covered in dust. It would be a hot day again and she had limited water. One by one she pulled items from her pack and laid them upon the earth. She was in no danger of being attacked or robbed as there was no one as far as she could see. Perhaps The Flickering Saint's plan to kill her would still work—but just a bit more indirectly as she would starve or die from lack of water.

She removed her water skin, her small bag of coins, her compass and her book. The key she believed to have summoned The Saint on High had been left with her horse with more coins, food and water, and her old sword. She looked off into the distance again for the horse.

Ana put her head in her hands and cried. She gained one sword only to lose the other. They were both equally important to her—she realized. The other sword was all but useless now and yet still held much meaning in her heart.

She looked at the odd and meager items in front of her as her tears made rivulets down her cheeks through the dust. She had argued with Stojan about keeping coins in her pack as they made too much noise. She refused to wear anything at her belt save for her sword for many reasons, and keeping all of her money in her saddlebags was unsafe. Her compromise was to keep just a few and roll the bag so tightly that they would not move. She was grateful for this as she literally now wore all of her possessions upon her.

She laughed again and blinked the dust from her eyes. She stared at the items before her and turned her book so it didn't blow in the breeze. There was water, the compass still worked, the book was intact and she had some monies.

Ana shook her head.

"Enough."

She spoke it to the wind, to her fate, and to herself.

The wind blew and did not hear her.

Amira

HE WHO SOARS

After sitting in the sun entirely too long, Ana had used up most of her water. She could not seek the shelter of the building, nor could she ride to the nearby town. Instead she was seeking the shade of a grove of trees and then would hopefully find a river. Her map had unfortunately been kept in her saddle bag with the rest of her belongings as it was rather large, but her compass would help her find her way.

Her most immediate concern was not dehydrating and —if at all possible —finding her horse.

That day saw no horse and very few animals, and her camp was minimal as everything was carried upon her. It was a sort of luxury in that she didn't have to return to her possessions because everything traveled with her person. That night she heard thunder and saw lightning in the sky, but no rain fell. She was up with the sun and large clouds greeted her. They hovered in the sky like giant cities made of cotton and brought shade in regular intervals. Her decision to stay for the night made the most sense as she was far more exhausted than she thought.

A smile crossed her face as she looked at the thing she hugged while she slept—her sheath. It was entirely too uncomfortable to wear it and sleep, and she would not part with it so it was her sleeping companion that night. Standing and unsheathing it carefully, she looked upon it as if it had been delivered out of her dreams. It was indeed real and she ran her hand along it. So much like her other sword—it was simply longer. It was perfect and completely unharmed from the events of the previous day. Ana sheathed it and attached her belt. Today she would make the journey to the nearest town to the north and ignore the pleas of her stomach. Her head hurt slightly as she drank the last of her water. She and Stojan had stayed quite a few nights in the wilderness, but always with a plan. He had taught her a number of rules for survival and she'd broken more than one—not intentionally however.

She started walking and noticed the majestic clouds. The building in the distance had not resurfaced, but today there were birds and some were in the sky. A rather large one approached from the west and soared like a bird of prey. She glanced back in front of her lest she stumble. The sounds of the birds were a welcome change from the silence of the previous day. Whatever happened with the door had spooked animals for kilometers. Most had returned, or at least the birds had. She glanced up again to the bird of prey—perhaps it would lead her to a lake or river. It was gone, however. She looked back to see if it turned abruptly but could not find it. If she was near a body of water it would make more sense to go the short distance before continuing. Her frustration was increasing, along with her headache. Ana's annoyance got the best of her as she just froze and scanned for the bird. That was when she heard a noise she was familiar with. She'd heard it before, but it was muffled and louder then.

She ran. The bird was ahead of her and much lower. And it was not a bird.

The arrow plane had returned. Dust was kicked up as she entered a flat area with no trees. She ran towards where it headed and it appeared to be making its descent between her and the location of the door. It shone in the sun and was the beautiful sculpture in metal and other Amiran materials she'd come to appreciate. Seeing it far away as it performed its graceful and majestic flight was new, however. She had only seen it up close and then from within. It was truly a magic conveyance that had no equal. Unlike a bird, it did not alight when it landed but instead took much time to come parallel with the earth and roll to a stop.

Only a short distance away she stopped. Dagmar was certainly not within. Who could it be then? Who could also steer the craft of the sky? Even Dagmar seemed terrified, though he hid it well. The saints could easily do this. Had the flickering saint returned so quickly? She had just assumed the visitor was friendly. She realized this was a mistake, and it was too late; whoever was inside had already seen her. She reached for her sword and drew it. The door eventually opened and two figures emerged.

Even at this distance she recognized the dress of both and the face of one. Smiling broadly she resheathed her sword and ran towards them. She did not stop until she hugged the older of the two. And like so many others, he looked relieved when she did this as her movements were so quick and intense. He groaned as she squeezed.

She pulled back and realized that she may have hurt the elderly gentleman.

"Sunflower, you have grown as tall as your namesake."

He looked spooked, relieved and full of joy.

"Stanley Two Rivers!"

His craggy face proudly smiled upon her. She smiled back slightly confused, relieved and sad.

"You live! I wasn't sure. When he said the elder was... Oh, Fox. Poor Fox. I am so sorry." They were holding hands now—the remnants of the embrace. She looked into his eyes.

"He was a warrior."

"Yes, my son died honorably and I am proud of him. His loss was felt by many, including his cousin."

With that he turned to the younger man next to him and then disengaged their hands. The younger man smiled and seemed to be shaking his head in disbelief. He spoke with difficulty as if he was out of breath or had recently taken a blow to his stomach.

"I am..."

The elder smiled and completed the sentence for him.

"...quite beside himself."

"Uncle!"

Ana and Stanley Two Rivers laughed. The man attempted to compose himself as the elder continued.

"He Who Soars is affected more by the journey than I am, in spite of his name."

He winked at the younger man, who picked up on the queue. Ana saw it as an opening and hugged him as well. The man's eyes were wide and he simply mouthed '*Uncle!*' as he hugged her back. She pulled away and nodded to him. Ana glanced from older to younger man.

"How did you find me? How did you find the arrow plane? And how did you come to master it and fly it properly?"

The two men looked at each other and the younger replied matter-of-factly.

"We read the manual."

"Yes, He Who Soars was an excellent study and committed to it. We have been watching it for some time and when you and your friend soared above us with it, we decided to approach him about the manual. We had instructions while he possessed the actual craft."

The younger man looked quite proud now while the older man continued.

"But much happened before we could do that. We are sad that you have lost your friend. He was a good man and we honor the sacrifice he made."

"You know of this? How do you know?"

"All who still dwell in Luxor are aware of what happened—including the sky arrow you set upon them. More than one of his men left his service in time not to be destroyed. And for that they were thankful—and talkative."

Ana was taken aback. In her mind she had pronounced that saint and all who were loyal dead and gone. She might not have been so vocal about what she did or where she was going had she known there were those that escaped the wrath of the sky arrow. Seeing her face, the elder continued.

"They are of no matter Ana; they are but a handful and seeing the destruction wrought, they spread a message quite different than the last."

"And that is?"

"That the saints are mortal. That The Sunflower has rained terror and destruction from the sky. That it is she who the saints should fear now and not Watchful Raven."

Anastazja smiled at the mention of Stojan's true name. It harkened back to her time with The People and many memories flooded into her pounding head.

"Ana, come with us!"

"Where… where are we going?"

"Well, nowhere right now, but it is much cooler in here."

He Who Soars gestured with his hand as she walked up the short stairs and into the conveyance. He traded glances with his uncle. Once on board they closed the door and Ana felt the cold of the interior. She removed her belt so that she could sit properly and the leather of the seat was cold on her legs. Before she could speak, the younger man handed her a water skin. She accepted it gratefully.

"It is cold!"

"Yes, there is a special container that will not allow its contents to be warm if you wait long enough."

She drank the cold water and it was almost painful, but the enjoyment of quenching her thirst combined with the air inside of the conveyance made for a most pleasurable experience. He Who Soars went an inordinate amount of effort watching her drink—as well as keeping an eye on the water that missed her mouth and ran down her chin. She pulled the skin away and stared at them with her mouth open as she caught her breath. The elder smiled and looked like he was quite happy she was quenching her thirst while his nephew seemed transfixed and slightly concerned.

"How did you find me?"

"The city was marked on the map in the arrow plane."

"Yes, but you landed so near me."

"We landed near The Great Doorway. It is visible from the sky—even very high up."

"It is?"

"Yes. It is a circle larger than any city. It is as if someone has drawn a circle some fifty miles long or more."

"Oh."

"Yes, it looks like it has collapsed inward as we could see that it was like a trench with trees and earth caved in towards it."

Ana thought back to the smoke trail that travelled away from her when the building collapsed.

"We came to see if you reached the doorway."

"Who told you I would be here? How did you know?"

"Sedona. All of Sedona and Luxor knows of your quest to destroy the saints."

Clearly she had left enough breadcrumbs.

"And Stojan? Do you know of him? Where is he?"

The two men traded slow glances.

"No, please. Please do not tell me that he is…"

The elder man shook his head almost imperceptibly.

"No no. We have not heard of his demise, but in fact have good news for you. He has escaped to the north."

"Escaped to the north? From his capture? How did you come upon this information?"

Again, they traded glances.

"It is good we found you Ana. You are hungry."

It wasn't a question and as always the elder just knew. He hadn't answered the question, but she nodded as he broke out some food. It was some very thin flatbread and root vegetables. She happily ate them and listened.

"Ana can please tell us what happened here? When you are done of course."

The elder happily watched her eat and relax. He had not mentioned how different she looked of late. Ana had grown even more in the short time she was gone, and her attire had been tweaked by her to match her style. She also looked like she had just been through an ordeal—which of course she had. She removed her hat, placed it on the seat and ran her hand through her hair rapidly to bring body back into it.

Ana had a lot to tell her visitors—and the fresh food, cold water and comfortable environment made for an ideal setting to share. They both sat quietly, interjecting only here and there for some of the more absurd and amazing aspects of her story. She was tireless in her discussing and unloading of information and her audience was eager to learn. The younger man's mouth stayed open for most of it. He'd been exposed to the arrow plane and much reading on Amiran tec, but his experience with saints was nonexistent. Here, in front of him, was someone who had met not one but *four* of them—and was indirectly responsible for the demise of three. And some of the things she described verified what he had just read, as the manual for the arrow plane wasn't the only one he had absorbed.

When she finished, the younger man closed his mouth, traded glances with the other occupants and allowed the elder to speak first. He did so —warmly and slowly.

"Sunflower, you have had quite an adventure. I am most proud of what you have done. To travel alone in a country such as Amira is an impressive feat. You have grown in many ways."

She smiled and looked embarrassed when she realized he was just getting started on his accolades.

"We have been with you for many months. When word reached us of Fox and your quest to see the coast we made many…observations."

"You were there? You were watching me?"

"We were keeping an eye on you, especially when you were near us. You did very well. We did not follow you. We watched you pass though. But what you tell us is validating."

He became very serious as she looked at the other man before speaking.

"We found many more saints influencing the people of Amira. If what he told you is true, that means they are all one—The Flickering Saint. It explains many things we did not understand."

It was He Who Soars turn to speak now.

"We have learned much from our library, Anastazja. What Amira is capable of is amazing and it should have risen as a great nation again, but something…"

She tilted her head at him as he finished.

"…held it back."

She listened as she did not quite understand.

"We think that was on purpose now. The Flickering Saint has worked hard to set those in Amira upon themselves. Since he himself could not have a congregation he simply nudged and influenced—keeping the nation in chaos and setting them against each other…and us."

"Us?"

"Yes, the Amirans and The People have long been at odds with each other. The ways of The People of the Ants are different than the ways of the Amirans you have been among for some time. A difference does not make an enemy. But distrust for us has been ruled by the saints. And no saint has provided more fuel than the one that flickers."

"He was very angry."

She nodded with some humor.

"I wonder how these interlopers have remained sane after a millennia?"

The elder turned to He Who Soars.

"No, I do not think you understand even. From what Ana has told us, he has no control to where he alights. He is forever destined to spend but moments in a single place. It was only due to recent happenings that allowed him to stay as long as he did within the doll with Ana. And he sacrificed The Saint on High to do so. A millennia of constant movement between the soft spaces. It has made him desperate, and like the wolf you once met, Sunflower, he is rabid beyond any sanity—even for a saint."

Stanley Two Rivers reminded her of the rabid wolf that she had dispatched. The vision of her perched atop it with her sword thrust down into it and into the earth was before him now. It was the vision that convinced them all that she was indeed The Autumn Wind.

It then occurred to her that this saint would do everything in his power to keep her away from Stojan. And then he would flitter about all of Amira turning those who would listen against them. He meant to snuff out both Anastazja and Stojan. It was the latter that truly affected her.

Anastazja looked at both men and her face changed. He Who Soars sat up slightly—as if sensing something was about to happen. He had been leaning into the conversation, but was now sitting more upright and tense. Anastazja's face became grave, and for the first time the younger man saw what the elder had seen many times before. She inhaled slowly as her hair became that of crimson. It was alive and it had changed. The process of changing was something to behold. The blonde had simply melted away into the deep and impossible reds. Even as disheveled as it looked, it still glistened in the light that came through the windows of the conveyance, but much was lost in its depths. If this had been an animal in the wild and he'd seen it for the first time there would be no doubt that it was a warning just before a vicious attack. The change and the deep and darkly intense look on her face clarified that what he had been told was real. She spoke in a voice commensurate with the intensity she displayed.

"Then he will meet the same fate."

Amira

NORTH BY NORTHWEST

"I need to go to the north."

Ana's hair was slowly turning back to the natural blonde, and He Who Soars also noticed a change in her demeanor. Stanley Two Rivers waited to make sure Ana had exhausted what she needed to say, and just when the silence was about to become unbearable he finally spoke with a grandfatherly smile.

"Word of the destruction of the pyramid will reach Stojan quickly—even if he is still captive. From what you have told us of The Flickering Saint, he will do everything he can to set everyone against each other. He will explain to the others that you are to blame, and the one thing that will draw you out is your father."

The younger man looked on with quiet interest as he continued.

"But this is good news for us."

He smiled again. His tone was comforting which was appreciated by all within the conveyance.

"This means that Stojan will *not* go to the pyramid, and he will be updated on your movements."

"Then will he not just seek me out where I go? Why not lessen the time by traveling to the north?"

Frustration crept back into her voice. Again the old man thought, but clearly had prepared his thoughts in advance. He had a plan.

"Because we can use this to our advantage. The saints have no presence among The People. The information they gain will be what we choose to share. So I ask that you please be patient."

"And do what?"

The two men exchanged glances.

"Come with us. Back to The People."

Ana was at once skeptical and overjoyed. She had missed them and their ways, and wondered many times about how to reach them, or why they had not reached out for them. As she found out, they had been watching her for some time. The decision was clearly one of internal conflict and she stared at them both as she thought about the decision. They had literally dropped out of the sky and she was now forced to change her plans if she agreed.

"I am honored, Stanley Two Rivers. Truly. But I must find Stojan."

"I understand your decision."

He nodded his head slowly, with compassion, and then spoke as if remembering a question he had for her.

"Tell me Ana, when you are shaping your metal, what happens if the fire is not hot enough?"

She looked confused at the abrupt subject change. The question seemed to be out of nowhere, but she proudly stepped up with her knowledge of blacksmithing.

"Well, nothing will happen. Or it will take forever! If the iron is not hot enough you will take a very long time to…"

She trailed off at the smile, as she narrowed her eyes in mock suspicion. He finished her thought for her.

"We ask simply that you strike when the iron is hot."

It was a lot to ask of her. She desperately wanted to find Stojan and had an inkling that he was to the north somewhere from what both The Saint on High and The Flickering Saint had alluded to.

She sighed and sat back in her seat for the first time.

Finally, she realized that he was right. Her lack of patience would actually create a longer and more difficult time in finding Stojan. And she would once again see the people she cared much for. And perhaps they would help in some small way?

"I will come with you. I trust you and The People, Stanley Two Rivers."

Because the conveyance needed to bathe in the sunlight to replenish itself, they did the best they could to move it to the side and make a camp near it. They explained that it was better to be outside of it to defend it against both man and beast that might be curious or attack. He Who Soars explained that the conveyance was actually quite fragile—despite its appearance to the contrary—and that even a simple strike with a sword could render it useless. She thought him overprotective and obsessive about the Amiran tec, and in that way he reminded her of Dagmar.

The conversation of the campsite was one of reconnecting, catching up and revisiting the ways of the Navajo.

Fortunately, it would not take much longer than a day or so to replenish it, as their trip had been from nearby instead of directly from the village she was familiar with. They had "hopped around and rested" according to He Who Soars.

————

The journey from The Great Door of Waxahachie and the land of The People was just as pretty and as amazing as she had remembered. He Who Soars was even more adept at steering the conveyance than Dagmar and as they left, he did more than move it in a straight line; he caused it to circle around and pass over the great doorway. Ana was able to see just how large the circle was that had collapsed. It was so large they could see it all the way up in the sky. The elder explained that this was actually all part of the door, and that she had only seen where things converged. Ana knew not what this meant, but was amazed at the view and the immensity of it. The Amirans of the Old World were masters of construction and seemed to have no limits in what they could create. Somehow, The Flickering Saint had kept it pristine for a very long time.

Instead of the protective building in Sedona from whence came the craft, the destination was actually quite near to the city of elders. They explained that there was a flat place that allowed the conveyance to properly return to the earth and that they had some business there. She was happy to not only reconnect with the Navajo, but also with the elders of that city as she had grown fond and protective of them.

As they approached, the conveyance bounced up and down and she learned quickly the importance of the belt she was always told to wear.

They all traded glances as this happened and He Who Soars was particularly focused on his steering. She asked the elder about it and he quickly responded with some animation in his face.

"I have seen worse."

She smiled as she realized that he must have had many trips with the young man and not all of them were to his liking.

The conveyance passed over the exceedingly colorful city and eventually rested to a stop on the other side of it. The buildings were more vivid from the sky and the sun—now low in the sky—helped to bring out even more color. As they passed, she noticed very little activity in the streets, however. Perhaps the people were settling down for the day, or were mostly inside as part of their daily routine? Ana had hoped to at least see a few in the streets as they approached. Only one or two people were seen and they looked to already be sleeping on their shaded porches outside. So focused was she that Ana did not notice the faces of the two Navajo in front of her in the craft.

Exiting, she stretched her legs and arms and then reattached her sword belt. The craft was one of the few places she felt comfortable removing her backpack. This she wore before even exiting.

The air was cooler than it had been in the area near the door and this was her first experience traveling from one climate to another without being exposed to the outside. In fact, she noticed the vegetation changes as well—something that would have happened gradually. It was a little disorienting and surreal.

The two others had been quiet and moved the craft quickly to a building they had repurposed as a home for the thing. The two men seemed hurried and concerned and she did her best to help in any way, as she waited for the people of the village to greet them. But none came.

Surely there was some sort of procedure for them returning in place?

This was when she noticed the body.

An elder was slumped over on an outside porch. The three approached it and she drew her sword. No words were exchanged, but it was agreed upon that something was not right.

Her companions exchanged glances and the younger one moved to the prone man in an attempt to wake him. He would not, and the bruise to his head was brutal. The old man was dead. The elder put his finger to his lips as the three entered the building. Much was strewn about as if a battle had taken place. Others were on the floor and none were alive. They moved from building to building as the sun drooped lower in the sky, and each building revealed the same scene—those inside were dead from bludgeon or stab wounds and sometimes it looked like a scuffle had taken place. Oftentimes, there was no scuffle as if the people were taken by surprise. With each elderly Navajo found, Ana's heart sank. She was so saddened by it she had no energy for anger. This would pass, however. She whispered the question on everyone's mind.

"What has happened here?"

"I do not know. Many have come and gone it seems. They left little trace but the death of all who dwell here was their clear purpose."

As they moved through the town, they came upon dwellings of these that they knew most and again and again their hopes were dashed as they found the same scene.

"Very little has been stolen."

It was He Who Soars now, and he had noticed the lack of pillaging.

"Some things have been destroyed and some are missing."

"But most are not, He Who Soars."

Ana remained silent as the two discussed the obvious.

It had been a few hours since they arrived and their methodic searching of the city finally revealed movement. It was an elderly woman who was all but crumpled into a corner. She grasped a small doll in her hand that barely filled her palm. She looked as if she had been crying—alone and hopeless—for some time and the pronounced ridges under her eyes were discolored.

Ana sheathed her sword and ran to her—crouching on the floor to meet her eyes. She put a hand on the woman's arm.

"What has happened here?"

The two men gathered as well—with the younger stealing glances around the room to be sure no one else occupied it. The woman spoke in even tones and her breathy voice suggested that she had been involved in the conflict herself.

"They came…"

Ana tried to help her up, but she shook her head and wanted to remain on the floor. The cringe in her face suggested some pains of moving. She spoke and took short breaths—never saying more than a few words at a time.

"They came here. So many of them. They were looking for something. At first they said they were passing through. Then when they were all here they attacked. All at once."

She breathed and closed her eyes, then opened them again.

"I heard them speak to each other. They were here in search of something—many somethings. They wanted us all dead. They were told to kill us all."

"Please, let me help you up."

Ana looked upon the woman and her obvious pain. She wanted to make her feel better and to end her suffering but the woman refused and would only remain in the prone, crumpled position in the corner like a forgotten thing.

"No. I heard the screams. I heard them invade the homes. I heard things smash."

"Why? Why did they do this? Why did they kill so many? What were they looking for?"

The woman opened her hand and looked into it.

"This."

The three looked upon the item in her hand. The tiny painted doll looked like something a little girl might favor on her shelves.

"They said it was too small. But they wanted to destroy them anyway. They wanted to destroy all of them."

Ana knew immediately. She had travelled for a month with something that was unnaturally animated and possessed. She whispered her response.

"A vessel."

"Yes, that is what they called it. They meant to make sure we had none and were hiding none. It is the saints."

The elder was crouched down now and he placed his hands upon her face —gently cupping her jawlines in his hands.

"Which saint, dear lady?"

"All of them I think."

The elder was holding her head with more strength as she started to drift off.

"They are at war."

Those were the last words of the last surviving member of the city of elders—a city that was intended as a gentle resting place for those that had given so much to the community of the people. It was a bright city and despite their age, it was colorful and full of vibrancy in so many ways. But no more.

Anastazja stared and absorbed what had happened. It was devastating. In a city that housed hundreds and hundreds of people, she felt alone with the two men in which she shared the space.

What followed was a tedious and heartbreaking search and accounting of all people. Indeed the woman was the only one that was left—whether it was on purpose to pass on a message, or by chance. But she too now was dead.

Stanley Two Rivers left on horseback to seek out more of The People. He Who Soars explained to Ana that they were not far from here and had kept an open means of communication on an almost a daily basis. The elders of the colorful city were not alone.

Before the sun had set Stanley returned with many men and women. They quickly went to work collecting all those that had passed. Ana insisted on helping even though she was cautioned not to. She reminded them that she had seen her fair share of death. She did not mention, however, that she was typically the cause of it.

They worked tirelessly into the night and as they did more, more came from the nearby village. Some brought food, some brought supplies, and still others were clearly family members. By the time they were done the city had been refilled with people equal to or greater than the number who originally dwelt there. The next morning she woke to the smells of food and fire. The village was lively and in spite of the grave circumstances, those that were there were friendly and kind. She mingled and ate and met with many people and learned that she was actually the youngest present. The hundreds that had come were quite organized and groups had specific duties such as physical labor, preparing the funeral and cleaning up. Other groups were there to support them and prepared food and provided materials—some of which were made on the spot. They were exceedingly efficient and took nothing for granted. It was very much as she remembered when living among them.

That night saw a mass funeral which brought even more people to the village—this time children as well. She was told that these were the direct family members of the deceased. As the sun set, many words were spoken about those that had lost their lives and Stanley Two Rivers was not the only elder in attendance. The others also oversaw and spoke to such a momentous and overwhelming occurrence. In her time with them, Ana had seen more than one funeral but never a mass funeral such as this. Words were spoken loudly about all, and then families broke into individual rites and words about their beloved.

It was a shorter affair than she expected, yet all were handled with dignity and grace. The dead were then buried at the back of the town near where the arrow plane had made its landing. So many strong arms made short work of it and it reminded Ana of the burial plots she had heard of that were a common occurrence in Amira.

Many would remain in the city and continue cleaning up. The next day about half of those left for the village of The People and with them so went Ana. The elder strongly suggested she do so before she continue her journey to the north. Finding the village was easy and obvious when she was with them, but on her own she felt she would have never found it as it was strangely hidden in plain sight. It was a skill she would one day hope to master.

So draining had been the events of just the past few days that it was easy to remain and rest. Her desire to find Stojan still burned within her, but she had understood now the enormity of the distance, and the slow passage of time. She would not just be reunited tomorrow—it could be months. And this realization allowed her to begrudgingly focus on the now.

Her welcome to the village was nothing short of wonderful. Many of her friends were reunited with her, and when she questioned how some of them had come to be at this spot, they told her that news continued to travel quickly and they were alerted to her presence right after she and Stojan had passed through the city. Some had come just on the chance that they would run into her. For that she was grateful.

As the colder season would be starting soon, the elders suggested that she stay for a while to focus on the direction. Ana was not particularly fond of the idea.

"I am grateful to you all for welcoming me back among those I hold dear."

Her respect regarding them made them quite proud of her and served to help buffer the friction they were to endure in the conversation.

"We are most grateful for your return, Sunflower. You have returned to us, taller, more worldly and most importantly in one piece."

She smiled broadly at this.

"We have news to share with you as we are sure you wish to share with us."

Ana realized that she was in essence a guest of honor at a meeting of elders, and they hinted more may be on the way in the future.

"Your story has been relayed to us. What you have done is extraordinary and proven the prophecy to us. We who believed knew that you would be the one to deliver the Amirans from the saints, but we did not know that you would reign destruction upon them from the sky."

Ana thought of Dagmar, and his tedious and obsessive work with the sky arrow—just like all of his work with Amiran tec and things of the Old World.

"I thank you gratefully for your words, respected elder. I mean to travel to the north to find Stojan."

"To that end we have something to say. You see, the one who flickers has vengefully spread the word of you and Stojan. In fact, he has spread the word so efficiently and effectively that he has lit up all of Amira as to your whereabouts and the workings of the saints."

She listened intently to this and folded her arms in front of her.

"So angry is he that he tirelessly exposes the movements and thoughts of the other saints. It appears he has nothing to hide and in so doing even exposes himself."

"To what end does he do this?"

The elders exchanged glances, and another spoke now.

"He is stirring up as much conflict as possible—between not only the saints, but the saints and the Amirans."

"And The People."

It was another elder now, but his words were not appreciated by the others. He was a lone voice in this belief. They continued as if they had not heard him—something that surprised her.

"The conflict is mounting every moment. Nothing that exists could possibly fan the flames of conflict…"

"War."

She interrupted the speaker and then regretted her behavior. Her habit was hard to suppress. He continued.

"Each day the Amirans fight among themselves. What has happened here is happening out there. Saints that were content to keep to themselves and their congregations are now sending followers to conflict with others, but we do know one thing due to the ready and daily flow of information from the vengeful flickering saint."

"What is that?"

"There are but four left. And The Flickering Saint has revealed his secret —that he is the one saint that had been known as hundreds of saints."

"What does he have to gain from all of this?"

At this, they looked disturbed.

"We have talked among ourselves for much time now. We believe that the doorway is not only closed, but destroyed. Because he believes he no longer has a way home, he intends to set Amira on fire."

She searched the faces of all of the leaders who sat around the large gathering that night. Their features were lit with the small fires that burned—helping the starlight that had come so far to brighten them. Her mouth was open with shock.

"Truly Sunflower, he is mad. He has tirelessly flickered about and is in contact with the other saints. He reveals their intentions and inner thoughts. And every discussion he has is to sow the seeds of dissent and anger. Even as we speak, Amirans fight other Amirans; followers are turned against followers and cities against other cities."

"But… but why?"

"We think that if he cannot go home, he will just destroy everything so that not even the saints can live here. Or perhaps he will be the only one left."

She was taken aback. The whole world—or at least Amira—seemed to have changed almost over night.

"Your great sweep in Poliska is what prevented such a thing from happening there. Perhaps he means to force those in Amira to do the same thing—thus killing him and the others. But we think that his spite and vengefulness causes him to want to see the conflict and suffering for many hundreds of years to come."

It was a grim and dark pronouncement. The amazing land of Amira would be plunged into constant turmoil and conflict. Those few that were steadily rebuilding mankind would diminish to even smaller numbers, and the gains that had been made would be lost—just like so much of the Amiran tec.

Ana did not know what to say. She could not fight them all. She wanted to find Stojan and knew he was out there somewhere. Oddly, there being a conflict as described did not cause her to worry more for him. He would survive in spite of the conflict and in fact may survive because of it.

Days past as she readjusted to life in the village of the people. It was much like the village she was used to, and much less like the true people of the ants who dwelled within caves.

As difficult as it was, she decided she would stay through the cold months. She had been convinced by Stanley Two Rivers himself as he was the purveyor of good news. Stojan was indeed still alive. That was all that was revealed. Try as she might, she did not learn anything new, and he explained that the saint only spread that news to draw her out into the conflict. Most nights she would go to bed thinking of him.

Ana was most grateful for her practice and her walks by herself. Something about having someone waiting for her to return made them special, and there was always someone in the village waiting to greet her.

When spring arrived, she once again proposed to the elders that she was leaving. They once again requested that she remain, and that perhaps Stojan would instead find her. Time and time again she suggested they use the arrow plane to cover much of Amira. Time and time again her requests were denied. Slowly and surely she grew more restless, and each day a portion of her hair remained red, until finally even when she awakened from sleep, all of the blonde was gone.

 One day, she met with the elders to discuss her plans. What occurred demonstrated that her patience had been used up before she realized it.

"I would leave you in the next week. The spring has come and even the north of Amira is warming up now."

"Ana, we believe you should remain with us. Stojan will find you and we will somehow have word reach him."

"How? How will you do this?"

Her tone was accusatory and challenging.

"We would send but a few to…"

"To seek him out? To listen to the rambling of the mad saint? Then why would I not go in their place? Why send others to do what I *want* to do? And if they would find him, then so would I!"

They were shocked at her tone.

"This makes no sense. I am right, am I not? You send a few to…"

She trailed off as more than one elder was listening to a man who she did not recognize—an emissary from another one of the villages. Watching their faces change, she knew there was more grave news.

"They have attacked you again, haven't they?"

She pointed her finger at the conversation and yelled loudly. Her patience was now gone. They turned their heads reflexively, but did not respond.

"Why do you let them do this? Why do you hide here?"

Before they could speak she continued.

"Enough! Enough of this! You let them kill your people?!"

Some of the elders gasped. She dropped her arm and started pacing.

"You must fight back. This is the land of your people as well. You cannot hide forever and your peaceful ways are not compatible with what is now going on. They will find you eventually. Their madness will spread. You have told me over and over again that Stojan is alive, yet I hide here like some sort of wounded animal. You are a strong people, and I am better because of you. But enough is enough. I will not see my dear people extinguished."

She stopped and narrowed her eyes.

"I will not live in fear."

If they had a response, she did not hear it as she stormed out of the gathering to collect her things.

That day, the one known affectionately as Sunflower—the light-skinned foreigner who came to be part of The People—left the village to seek her father out in Amira. The one that had been named The Autumn Wind as part of the prophecy, now left them and there was much discussion. She refused anything other than supplies and the horse she had become accustomed to. Though she was angry, she found enough love in her heart to bid farewell to those that had cared for her so kindly for all of those years.

They watched her crimson hair bounce as she rode away.

Mark Bradford

Amira

THE SAINTS OF THE NORTH

The man rode behind the woman in front of him. They approached the city together, yet they did not know each other—they just happened to have the same destination at the same time. He had watched as other trailers had greeted her in passing, but she made no commensurate movement in return. She was ignoring them.

He greeted those that then passed him and in some cases shrugged. He even pulled back a bit so that they would not think them together.

As they approached and entered the city, she stopped her horse, drew a sword from her saddlebag and yelled at the statue.

After a few seconds, she swung the thick sword and beheaded it. His eyes opened all the more as it was a strong swing and positioned perfectly. Perhaps the statue was weak and was cracked?

He realized he did not want to follow the redhead any longer.

As she had done for many days and weeks, she traveled from city to city on her way to the north. If needed, she would camp outside of the city, otherwise she found an inn and remained. No longer did she care about her walk, instead she would use her time to train, and ask and inquire.

Each time she came across a statue she would ask it the same question. Each time the outcome was the same.

Staying in an inn sometimes proved to be a challenge, as it was in a small city over two month's ride into her journey.

"Move away from my horse."

The three men stood by her horse. They were eyeing up the longsword that protruded from the saddle bag. She had yet to drag it into the inn along with the one she wore at her side. They could see that it was rather thick and had been mistreated. Surely it belonged to her partner or husband, but none was present.

They grinned and the largest of the three smiled a toothy smile as his beard expanded with the expression.

"Oh. Relax yourself. Whose sword is that now?"

She continued walking towards them. It was a slow, but intentional gait and her muscles were an odd mixture of relaxed and tense. They eyed her up and down—a tall girl dressed unusually. Her hat was not quite like those around her, and she wore a combination of soft and hard leathers. Her skirt was a skirt made of intricate overlapping lengths of leather or a similar substance. It was not apparent to them what items had been constructed by her, her Navajo teachers or Dagmar. It was a subtle but carefully planned fixture of style, Amiran tec and Navajo ingenuity. Her boots were topped with fur and around her neck was draped a small ornamental portion of the giant rabid wolf she had killed with one sword thrust. Her hair was of an amber of intricate colors that all competed for the attention of the sun itself.

"I said move away from my horse."

She walked up to the post and quickly untied him, then walked back towards the man. She had not blinked and the two other men seemed to be trying to smile, but were not feeling the joviality they hoped.

The big man reached for the sword.

"Ben."

Arm still half outstretched to the pommel of the sword in the saddle bag, the man turned to his friend behind him who had called his name. The smile drained away as he looked at the man behind him. His gaze was not returned as he was transfixed on what stood in front of the one named Ben.

Her hair was now of a color they had never seen. Only those with hair approaching this hue were typically unusually light skinned and preferred to be indoors. She was clearly neither. And this was a vivid red and like many before them, it seemed like a warning. She did not look happy.

He would relate later that he had never seen anyone move so fast. Animals? *Yes*, he would respond—but not a person. In one fluid movement, she had unsheathed her sword, leapt onto her horse and spun around into a seated position with the sword blade coming to an abrupt halt upon his throat. He was pressed back into the horse's body and had a look of terror on his face as surely his throat had been sliced.

It had not. In her swift movement, she had thought to turn the blade so that the flat side pressed against his neck instead of the exceedingly sharp edge. She was, apparently, in a good mood this day. He drew an experimental breath and when no blood entered his lungs he just stared at the upper left, but would not turn his head lest she simply turn and withdraw her blade and cut him through.

"I said move away from my horse."

She withdrew the blade safely and sheathed it. He peeled his body away from the horse and looked to where she had been standing in an attempt to make sense of the leap she had to make to position herself upon it.

She turned to the three men and asked a question firmly.

"How far is the next town to the north east and is there a statue there?"

"A…statue?"

"Less than a day's ride."

"Are you..?"

Satisfied with the answers, she rode off.

In town after town she entered the same way—seeking out any statues, asking them the single question, then destroying them. Each time she left it was also the same—she inquired as to the distance and whether a statue was found there. Sometimes she would stay in the town and sometimes she would camp between them. Her time in the cities was spent inquiring as to the whereabouts of a rather tall foreigner that answered to the name 'Stojan.' No one as of yet had seen him, though one of two strangers had thought they heard of him. Her conflicts were few and typically ended quickly.

Her plan of moving to the north east seemed to make the most sense and had the most return. This was the direction she was told Stojan would be taken, it was the direction that the saint who had taken him dwelt, and it was also the direction of the water conveyance. Retracing her steps back to it gave her some sense of familiarity.

Her travels had given her direct exposure to the conflict described by the elders. For all of their wisdom she saw a fatal flaw—their exposure recently was very limited and their seclusion had curtailed their knowledge. What she found out in the world was that indeed there was conflict, but that this was taking place in various pockets. Not surprisingly, where there was no conflict there was no statue. And where there was the most direct conflict, the statue had recently spoken.

It was some time before her question to a statue was finally answered.

Witchpaw was one of the largest cities she would visit, she was told. It was the next town to the north east and a very popular trading city. The small village just before it boasted very little other than its proximity to said city. However, it did have something she was interested in.

As she rode to the entrance, she noticed the small statue of a man holding his arms to his sides and looking up to the sky. It was not on a large pedestal, but was directly on the path and in a perfect position to greet those that walked upon the road. She dismounted her horse and pulled out the oversized weapon.

"Do you know the location of Stojan?"

"Yes. Of course."

It smiled and turned towards her. Ana had grown so accustomed to the statue being inert that it almost startled her.

"So nice to see you again Anastazja."

"Where?"

"You're on the right path."

"I said *where*."

Her arm tingled as her patience immediately left her.

"Do you do this in every city you visit? You do, don't you? And yet, this is the first time we have met."

"Yes. Are you going to tell me?"

It continued smiling and looking her up and down. The Flickering Saint had finally appeared to her and proved that he had survived the destruction of the doll. She asked another question before he could answer.

"What happened to The Saint on High?"

His face changed from smiling to one of enjoyment.

"You will be happy to know that he is truly gone. He was unable to flit about as I do, so I... *helped* him. Do you not think my timing was perfect?"

"You did that? You killed him?"

"I did not. It was the door, which you destroyed. You were there to help."

He again looked her up and down.

"Is something different about you?"

"I asked you where Stojan is? Where is he?"

The saint clearly was enjoying the interaction and drawing out the moments as long as possible. He was taking his time in answering and deciding what he should share and how he could affect her actions. Manipulation was a skill he developed over time. Ana was weighing her actions and suddenly felt trapped. The saint looked behind her at the approaching man on horseback. That was when she struck. The large sword was swung and he genuinely looked surprised as he raised his arms in defense. The blunted and dented sword made short work of his arms and then continued through to his neck. The statue was life size so it easily shattered.

It had been a split-second decision. She weighed the information leading to Stojan with the possibility of taking him off-guard and destroying him. The other statues were destroyed so that he would not have a place to return; this was destroyed in the hopes of taking him with it.

She would not know for some time if she succeeded.

She returned to her horse and ignored the man behind her. As she rode ,she thought about the conversation. Would he tell her where Stojan was? What was his actual plan? Had she destroyed him just then? His words were odd, and he taunted her—but sometimes he revealed something. *Is there something different about you?* She absentmindedly brushed her right arm with her hand. Was that a taunt, or something else? She coaxed her horse forward to put distance between her and the man behind her who was now examining the statue.

As it came to pass, the city had little else to her liking and she exited shortly after entering. Tonight she would camp on her way to the larger city and enjoy a good walk. At least that was her intention.

The countryside was similar to what she had seen recently—the colors of the Red Lands were replaced with green trees and grass. Finding an area of thicker forest was a bit of a challenge, but she did find one near what she reckoned to be halfway to the larger city.

Making camp and leaving her horse to walk always reminded her of losing Stojan, and those thoughts of abandonment were reinforced by what had happened by The Great Door. Each time she left, she wondered if her horse would be there upon returning. For that reason, the only thing typically left in the saddlebag was the oversized and battered sword.

Lately her hair revealed that she was angry more often than not. It was this anger that drove her to find Stojan and to survive alone in the wilderness and the large cities of Amira. It had been this anger that drove her to abruptly leave The People. She gave much thought to it, and how her hair became such a wonderful tool in her training with Stojan. Had she lost this control now? Or had she just embraced her mood, her drive, her anger?

She missed the happier times with Stojan in which she could leave all the stoicism to him, and she was just left with cheerful, curious questions about the world.

But this was how the world worked. She was in Amira now, and had seen things never imagined. Perhaps she would try to focus the way Stojan had taught her. She imagined him to be with her as she made her way through the forest.

It had been a very good practice session and her sword moved fluidly with her. Just as he had predicted, her style returned to her as the new sword took its rightful place in her routine. It was as if she practiced with it from the beginning. Her body had grown and so had her sword. It would have been the ideal session had it not been for the interruption.

Whether it was a smell, or a sound, or something about the wind—she did not know. She just knew there were people nearby.

Carefully making her way, she went towards the sounds she was now hearing. It wasn't near her campsite, but instead near a road. A group of men fought with one another. There was yelling, and accusations. Weapons had been drawn and some had dismounted. Apparently one group was attempting to pass the others and neither would give way. Things escalated once one group brought the name of a saint into things.

"Saint Louis will prevail. You are simple to think otherwise."

"Saint Louis? That may work in the north, but these lands are free."

"Free from sanity!"

"Your kind are not welcome here. Go back."

After a pause, a woman from the group spoke less angrily and more inquisitively.

"And yet we have been accepted before..?"

"That is because you listen to the saints."

It was a new voice. The speaker was from neither group, and in spite of her better judgement, she decided to speak up.

All eyes turned to her. She was standing to the side between the two groups. Ana had given up a position of stealth and had not even drawn her sword. Stojan would not be pleased. All eyes were upon her now.

"Who are you? Where did you come from? How did you..."

Many necks craned around searching for her horse.

"They have set you upon one another! They mean to keep you fighting."

She spoke loudly and with much passion. It was a discussion she had many times silently and now had finally brought it to their ears.

A man in the lead of the group to the right pointed to her.

"You there. What is this you speak? What do you know of Saint Louis?"

She smiled.

"Thank you. I know nothing of him. But now I know his name."

"You know nothing of Saints? Then why do you speak so?"

It was the group to the left now.

"I did not say I knew nothing of them, I simply did not yet know anything of *this* one."

"*This* one. Pfft."

The leader of the group to the right was clearly disgusted by the suggestion of more than one saint. Another from the group to the left continued.

"Then what do you know of the saints that you speak of to us—that you appear here?"

"Because I have destroyed them."

They gasped and some started talking all at once, but she was not finished.

"Saint John, The Saint on High, Luxor. They are all gone forever. And thanks to you, Saint Louis will be next."

The reactions were distinctly different and demonstrated the difference in beliefs of each group.

The group to the left fell silent save for whispers, and the group to the right became agitated as their apparent leader shouted.

"Your mutterings will cost you, girl."

"Then dismount, brave man, and face me."

"I would not do…"

She drew her sword.

"If you best me I will admit to the greatness of the one you follow, and I will join your cause. If I best you, then you will lead me to him."

Ana blinked slowly. The man dismounted with a smirk. A woman next to him shook her head and whispered something. She was not as fervent about her saint as her husband.

The man drew his sword and looked to the heavens.

"This is a test! I accept this, oh lord."

Ana walked towards the man, slowly and methodically.

"This is not worth it. We should have let them pass."

Quiet comments arose from the other group, as the two neared each other.

"'Tis an easy test. A test from a girl…"

His sword sang from her first strike—far faster than he imagined. Again she struck, and again. The more she struck, the larger her smile. He noticed her hair then. She was a redhead, but the color was that of something unnatural, and the bright sun only added to the vividness.

He attempted to gain some ground, but not only were her strikes precise, they were with much force and his ground was given up as he backed away—sometimes without his consent. He was doing so because it was the only way to survive the barrage. She was clearly not what she appeared to be. She was much stronger than he had thought, and her skill was impeccable. The most difficult part of it was that she was enjoying it. Finally he stood his ground and had enough. Unfortunately, it plunged him directly into the center of the battle and she cut him on his arm, his chest and his leg.

"Enough!"

With that, she had performed a circular motion that disarmed him. Her blade was in his face and he thought to bring his hands up to grab it. The absurd thought left him as he looked into her eyes. She had killed before, perhaps many times. He knew it. He had failed the test. It was unfair.

"Now. You will take me to this Saint Louis and we will see if he holds capture to my father."

"Your father..?"

"I have won. You agreed to this. If you want to die then so be it!"

She raised her sword as he and a woman from his group both uttered.

"No…"

"Then honor your bargain!"

"We were on our way to… to the south. We have business there for our family. We cannot just turn around. It is many miles to Saint Louis—hundreds."

The man looked defeated and scared. She wanted to kill him because he believed in the interlopers and was an agent of their evil. She had never faced off against common folk who were followers. Her heart was not in it and she began to feel sorry for him. He had a family—no doubt his wife was with him. She could not rob her of her husband that day. The fear and uncertainty in the man's eyes told her he wanted to live, and was confused. His boasting was empty and his swordplay was poor. He was not a warrior. Perhaps the two groups would not have come to blows and only hurled insults had she just watched. He was a pawn like so many others, and with The Flickering Saint fanning the flames, even more were drawn into it. He dropped to his knees.

She looked behind him—the group came into focus and all faces looked back in horror. Slowly she turned her head around without moving the rest of her body—her sword was still in mid-strike. Those behind her also looked on with concern and shock. These people were even less prone to violence. Their faces and the emotions they felt were crystal clear to her now, and she slowly turned her head back to the man before her.

"Your hair…"

She looked upon him no with hate or malice—but with understanding. She was about to strike him down as if he was directly responsible for Stojan. He was not a saint nor a bishop, but just a follower.

She inhaled as did the others, as murmurs and gasps were heard on both sides. Ana lowered her sword and grasped some of her hair with her other hand. It was indeed blonde now. Ana exhaled, sheathed her sword and then extended her hand to the man. He took it apprehensively as he came to his feet and was not surprised at her strength in helping him up.

"You are the one we have heard of."

He looked into her eyes and at her hair, and then looked her up and down as if seeing her for the first time. She was more real to him than the saint had ever been, and her hair was a demonstration of something impossible.

"You can be on your way. I have no intention of keeping you from your family."

She looked into his eyes solemnly and for many moments and he saw vulnerability for the first time.

"I'm just trying to find mine."

She did not remember how much time passed, or even when it happened, but all who were present had dismounted and were surrounding her. Some were even touching her on the shoulders.

———

That day Ana returned to her camp, gathered her things and came back to the road in which she'd had the encounter. After some discussion, the group coming from the south volunteered to take Ana to Saint Louis. The group from the south shared what knowledge they had with them, and even provided some monies to them to help them find Stojan. The group refused and many salutations were heard upon departure. Ana had done what they could not. They were united as people of Amira. It was a tiny manifestation of a much larger possibility and it was too big a thing for her to think of at that time. She was grateful for the company.

The group learned that Stojan was alive and being held captive, but the constant attacks sent from the saint to the north made for a dire situation. All the more, she wanted to reach this new saint, and asked much about his fortress and his followers.

Her new compatriots numbered six, and were traders who dealt in gems of the south. They were familiar to Ana and she had seen some of the most gorgeous and oversized specimens during her time in Sedona. She thought them mysterious and pretty, but would not believe in any of their magic—as thanks to Dagmar, she saw the world differently.

The group she traveled with were friendly and respected her time alone when she required it. Though she trusted them, she would leave only her oversized sword with her horse when she walked. Some of the traders came and went and being in their company did not stop her from her commitment to asking the question of the statues she would find. Eventually however, she became a lone traveler and although they were enthusiastic, they had no interest in being part of her vandalism of public property.

They needn't have worried as shortly thereafter it seemed someone was doing her job for her. A person or group was not taking kindly to the likes of statues.

None of the group was with her when she finally rode into the great city of Saint Louis. Like Luxor, it was not just the name of the saint, but also of the place in which he dwelled.

Amira

SAINT LOUIS

It was not difficult to find the location of the saint's dwelling. His beautiful cathedral was not one, but two buildings—at least that was what travelers had told her. Others had said it was the most beautiful statue and monument to anything in all of Amira. Ana mused that those in Luxor most probably thought the same. As much as she appreciated Amiran tec and the buildings of the Old World, what she had seen in the Red Lands were far more magnificent and if what she had been taught by both the Navajo and Dagmar was to be believed, those sculptures of nature dated them by hundreds of thousands of years. It was not conceivable.

The city was large and vibrant and at the very heart of it was not only the cathedral, but the thing that made it so wondrous - the culture that was a building that was an arch. Just when Ana thought she understood the limits of Amiran tec, she was reminded that she had more to see. It was immense, slim, and beautiful. It shined in the sun as it came forth from the earth, curved above it, then returned again. Perhaps it was a giant lopsided hoop and half of it was buried deep within the ground. Had it laid flat like the door at one point and only erupted due to the saints, or a rumbling in the ground? Ana's head was filled with possibilities and the similarities between this and the door to the south.

Every statue she had approached on the way had already been destroyed. So, though she was unable to gain any new information from The Flickering Saint, she was able to inquire with many townsfolk during her journey. Saint Louis was described as a very densely-populated area with a vibrant community, and had been that way for as long as anyone remembered. The saint ruled over it with the Lady Bishop as its arbiter of his word. Though she found them all to be supremely paranoid, this saint was not only so, but believed he was the only saint in not only all of Amira, but in the world. Or, at least that was what the citizens were strongly encouraged to believe.

Because of this, it was common to come across those that ventured outward to spread the word. Surprisingly, the saint was not very interested in increasing his followers, but instead simply wanted his city to remain separate from the beliefs of others. If you did not believe that he was the only saint, then you were cast out. Most who dealt with trade were well informed as to the supposed existence of the others, so they happily agreed and just simply kept that knowledge to themselves. The result—unbeknownst to those that ruled them—was that the vast majority thought one way and behaved another. It was a public secret.

Anastazja decided she would find this bishop to discuss the whereabouts of Stojan. She was well aware of the fact that the information being spread by The Flickering Saint was probably designed to draw her here. Her thought on the matter was that they wanted the two of them in one place to make it easier to extinguish them. Stojan had taught her about traps—large and small—within a battle. She was willing to allow herself to be trapped to find the larger plan. Of late, she was tired of the journey and wanted to destroy those who would stand in the way. It had made her discussions tenuous at best. She sorely needed exposure to Stojan's stoicism.

The city was far more quiet than she expected. Instead of hundreds milling about their daily activities, she saw almost vacant streets. As she moved closer to the center of the city—and thus the cathedral—the normal density of the population returned. There were no smiles or greetings. No one made an effort to look upon her for more than a moment or two. Periodically she saw recognition. It was time to go over her plan again.

From what she had been told, The Flickering Saint discovered that the doorway was truly destroyed. At once, she was both thrilled and disappointed at this. If the door worked the way it had been described, then all of the saints would have been forced through it. However, it was hard to trust a saint—let alone such a mad one. But now that the door was destroyed, it would take Amiran tec to rebuild it—and no such artisans existed. So instead, it seemed he turned his efforts to trying to destroy Stojan and Anastazja. His manipulations worked for the general populace of Amira, but he could not do this thusly for the remaining saints—they knew his thoughts as he knew theirs. You cannot fool someone who knows your very thoughts and actions. Because of this, she believed he simply turned to chaos and mayhem—fueled by his anger and frustration. His concept of time was infinite. Perhaps he would spend only a few hundred years being angry, and in the mean time bring death, hatred and destruction to all who dwelt in Amira.

What the other saints were thinking, she knew not. However, someone was destroying the statues. Her guess was that it was the other saints—or at least their followers as directed by them. The less that remained, the less vessels through which to spread his chaos. They meant to mute his ability to reach the people. What would happen when the last statue was destroyed? Would he finally be dispatched? Her excitement over this thought faded quickly as she realized the saint probably had vessels all over Amira and some of them had never been seen by anyone—ever. That meant he would always have a hiding place, and once one was discovered, he could slowly but surely enlist new followers. He would be here forever.

She narrowed her eyes at her renewed anger.

But what of the saint she now approached? What was *his* plan? Surely he meant to repel the influence of the saint that caused so much mayhem now. And he had one thing in common with him—he also wanted her and Stojan dead.

She shrugged, and then smiled. The tumultuous thoughts were pushed out by the scene in front of her.

The populous was armed. That was not to say that the average person might not normally carry some sort of weapon; instead the people before her all looked like they prepared for combat. Each wore some sort of sword and wore at least something that resembled armor. They were ready in spirit for a fight at least. How skilled they were remained to be seen.

She turned behind her and saw what she expected—a number of people were following her, grouping up and closing in. They meant to encircle her and bring her in. Her trap had materialized far too quickly. Subtlety, it seemed, was not the forté of Saint Louis. Either that, or something else was afoot.

She stopped her horse in the middle of the street. The trees that lined the streets were quite lovely. The houses and buildings were of a design that was unfamiliar, yet reminded her of home. It was probably of the old world, yet not pretentious or otherworldly like some of the buildings. It made her wonder about the people here. Did they prosper? How involved was the saint in their daily lives?

"Stop!"

She almost laughed at the man who commanded her.

"I've already done so."

Emboldened by her apparent gentleness, he walked towards her. The blonde woman on the horse looked almost friendly. But it was she who decided to command now.

"Come no further. I am here to find my father. Those who get in the way of this will not tell of it."

He was taken aback by the almost instant change in demeanor, and it literally caused him to stop in his tracks. He thought for a moment and looked around at the others.

"I am charged with stopping you."

"Stopping me from finding Stojan?"

"No... no, not..."

He looked slightly confused, but continued.

"Stopping you from bringing any harm to Saint Louis."

"So you admit your saint is mortal like you?"

The conversation had taken an odd turn for the man. The woman on horseback was not like he was told. Some said she was ruthless, others said she was a child, and still others said she possessed physical abilities that were unheard of. Some even said she spent time around the Navajo and learned special skills unknown to Amirans for hundreds of years. He gathered his thoughts and attempted once again to make his simple point.

"You will yield to us. Dismount now and no harm may come to you."

"I will ask you one question. If you do not answer it to my liking you will be the first to die."

Her bravado was not effective, as she spoke too matter-of-factly and too calmly. She did not even brandish her sword. Those who surrounded her had also stopped and were listening. This was a girl out of place—perhaps misguided. She had come a long way in search of her father and her head was filled with wild ideas.

The redheaded woman was deluded if she thought she would fight them all. He looked at her again and blinked. He stared as whatever little emotion he showed in his face disappeared.

To Ana, the man seemed very confused. She looked around at those who surrounded her—many against one; with no clear escape. Even if she could make it to the cathedral, she would just be trapped there. And smashing a statue—assuming there was one within the cathedral—would only dispatch the saint if he was foolish enough to inhabit it. Only one saint was so bold because he could simply leap to another vessel unrestricted.

She was again reminded that Stojan would not approve. She would attempt to prove him wrong.

"Allow me to speak with your saint."

"Speak with him...? The bishop is..."

Another finished his sentence.

"The bishop is gone. He fights for us and the..."

"No, *SHE* is gone. *She* is the real bishop. Lady Madison..."

"She was a false bishop and..."

"False?"

Yet another clicked their tongue at this. Many more nodded, but it was unclear as to when they agreed with.

"Lady Madison was sent on a false mission—that is the only thing false about..."

"HA!"

Much dissent rose at the discussion. Ana had no bearing on what was occurring, but listened and continued to dart her eyes from person to person as they erupted. Their stances slowly began to change as they entered into the argument. Clearly, there were factions with opposing views. They relaxed their weapons as they addressed each other. One shouted not to the others, but to her.

"What will you discuss with Saint Louis?"

She smiled. Then yelled so that all could hear her.

"Come with me and see."

After a pause, someone yelled back to her in uncertain tones.

"You will attempt to destroy him. You…"

He was hushed by the others as Ana formed a reply. They were anxious for some reason.

"I promise you that I will merely have a discussion with him; if he is game for a conversation."

Again, some murmuring and the one that initially challenged her spoke.

"We will all come with you. We agree, but you must leave your great sword outside. We know."

Great sword?

"We know you will not use your father's sword to destroy him."

They pointed to the one she carried and had unsheathed without them realizing. Then they looked at the large, battered sword sticking out of her saddle bags. They knew, somehow, that she would never again try to use her sword to smash something of stone. That was why she had purchased the massive sword. Its purpose was to take the punishment her sword did not deserve. She would not soil it thusly.

Clearly The Flickering Saint had been very busy. Anything he knew was shared to the other saints, and he happily spread the information to anyone who would bow before the random statues spread throughout Amira. The entire country knew of her now. The amount of chaos she saw before her amazed her. She nodded and the group followed her as she rode toward the cathedral. It was a beautiful town center and the great metal hoop that sprung from the ground gleamed in the sun. Like the great pyramid, it fooled with one's senses and lied to one's eyes.

Those that witnessed the event that day from afar saw the people accumulate. They saw those who worked in the stores; those out in the open with their carts. They saw the people not only in the streets, but those in buildings simply abandon what they were doing to accompany the redhead on the horse. They followed her and clogged the streets until there was no room. Those that hid from the chaos felt a certain unity had returned as they joined the ranks of those all moving in the same direction—to the wonderful cathedral of Saint Louis. Anastazja would have an audience with the saint and the cathedral would be filled to bursting with the citizens of the town.

Though their numbers had diminished, they were still far more than were ever allowed in the revered building at once.

She dismounted her horse upon reaching it, and much of the crowd eyed the sword that protruded from the saddle bag. They waited expectantly, as if she was about to grab it and run into the cathedral. She did not and more than one remarked that her hair had mostly changed to the ambers and golds.

Ana took a deep breath and looked behind her. She was indeed surrounded by hundreds and hundreds now as if the entire city was there for the event. It was. She took another breath and imagined that she was not able to get enough air. It reminded her of the caverns she was asked to sleep within while with The People. These people could easily rush her and snuff her out just by the lack of air. But if these people meant to do her in, they could have. By sheer numbers they would win— assuming each fought with the ferocity she brought.

She took another breath.

The doors seemed inviting for some reason. A mother and young daughter looked at her and smiled. She returned it and entered.

The cathedral was beautiful on the inside as well, and row upon row of long chairs greeted her along with the gold appointments to the ceiling, the columns and the walls. Multicolored glass brought a rainbow of warm light to the massive room. Like other cathedrals she had seen, this one had a special statue upon a dais in front. She learned from Dagmar that these were usually found nearby and placed upon the stage, and that in the Old World this was not the case but a modification saints made so that they could address their followers directly. It was a powerful kind of influential magic.

The crowd followed her as they whispered. If seen from above, she was like a brush trailing a wide swath of multicolored paint in her wake. The paint became people as they filed into the long chairs. Those walking near her reminded her that she promised no harm, and she nodded while staring ahead. Her hair demonstrated that she was honorable as the blonde absorbed and reflected the various colors of the windows. Never had such a great crowd filed so quietly and orderly into a building. Ana was not alone in watching the statue at the front of the cathedral. At any moment it would come alive no doubt. She continued walking towards it. Unlike the doll, she assumed this one was rooted in place. More and more filed and packed themselves into the long wooden lengths as their breathless voices were muted by the very apprehension they all experienced. Some believed the woman was being deceptive, while others were sure she would see the light. The vast majority were exhausted as their world had been recently turned upside down. For the first time, some of them wanted to be truly free.

She stopped at the wide, shallow stairs at the stage. What she saw amazed her.

It was so normal—this statue—and majestic. It looked like a royal from a large city in Poliska. And he was atop a horse. The statue in full was mounted upon a slab of metal constructed out of the same material. One leg was raised as if it was trotting forth, and it wore drapes and armor and bindings even upon its head. The helmet had holes for the horse to peer through and a large simple symbol was engraved upon it—the tall crossing of two planks she had seen in other cathedrals.

The man wore a fur-lined robe and a crown was atop his head. While one hand held the reins, the other held a thin sword with an oversized hilt. It was the kind of hilt her father had told her was favored by some, but the design unbalanced all but the longest of swords. She made sure to keep her ground and under normal circumstances would never approach a raised enemy like this so closely. She was at a terrible disadvantage—made worse by being at the bottom of the shallow stairs.

It was the most impressive statue she had seen, and strangely even more so than the statue in the great pyramid. Her hand went to her sword as she waited.

The long rows were filled with people and still more stood in the approaching aisle as others spilled around her. Only the stage area was empty, save for the regal man on his metal horse.

"I would speak with you."

There were those that followed Anastazja to the front and stood closely by. They did not trust her and would try to intervene if they saw any signs of deceit or violence. They stared at the saint, and then to her.

And all in the room waited.

Something loud was dropped at the back of the cathedral. Most of the crowd turned as the tense silence was broken—much to the chagrin of those that jumped. Even those at the front smiled at the relief. They turned their heads back to the man on the horse.

He was shaking his head.

The group at the front stared as Anastazja squinted. She was ready for the conversation.

"I am here now!"

He had spoken to her, and to them, as if proclaiming the obvious. It was odd to her and it took much effort not to draw her sword. She spoke in even tones, and her ease at which she spoke to the animated statue surprised her.

"Yes you are. Where is Stojan?"

It turned its head down to her, as if seeing her for the first time. Upon seeing the source of the question, it snarled.

"Is that all you can say?"

She tilted her head in confusion. Some shushing was heard from the back of the cathedral as they all struggled to listen in.

"My…my lord. Saint Louis, we have come to…"

The seemingly-metal man turned his head to the man speaking now.

"Why do you all come here? You have all followed her?"

It spoke with discomfort, as if some of its concentration was elsewhere. He was almost squirming as he spoke in aloof and disrespectful tones.

"You waste your time here, and should be on your way to Saint Michael."

Many glances were stolen between those that accompanied her. Some bowed their heads.

"Saint Michael?

"Yes. Yes!"

He looked to the entire audience now and after giving her a quick glance, ignored Anastazja.

"You must march to Saint Michael to the north!"

"But we were told to protect you."

The man was genuinely concerned, and like most in the city, looked exhausted.

"I need no protecting. Certainly not from her. What do you protect me from?"

"But…"

"Seek out my bishop. He is to the north."

"What of Lady Madison?"

He turned his head and gave an unconvincing look of sadness.

"Oh she has been lost—lost to the wilderness between the cities. Her mission failed. Oh yes. She failed me. And in doing so failed you!"

The last part he yelled as he addressed the audience. There was a sprinkling of clapping, while others murmured. Clearly there was much confusion. He attempted to raise his sword, but it would not move from its sculpted attachment to the horse. Ana narrowed her eyes, and then as if she had been pricked, opened them wide.

She looked over at the default leader of the crowd standing only a meter from her, then back to the man on horseback.

"You…"

He smiled down to her in agreement. She drew her sword.

"No."

A few in the crowd with her objected. She had no interest in striking and knew she could do little to it. If she was right, then he would be immune. She pointed at it with her sword, and her arm tingled.

"This is not your saint."

Of all of the proclamations or arguments she could have produced, of all the things they were ready to deny, this was not something they considered.

"Of course it is. He is the only…"

"No, you must destroy Saint Michael!"

"But you are the only one!"

His most fervent followers were not so ready to be told the opposite of what they'd been told for a thousand years. Those in the audience—who were common folk that lived in the shadows, and had learned the truth—they already knew.

"No. No he is not."

Voices of dissension now reached the podium. Ana turned to the man next to her.

"He is The Flickering Saint."

"What…?"

Much confusion was had now as the audience started to erupt. More had pushed forward from behind her.

"I said go to the north!"

The man on horse now became angry. It screamed in frustration.

"You listen to *him* without question? But when *I* speak, you sit like dogs with your mouths agape? You all deserve the destruction you've brought upon yourselves."

He tried to move his other hand, but it too was affixed to something, and the reins he held had not ever been released.

"You! You persist. These idiots will kill each other as they listen to those less ambitious than I. Perhaps your great, great grandchild will help me rebuild the door. I'll put her to good use."

He looked at those around him—they had closed in even more.

"And her children, and her grandchildren. I will never stop."

He laughed, but then became serious.

"Still, there is something different about..."

She moved closer to him, and in doing so her arm tingled all the more.

"Please! Please do not talk like this, my lord. Surely you just wish to..."

The man trailed off as he surveyed the other faces. This was not a cathedral of followers who experienced the weekly gatherings. These were townsfolk and merchants banished to never enter the cathedral. And they too were angry. He was in the minority.

The eyes of the statue widened as she continued her approach.

"You brought it with you? Even now it wanes, but I can still feel it."

He panicked.

"Back! Back away. I cannot..."

He continued squirming and looked to the audience that surrounded him. She was almost touching him now and her sword hummed.

"Oh no... No. This is not the way it should work. The door is collapsed and destroyed. But you carry some of..."

He contorted and those around them saw something they were told the immortal saints never experienced: fear.

"I cannot."

Ana considered her sword and turned it in her hand slightly as if seeing it for the first time. The humming was most intense now and her arm continued to tingle. She looked back at him with understanding.

"You're afraid, aren't you? For the first time. You could always get away. But now, because some of the power of the door is…"

She cut herself off and shoved the sword close to the painted stone, almost touching him.

"You cannot leave."

She looked quickly around and began talking loudly to the crowd; to the faces nearby.

"He has deceived you! This saint is not your saint! He occupies the statue!"

More than one member of the group was touching it now, even tapping the horse to see what it felt like. The statue barely moved now save for the small contortions.

Suddenly a rhythm occurred—silently and without verbal agreement. They were pushing on the horse. Some pushed and some pulled. It was surrounded now. It moved. Though it was heavy, many hands working in concert—testing, prodding and pulling—had found a back and forth that made it move. Just slightly at first, then then more and more it rocked back and forth. All faces were blank around the statue as the voices in the crowd became louder and louder.

It was as a child silently plays with something they are forbidden to touch—or a scab is picked at. Morbidly, they continued to push and push as the man and horse rocked more and more—naturally rocking along the axis of the length of the small rectangle it was perched atop. It rocked precariously as she watched and kept her sword out. Suddenly, those to the right of it parted and did their best to press back against the other as it toppled.

Ana watched down the length of her sword as the man's eyes stayed locked onto hers as it became tilted, then horizontal, and fell with much force against the stairs and shattered. The statue revealed its nature of painted stone as the one piece became countless others.

And thus the saint who had never found purchase in one soft spot, the one gone mad with constantly changing and never remaining in one place for more than a few minutes, the one known as The Flickering Saint… flickered no more.

Due to the waning power of the door absorbed by her sword, he was not allowed to leave the vessel as those around him shoved and prodded as their minds pushed them to test the limits.

The gasps were as deafening as the silence that followed.

Anastazja—still holding her sword—surveyed the faces of all who were present. They looked amazed and stunned. Finally the silence was broken by one in the crowd who yelled three simple words.

"Burn it down."

Amira

GUIDANCE

Ana—to her substantial relief—was able to exit the cathedral without causing harm to any of the occupants. What was to be a wading through a crowd turned into a timely and efficient exit through a side door next to the stage area.

With no bishop present, and almost all of the followers sent on missions, the abandoned and demoralized workers turned their attention on the cathedral.

It was a beautiful cathedral and as she rode away it made her sad to see it erupt into flames. Her eyes were tearful at the loss of such beauty, but with Saint Louis trapped within the building, the denizens were destroying it and in turn the saint himself.

However, the great metal hoop would stand as a cold testament to a city that no longer contained a saint, but now boasted a proud monument to his absence.

The Flickering Saint and Saint Louis were no more. Only two remained —Saint Michael and an as yet unnamed saint.

To the best of her knowledge, Stojan was still to the north a bit. He had been last seen just before winter had ravaged this part of the country. Though Ana worried, she was repeatedly told that it was not uncommon for people here to dig in and hibernate for the winter. In that way, the people she sought out were very much like bears. But now they would have emerged and she would be able to seek him out. Because of the extreme dissemination of information by The Flickering Saint, she knew he had not been captured by Saint Michael. The saint's discussions with his minions had been told and spread like gossip all around the country. And part of this information told of an escape by Stojan and a lady Bishop. This bishop had been sent by Saint Louis in an effort to see her die trying, for she had learned the secret of multiple saints. It was not in the best interest of her master for his following to learn of other options for worship.

She would travel almost due north to a city large like the one she had just left. If she traveled too far she would know it as a piece of the ocean itself had been trapped by the great country of Amira. It was not the ocean, but a lake so massive as to seem like it was. Amira was just so large that things like this were possible. The Navajo had taught her much of the geography, and she was grateful for this as it gave her bearings in her travels.

The people of Saint Louis had kindly provided some supplies to her and had insisted on filling her saddle bags. So accustomed was she of losing her horse that she all but regretted accepting. This made her smile as the thought of misplacing a horse as if it is was gardening tool was absurd, yet she had done this numerous times since arriving.

Her trip would take her less than a week and she welcomed her nightly forest stays. The area continued to provide think foliage—bushes, shrubs, trees and grass. It was a paradise of greens and browns. With it came many large animals of the forest and once again she felt in tune and gave the deadly creatures much respect. It did not, however, prevent her from sneaking up and touching them. Her old habit could not be tamed.

With her new sword, she practiced hard each day. It was not long before she fell comfortably into the same routine she'd had with Stojan, and every day she used her pristine sword it filled her with happiness and hope. Each day she remembered something new that Stojan taught, each day she heard his voice.

The north forest made her feel quite secure, and by following trails and using Dagmar's compass, she was able to embrace nature, stay away from the affairs of mankind and focus on what was important. To anyone and everyone who might want to find her, she essentially disappeared. To find her would take extraordinary tracking skills even beyond some of the best trackers.

The day's travel through the trails and clearings in the forest were abundant with the sounds and calls of animals. She knew many of them and found the woods were not only filled with animals that made their way on the ground, but also of those that traveled by air. Today was no different and she was starting to recognize the calls and mutterings of a specific bird. In fact, it had caused her to play a game of seeking it out. What she thought were numerous species turned out to be a single kindred. And now she was starting to wonder just how many birds there were. They were always just in front of her—sometimes to the side a bit ,but always just in front.

It seemed that the more the birds were off to the side, the louder and more obnoxious they became. Then one day they became quiet. Ana wondered if they were defending a nesting area and had finally moved through it, or if they just objected to her and her horse in moving so deeply through the forest. It reminded her very much of a time back in Poliska.

TWO BECOME ONE

"What is it? Why do you not prepare?"

The woman with disheveled, curly hair yelled to an empty room. The cabin was small, but comfortable, and had been constructed with massive logs. The interior was an open design with a loft on top. Various trophies from the wilderness had been mounted on the walls, along with a number of planters and oversized utensils. It looked like the cottage or home of a Tinker—those that made their way by offering to fix various things of metal. This one had painted and mounted some of his findings on the wall. He turned the older broken items into a sort of art. The woman currently yelling was his niece and had inherited the structure.

Stojan emerged from the bedroom and looked about. The cause of the confusion was a lack of items packed and prepared.

He looked to her with concern. She was used to his demeanor, as she spent the entire winter in the small home with him.

He shook his head.

"I feel we should wait a bit longer."

"Are you not feeling well?"

"I am quite well, thank you, Madison."

She remembered the day he stopped saying the 'Lady' before saying her name. It was shortly after he started to regain his health and she knew he would live.

Soon after their escape he was struck with an illness. Though they regained their freedom thanks to Stojan's quick wit and equally dexterous swordplay, she decided to take him to those that could help—and much to his objection they were located to the north. He fought her urgings and her direction. He wanted to go to the south—to the pyramid and to where he believed Anastazja resided. But in his weakness could not have made the journey on his own, and left to himself would surely have perished. They made the long trek back towards the north in time for winter to arrive, and all the while he objected quite loudly.

She told him numerous times that she liked him much better when he was healthy and even preferred when he was "considering killing her." She knew the severity of his sickness when verbal battles like that were easily won. In spite of the resistance and difficulty, she knew Stojan had saved her life twice and she was more than grateful to return the favor and committed wholeheartedly to that. They were both wanted and she no longer had a place with her saint.

When Stojan was no longer in danger of losing his life, she decided they would steal away for the winter. This again was not received well as his unending desire to find Anastazja superseded all other conversations and efforts. But he was in no condition to argue and the winter made their stay almost a necessity. Fortunately, she had the foresight to keep it well stocked.

But now the day had come that they would leave. Spring had returned and so did Stojan to practicing his swordplay. Yesterday their discussion was one of the next step.

———

"It is beautiful out today."

"Indeed it is."

Stojan ate and was pleased that Madison once again allowed him to cook. Her palette was a bit bland, thought he, and it was the source of much chiding. She was sad at what was to come now and dreaded the obvious.

"Stojan, what will you do when you find Ana?"

He chewed and thought for a moment. He had been expecting the conversation and himself also dreaded it.

"We will continue where we left off I suppose."

"And..?"

He swallowed. There was no avoiding it. Stojan put down his food and looked at her. She smiled delicately. Her eyes had fear and she looked fragile.

"Madison, as we have discussed, I have thought no further than that, because the future is ever-changing."

"Stojan, you know that not to be true."

"Then I know enough to know that I have little control over it."

Satisfied with his answer he began eating again. She, however, had much to say.

"I am happy for the time we have spent together."

"As am I."

"Are you?"

"Yes, I am grateful."

"For what?"

He stopped eating again. Some traps were unavoidable. He reached out to her and her hand met his. Stojan smiled sincerely as he looked into her eyes.

"Madison, I owe you my life. More than that I am grateful that I have come to know you. You are one of the few people that I have encountered that have…"

He stopped and searched for words. It was a rarity and that helped to verify his feelings that day.

"…made a difference."

Her eyes welled with the beginnings of tears.

"I know what you must do, and I know what I must."

He moved closer to her.

"Our paths are different. We both have something waiting for us."

They did not finish their meal that day.

———

Today, she prepared for them to seek their fortunes and part ways. It was with a mixture of trepidation, relief, emptiness and satisfaction that she greeted the day. But now something was different.

"Stojan?"

He smiled and waited for her to finish.

"Are we not leaving..? Did you dream again?"

He approached her and held her shoulders.

"I did. I feel we should wait one more day."

She mentally shrugged. The longer they delayed, the more difficult it would be.

"Wait? What difference will this day make?"

She wanted to kiss him, and then forget about any timelines and urgency. Her world had changed and his daughter was out there somewhere. And they she just wanted to stay there with him in the little cottage. Their paths had crossed and would soon uncross. He inhaled and closed his eyes momentarily. When he opened them, he spoke gently.

"I understand it is odd, but I believe that my chance of finding her greatly increases if I wait until tomorrow."

"Because of your dream?"

He nodded, but his face revealed something else. She was mostly right. He could not tell her the real reason.

The next morning they woke early.

As he held her he spoke to her in gentle, earnest terms.

"This is as difficult for me as it is for you. I will tell you that I thought of doing something to make you angry, to make you upset and to make you change your opinion of me."

She ran her hand down his ribs, to his stomach and then back again as she listened.

"I wondered, even, if I could make you hate me."

Her hand stopped.

"Because it would be easier?"

"Yes, for us both."

She watched him breathe, she felt the pressure of his arms, the warmth of him next to her.

"Thank you for not. I prefer the pain of seeing you go."

It was over an hour before they left the bed.

———

It was decided that Madison would travel to Saint Louis and Stojan would travel to the cathedral of Saint Michael.

His dream had revealed imagery that he interpreted to mean he should move towards Saint Michael. Or rather, it showed him what would happen if he did not. It seemed he had to let go to receive. His time with Madison had been something he could never have foreseen and he would always carry the essence of their encounter with him. The more he cherished it, the more he found the strength to let it go. It was an odd thing and not since he lost his wife so many years ago did he feel what he felt for her. It seemed a stupid thing on the surface to let her go—this woman that he'd fallen for. His best tactical advice to himself was ignored and it was absurd. The raw, naked truth was told and he was better for it. He lied in battle, but would not here.

In an odd way, he enjoyed the pain of seeing her go because he was still whole inside and it made him happy. And it was for the best.

Finding Anastazja would help him heal the wound he was about to create.

He only hoped Madison would find the same solace.

"I will see you again."

Madison said it with such conviction, such certainty, that he pulled back for her and looked at her incredulously.

They both laughed as the moment caught them off guard. They had been embracing outside of the cottage as a farewell. Her strength in the matter, and her appreciation of his honesty, solidified how he felt about her.

There were an infinite amount of things to say upon parting, and they said them all with their embrace. Stojan and Lady Madison did not say goodbye this day.

———

Anastazja had finally come upon a junction in the forest that caused her to seek the nearest road. Her sleep had been interrupted by animals that were restless and she saw it as a portent of something to come. The noises and sounds and calls of animals were something she knew well and considered herself attuned to. But this night, things were different and there was an urgency to the tweets and calls heard in the air. She found herself far more annoyed than she waned to admit, and her morning routine was less dictated by her and more controlled by the urgings of the animals.

She found the road and had little direction other than knowing that if she went too far there would be much water in the way. If Stojan was not to be found, she was devoid of any further plan. And she was out of faith, out of energy and would just want to give up. However, it was a warm sunny day and Anastazja made a finding that brought happiness and cheer to her. The beautiful yellows and the faces brought warmth to her heart. It was a clearing very close to where she had emerged and it was full of sunflowers. They were vibrant in the sun and their pull on her was magnetic. She rode slowly though them as the minor road cut a path. It made her reflect on her past and her namesake and it was a most enjoyable natural feature in contrast to the rich greens and browns she had been immersed in for some time. Ana thought she felt the light on her skin from both the sun and the flowers, and she closed her eyes to bath in it.

"Go back!"

Her enjoyment was interrupted by a man coming the other way on horseback. She tensed and grabbed her hat in greeting. He meant no malice, but had fear in his voice as he stopped along side her.

"What do you mean?"

"You do not want what is up ahead. They are no longer a city."

The older man looked haggard.

"Why, what has happened?"

"Saint Michael has declared war."

"On which peoples? Which saint?"

"Which..? All of them. Everyone. Just leave. It is no place for a lone traveler. I am a merchant and I cannot stay there."

He was imploring her for her own good. It was absurd to him that a traveler would not know what was up ahead.

"Then pass by, stranger."

She attempt to dismiss him. Soon she would rejoin Stojan.

"No, come with me."

"I think not. If you wish to go where there is no saint then travel to Saint Louis."

He paused as if she had joked, and then stated the obvious.

"But there is…"

"Not any more."

She rode away, as she had no more use for conversation. Unfortunately, his words were true and she discovered a city that sprawled with what seemed like tens of thousands of people. And Ana could only go so far. They had no interest in lone travelers, and after only a little time it was clear that they were quite militant. So many were armed. While the relatively small amount of people of Saint Louis were downtrodden, exhausted and demoralized, these were different. Instead, they had been whipped into a fervor and every one she encountered had fanaticism in their eyes. They were bent on a kind of domination she'd never experienced. Only the teachings of the Navajo had exposed her to such a concept, and it was a thing of the distant past. There were conflicts from city to city in Amira as those of one area opposed the others, but those efforts soon diminished as the distances were great. In Poliska, very little conflict occurred as most considered themselves one people.

But now she saw the beginnings of a large scale war. The massive city ahead apparently ruled by Saint Michael was collecting and amassing a group of people trained and instructed for one purpose—to forcibly overtake the nearby cities. And the Navajo had a word for this—military. At one time, in the Old World, and before each country had its own military, and great wars were waged. However, she knew little if anything about wars *within* Amira.

She tried to understand the timing of such a thing. With all the saints diminishing in power she thought this one would barricade himself as Saint Louis had.

Her decision to enter the city to look for Stojan would simply not work; she had not the luxury of roaming unmolested or challenged—and asking questions had resulted in skirmishes.

For days she camped near the field on sunflowers. Every day it greeted her, and every day she made a trip into the city. The raids were to find what she could about the city, its leader and their intentions. Though the vine of information The Flickering Saint had established was destroyed, it was easy enough to know that Stojan had not made his way here yet, for surely they would boast about his capture. He was as much as an unknown as she was, or at least she had been. Word of her appearances traveled very quickly and the raids became more and more difficult as the people's awareness of her increased with their viciousness. How a city that size sustained itself she did not know, and guessed that perhaps in the heart of the city lived the common folk and farmers. It reminded her a bit of Luxor, but in reverse; instead of a fortress surrounded by farmers and peasants it was a militia surrounding the heart of things.

Her camp was just far enough to give her security but allow her an easy ride in. More than once she chastised herself for pushing so hard in the city. Her anger had the best of her and eventually they would catch on. Unfortunately those thoughts came too late.

Another beautiful day saw her walking though the field of sunflowers that did not quite yet reach her height. Another month and they would envelop her. That was when she saw them approaching. They trampled the flowers with their horses as they boldly came towards her. It was a large group of at least seven—perhaps more. They came in fast and hard and obviously meant to cut her down in the field.

The only advantage was that they all grouped together and weren't trying to surround her. It was a small thing, but she would try to use it.

She immediately ran to the left of them, then dropped down into the grass. Hunched as far down as she could, she ran in the opposite direction as she cursed the height of the flowers. Her thighs complained as she ran as fast as she could in this hunched manner. It fortunately worked and she had bought some time with the diversion; they continued forward and veered slightly to the left in an attempt to trample her. She watched as they overshot, stopped and began yelling as they spread out. It was more than she hoped. Her intention was to just gain some distance and at best to somehow lose them in confusion as she made her way to the camp. She shook her head in anger as she realized her raids were too often. Despite her hunching, one of the men saw her and came at her. He had a sickly smile upon his face as he drew his sword. The delight in his eyes told her there was probably a bounty.

She stood and drew her sword and the sight of so many flowers being trampled added to her rage.

He rode towards her and tried to angle his horse so that he could sweep his sword as he passed, but combat from horseback was difficult at best and Ana always chose to dismount. The man was learning this lesson as well. Upon missing her, he turned again but this time came up slower. It gave her ample time to dart to the other side at the last moment. Again he could not connect. Again he returned with a frustrated look as he slowed considerably. Unfortunately, it was slow enough for her to mount his moving horse and she was now behind him and used her sword to hold on—by placing it under his chin. She jumped off and took him with her and he made no sound as he fell away. He was dead by the time he reached the ground. She ran to the horse and slapped it hard to motivate it to run away, and indeed it did into the other searchers. She did not have time to see if they saw her and she ran towards her camp.

The crimson haired girl was not hard to find.   Though she thought herself near invisible while wading though the similarly colored sunflowers, her thoughts and anger had betrayed her earlier than she even realized. And now her bright colors were in full display—a pinpoint of red in a sea of yellow.

It would only be moments before they realized what happened and follow her into the nearby woods.

She made it into the forested area and continued running towards her camp. As she pushed herself, she knew she had no time to plan but just focused on moving as fast as she could without running into a tree.

The sounds of them following reached her ears as she almost made her way to her actual camp. She would be unable to lose them and would have to fight again. But this time they were smarter. They spread out and had her surrounded. She had no grass to escape into and the trees were sparse and would not help her. Soon, they encircled her as she stood under one. They looked possessed, greedy and had bloodlust in their eyes. They would kill her this day. At the very least, they would seriously injure her and drag her to this saint. Her plans would not stand and her grand trek across Amira had come to an end.

"What are your intentions with my daughter?"

They turned to the voice. Their irritation turned to surprise. She saw fear in some of the faces. Cornering one combatant was like a game. But now there were two, and any lack of recognition quickly dissolved. Their denial that the redhead was the one that swept through Amira, the one that destroyed saint after saint, the one with combat skills that were described with absurd abilities and outcomes had now hit them hard. She was the one they cornered, and her partner—her father, the man that had destroyed the first saint—was upon them now.

She had found him and nothing would stand in the way.   The girl became a cornered animal as she grunted softly with swings and sweeps of a sword that was constructed perfectly for her. Her skills were used most precisely and every one of the stories the men were aware of now became real as she demonstrated before them. The trees and grass were now a stage as her performance was shown to them as unwilling participants. It was a tragic play as they were all were destined to die. Though outnumbered, they were no match for the fearless blurs that wanted nothing more than to see each other at last and the men that surrounded them had made the unfortunate effort to be the volunteers that stood in their way. They could not have been more motivated that day and had one lived to tell about it, the story would never had been believed.

When they were done they slowly approached at first, but then she ran to him and embraced. As if on queue both dropped their swords. The force of the impact from her hug almost knocked him to the ground. Her embrace was much more intense to what he had grown accustomed to in the last few months, and he exhaled. She wanted to pull away and see his face but did not want to end the contact, so for many moments they stood and hugged and breathed rapidly from their exertions. Even her hair had turned back to golds and ambers, and their breathing was at rest, and they had truly tested reality with their embrace—it had told them that indeed they were real. They finally pulled apart.

She looked up at him with tears still in her eyes and noticed the same on him, and this made her even more emotional. Finally she stepped back a single step, put her hand on her hip and her face changed completely.

"Can you not even allow me to rescue you?"

Her voice was filled with mock exasperation as her face lit up. She could not hold the look long as they both broke into laughter. Finally he responded with a bite of his own.

"While you have excellent skills in battle, you have much to learn regarding your skills as a tactician."

The grim duty of dragging the bodies as far away from camp was handled by them both. Ana was reminded of how thoroughly Stojan checked for monies and supplies and so forth. It was not a habit she had acquired from him—even during lean times.

They carefully made their way back to her camp.

"When they do not return, I am sure they will send others."

Though she could not stop smiling, she understood the gravity of the situation. She did not care, however, for she had found Stojan. Or he had found her? In passing she remarked.

"There are a lot of birds nearby, have you noticed that?"

To that he eventually mumbled something quietly, and when she asked him to speak up, he replied without looking.

"No, no, just one."

With much work their camp was moved.

Stojan and Ana rode north a bit with the horses and set them free, then rode south past when they had they encounter.

At the camp that night, they regaled each other with stories. Stojan remarked how fearless Ana had become, and she in turn remarked how his stoicism was now tempered with a warmth she'd never outwardly seen. When she had finished her stories, it was Stojan's turn. He explained that he'd fallen ill due to something that they assumed was a poison, and how he was forced to stay dormant for the winter. His talk was vague and she thought not to press him further. He was not one who fell victim to too much elaboration.

"They will continue to come for us I think. I have raided too many times."

Stojan nodded and thought.

"I have not gone to the city yet. It is most fortunate we encountered each other before that."

"No we do not have to now."

"No? You have given up your quest to rid Amira of all saints so easily?"

Ana was not sure if he joked.

"I have already found you, Stojan."

"And I, you. Yet I feel that with what you describe, things will not be so safe for us."

"Then we can return to the south—to the Red lands, or even…"

He smiled for what was to come.

"On vacation at The Coast!"

He smiled and shook his head. The sun had gone down and he inhaled the cooler air. He was truly grateful for what fate had delivered to him.

"Perhaps we should sleep on this and think more on it in the morning."

Ana smiled and eventually fell asleep as Stojan remained awake for a bit. He would wake her slightly past midnight for her shift. He wanted to allow her to sleep but knew it was better to get at least some rest, and they were both used to having sentinel duties.

Amira

SAINT MICHAEL

Stojan woke to a familiar sound—though it was a sound he normally produced. Ana was sharpening her blade in a manner similar to him. She'd clearly used it to wake him, and as predicted by her, he'd thought she was sharpening his blade. The moment of confusion made him smile. Their plan was to pack at first light and head south. Regardless of Anastazja's decision, they would at least seek safer grounds until they decided. Stojan was not in a hurry to plan their entire future. They had, after all, just reunited.

But the threat of the saint loomed over them and if what Ana had said was true, then they had reached all the way to the Red Lands. This saint was like no other in his ambition and in spite of—or perhaps because of—Anastazja's actions—he meant to spread out.

Though he felt an anxiousness, he agreed to allow her a short walk. He needn't have worried as she returned far earlier than expected, like a faun leaping around trees quietly and efficiently.

"What is wrong?"

"They are here. They are already here."

"More?"

Stojan knew the answer to the question as he asked it. He knew more would come for them, but as they had relocated farther away, he thought them less wise to look for them this far.

"I saw them on the road. There are many of them. I have never seen so many traveling together. And they all trot their horses together in turn."

"Trot together?"

Stojan thought back on the synchronized trotting the guards would perform with their horses once a year for the people of the city—so many years ago. It was a demonstration of unity as well as power. To him it was just a show, but it was required each year.

"How close did you get?"

"Not close enough to hear them."

"They may be dispatching that group to the nearest city. They may not be meant for us."

"Saint Louis?"

"Yes, if he is truly gone and the townsfolk have revolted, then that city is ripe for the taking."

It was then that Stojan's stomach turned at the thought of Madison venturing there alone, and what she would find, and what was to come. He suddenly felt foolish to think that they would have any choice in the matter—to be able to continue to freely roam Amira. And letting Madison go off on her own into the apparent chaos was a terrible decision.

"We must leave immediately."

"To where?"

"Away."

He packed things quickly as she did the same. He then continued.

"We should make our way back to Saint Louis if we can. You said you travelled though the forest from there?"

"Yes mostly."

"We should be much safer that way."

As much as they tried, as stealthy as their escape had been intended, too much time had passed and too many men were involved. The land to the south was blocked my not tens, but hundreds of men. Some were on foot and some were on horseback. Ana's walk had been to the north and it only made her privy to the large group that traveled downward. But this new group was even larger and was coming from the opposite direction.

The sounds reached them first, then the voices. Their frantic rides in various directions only showed them that an absurd number of men were closing in on them. Escape without confrontation was not an option.

Much to Stojan's dismay, he hadn't even thought to set traps—so enthralled with Ana's stories was he. And then they saw them.

The men were careful and methodical. They observed a sort of discipline that again reminded him of his service to the guards of Poliska. These men were trained—more so than the last group. They said very little other than to warn Stojan and Anastazja that they were not be harmed unless they tried to escape.

"I have orders to kill you on the spot if you try to escape. If you come with us peacefully, then no harm will come to either of you."

Ana snarled and wondered just how many she could cut down. Could she cut enough to form an escape route? She knew of the men to the north. Even more awaited. But where had these come from? The answer came soon enough.

"You have no place to go. We have been searching for you for days and each day we have added another battalion."

Stojan appreciated the man's even tempered way of dealing with them. He would make an excellent guard and was clearly someone of some sort of rank. Perhaps he had been a captain of the guard in the city?

It took much convincing to persuade Ana to agree to be taken. At least this time they were together.

"What is your plan? What is your master's plan?"

When one of the men started to speak up the leader shook his head. They observed a good deal of discipline.
No one got close enough to attempt to disarm them, but instead they kept them in the center of a tight circle. More than once Ana thought about

leaping to a horse and killing the man next to her, but the amount of men present were more than she had ever seen before. They were all armed and the ones near her kept their swords out the entire time. Surely they were tired. At one point they were exchanged for other riders who then unsheathed their swords. They were prepared, trained and were taking no chances. After a short ride, they came upon the group in front, and the leader rode ahead to speak with the leader of that group.

"Stojan?"

She looked at him and hoped for some sort of plan, as she had none.

"Oddly, Ana, I think we will have better odds once we arrive. I have no intention of dying shortly after I have found you."

Internally it cheered her, externally it was obvious just how angry she was. The men seemed unfazed by her hair color though most hadn't seen it change. Perhaps they had all been told a redhead and tall man were on the loose?

Eventually they came to the city outskirts and making their way over a large hill presented a lot of the city to them. It was immense and most of what they saw were men like the ones that surrounded them—their attire was similar and all reminded Stojan of city guards. However, even a city of this size would not require such numbers. Many fires burned in makeshift buildings and camps. Had she not known better Ana would have thought that these men took over the city, and were not produced by it.

They stopped and waited.

Ana and Stojan exchanged glances. They were nowhere near a cathedral and had just barely entered the city. Finally a man on horseback arrived. He looked tired, important and thrilled. The leader approached him, dismounted and then kissed his hand. It was clearly the bishop of this saint. Maintaining his distance, he spoke to them.

"Stojan and Anastazja. You are now the guests of Saint Michael."

He was proud and firm. Ana did not like the way he said 'guests.'

"When will we meet him?"
Some of the men looked surprised and Ana saw fear in their eyes.

"Oh you will not."

He smiled and looked at some of the men.

"My saint is learned. You will never have an audience with him."

He laughed.

"You will never be permitted to be anywhere near him, or his great cathedral."

He smiled a very satisfied grin. That was when they both felt the hands on them and saw the metal in their faces. These people took no chances and had planned it. Stojan was torn between protecting Ana, the designs of the saint, the whereabouts and safety of another, and what was to come. He assumed they would be disarmed and placed into a cell.

Ana tried to shrug off the hands and almost spun her eye into a sword point. Any move would end in a serious wound—before she even made her escape. They were taken down from the horse and kept within a good distance of the bishop. He remained on horseback. They were very careful.

"My saint will soon rule all of Amira. And you can watch."

"It was you, wasn't it? It was you who killed all the elders in the village!"

Ana fumed as she realized what had happened.

"Yes! We have made great strides. That wasn't even a battle. Old people, waiting to die. And they were not the first. Do you know how ill-prepared we in Amira were before this? Not any longer."

Ana was taken aback at the sadness she felt. The kind people of the village, the slaughter—these people of the north were calculating and life meant nothing to them. A battle to save one's life was vastly different than a calculated plan to wipe out cities of passive peoples. Her sadness mixed with the most bitter of guilt; for she had paved the way. With each saint destroyed there was one less island fortress to overcome; one less reason for the people to defend themselves. She had done it all, save for this and another.
"What of the other saint?!"

"They other? Surely you are mistaken. My saint is the *only* saint now, the one true saint, the one who rules over all of Amira. We just have to insure that all know that."

She shook her head as the men nodded in agreement and grunted. There were two left, not one. The Saint on High and The Flickering Saint had confirmed that. With all his madness, The Flickering Saint had an obsession with telling the truth and providing information. There was another still out there.

She had come so far. She had finally found Stojan and now they understood how to contain them. These people took no chances; provided no openings. And now hands were upon them, disarming them. She felt sickened. Their hands were on her and her father's sword.

"Ah. Lay those down here."

The men brought the two swords to the ground and laid them in front of the horse's hooves. Ana looked upon the massive spiraling city—the various fires lit. She knew there were many forges established. They meant to create many more weapons. Her thoughts were broken by his continued grandstanding.

"They will make grand ornaments in the cathedral—more proof of…"

He looked above their heads, passed them and beyond.

"Eh? Who approaches?"

They turned. It was a man. He was on foot and ornately dressed. His leather pants were lined with furs; around his neck was both a necklace of teeth and the pelt of an animal. Upon his head he wore something the men thought absurd—a great plume of feathers that spouted and reached for the sky. Though delicate looking it stayed firmly upon his head.

In his right hand was a staff with a large crystal upon it, and it reflected the sun. In some ways, his dress was similar to what Ana favored. The man was older but not elderly and had a great energy about him. His confidence poured forth as he entered from the hill. He walked directly to the large group of men and they parted slightly as he walked. He nodded hellos to each and every one of them as he passed, and in one case patted the neck of a horse. For the first time, the bishop and his right hand man were unprepared. The men looked for a horse, but the man had clearly left it just beyond the hill.

He stopped, and smiled at Stojan and Anastazja, then looked at the bishop.

"Let me friends go."

For the first time, Anastazja's hair had reverted back to her normal blonde and some of the men seemed taken aback.

The bishop stole an irritated glance at his apparent captain and then looked upon the older man who looked so very out of place.

"Who are you? Where did you come from?"

"I ask you one more time. Let me friends go."

It was a simple request, but carried a disarming weight to it. Ana felt it because she had said similar, simple things to men before she killed them —as had Stojan. But the man was unarmed save for the staff.

The bishop wrinkled his nose in disgust. He had enough of the charade of the wandering man who had obviously seen a group and wanted to be part of it. In distasteful tones, the bishop propositioned him as if he was a disobedient animal.

"Or what? Or you will walk all the way back to your horse and ride away?"

He winked at Ana.

"Oh I didn't say I arrived by horse."

With that he raised his staff high into the air and turned it around. The shiny gem at the top reflected the sun in many directions—to the men, to the sky and to the hill behind him.

Though slightly frightened by what he thought was a nasty surprise, the bishop quickly regained his composure and looked at the man. He stared at him, but he had no further actions. The bishop opened his mouth as he noticed the slight change in the hill. It was growing, and moving.

The men all turned to witness it as well. The hill itself was not changing —just the surface. Dust was being thrown up in all directions—great clouds of dirt were being disturbed by something moving over the top and now descending down this side.

The men continued to watch. There were men on horseback. Hundreds came, and behind them hundreds more. They rode together and in the center of their ranks moved a thing the size of a house. The ground rumbled at the thousands of hooves all hitting the ground like raindrops. More and more were added in a continuous blankets of men, horses and large objects that were dull in the sun.

Ana stole a glance at those around her. The men were transfixed, and behind the bishop came some men who were walking up in curiosity. They too stared at the sight never seen before.

"What is that…?"

The bishop whispered out of the side of his mouth. His captain had no answer and just continued to stare. Some of the men turned their horses to watch.

The massive forces on horseback continued to approach and the thing in front could now be heard. It rumbled and moved smoothly through the sparse grass. It was colored grey and greens and was sometimes hard to see, and it wasn't the only one. There were two more behind it.

"Get your men get your men get your men!"

The bishop panicked when he realized the blanket of invaders coming towards them outnumbered their men by an order of magnitude.

"T… t… to do what…?"

The man who had respected and lived in fear of the bishop did not look at him when he responded. He knew what not to do. Even if he could gather them in the next few minutes, to muster everyone fit to combat this group would be suicide. The man simply resolved to wait.

Within a short time the group arrived. They kept their distance as the great edge of them stopped barely a block away. They could see the faces of the riders—all similarly dressed as the man, but not as ostentatiously. And now they could see the thing that rolled to a stop. Unlike a cart, it had many wheels—perhaps seven or more, and two did not touch the ground. In fact none of the wheels touched the earth but instead rode inside of great bands made of strips. It was low, and wide and painted with splotches in colors of greens and browns. Upon it was attached a great flattened hammer and the handle of the hammer protruded directly in front of it. Those on horseback kept their distance on the side of it and it was given great respect.

At least one man thought he saw the flattened hammer turn slightly upon arriving.

The dust clouds were blown slowly away by the gentle wind as the group stood in silence. It was indeed a massive and unprecedented gathering.

The bishop dismounted and moved towards Stojan and Ana. He shoved her to the ground and the sword points prevented her from objecting, other than raising her hands to her face. The man behind Stojan followed suit and he too was shoved down. With the two on their knees, unarmed and surrounded with drawn swords, the bishop drew his own sword. His face looked crazed and desperate now, and the expression was one that meant to kill them both. At least he would have that.

The bishop did not see the visitor raise his staff a second time, nor did he see him motion to Stojan and Ana to cover their ears. Confused, they followed the direction and were grateful for it. For soon after that a great sound was heard. It was as if lightning had struck behind them. All of their group ducked instinctively save for the man in the headdress and the two on their knees who were covering their ears. They heard it a second, and then a third time. It was a powerful and terrible sound and the men saw that it came from the end of the hammer handle. A plume of smoke emanated from it and those quick enough noticed the thin trail of smoke that drew upon the wind and the air—tracing a line as an arc as it entered the city. They watched as a sound was heard thrice—this time in the very center of the city, as a cloud of bright orange and smoke erupted.

Anastazja watched the sword points around her dip down, as the men's mouths were agape. They had all traced the thunder of the thing and seen the lines. They all knew what had happened, and that included the bishop. He had been in mid strike when the sound occurred, and his legs buckled as he dropped his sword in fear.

No one saw her move; none saw her weave her way through the now relaxed stances, the dipping swords, the noise of the thunder, the horrifying cloud of light and then the deafening silence. The bishop had been knocked backward with such force that he landed a few meters way. She found her sword as the others gasped.

The captain—having just dismounted to follow his liege—raised his sword to take Ana from above. The man of the feathers, whose staff had called upon a great army once, and then called destruction upon them the second time, looked at him and shook his head. It was enough for him to freeze. The man spoke to the prone bishop now.

"You have made war and brought war upon you. You have preyed upon those that are peaceful. Do not mistake peace for weakness."

Sword in hand she meant to do the bishop in, but then thought better of it as she looked at her sword. She would not soil it on him this day. She turned to the men and the great army assembled. She looked at the leader of the Navajos and smiled. She did not see the bishop rise with hate in his eyes as everything he believed in was lost. She did not see him scoop up the other sword that he'd landed on. She stood with her back to him as she continued to watch the army and the men before her. Stojan thought he saw her close her eyes as the sword was struck. It was not an overly long sword held in the awkward hands of a man filled with hate. It was not thrust into the back of a girl who seemed oblivious.

It was a sword made with love, from a man who had never seen his girl grow up. It was a sword that was a perfect fit in her hands, and sung with the expert training and strength she applied to it. And it was swung behind her, without a look. It was a backhanded motion fitting for a man who would do such terrible deeds. The swing was fast, and powerful, and took all by surprise save for two people—the one who swung it, and the man who had done the same thing almost three years previously.

The bishop was cut down as her sword decapitated him that day—to the horror of all that watched, as her blonde hair remained in place with the rest of her body.

Those that held a sword either dropped them or sheathed them. Many ran in the city looking for protection from what had happened, and many secretly rejoiced; for the cathedral and the saint were no more. And soon they would find the same fate had befallen the bishop.

As he stood, his sword was returned to him by Ana, as the visitor approached them both.

"I am Vincent Defender of Eagles, and I am honored to meet the ones known as Watchful Raven and Autumn Wind."
He waved to the great army amassed nearby and they approached further.

Stojan wondered what would happen if he raised his staff another time, and would joke about it later.

"Are they gone?"

It was the captain now. His question was honest and sounded like a child asking a parent, and there was an unusual tone to his voice: hope. The visitor turned to him and spoke in reassuring tones.

"Amira is free of the saints. You can rejoice now."

Ana smiled, but in her eyes were hints of doubt. His wording was not to her liking. That day there was much discussion and to the surprise of the denizens of the city, the Navajo had no interest in conquest. Their show of force was in defiance to the beginnings of a great Amiran war. This show of strength would prevent the loss of thousands of lives. Those of Amira would now adjust to live without the rule of the saints, and perhaps in time the Navajo would welcome more into their ways, their cities and even their library. But this would happen in time.

Unfortunately, there was something of more immediate need.

At a great gathering that night there was celebration and familiar faces.

Stanley Two Rivers was also present and Ana happily reintroduced him to Stojan. Other leaders had come along with those who orchestrated the great army.

As they watched the fire and the embers of the encampment, Ana spoke seriously to the one known as Vincent.

"I must know of the saints."

"Please, of course. I have news to share with you on that. I wished to wait."

"To wait?"

"Yes, having removed such a burden from your shoulders today I dreaded placing it back once again."

Ana looked concerned as Stojan stood by.

"Please. Please tell us."

"I spoke the truth when I said Amira was now free of the saints, but one more remains."

"But if Amira is free then where…"

The man closed his eyes before he spoke as Ana interrupted.

"Oh no…"

"I am sorry. Word just reached us days ago. Yes, one still lives."

Ana was reminded of her discussion with The Flickering Saint.

"Yes. I was told this. The one that opened the door in the first place."

"Yes. It has escaped. It no longer resides in Amira."

"How long?"

"Perhaps less than a season."

This time it was Stojan who asked. He needed clarification.

"Where?"

"I am sorry dear Ana and Stojan, but it has gone to Poliska."

They were stunned, and Ana was filled with questions.

"But Poliska? How? A vessel? Why would it go there?"

It was then that Stojan smiled a most distasteful smile—though he did not speak.

"We do not know. But if this one is powerful enough to open the door…"

"The door is no more! We saw it for ourselves. Even The Flickering Saint would take hundreds of years to rebuild such a thing."

"Yes Ana, but it makes it no less dangerous, no less troublesome. Its power is unknown."

Stojan remained silent and was clearly very upset.

"What? What do you know Stojan?!"

Ana seemed panicked now. She always believed that no matter what happened, her homeland would always be free of the saints.

"Ana, I must think on this tonight."

"But... we will go, yes? We must go!"

"But how? How would you return to Poliska?"

"The conveyance!"

She was almost shouting now, but the festivities were loud enough to mask her. Stojan looked at her.

"That was some time ago. We do not know if it even operates, or where it is. And it is probably a thousand or more kilometers from us, Ana."

It sickened him inside to think of what might be happening as they spoke.

"It does."

It was a new voice and one familiar to Ana. In fact, the two men that joined them greeted them warmly. Stojan had met Stanley Two Rivers, but not the younger man. He Who Soars introduced himself as Stanley apologized for interrupting.

"Forgive us, but we have seen the conveyance. It still makes the trip from Poliska to Amira and back again, and we believe this is how the saint left some time ago."

"We are out of time then. It will take months just to reach it, it is already the beginnings fall and winter will come before we even arrive. I know first hand of this."

Stojan's words weighed heavily. Ana brightened as she looked at He Who Soars and smiled warmly.

"No Stojan! We have a means. The conveyance!"

"I know of the conveyance Ana, but we must reach it first."

"No, not that conveyance. That is a conveyance of the water. There is a conveyance of the air."

"Of the air? You mean..?"

"Yes! The arrow plane!"

She nodded vigorously as those present looked on with confusion and apprehension.

He Who Soars spoke now.

"That is a long journey but we could make it."

"You could take us to Poliska in the sky?!"

Stojan was incredulous.

"No, we cannot do that. It is too far and…"

He swallowed.

"I would not make a journey over water—over the ocean."

"But we can go inside it! Inside the ocean!"

Ana's enthusiasm was contagious, and Stojan spoke to truly understand.

"You would be able to take us to the conveyance before winter?"

"It refreshed today, so yes tomorrow."

"We could leave tomorrow?"

"Yes."

"And when would we be there?"

"Tomorrow."

"WHAT?!"

Ana smiled, nodded, and hugged him as he stared at He Who Soars.

———

Any and all feelings Stojan had about heights were literally dwarfed by his experience in the arrow plane. He wondered aloud many times why they would build such a thing with so many windows. The purpose of a fragile thing like glass within such a fragile thing was absurd. Truly he thought they jested when he was first shown it. To make matters worse, it seemed that Anastazja immensely enjoyed his discomfort and was happy to ask questions of He Who Soars during the journey. The only saving grace was that the journey was made it such a short time.

Stojan's fear and nervousness also affected He Who Soars and Ana was the only one present who just simply enjoyed the journey for what it was. The descending of the arrow plane was a horrible experience—made worse by the nervousness of the one that controlled it, and his nervousness was enhanced by Stojan himself.

"It is normally not like this," was said again and again throughout the course of the trip and upon finally touching the Earth and coming to a stop, Stojan was the first to exit. He required time alone and eventually returned.

Unfortunately, something about the wheels was thought to be damaged with the roughness of their landing, so Stanley Two Rivers and He Who Soars had much work to do as they waited for it to refresh. They promised that they would be well and safe as they said their goodbyes to the two passengers.

It was only a short distance to the port, but they made it on foot as a horse would not fit in the conveyance. Stojan remarked that it was not just space and that a horse simply would not allow it.

"They are smarter creatures than we think."

Anastazja happily carried whatever belongings she had. They were burdened, but knew that it would not be long to reach the conveyance.

To their surprise, the building they remembered was still occupied by those they had met, and they were more than happy to allow them passage for a sizable fee. Stojan had bargained for some time and begrudgingly paid them a considerable amount. Once again they would travel within the ocean.

The two argued on the way as to their favorite conveyance, with Stojan being shocked at Anastazja's choice of something so dangerous as she shared her equal shock at his like of a windowless craft. The enclosed space did not bother him just as being in the clouds did not bother her. It made for a nightly ritual and they both enjoyed the argument. It was again a time for talk, and remembrance and discussion, and his heart was filled with the happiness she provided. For her, Stojan was back and her life could continue. And they were going home.

Fortunately, the two men they traveled with had little interest in them, and had little knowledge of their exploits. They had agreed to remain as incognito as possible, or at least describe themselves as travelers that had sold everything to return to their home. The conveyance now was well known to those that had the means to pay for it and was no longer a merchant's secret. How it was maintained and repaired without the influence of a saint remained to be seen, and by some of the noises Stojan heard upon arriving, he thought its days were numbered.

They were able to purchase horses at the dock itself, as it was not uncommon for travelers to sell them upon leaving. It took most of the remaining money to do so and they rode to find a town on the way.

Ana looked at the trees, and the countryside and the grasses. She looked upon the sky and the clouds. It was fall in Poliska and it was beautiful. Though there was nothing like the sights of Amira, somehow Poliska was different, and it smelled of home. Stojan watched as Ana wept quietly and he realized they were tears of joy, so he let her be. He too was reminded of many things and fall had a special memory for him. Finally she spoke.

"Stojan? How will we find it? Poliska is so much smaller than Amira."

"We need not find it, for I know where it is."

"You do?"

"I think."

"You think? Tell me Stojan."

"It is how I came to meet you."
"But that was the bishop. We go to see the bishop?"

"Yes. I do not think he was able to do this on his own. I think I was in the presence of a saint those many years ago."

"In the fall?"

"Yes, just like this."

It would take them less than a few weeks at most to reach the bishop. As the journey went on, Ana was able to walk and venture again. She trained with Stojan and the two of them spent very little time in the towns. Many things came back to him and his nomadic ways helped him to find the proper routes and avoid others easily. He had no desire to alert him, or to have to answer too many questions.

Ana was restless at night as she dreaded what was to come. Her imagination filled in more than she liked, and her dreams reflected that.

Stojan, however, seemed calmer than ever—almost to the point of a lack of concern for them. This peace seemed to happen one day in his heart, as if he'd gone to bed as worried as she, and then woke up with the burden of it removed. He would not volunteer anything related to this, but it sometimes unnerved her and sometimes cheered her. She just wished her spirit would pick one.

At last they came to a very small city and made their way to the outskirts.

"Tonight we go."

"Why not now."

"Night time seems the proper time, Ana."

It was then that she realized many things, and from that point on it all seemed surreal.

Amira

THE TOWER

It was a cool autumn night in which Anastazja and Stojan reached an all-too-familiar building.

"Stojan, is it truly… that day? Do you want to know?"

She motioned towards the tower as if this would explain her words, and continued.

"Should we consult a calendar?"

Stojan smiled broadly—far more than he expected to.

"Ana, are you afraid you will have to deal with two of me?"

Taken aback from this, her face changed from clandestine concern to one of mild amusement and confusion. She tilted her head and brought her chin into her chest.

"Well, I…"

"It matters not what day it is to me Ana. As we have discussed, we have far less control over things than we have ever imagined. It is what it is."

She frowned slightly.

"True."

"However, I am owed a small fortune from the man who sent me to kill you and I mean to retrieve it."

Walking up to the building, Stojan showed no signs of attempting to be covert. Instead, he was direct as if he was popping into an inn for a quick pint.

Ana walked beside him—looking around in an attempt to find the hidden traps and mercenaries that would then jump out to challenge her. She needn't have worried as they had all been dispatched the previous day.

Stojan knocked at the door, and neither had their sword out. It made Ana nervous to be so nonchalant about the entire affair. Surely they should have entered through a back door, or forced their way in under the cover of midnight. The sun was just setting.

To Stojan it simply felt like the right thing to do. And in his heart he had been given a great gift. He was prepared to die so that Ana could live on, and these last years could not be taken from him—powerful magic and time travel not withstanding.

Just a cordial conversation, he thought to himself. Despite his penchant for planning, foresight and caution, he meant to simply walk in and at the least retrieve his monies. If the bishop perished in the ensuing cordial conversation, then so be it. He felt almost possessed—in the same way a rowboat is possessed by a river.

Ana swung her torso back and forth in waiting—keeping one hand on her sword.

Just then the door opened. The face of a man with a slight build greeted them. Said face showed irritation, then concern, then utter shock.

He clearly remembered the assassin that had just been hired a few days ago - except that something was very different. The man that stood before him looked a little older and did something the assassin seemed incapable of.

He was smiling—slightly.

"I would see your master."

The servant backed up—fear showing on his face—as his eyes darted from Stojan to the blonde woman that accompanied him. Back and forth his eyes did move as he stumbled backwards.

To Ana, the interior was familiar; she had been in enough cathedrals to recognize the windows, the long chairs and the stage at the front. This one was relatively small and she had the impression the gatherings were infrequent. It just felt empty.

"I…"

Words slowly seeped out of the small man.

"You… you are, you have…"

"I assume he is upstairs?"

The memory of the layout of the building was fresh in Stojan's memory as if he'd just seen it yesterday. In a way he had.

Ana smiled at the man, she was slightly taller than he. He looked at her —her body and her sword. Stojan simply walked to the door leading up, opened it and walked up the stairs. Ana followed and was a bit surprised at the lack of plan. She walked a few steps behind him—leaving the servant to stand dumbfounded as he looked on.

He watched them go. For many moments he stared at the closed door. The last time he'd seen the man he looked younger and was dressed differently. Or perhaps he was older? This man looked like a more mature version, but unlike the previous man, he looked different somehow. His face? His demeanor? For many moments he stood in silence trying to figure out what significant difference this man displayed. And finally it occurred to him.

He looked whole.

His initial reaction was to run up after him, but instead he took a deep breath and closed his eyes. He was terrified of the bishop, and also terrified of this man. If he had come back because the payment was no good, or the bishop had used some sort of trickery, he wanted no part of it. If he came back to inform the bishop that the deed was done, then his master would be most happy and would want the private moment with the assassin.

The servant thought all of these reasonable justifications were utter nonsense and just an excuse for remaining in place as to not wet himself with fear.   Perhaps today he would end his employment with the bishop, which was to say he would fling himself out of a second-story window first thing in the morning.

Assuming he was still alive.

———

Stojan waited for Ana to catch up to him, and at the door he simply said, "Stay behind me. I would like to introduce you. Be careful, dear Ana."

Ana had not needed to argue with Stojan to convince him to allow her to accompany him.   She was sure he would have absolutely insisted she stay behind and allow him to enter the building on his own. Yet, he was uncharacteristically accommodating.   This made no sense.   Stojan did not play games, and he always had a plan.

Stojan slowly entered the chamber—making the turn to enter from the pseudo hallway created for privacy.   It prevented anyone from just opening the door and casting their eyes upon the bishop.   Instead he would always insist his servant enter and then call to him from behind the short wall.

The servant was convinced this particular tower room was once a bedroom or dressing room for those that lived or worked here. Regardless, it kept him separate from the bizarre rituals the bishop participated in.   It also provided cover for Stojan and his young companion.

Stojan walked in, taking in the lighting and smells of the room.   The ever-present candles, the cloths, the dim lighting—it was like so many of the cathedrals they'd been in.   This room, however, looked as if it was made to look like one.   There was a certain lack of authenticity.

The thought that he was now a connoisseur of the inner workings of cathedrals would have made him smile slightly, had he not a grim job to do.

At that, he heard quiet talking.   It was indeed the bishop and he was exactly where he had left him; standing behind the great statue covered in drapes.

At the time he thought him mad; but Stojan himself had carried on conversations with statues more than once in the many years.

He walked towards the bishop who was concentrating on the massive sculpture—a statue that was covered and had its back to Stojan. With this viewing he had the luxury of studying it a bit more as he crept up. The statue was probably the largest he had encountered—it was at least three meters high and extremely broad-shouldered. In fact, unless it was a trick of the drapery, this particular statue had some sort of shell upon its back. Perhaps it meant its reach was two-fold. He would have to keep his distance. It was quite curious that this statue had been brought into the room. It did not belong, clearly. And knowing the vast ego of the interlopers, they preferred to be center-stage. This one was subdued.

"And then what will you do, Lucjan?"

Stojan froze and listened to the quiet conversation. The saint within the statue had a demeanor unlike the others. He had been struggling to listen as he approached and now the words were clear.

"What will I do? I will do whatever I please. Unlike the others, I will have reversed the roles."

The smugness of the man brought Stojan back to their last conversation.

"At what cost?"

It was, of course, a perfect opening.

"Speaking of costs."

At this, the bishop jumped backwards and raised both arms in front of his face. He was quite taken aback by the sudden deep voice.

Stojan made sure to stay far enough away from the statue as not to be within the physical reach. It was the non-physical reach that concerned him even more.

The bishop looked out from the protection of his forearms and slowly un-arched his back. He straightened to his normal height as his arms found their way to his sides. A look of recognition crossed his face as his eyes took in the tall assassin.

Stojan noted the look in his eyes—it was a crazed, animalistic demeanor

—the kind one would expect of someone lost in the wilderness, or running from a murderer as his stamina is just about to give out.

Up and down he looked as his face turned from recognition to irritation.

"It did not work?!"

The bishop's eyes darted briefly to the statue as his little mouth tightly closed.

Stojan remained nonplussed and simply waited for whatever the bishop had in store for him.

His younger companion listened on from behind him—out of the sight of the bishop, for now. She found Stojan's confidence out of place and unnerving.

"What is it you want...?"

Again his eyes darted to the statue and back to Stojan.

"Why aren't you there? He will be here any moment. How will you defeat this warrior at his weakest when you have stupidly returned?"

Stojan detected a flash of fear in the man's eyes as he expected retribution, but rational thought did not guide him this day. Instead, his brain was governed by a lack of sleep, desperation and absolute fear of the events to come. He was even willing to die at the hands of the master assassin it seemed. Or perhaps he had a talisman against it? The protection of a saint would surely be enough?

"I am here for my payment. It seems it did not travel with me. Whatever saintly magics you invoked to send me did not include safe passage for my monies. A shame."

"Did you do the deed?"

A look of hope crossed the man's face. It was the tiniest glimmer.

"Yasssss... Your face; your clothing..."

He looked again at the saint—this time longer.

"Yesssss... it *has*."

His face was an explosion of excitement, heightened by his present state of mind it created a most horrid mask of ecstatic insanity.

"It worked!   After all this time you have returned to me.   But for me it has been a day."

His words became warm—almost fatherly—as he inhaled and seemed to be filled with pride at the great power he wielded.

"Of course! Your payment…"

He looked around the room as if he had misplaced it. Stojan watched his eyes take on a life of their own as they darted to and fro in the chamber as his body became agitated.   It seemed he truly meant to find the payment—assuming it ever existed.

Stojan took two steps back.

The man started to move around and fortunately for his visitors the statue did not.

Again Stojan took another step back—always keeping his distance from the great hulking statue as well as the rambling bishop. He gave him wide berth to rummage about the room—so much so that he eventually came upon his companion.

Their eyes met.

Hunched over and about to open a rather large, hinged tuffet he had turned his head slightly—thinking he would look upon his servant.

Instead what he saw stunned him.   It was a woman.   She was tall in stature and dressed strangely.   Clearly a warrior, she was clad in thin leathers, tight leggings and adorned with furs.   Around her neck was a primitive necklace.

Her face was perfection and her eyes were massive—pools of bight blue that challenged the sky as the rightful blanket of the Earth. Her hair was crimson of a most unusual kind as here and there were the tiniest tendrils of blonde throughout. It hung there upon her as a protective helmet.

This girl of crimson hair was the most fascinating creature he had ever seen, and she could be no more than 21 years of age.

He stood up, and keeping his eyes on her he yelled to Stojan.

"Who is this? A companion?"

Anastazja felt the rage welling within her. She was face to face with the man that had tormented Stojan; had sent him to kill her and was in the process of releasing the saints upon her dear Poliska once again. She'd quietly remained in the alcove waiting, fuming and focusing.

She had her hand on her sword. She said nothing.

"Eh? Who is this, Stojan?"

He asked again, while still looking at the girl. Then his eyes narrowed.

"A trick?!"

He stumbled backwards. Ana took steps forward, slowly moving towards him—almost following him like prey. Without realizing it, Ana and Stojan had triangulated positions so that they were flanking the bishop away from the statue, and into the corner of the room by a large window. The statue remained still in the opposite corner as the bishop glanced at its back for help.

"Ha!" He pointed at her, then Stojan, backing into the corner.

"I am protected by the prophecy!"

Recognition of the word shown in her face and he noticed.

"You know! You know, don't you?"

He looked at Stojan, who looked slightly disappointed.

"Your plan has not worked. I am protected by my pact, and whatever the prophecy holds it does not do so for me."

He relaxed and put his hands on his hips, looking to and fro to his potential attackers. He smiled a smile of triumph, but Stojan still saw fear in his wide eyes.

She wanted to kill this man, slowly, quickly—in whatever way was best at the moment. She'd reviewed in her mind the hundreds of ways she would do it the moment she'd stepped into the chamber. Nay, the planning had started the moment she stepped into the building.

Thoughts of the man that killed Fox filled her head and the sword she placed in his throat. Images of the wolf that would harm Stojan appeared, and the feeling of her leaving the Earth weightlessly to land upon it and drive her sword so powerfully into it as to impale the ground itself.

"You've brought her here to help you kill me? But it will not work."

"Oh no, that is not why she is here."

He turned his head sharply to Stojan the way a teacher directs his attention to a student who has spoken out of turn.

All thoughts of payment forgotten, the bishop snapped at him.

"No?!"

"No, Lucjan."

He turned his palm upward and motioned to Ana.

"She simply wants to read to you."

Even Anastazja was surprised at this—her quiet rage convoluting with a drop of curiosity.

"Yes please, Ana. I think his holiness would appreciate your poem."

"You've written a poem?"

He looked her up and down suspiciously, then with some mirth. He was bathed in a colored glow from the window as it did its best job to filter the full moonlight that night. He took on a multi-colored visage, and the purples, reds and oranges were not kind to his face.

"My my Stojan, you've taken her under your wing and taught her all manner of civilized skills."

Stojan looked at Ana's hair as the bishop spoke. Ana returned his intense gaze as moments seemed like hours. Something was afoot and not right. They were not taking the clear opportunity to…

Realization set in.

Had the bishop been looking at her at the time he would have ben alerted to whatever had crossed her mind. Instead he continued to gloat and to patronize. She took her hand away from her sword, and taking a step back she deftly removed the tiny backpack.

Keeping her eyes on the bishop the entire time, she brought it forth, unhooked it and removed the book from within.

She dropped the backpack to her feet.

He eyed the book curiously. Stojan watched as his face became a mixture of apprehension and interest.

"What a delightful show you have brought me."

Anastazja reverently flipped through the pages, being careful to find the right page. The poem in question had always been her favorite. It was simple, and the imagery seemed direct.

And—as she had told Stojan more than once—it had her name in it.

She began. She formed her words confidently, but slowly. In reading she found she was far more upset than she realized. It was taxing to concentrate. Stojan, the proximity to this evil man, her memories of how this all started—all came together now. And this amalgamation of memories and feelings gave her a supreme loss of control. Never had she felt this way, but she strived to do her best. Her soft voice read aloud.

Strike at the warrior when n'er be more weak
Motion is set when ye find what ye seek

The lion will pass but the flower survives…

At this, the bishop became enraged.

"What!? What is this? You read the prophecy?"

He grabbed the book from Ana who immediately reached for her sword. So taken aback was she that she had little time to react. He now had her precious book, and she bored holes in him with her stare. She imagined him tearing the book, tearing the pages out—even setting it afire.

She wanted to act, but found that she could not. Clearly some sort of hex was here in the room. The saint present had clearly enhanced the room with some sort of protection. Try as she might she could not act on her desire—which was to end the life of the man before her, efficiently and expertly. It was maddening to be restrained in such a subtle, yet powerful way.

The bishop held the book in his hands, flipped it over to read the cover, then flipped it back to the page that was open. He looked at Stojan and then Ana.

"You bring me the entire prophecy intact? Translated? And because of your travels and the powerful forces I control you've done the work for me? This is unimaginable."

He smiled a satisfied smile and took a deep breath. The protection that was promised was truly in force. The assassin and his redheaded accomplice could do nothing to him. It was just as the Saint had spoken —albeit less clearly than he would have preferred. He not only had destroyed the warrior before he could reach him, but the entire prophecy had literally been hand-delivered to him. Was there nothing he could not accomplish now? He felt the rightful confidence of one in such an esteemed and protected position. He was elated.

Lucjan looked to Stojan, who appeared unusually calm. He looked at the redheaded woman who seemed to struggle with rage—she was clearly feeling the effects. She looked over hopelessly to Stojan, and then back to him. He pronounced the entire situation in one word.

"Magnificent."

With a large smile he glanced at the light coming in from the window, and held the book just so within the moonlight and continued the poem. He read it with delight and fascination. It was beautiful, simple and powerful.

...A sword turns to shovel, as a warrior arrives

A sacrifice thwarted, two become three
New skills are learned, and taught with much glee

Each verse was read as an accomplishment, as if he was constructing something as he spoke.

The distance substantial; their efforts are mocked
The road must be travelled but cannot be walked

Brick and mortar, again and all
The path becomes shortened as the patrons fall

A love is still lost, redemption was earned
Companionship lent must now be returned

It was almost as if he was performing an incantation that altered reality. The more he read, the more intoxicating it became.

The fall at last takes him and three become two
Patience they find is the only virtue

A circle's the path, a tower at night
A world upside down may now be set right

The words read aloud by he who has sinned
A final blow from the autumn wind

That was when he looked up and saw her.

His face so full of fascination and passion—so contorted into concentration and glee—dropped immediately. Every muscle in his face became relaxed as his expression changed dramatically.

She was still there standing in front of him, but she was no longer a redhead.

He stared, dumbfounded.

She no longer looked enraged but instead was calm. What he witnessed then was a ballet of movement slowed down in beautiful, horrible dance. Each movement was with intent; each muscle flexed with memory—with freedom and quiet power.

With infinite patience she unsheathed her sword and he watched it travel through the air. It turned and swept and rotated.

All in the room was still save for the girl before him and her ballet of intent.

The sword effortlessly traveled and the metal was bright in the darkened room. It reflected the multicolored moonlight as it traveled. He heard no sounds; took no breath; thought no thoughts.

He simply watched as the only two things in focus in the surreal blurry scene made their impact on him.

His shirt and robes were parted as easily as his flesh. Seconds were hours as the sword entered, joined and passed though him. His impalement was complete as the smooth metal was introduced to his chest. It felt as if the metal entered his heart and he could feel the cold of it. It made the smallest of sounds behind him as the point impacted the glass.

Her wide, blue eyes looked into his. There was no hate, no anger and no rage. Instead it was a calm, serene, intense stare as she completed a movement that started with freeing her sword.

Lucjan's face continued expressionless as he felt the life drain out of him. The enormity of what had happened weighed upon him all at once. The intensity was overwhelming as he expired in slow motion. The second impact was made by the final words he heard as she looked into his eyes through her blonde hair.

"For my father."

They were stated together but separated by infinity.

"Both of them."

Before he could collapse, the sword was withdrawn. Though she was disgusted by what remained on it, she did not clear it. Instead, she watched as he stumbled backwards—his steps competing to balance him, but instead giving him momentum. She reached quickly to snatch the book before it reached the floor. His back hit the window hard— shattering it with more weight than he should have possessed. She watched him tumble out—legs exiting along with a sizable bag at his waist.

With that, her head slowly turned to Stojan. He remained with arms folded across his chest—something that she had never seen before in a combat situation.

He looked moved by her actions. Perhaps it was her words?

Ana watched as he moved towards her. He looked upon her hair and smiled.

"Well done."

They moved towards the window to peer outward and found the bishop splayed across the ground outside—his arms and legs contorted into odd positions—as coins and jewels spilled forth from his waist. They glittered in the moonlight that night.

A breeze of fresh air entered the room—rustling the coverings of the thing in the corner. She could hear the sounds of the night as well, and thought she heard one thing in particular.

Anastazja was thoroughly amazed at the wisdom of Stojan. It all made sense save for one thing.

The saint.

It remained huddled in the corner, but the the sheets and cloths that swathed it had now fallen due to the breeze.

Surely if the thing had been held in some sort of spell that contained it, the death of Lucjan would have just released it.

Ana bent and wiped her sword on the luxurious tuffet before her. It was a shame to stain it so, but to her it was all the gaudy trappings of an evil man.

Stojan waited patiently as she replaced her book, sheathed her sword, and refastened her tiny backpack.

"How did you know?"

It was all she could say as she embraced him. She repeated the question and added more as they pulled apart.

"How did you know? You knew from the moment we entered. You had no stance. I've never seen you like this. How?"

"Because he accepts wisdom, regardless of the source."

Ana tensed and looked around the room. Her stance became one of defense and most of her relief dissipated. She had all but forgotten about the saint in the room—so dormant had it been the entire time. It was certainly an odd placement to have it sequestered into a small chamber. Their travels had taught them that when a saint took the form to interact, they most strongly preferred to be the center of attention.

Stojan looked to the hulking figure in the corner. As with the other saints, they could not really tell from where the voice emanated. They stood in silence and looked around. After many moments Stojan's face turned to agreement with a slight bottom-lip frown as his eyes tilted upward in waiting for more.

The voice seemed very weak and quite different than the others. Perhaps this was due to whatever incantations the bishop had applied. Ana seemed to read his thoughts.

"Stojan? Have we released the saint from the binding of the bishop?"

She was rightly concerned. Having dispatched one evil they had inadvertently released a far greater one upon Poliska—perhaps the greatest. At least, that was her fear.

That was when it flew in.

Taken aback at the sound, both flinched as the large black bird flew in the now open window. It passed by them and landed on top of the statue. They watched with some amusement as it waddled to and fro—repositioning its feet to get the best purchase. And there it stood, looking quite at home.

Anastazja marveled at the size. It was the largest raven she'd ever seen and it was quite beautiful.

"She wants to say good bye."

Again it was the voice they'd heard before. The two traded glances and both showed a look of mutual concern.

"She?"

It was Anastazja asking the one-word question.

Slowly and apprehensively the two made their way around to the front of the statue. The bird tracked their movements contentedly as they made their small arc. Both had their swords drawn reflexively as their eyes went from bird to statue and back again. Something about the wild animal alighting upon it made it seem less likely to strike out, but they would not be fooled this day.

Finally they saw it. It remained still as they looked upon its face.

It was a woman with her hands folded together in front of her. She had a look of serene sadness and her head was hung low. The statue was quite impressive as the features were carved with exquisite detail.

Her robes were loose against her and she was wrapped not in cloth but in something she had in common with the great bird perched upon her: wings. They protruded and wrapped around her like a great shell-covering her and protecting her petite body. They encircled her leaving only her arms and face exposed. It seemed she stood here alone, facing the corner and both her stance and expression matched her surroundings. Clearly she had been positioned here, yet she did not look out of place.

The bird cawed at them.

"It was you, was it not?"

Stojan spoke not with anger or challenge, but with curiosity. He wasn't sure if he spoke to the statue, the saint or the bird.

Again the voice spoke, but this time the statue's eyes slowly opened and looked up and to Stojan. Its slight mouth moved with the words. It was meek.

"Yes."

"You. You visited me that day in the barn."

"No Stojan, she did. She wished to go with you, and through her I could contact you."

Stojan was silent, and considered the words carefully.

Ana watched the exchange and felt as if something was different; something was missing. There was an emptiness and finality to this saint.

"I don't understand."

The statue looked at Ana, then back to Stojan. Again she spoke with head slightly tilted down, as if she carried a great burden and sadness. Her movements were slow, as if she was tired.

"It was her death that awakened me—in a way that I did not know I could be reached. I thought it best to hibernate in this world, for I knew once I was found by the others, they would try once again to open the door."

"It was you? It was you who closed the door… from the other side? *This* side."

Anastazja offered her clarification to the conversation as she glanced at Stojan.

"Yes. I was powerless to do anything, and being connected they could only draw from my energy and my knowledge. If I remained inert, they would be trapped."

"But how were you awakened then? Why did you…"

"There was so much sadness, yet so much love. It was overwhelming. And she was the first to contact me."

The bird shifted its stance slightly.

Stojan's brows drew together as he looked at the raven. His voice was softer and his sword had dropped.

A tear found its way down Stojan's cheek as he seemed to be deep in thought, remembering the events and conversations

"Goodbye?"

"She wishes to say goodbye. She's been with you in your travels and came with you when I sent you back. I promised her that you'd be safe, but she wanted to be sure."

"But why send me? Surely this was your doing?"

She looked into Stojan's eyes and then rested her own on Anastazja's.

"The bishop knew you would go because you no longer had a heart. I chose you because I knew you would once again find it."

She smiled at Anastazja.

Stojan was numb as he took in the reality of what was before him. If the saint meant to trick him, it had worked. So intense was his relief that he no longer cared if it was a ruse. He held and honored the memory of his daughter and cherished that Anastazja was beside him.

He was overwhelmed with emotion.

He looked at the raven. It stared into his eyes one long last time, and then took flight. It soared through the broken window and into the night.

The pair watched it leave and did hear it call from a distance.

They looked back to the saint. She was the last one. She would not open the door and had sacrificed herself. Would she live in a statue for eternity?

"Now Stojan I must ask a favor of you."

It was then that Stojan thought surely payment was due.

She smiled a timid smile and asked of him quietly.

"Strike me down. Make it quick and final. It is the only way that this cannot happen again."

"No!"

Ana spoke without thinking. Her involuntary reaction was to object. She looked to Stojan, his sword then the statue. His arm was at his side and his sword point pierced the floor—hanging down heavily.

"It is the only way."

"But you deserve to live! You are the only one—truly—that does!"

Stojan swallowed and took a breath. His tear-filled eyes met Ana's.

"Ana, for the first time I find myself unsure of what to do."

"Please, it is for the good of all."

It was then that Stojan truly heard the saint's voice. It was not the resonant powerful voice of hate. Instead it was one of warmth, of softness and of kindness. It was the voice of sacrifice.

They stood in silence for many moments, both weeping for what was to come and for what had unfolded.

Finally Stojan looked to Ana and spoke quietly.

"Ana, may I?"

She stared at Stojan for many moments, then at last turned to the statue and spoke her parting words.

"Thank you. Thank you for bringing him to me, for bringing him into my life."

Ana nodded and closed her eyes—and waited. She tried to remember to breathe as the moments went on. Finally she heard the familiar strike and resulting shattering. She opened her eyes involuntarily lest she be pelted with the jagged fragments.

But the saint remained.

It was not to say that the statue hadn't been shattered—it had indeed been destroyed. In its place stood the saint.

It wasn't a being with tormented expression; nor was it an otherworldly creature with dimensions unimaginable. Instead it was the same form they had looked upon the entire time. Though identical, this one was translucent and shimmered in the darkened chamber. Anastazja could see elements of the room because she could look through it.

She traded glances with Stojan who looked equally astonished and perhaps relieved.

It was a woman with wings and she rose upward—her hands now outstretched with her palms to them. Behind her, the massive wings reached their full expanse as they majestically stretched outward. They did not flap as a bird, but instead remained motionless once reaching their great span.

She smiled down upon them and her expression was one of joy; her face was the face of love. She looked upon Anastazja, then Stojan. Her surprise at her current condition made them trade glances and they too smiled.

"I did not know…"

———

In a small village in Poliska, in a year of all saints that no longer mattered, an angel did rise from a small church—signaling the end of the saints and their reign as interlopers.   The people of Amira and Poliska would no longer feel their influence.

But perhaps a raven would visit from time to time.

The End.

Amira

Thank you for reading this. <u>It means a lot to me that you did</u>. If you liked this book I would appreciate if you took a minute to review it. Your input really helps and is valuable.

Amira

AFTERWARD

After I wrote four nonfictions, I decided to focus on marketing them—as I had been told (and scolded) often.

That lasted two weeks. It seems that writing is not just something you turn off. But something unusual happened. As I like to do, I took a walk in the cemetery near my house. My mind was unusually clear and after a while I saw a scene where there had been emptiness. It was fascinating, and powerful, and amazing. Then I heard the voices of two people chatting.

It seemed that I had heard the end of a wonderful story.

When I returned home I sat down and wrote a poem. It took less than ten minutes to write it—as if my mind was composing it along my walk. I smiled at it and felt the enormity of what I'd just written. It was the very basis of this book and the exact poem you just heard read aloud by Ana.

I shared it with two people I know and for one day it was included in the description of *The Sword and the Sunflower*. I quickly decided that it was too important to reveal at the very beginning.

The Sword and the Sunflower was written with strict prosaic medieval atmosphere in mind, as I believe that Poliska was more of a traditional European society due to a number of factors. You may have noticed that 'Saint' is sometimes capitalized and sometimes not, and this is due to the reverence held by the speaker. While Stojan never has any, Ana's reverence is diminished by the time she explores Amira.

Amira was written with more relaxed modern wording reflecting the people and atmosphere of the vast country, as well as Ana's comfort with it.

So thank you for traveling along with me, Stojan and Anastazja for the journey set forth by a prophecy as described by a poem.

I hope I did an ample job relaying the vividness of their journey and the depth of their experiences.

With much warmth,

- Mark Bradford

Mark Bradford

Amira

ABOUT THE AUTHOR

Mark Bradford is an author, speaker, podcast host, coach and builder. He invests a great deal of time and effort researching a subject to come up with an explanation for it that everyone can understand. His podcast interviews as well as his experiences have taught him what life's made of, time management tricks, what multitasking really is, and even how both order and chaos benefit our lives. 15+ year business owner, he also is a full stack web developer.

It is in his nature to build things that fix, augment or create a solution. The fruits of his labors have been a role playing game with three custom 12-sided dice, a writing site, a dating site, six books and a card game.

Mark speaks to professional associations, groups and businesses about status, time, energy and resources, and how we all connect.

Mark produces and hosts a weekly podcast about Time, Energy and Resources that also features interviews with amazing people. Listen to *The Alchemy for Life* podcast for more insight, on iTunes and most other podcast providers. Subscribe and you won't miss them.

www.alchemyfor.life

Mark produces *The Status Game* series of books and card game that helps demonstrate, educate and enlighten people about an invisible but very real aspect on how we connect, and what we like.

His answers have almost two million answer views on Quora—a question and answer community.

Follow Mark on Instagram for announcements and things related to his content—books, podcasts, etc.

@authormarkbradford

For all things Mark Bradford go to:

MarkBradford.org

Books by Mark Bradford

Nonfiction:

The Status Game II
How status is the key to all relationships—business and personal.

OneSelf
Faith of a simpler, more direct kind. Or just nonsense.

Alchemy for Life
Everything you need to know about Life Coaching in one book. And 16 formulas for success.

Fiction:

The Sword and the Sunflower
Amira

Amira

Mark Bradford

Made in the USA
Columbia, SC
22 March 2022

58016320R00251